CW00493122

M.A. Nichols

Books by M.A. Nichols

Generations of Love Series

The Kingsleys

Flame and Ember

Hearts Entwined

A Stolen Kiss

The Ashbrooks

A True Gentleman

The Shameless Flirt

A Twist of Fate

The Honorable Choice

The Finches

The Jack of All Trades

Tempest and Sunshine

The Christmas Wish

The Leighs

An Accidental Courtship

Love in Disguise

His Mystery Lady

A Debt of Honor

Table of Contents

Prologue

London
Spring 1805

A gentleman's study is more than a mere sanctuary for its master. For it to be that true beacon of masculinity the room must be formidable and austere; a place that conveys all the proper pride, pomp, and circumstance that is due to its denizen as he conducts his business and intimidates his underlings. No self-respecting gentleman would accept anything less, and Horatio Granger was no exception.

However, young Miss Tabitha had never felt such trepidation in her father's study. From an outsider's perspective, Mr. Granger's room was the epitome of what a study should be—managing its function to perfection. But for Tabby, it was a place filled with fond memories of sitting with her father by the fire as they gorged themselves on books and teacakes. Though plenty of people found Mr. Granger to be an imposing man, Tabby knew her papa to be more bluster than bile, and visiting him in his study had never caused Tabby an ounce of dread or dismay.

Until this moment.

Clenching her fists in her skirts, Tabby watched her father's face. It was thin and lined, though that had more to do with the angry pull of his eyebrows than age. She had to make him see. Her happiness depended on it. Leaning on his desk, he watched her as if peering into her soul, and Tabby pushed away her nerves to radiate the confidence she felt in her choice. This was the right one. There was no other.

Tabby's heart rested on the edge of a knife, ready to be cleaved in two if things went awry. She knew that if the worst should happen, there would be no piecing it back together. Her heart would be irrevocably ruined, and she would be lost.

"You wish to marry Joshua Russell?" Her papa huffed and shook his head. "That jackanapes?"

"He is a gentleman," insisted Tabby. "A good man."

"No man with his reputation can be called either of those things, Tabitha," he said with a scowl. "You cannot be serious about marrying him. He should never have been introduced to you in the first place! And he should have had the decency to speak with me before paying his addresses, rather than hiding in the shadows like a sneak."

"If he had come forward sooner, you would have denied him as you are now."

"What good father would do anything less?" He puffed his cheeks, glaring at his desk. "If I'd had any clue that he was sniffing around, I would have packed you off into the country posthaste."

Tabby held herself in her chair, though she felt compelled to get on her knees and beg. She'd never had such an urge before, but the thought of losing this battle left her feeling as though a vice were clamped around her heart, squeezing it until it was liable to burst.

"He has changed, Papa. I am not ignorant of how Mr. Russell has behaved in the past, but he is different now."

Her father huffed again and shook his head. "Altering oneself to impress a young lady is not a sign of a true change of heart. I hate to be the bearer of bad news, my girl, but such a shift in character does not last after the lady is won."

Her fists clenched tighter, and Tabby fought to keep her composure. She would not prostrate herself before her father, even if every part of her heart and soul was desperate to show her conviction. "He has no desire to gamble anymore, and he has been attending church services every Sunday."

"To impress you."

"He gave up drink," Tabby continued. "Except for a bit of port with the gentlemen after dinner, he abstains from any spirits. His former friends have all but shunned him because of his new behavior, and yet it has not weakened his resolve. Surely, that is a sign of a changed man."

Just thinking about Joshua's struggle filled Tabby with irrepressible love. He was such a sociable creature, and to be so isolated from his former friends and acquaintances cut him to the core. He did not deserve such treatment nor her papa's distrust. Joshua was human. He had been frail and weak, but Tabby knew that any gentleman could change if he wished to be better. She knew Joshua was becoming something more than he had been a few months ago. Watching that transformation was one of the most humbling and remarkable things Tabby had witnessed in her twenty years of life.

"Tabitha—" her father began, his tone all but telling her what was to come.

But Tabby did not want to hear it. Surrendering all sense of decorum and self-respect, she rushed to him. Gripping his hand, Tabby knelt beside his chair. "Please, Papa. I love him so much, and it is not fair to hold his past against him. None of us are perfect, and he is changing. He truly is. And we love each other so very much."

Tears blurred her vision, making it impossible to see her father's reaction.

"Dearest Tabby," he said while mopping at her face with a handkerchief. "I understand—I do—but you are too important to me and your mother. We cannot allow you to marry someone whom we distrust, and neither of us feel he is the good man you believe him to be."

"I cannot bear to live my life without him," she said, her words broken. "I love him."

Her papa sighed and stood, pulling her to her feet and escorting her to their sofa by the fire. Seated beside her, he took one of her hands in his while surrendering his handkerchief as she continued to sniffle.

"It is not love that I worry about," he said. "Any fool can see that Mr. Russell loves you. He made it very clear when he spent the morning begging for permission to marry you. However, love is not enough."

"That is not—" Tabby began, but stopped when her father raised a silencing hand.

"Tabitha, I know that at your age you feel it is, but trust someone who has a little more life experience than you. Love is not enough because romantic love is not always constant," he said. "When you marry someone, you bind yourself to them irrevocably. It is easy to love them through the good times, but when the struggles of life come, you need someone who will stick it out."

"Joshua—" At the sharp look from her papa, Tabby began again. "Mr. Russell will do that. I do not believe I have ever seen a man work so hard for the woman he loves."

"I have," replied her father. "Many times. People get wrapped in the glow of love and alter themselves dramatically in order to win the object of their affection. Then they marry only to realize that the energetic infatuation fades with the reality of daily life, and eventually, they revert to what they once were. They changed solely to make the other happy, and at some point, that will not be enough of a reason to maintain the lifestyle they did not desire in the first place."

Tabby crushed the handkerchief and shook her head. "That is not the case with Mr. Russell. He is so much happier now. He does not want his old life."

"Sweetheart, I know you believe that with all your heart, but resentment grows quickly in the wrong circumstances, and I have never witnessed a happy ending for couples who start off with such different desires in life. You want a home and family, and he wants pleasure and idleness. What happens in a few years, when life has settled you both firmly in that quiet country life and Mr. Russell begins to miss his old one?"

"You don't believe people can change?" asked Tabby.

"Of course people can change," he said, giving her hand a squeeze. "But doing so for someone else is not a true reformation. Such things can only come from within, independent of what others desire of you. It is one thing for him to be inspired by your good example and alter himself because he wishes to be better, but everything he has done has been to win your good opinion. What happens if he decides it is no longer worth the sacrifice?"

"Papa, every marriage is a gamble," said Tabby. "There are gentlemen who feign goodness in public, and good men who become wicked, so marrying a seemingly perfect husband with a perfect past is no guarantee he will remain so and that our marriage will succeed."

"But you increase the risk of failure if your husband is an unabashed libertine and rake."

Tabby shot to her feet. "I will not listen to you condemn him. No matter what he may have been, he has changed, and it is unfeeling of you to hold it against him."

Her papa stood and tried to draw closer, but she stepped away. "I am your father, and it is my duty to protect you."

"I am not a child."

"Only children say that," he replied.

Ignoring that, Tabby continued. "I want your blessing—we both do—but I am nearly of age and shan't need it. If you and Mother will not give it to us, we will simply wait until the law is on our side."

She had hoped not to need to resort to such tactics. Over the years, she had dreamt of the moment when the man she loved would ask for permission to marry her, but Tabby had never thought that she would have to beg, plead, and cajole her papa into accepting it. This should be a happy event, and the look on her father's face was anything but. His brow wrinkled further, and his eyes were dimmed with disappointment, not shining with joy.

"Are you so determined to have him?" asked her father, his voice sounding weaker than Tabby had ever heard before.

Tabby ran her father's handkerchief through her fingers and then lifted it to wipe away a new wave of tears. This was not at all what she wanted, but she knew her Joshua was worth it. Stepping closer to her father, she took his hand in hers.

"I cannot imagine my life without him," she said. "I have met many gentlemen, but none of them have stirred my heart so. You and Mother may not trust him, but I do. He is a good man, and I want to marry him more than I have wanted anything in my life. I know that we shall be happy, Papa, and one way or another, I shall marry him."

Her father turned away and stared into the fire, leaving Tabby blind to what he was thinking. She wanted to push him, but she knew she must wait. If there was any chance of this ending happily, she had to be patient. Tabby's breath caught as she watched him, her heart ceasing to beat as he deliberated.

When he met her eyes again, Tabby saw the resignation. It was not the emotion she had hoped for, but the nod of his head had her springing into his arms. With kisses on his cheeks and a flurry of excited words promising him heaven and earth, Tabby's elation enveloped him as she assured him of all the blissful years that were yet to come.

Turning away, she ran for the study door, bursting through it as her father slumped onto the sofa. In the moment, she did not notice the tears in his eyes and the way his head hung low, but in the years to follow, her memory would dredge it up on many an occasion. At present, the only thoughts in her head were of Joshua standing just outside the door, his eyes red and face twisted in uncertain agony. In two steps, she threw herself into his arms.

"We must marry the moment we can get a license," she said, hugging him tight.

"He gave his permission?" Joshua's voice trembled.

Pulling away, Tabby nodded through a wave of new tears and saw matching ones in Joshua's eyes. With a triumphant shout, he spun her around, crushing her in his arms. When they stopped, Joshua's hands framed her face in his strong fingers.

"I love you, my darling," he said, saying the endearment as if it were as sacred as a prayer.

"I love you, too," replied Tabby before he pressed his lips to hers.

...

Thornwood, Devon
Eleven years later

Tabby Russell stood at the library window, capturing the image of her gardens firmly in her mind. She had stood thusly many times during her eleven years as mistress of Kelland Hall. In summer, the blossoms filled the beds in a rainbow of colors. In winter, the landscape grew barren, but the grass and moss became all the more vibrant under the winter rainfalls. And then there were the days when the snow coated the hedges and ground like a down blanket, all cozy and inviting. But for a few weeks in spring and fall, the seasonal transition seized the world in a gloomy mess of mud and decay. Tabby wished her last memories of her home were more colorful or comforting, but it was a fitting end.

Crates were scattered across the library, the bits and pieces of her life stuffed inside, hastily packed to make way for a new family that would fill these rooms. Walking over to the last of the boxes, Tabby wrapped a rag around a vase before nestling it among the straw. Gathering extra bits of padding, she made double and triple sure that it was safe from harm. Having no intrinsic value, her mother's favorite vase had escaped the ravages of the creditors, and Tabby could not bear to see the heirloom damaged.

Retrench.

Tabby had grown up hearing stories of great families brought low, and that word was spoken in hushed voices with raised eyebrows as neighbors tittered about their downfall. Tabby herself had participated in such conversations—not in a mean-spirited manner, but with the morbid fascination of those who cannot imagine such hardships befalling them. Yet, here it was at her doorstep. Retrenching.

It was a temporary step. Nothing more. By downgrading their expenses and adding the income of a renter, they would make do. It would take time, economy, and sacrifice, but Tabby knew they would gain a more secure financial footing. They would manage.

Kneeling beside the crate, Tabby reached for the next leftover bit of her life when she heard tiny footsteps echoing in the vacant hallway. Tabby looked behind her to see her little man run past the doorway. Phillip peeked out at her, and Tabby glanced at a stack of her father's books that they'd been unable to sell. Pretending to examine them, she kept her eyes fixed on the crates as Phillip crept across the room. She turned the books over, studying them with the intensity of a scholar while the floorboards thumped and stifled giggles drew closer.

And then Phillip pounced. Throwing his arms around her neck, he leapt onto her with a squeal.

"Mama!" he shouted, squeezing her neck.

Swinging him around, Tabby nibbled at her favorite spot on his cheek and tickled his sides. Phillip wiggled and laughed, his joy raising her spirits. Holding him tight, Tabby gazed at the boy who looked so like his father. They shared the same curly chestnut locks and crystalline eyes that were the color of a clear summer sky; when he was grown, Phillip would be just as handsome as Joshua had been.

Phillip wriggled in earnest, so Tabby gave him one last kiss and released him; the three-year-old promptly began digging through the crates.

"What are you doing, Mama?" he asked, scattering a bit of straw.

Tabby scooped the mess with one hand and secured Phillip's wrists with the other. "I am packing our things."

"Why?" he asked while tugging at her grip.

Tabby handed him one of the books she did not care about, but Phillip pushed it aside and reached for the straw. "We've talked about this, dearest."

Phillip looked at her, his brow scrunched, but Tabby did not have the time and patience to go over this conversation again. This change in their circumstances was difficult enough, and Tabby did not have it in her to withstand another tantrum.

"Where's Papa?" she asked, diverting Phillip's attention.

"In his study," he said. "He's sick."

Tabby sighed. She had thought Joshua would be able to watch their child so she could get the work done, but apparently, that was beyond his capability.

"Should we go find him?" asked Tabby, standing and holding out her hand to Phillip, giving his a squeeze as they left the library.

Rather than walking, Phillip hopped along, making a ribbit sound. When his little tongue darted out to catch an invisible fly, Tabby found herself smiling—until Phillip decided there was a fly on her hand, and she got a quick, wet lick.

"Phillip!"

But the frog in question pulled out of reach. With a grin, Tabby lunged for him, and the frog abandoned his hopping and ran. The two of them tore through the hall, around the corner, and up the stairs. She kept Phillip a few steps ahead, close enough to keep him worried, but far enough behind to make it look as though he were winning.

At Joshua's study door, Phillip paused, turning around to give Tabby another quick flick of his tongue, but she dodged out of the way and grabbed him. Tickling him until he shook, Tabby pretended to growl at his impertinence.

"Tongues belong in mouths," she said, probing Phillip's most tickly of spots under his ribs. He howled with laughter, and when he had done enough begging Tabby put him down again with a final tickle and knocked on the door. A vague reply came from inside, and Tabby stepped into the room to find her husband lying face down on the desk, a near empty bottle of cognac beside his head.

"Papa?" Phillip moved to his father's side, but Tabby dragged him back out of the room and went in search of a servant. No more than three months ago, it would have taken less than a minute for Tabby to stumble across some maid or footman, but now the hallways were empty. She was nearly at the kitchen before she found a maid sitting in a corner.

"Louisa," said Tabby, and the maid got to her feet with a mild curtsy. "Would you please look after Phillip for a few minutes while I speak with Mr. Russell?"

"I'm no good with children, ma'am," said Louisa, looking at Phillip. "Isn't there someone else who could watch him?"

"None that I have found," replied Tabby. "Please. It shall only be a few minutes, and I would rather Phillip not be there. Without his nanny around, I fear he will get into mischief."

Tabby spared herself a moment of self-pity. She had been reduced to begging for help from a maid. In other circumstances, Tabby would have simply ordered it, but as none of the staff's salaries had been paid for quite some time, she knew she was in no position to demand anything. She would not risk alienating one of the only servants who remained at Kelland. Likely, the girl still held out hope that she would receive her back pay, and it pained Tabby to know that it would not be forthcoming. Not in the near future, at any rate.

"I promise to fetch him in a trice," said Tabby.

Louisa stared at Phillip with a frown, but she gave a sour nod to her mistress and took Phillip by the hand to lead him to the nursery. He glanced at his mother, and Tabby gave him a smile while straightening her spine for the impending scene—

and there was no questioning that the impending conversation would lead to a scene.

Marching back to the study, she found her husband in the exact same position.

"I asked you to watch Phillip," said Tabby, walking to the desk.

"Demanded, more like it," mumbled Joshua, pushing upright. He rubbed at his face, scratching the stubble on his jaw and mussing his shaggy hair.

"He is your son, and I need help," she said. "There is so much packing to be done, and without Nanny Gilbert around to watch Phillip, I am finding it difficult to get much done with him underfoot, and I need you to watch him."

Joshua stretched and then settled into his chair to stare at his wife. His eyes were red and droopy, the lines at his eyes and mouth far deeper and craggier than a man his age should have. In the eleven years of their marriage, it was as though Joshua had aged twice that. If Tabby were honest with herself, she felt much the same, even if it did not show.

"I have enough to deal with," said Joshua. "I don't need to be doing a woman's job."

"You found a renter?" It was too much to hope for. Kelland Hall was not at the peak of repair and finding someone willing to take on the crumbling estate seemed an impossible feat.

"I am taking care of things," he said, reaching for the cognac bottle.

Tabby snatched it. "Drinking will not help the situation."

"It is the only thing that makes the 'situation' bearable," he said, giving her a gimlet eye.

"It is burying your head in the sand, Joshua!" Tabby stepped around his desk to throw open the curtains and point at the men gathered near the entrance to their home. "The creditors are quite literally on our doorstep. If it weren't for your connections, we'd be forced to flee the country, though I have no idea how we would pay for the trip."

Joshua's fist came down on the desk. "I am taking care of

it!"

Tabby took a breath and came around to stand before him. With another deep lungful, she sat on the chair facing him. They needed to discuss this like rational beings. "Joshua, please, I need to know what is happening."

Joshua glanced at the bottle in Tabby's hand. "I found a buyer."

She placed the bottle on the floor beside her, giving herself a moment to think as Joshua's eyes tracked her movements.

"A buyer?" she asked.

"No one is interested in renting. Apparently, the Russell family holding isn't worth what it should be." Joshua gave a self-pitying chuckle and crossed his arms. "The house needs too many repairs we cannot pay for, but the land is still worth something. I am selling the property in its entirety to Mr. Brexton."

Tabby held her composure, but it was a struggle. Their neighbors had coveted the Russell land for a long time, but she never thought Joshua would agree to sell. Casting a glance at the room around her, Tabby imagined the sad and lonely future for the home. The Brextons only wanted access to finer hunting, and she doubted they would care much about maintaining the building.

Her home. It held many bitter memories, but there were sweet ones, too. Those first years of marriage had been everything her young heart had dreamt of, and for a brief moment, Tabby reveled in the thoughts of those sunny days.

"Selling?" she whispered. It was one thing to accept a temporary displacement, but another to realize their home would be gone forever. And then another stark realization struck her. "But that means we shall lose our income."

Joshua snorted. "What income? Our tenants have all but fled us, and the estate's profits have dwindled to nothing. The house is the only thing of value we have, and selling it will barely cover our debts."

Tabby let out the breath she had been holding. "I suppose that is something of a blessing. With the debts gone and a little economy, we can live off the interest from my dowry."

Joshua's eyes fell to his desk for a moment before he reached into a drawer and retrieved another bottle. There was nothing more than a single swallow left in it, but he downed it and dropped it to the floor, where it hit the rug with a muted thud.

"There is no money left from your dowry," said Joshua, resting his head against the chair. Closing his eyes, he looked like he was ready to fall asleep, but Tabby was having none of it.

"No money left?" Tabby could not believe it. With no living siblings, her parents had been very generous with her dowry. There was no possible way that it and all of the Russell fortune could be gone in little more than a decade.

"Not a penny," mumbled Joshua. "My luck has been sour for the last few years, but it should turn soon."

"Luck?" Tabby's eyes widened, her breathing coming in fast bursts. "Are you saying you lost it all gambling?"

"Not all of it."

But Tabby heard the insinuation. Not all. But most. Tabby's heart sent out a silent prayer, pleading for it to be untrue. That he had lost vast amounts of their fortune was no secret, but this was far more than anything Tabby had anticipated. This was not retrenching. This was poverty.

"How much do we have left?" she asked, terrified to hear the truth.

"Enough."

"How much?"

"Enough," he said, opening his eyes and raising his head to give her a hard look. "I am certain one of our friends will put us up for a while. Or perhaps Cousin George will assist us."

Tabby's heart broke at the thought of having to beg their friends and relations for scraps. It was humiliating, but for Phillip's sake, she would do what she had to until they could get themselves established someplace new.

"And then what?" she asked.

Joshua's brow furrowed, but when he said nothing more, Tabby clarified. "That is no long-term solution, Joshua. We may find respite through charity, but we have no income and no property. How are we to live?"

He shrugged. "There is nothing more to do. You are fretting and worrying too much. It will work out. Things will be fine."

"We need income," Tabby insisted.

"Are you suggesting I work?" he asked. His lips quirked and he looked ready to laugh, but his mirth died when Tabby replied, "Yes."

"That is ludicrous," he said with a snort.

"Ludicrous is living without an income. We need money," she said.

"We will make do."

"Not without an income!" Tabby got to her feet. "Even if we can receive housing and food from others, will they pay for Phillip's clothing? His schooling? There is no other money coming to us. No long-awaited inheritances. Are we to live the rest of our lives off the charity of others? And what of our son's future?"

"And your solution is for me to become a common laborer?" he scoffed. "I am a gentleman."

"Not a laborer, but something. With our connections, I am certain we could find you a good profession."

Joshua looked at her as though she were speaking in tongues. Tabby was no fool and had known that he would not be keen on pursuing a trade, but she could not understand his blindness to their circumstances. They needed income and had no other option.

"Please, Joshua," she said, dropping to her chair once more. At this point in her life, it seemed as though she should be familiar with debasing herself, but begging hurt her pride every time.

Joshua's gaze darkened. "After all I have sacrificed for you, you would ask me to surrender the very core of who I am?"

Tabby needed no clarification. In the last few years, playing the martyr had become one of Joshua's favored pastimes. "And you are the only one who has sacrificed for this marriage? You poor soul for bearing the entirety of that hardship on your shoulders," she said with cold mockery.

Joshua slammed his fist against the table again, but Tabby would not be quiet.

"You made your choice, Joshua. As did I," she said. "I think it is time that you stop blaming me for your decisions."

"Get out!" he yelled, plucking the empty bottle from the floor and flinging it across the room.

Tabby did not flinch. It was nothing more than a tantrum, and Tabby would not be made to cower by a man acting more childish than his son, but neither would she listen to his pathetic self-pitying tirade. Getting to her feet, Tabby held Joshua's gaze for several quiet moments, making it clear that his outburst had no effect. Only then did she leave the study, closing the door behind her.

Walking through the empty halls, Tabby's tears finally broke through her defenses as she thought about her lost home. Life at Kelland Hall had been far from perfect, but it had been hers. Disappointing though it may be, she had built a life here, and it was painful to say goodbye to it forever. And then there was the terrifying future. The unknown and dark prospects loomed before her, bringing a wave of panic. She had no idea how to fix it all, but it was abundantly clear that it would be her responsibility.

The man she had married was gone. Memories of what Joshua had been haunted her. Perhaps it would be easier to bear the present if not for the fact that Tabby had been given a glimpse of the man he could be. The good, loving, considerate man she had married. Joshua had the capacity to be so much more than a drunken lout and was simply choosing to reject that goodness.

Tabby paused for a moment and closed her eyes against the wave of disappointment. Another tear slipped down her cheek, and she brushed it away. Memories of begging her father for his blessing came to mind, and some small, shameful part of her was grateful her parents had not witnessed Papa's predictions come to fruition. Tabby supposed they might be watching over her from beyond the grave, but she hoped they weren't. Better that they be preoccupied with their eternal paradise than their poor daughter; she was beyond their assistance now.

"Mama!"

Tabby had a moment to brace herself before Phillip threw himself at her. She reveled in the little arms and legs clutching her neck and waist. The love. The comfort of it. It was exactly what her poor soul needed in that moment. Regardless of what Joshua was, he had given her the most wonderful son a mother could ask for. That was something.

And with that thought, Tabby summoned other bits of happiness. Memories of the good that had come despite her foolhardy decision to ignore her father's advice. Perhaps if she gathered enough of them, they might outweigh her regrets.

Chapter 1

Bristow, Essex
One year later

Infernal racket. Captain Graham Ashbrook buried his head farther into the pillow, desperate to block out the sounds of maids puttering around him. His body throbbed as though he were still lying on the surgeon's table. Graham wanted nothing more than a bit of peace, but the noises pricked and poked at his consciousness.

The curtains flew open and light bored into his eyes. By the stars in heaven, he was going to draw blood!

"Get out!"

"Begging your pardon, sir," came the quivering response, "but Mrs. Kingsley specifically ordered your chamber to be cleaned today."

"Surely she did not mean at the crack of dawn," he said through clenched teeth. His head throbbed and he wanted nothing more than to be left alone. Quiet. Dark. Rest. That was what he needed, and he could not seem to go more than a few minutes without someone bothering him. A string of words came to his mind that would have Mina boxing his ears if she heard them aloud.

"But, sir..." The maid's voice was barely more than a whisper. "It's near time for dinner."

Graham fully opened his eyes and looked at the window. That could not be right. He lifted his head to see the clock on the mantle, but a stab of pain pulled at his muscles, and Graham dropped onto the pillow. His dratted body would not stop plaguing him. If he could get a single moment of peace, perhaps his mind would clear enough to think.

He grumbled something that no polite gentleman should say and shifted to get his left elbow under him.

"Send in James," he mumbled.

The maid trembled as she gave him a quick curtsy and ran from the room. Lily-livered coward. Graham was tired of querulous maids treating him as though he were a bear ready to devour them. He had simply given her an order, and she acted as though he had threatened her with his cutlass. He could only imagine what she would do if he greeted her in full naval regalia, sword in hand, bellowing orders as he had on the deck of his ship. A huff of laughter sent more shivers of pain through him.

Easing upright, Graham flexed his right arm. Months of effort and a fleet of surgeons had seen the last of the splinters removed from his injuries, but his limbs seemed hardly the better for it. Flexing and moving carefully, he swung his legs out from under the covers, even though he wished nothing more than to crawl back under them and sleep until everything was the way it should be. If it were not for Mina, Graham would've done just that, but his stubbornness might force his sister to drag him kicking and screaming out of bed.

How his men would laugh if they knew the truth. The brave Captain Ashbrook was terrified of his sister. But then, they had never met her on the field of battle. For all her timidity, Mina could be a formidable opponent when motivated and had grown even more so in the past few years.

Easing forward, Graham put weight on his leg. Prudence told him to wait until James could help him to his feet, but Graham was not one for such hesitation. Grabbing his cane, Graham's grip tightened as his right thigh screamed at him. Curses upon the heads of physicians, surgeons, apothecaries, and all the lot of the cussed boat-lickers. His dashed body was no more healed than when the Navy had cast him ashore to rest and recuperate last year. The devil take them all.

Hobbling forward, he made it across the room before the footman arrived to help him dress, as though he were a child or some fop who spent hours at his looking glass. Yet another blow to his pride. With each movement, his muscles limbered up, and by the time he was in his proper uniform, he was stable enough to walk the hallway himself, though not without relying heavily on his cane. The tip hit the wood floor, and Graham fought to keep his right leg from dragging—but there it was. Crack, drag. Crack, drag. The sound of the invalid echoed through the corridor, announcing to everyone that the crippled Captain Ashbrook was coming. Sound the alarm.

Much of his strength was spent in the trip, but the pain in his leg and arm had dulled enough that they were more of a background noise rather than a blaring trumpet. So, perhaps it had been worth it. His healthy limbs certainly appreciated the exercise. Even if it took so long that by the time he arrived in the parlor, Mina and Simon had already gone in to dinner.

A footman opened the door for him, and Graham found his sister and her husband sitting together at the far end of the table. Abandoning their first course, the pair rose from their chairs, and Mina rushed to his side.

"You are up," she said with a smile. "We assumed you were taking your dinner in bed today."

Graham allowed her to herd him towards his seat, which was directly beside her own.

"It was a near thing," said Graham, "but I thought if I hid for too long you'd drag me from bed."

Mina's eyebrows drew together. "Of course not. It has hardly been a fortnight since your last operation. You need your rest. Are you certain you should be up? I could send a tray to your room."

When they reached his chair, Mina pulled it out for him, and Graham's face burned red. He wanted to refuse, but with his temper not quite the thing at the moment, he dared not speak. But then she also placed the napkin across his lap and rearranged the dishes until they were nearly in his lap, as though he could not lean forward the scant distance. Though Graham was ashamed to admit that his right arm could not handle such a feat, his left was more than capable.

Graham sent a pleading look to Simon, who clearly shared and understood Graham's feelings.

"Mina, he is not a child," said Simon, coming over to lead her to her chair.

Giving her husband a hard look, Mina said, "Neither are you, but you never complain about the care I give when you are ill."

"But that is because I am hopeless," he said with a smile, raising her hand to place a kiss on her knuckles. "Graham is a naval man. He's made of much sterner stuff."

Graham stared at his plate, refusing to watch as his sister blushed before giving Simon a saucy wink.

"And I am not ill," he said. "I am injured. There is a world of difference."

"Of course," said Mina, returning to her seat. "A large, manly difference. Would it help if I started talking about battening the hatches and rigging the mainsails? Perhaps I could even manage to curse or spit. Would that make you feel better?"

She smiled at him, though it faltered as he glowered.

"Do you find this humorous?" he asked.

Mina's eyes widened and her eyebrows rose. "Of course not, I did not mean...of course, I would not presume to make light...I..."

"Graham." Simon's tone held a warning, his posture tightening.

He sighed. Graham had known the words were rude before he had spoken them, but he had been unable to stop himself after hearing her jest about his situation. She had meant no harm, though Graham struggled to erase his lingering frustration at her words. "Mina, I apologize. I did not mean to speak so harshly. I am just so bally uncomfortable."

"Graham," Simon repeated himself, and it took a moment for Graham to identify his newest offense.

"Apologies again," said Graham. And that put the final nail in the proverbial coffin. He missed his ship, his crew, his life. There was no need to watch one's language when aboard a vessel filled with men who thought "bally" was a weak word.

"Are you truly that bad off?" Mina asked, nibbling on the corner of her lip. "I know the last surgeon said that it could take another week or two to recover, but it seems as though you should be feeling somewhat better by now."

"I fear he may have done more damage than good," said Graham, taking a sip from his glass. In truth, his pain was worse than before the surgery, and there was a shocking lack of dexterity in his right hand that worried Graham, but he would not spread all his fears to his sister. She was worried enough.

"But it is too early to tell, Graham," she said, reaching over to lay her hand on his knee. "There is hope that all will be mended."

Graham nodded. He was counting on it. Hope is what drove him. It was all he had at this moment. Hope.

He reached for his spoon, but Mina scooted her chair closer to snatch the utensil from him.

"What are you doing?" he demanded as she scooped a bit of soup.

"Whether or not you want to admit it, you should not be using your hand yet," she said, offering the bite to his mouth.

"I have two hands, Mina," he said, leaning away.

"Oh," she replied, her eyes downcast as she placed the spoon in his bowl. "Of course. Apologies."

Graham gave Mina a sideways look as he tucked into his meal with his good hand. She stared at her soup as she ate, and he wondered what was going on in her head. Simon filled the silence with talk of the estate. Some vastly boring details about harvest and crop rotations or some such nonsense. Graham could not care less what it was, as long as it meant he could eat without being bothered.

And he did. Until the next course.

Staring at the beef on his plate, Graham retrieved his utensils. Using his bad hand to hold the meat steady, he sawed at it, but his grip on the fork faltered, and his hands slipped, knocking bits of potatoes and gravy onto his lap. The napkin caught most of it, but it could not stop his pride from getting more dinged and scarred.

Graham smacked the utensils on the table, making the dishes rattle, and he glowered at the plate of food. He felt Mina and Simon's eyes on him, but he could not speak. His temper was holding on by the weakest of threads, and it would not do to unleash it on his family.

A year. It had been a year since that cannonball slammed his ship. With quick thinking and a lot of luck, the vessel and crew had been saved, but Graham's body had borne the brunt of the damage. Heaven help him, he was more terrified in this moment than when he had awoken to the ship's surgeon cutting the massive bits of wood from his body. In that moment, he'd had the welfare of his crew and ship to keep him preoccupied. But sitting at home with nothing but time on his hands, Graham had to face the fact that his body had been severely broken.

Hands reached for the cutlery, and Graham barked at Mina before he could think better of it. "Stop coddling me, Mina. I do not need help!"

She retreated, and Graham's heart twisted. Simon reached for Mina's hand as he leveled a hard look at Graham. If he were not Mina's brother, he might be afraid of Simon calling him out for that. Mina kept her face turned away, but Graham saw the slump of her shoulders.

"Mina, I apologize," he said with a sigh. "I did not mean it. I am grateful for your help, and you have been too kind to put me up for so long. It is just frustrating to be an invalid."

"Then why do you keep putting yourself through these surgeries?" she asked, turning her eyes to him. "If you would stop having every quack in the country come cut on you, you could heal."

"And be a cripple for the rest of my life?" he asked. "Forsake my ship, my men, my career? My entire life?"

Mina's shoulders fell even farther, and she looked drained of all her spirit. "But they are not helping, Graham. You seem worse with each one."

"They are my only chance," he insisted. It was so frustrating to argue about this again. She did not understand. How could she? She had no idea what it was to have something you love so greatly be ripped away from you. To find yourself adrift. Graham would not let himself become one of those broken husks he had seen over the years. The dry-docked seamen who were left with nothing but their memories.

"Then you will not stop?" she asked, though it sounded as if she already knew his answer.

"I cannot. I have to return to the sea. It is my life, and I will not abandon it."

Mina nodded and squeezed Simon's hand. "Then perhaps it is time to reexamine our situation."

Graham's spine stiffened. "You wish for me to leave?"

"No," said Mina, wide-eyed. "Never."

"You always have a home here, Graham," added Simon, though his tone was far colder than Mina's.

Perhaps it was time to do a little mending of fences.

"Good," said Graham. "I far prefer it here. Between Louisa-Margaretta and the boys, I doubt I would get a moment of peace at Nicholas's. And Ambrose's bachelor lodgings are not an Eden for the injured."

But Mina did not respond to that. Her eyes slid to the side, and Graham could see her gathering her courage.

"I was thinking it might be a good idea to have you move into Gladwell House," she said.

"The dower house?" scoffed Graham. "Like some old lady?"

"I think it a splendid idea," said Simon. "It has been empty for years and could use some repairs, but it would give you a bit of independence while keeping us nearby to lend a hand while you continue with your...treatments."

Again, Graham heard the raucous laughter of his men echoing in his mind. Sequestered in a widow's villa and living off his sister. What a sight Captain Ashbrook made. Though he had the financial means to be independent, he did not have the physical capacity. Not to mention he hated the thought of renting a house. He would be at sea the moment he was well, and it was pointless to find something more permanent on land. He did not want anything holding him back when his health allowed him to return to his ship.

Graham wanted to refuse her offer, to pack his things, and find his own way, but if he ever hoped to heal, Graham knew he needed Mina's help, even if he did not want it. Perhaps this would be the best solution for them all. Support and a measure of independence. Enough distance without abandoning him on his own.

Giving an inward groan, Graham agreed. Heaven help him.

Chapter 2

Tabby held herself upright, refusing to allow the situation to break her spirit. There were worse things than abandoning one's pride. Starvation for one. And it was not as though she were resorting to truly horrific means to avoid that fate. She still had a modicum of dignity, and she was not the first genteel lady forced into service.

Standing in the middle of the sitting room, Tabby reminded herself not to sit. The instinct to rest for a moment was strong. Just like the instinct to go through the front entrance of Avebury Park. But she was no longer an honored guest or lady of equal footing. She was a servant—or hoped to be, at any rate—and such luxuries were not given to people of her station. No, she was to wait upon the whims of her betters.

Clutching her reticule, Tabby smoothed the edge of her cloak and waited. With one hand, she pulled out the letter and reassured herself that she had the correct time and name of the housekeeper, Mrs. Witmore.

Hold still and wait. The clock on the side table ticked away the seconds, its mechanisms making the only noise in the room.

The room was a cozy space. Not terribly different from any number Tabby had visited in her life, but there was something decidedly comfortable about it. Her mama would have described it as well-loved, which was her euphemism for something that was not of the finest quality but beloved all the same. Mama had claimed it sounded so much better than the less pleasant words the rest of their class used for describing anything that was not at the peak of perfection, and her mama had a weakness for that which was well-loved. When Tabby was younger, it had been an embarrassment, but she had come to appreciate her mother's tastes; the sentiment attached to well-loved objects made their value far greater than the money spent in purchasing it.

Tabby's heart grew heavy with the memories of her mother. Having lost her several years ago, the pain was not as acute as it had been, but grief was a crafty hunter, cropping up at unexpected moments to catch its prey unawares. But this would not do. One of the last things Tabby needed was to get emotional before meeting her potential employer. She took a cleansing breath, allowing the here and now to wash away thoughts of the past.

She eyed the sofa and wondered if she could sit. If she heard Mrs. Witmore coming, she could pop back up. It would be so nice to rest her feet. The walk here had been rather long, and Tabby could use a rest.

Then the door opened, and Tabby flinched. Thank the stars above that she'd remained standing because Mrs. Witmore had been completely silent in her approach. Turning to greet the woman, Tabby found instead a lady who could only be the mistress of the estate.

"Tabitha Russell?" she asked.

"Yes," she replied, tacking on a curtsy and belated, "madam."

With a gesture, the lady offered Tabby a seat. "I am Mrs. Kingsley—" She halted when she got a good look at Tabby's face. "Miss Granger?"

Tabby's eyes widened as she stared at Mrs. Kingsley. One of the prime enticements of taking a post at Avebury Park was its isolation from anyone of her acquaintance. The Kingsleys were known in society, but as they had never traveled in the same circles or been introduced, Tabby had assumed she would be safe from recognition and the accompanying embarrassment and questions. Apparently not, though Tabby could swear she had never met the lady seated before her.

"Yes, madam, but it is Russell," Tabby replied. "I married nearly twelve years ago."

Mrs. Kingsley clasped her hands in her lap, casting her eyes to the side with a furrowed brow. "Yes, I had forgotten that. The lady who tamed the infamous Mr. Joshua Russell."

Tabby's heart constricted, her soul twisting inside her, but she maintained a properly dignified exterior. When she was younger, hearing people say such things brought her pride and joy; the changes that had been wrought in Joshua had been no small thing. Now, it was nothing more than a mockery. Mrs. Kingsley said the words innocently enough, and Tabby did not detect any malice behind them, so it was easier to remain calm and collected.

"I would not say that, madam," she said.

Mrs. Kingsley's eyes returned to Tabby, snapping back from wherever her mind had wandered. "I'm afraid we were never formally introduced during our Seasons. I was Miss Mina Ashbrook in those days."

Tabby sifted through her memories of that time of her life, trying to place the name. "As in Mr. Nicholas Ashbrook's elder sister?"

Mrs. Kingsley laughed. "Yes, that is my grand claim to fame and generally the only reason anyone knows my name."

Tabby had not meant to offend, and she hurriedly pieced together an apology. This interview was not going as she had hoped.

But Mrs. Kingsley waved it away. "I did not mean that as anything more than a simple comment. You had your hands plenty full during your Seasons, and I do not blame you for not knowing me. When Mr. Kingsley announced our engagement, most everyone scratched their heads and asked, 'Who is she?'"

Tabby smiled. There was something about the lady that was so disarming. She had no airs and embraced a rather self-deprecating view of herself without wandering into self-pity. Frankly, Mrs. Kingsley was amusing, and Tabby quite liked the lady already. Until she asked the question Tabby dreaded answering.

"But I am confused," she said, "and I do apologize if I am being forward or presumptuous, but I understood Mrs. Tabitha Russell was looking for employment. Is that why you are here?"

If there had been any calculation or societal smugness in Mrs. Kingsley's demeanor, Tabby would have rebuffed her or simply not answered, but Mrs. Kingsley looked so genuinely concerned and confused that Tabby could not fault her for voicing the question aloud, even if most would not dare to speak of something so gauche as finances.

"I am looking for employment," said Tabby. "I saw your advertisement for a maid and thought it might be a good fit."

It was easy to see that Mrs. Kingsley wished to ask more questions. The push of curiosity and pull of compassion tugged at her. The lady had no artlessness and seemed unable to strike her emotions from her face; it was such a difference from the ladies of Tabby's acquaintance, and especially during this last year when so many of her former friends smiled to her face and laughed behind her back.

"I am so sorry..." Mrs. Kingsley's hands twisted in her lap, a frown tugging at her lips.

"I'm not looking for pity," said Tabby.

"Of course not," said Mrs. Kingsley. "I prefer to think of it as sympathy, for I cannot imagine how difficult your situation must be. Surely, there is someone who can offer you a better option than servitude."

Tabby shook her head. "My parents both passed a few years ago. I have a distant cousin who inherited the property, but he shows no inclination towards assisting me, and my husband's family and our friends have done what they can, but I cannot trespass upon their generosity any further."

Mrs. Kingsley's eyebrows rose. "That is admirable. There are not many who would feel that way. Most of the gentry seem conditioned to believe that they are entitled to their expensive lifestyles whether or not their coffers can maintain it."

This interview had veered off into uncharted territories, and Tabby could make no sense of Mrs. Kingsley, even if she appreciated the vote of confidence in the decision that had made her a pariah to their social circle.

"Yes, I am quite certain that I like you, Mrs. Russell," said Mrs. Kingsley with a smile. "Though I think you may be a good fit for a different position than a maid. When I read through your qualifications, I had thought you might be suited for it, but now that I have met you, I believe you will fit the bill quite nicely."

Tabby had no response, so she waited patiently as Mrs. Kingsley arrived at the point.

"I have been searching for a housekeeper that is not a housekeeper," said Mrs. Kingsley. "My brother is recovering from injuries he sustained at sea. He is a naval captain, you see, and he was severely wounded in a battle. The surgeons were able to save him, but they were not able to heal him fully. He has it in his head that he will be able to return to his ship even though any reputable medical practitioner says his body shall never be fit for it. In his determination, he has resorted to unsavory treatments that are doing him more harm than good, and it has reached a point where I cannot bear to watch him suffer anymore."

Mrs. Kingsley paused, her eyes falling to her tightly gripped hands resting in her lap, and she took a moment to compose herself. "But I cannot abandon him, either, for he will die of a fever or infection if he has no one to watch out for him. So, he is to move into our dower house where he will be close enough for my peace of mind but free to continue on as he sees fit."

Tabby gave a huff. "Men's pride. It takes a lot of work for women to work around them."

A flash of a smile broke through her pinched expression, and Mrs. Kingsley chuckled. "It does, indeed, and what I am hoping for is that you will serve as the housekeeper of that property. It has been empty for quite some time and needs cleaning and organization, and with your experience running a household, I am confident you have the skills to handle overseeing a cook, maid, and footman."

Tabby nodded.

"But more than that, you will also act as his nurse and companion. He is under the belief that your position will solely be a housekeeper, but I need someone there to watch over him."

"And be your spy," added Tabby with a smile.

"Precisely," she said with a responding smile, though her hands remained clenched. "I worry about him. He has always been a good hearted man, but I find that his injuries have hardened him. He seems lost and melancholy, but he will not allow me to comfort or aid him. I want someone who will help heal him and also pull him out of his doldrums. Can you do that?"

Listening to Mrs. Kingsley's worries and fears, Tabby felt a strong sense of responsibility. Though she had not known this lady for more than a few minutes, Tabby liked her and could see the pain caused by this situation. And then there was the mysterious brother—the man desperate to return to his work, doing whatever he could to fix his broken body. There was something admirable about that kind of passion even if it was misplaced.

"As to his emotional state, I cannot give any guarantees," said Tabby. "Change has to come from within a person, and I cannot do it for him." Tabby had ample experience with that truth, though none that she cared to share with Mrs. Kingsley. "But I am certain that I can act as his caregiver. My mother had a sickly constitution, and I often nursed her."

Mrs. Kingsley smiled and stood, causing Tabby to rise. "Then it sounds as though you are the perfect candidate for the position. Can you start tomorrow?"

A rush of relief filled Tabby as she and Mrs. Kingsley worked out the details. Employment. She would have income, and with her room and board included in her pay, the funds could go exclusively towards keeping a roof over her son's head and food in his stomach. Tabby wanted to hug Mrs. Kingsley. This arrangement was better than she could have hoped for, and Tabby felt buoyed over the fortunate turn of events. For once, things were coming together.

...

Gladwell House was a scant twenty minute walk from the main house, and Tabby enjoyed every second of it. Mrs. Kingsley led her along the pathway connecting the two buildings, giving a recitation of the various details Tabby needed to know, but she struggled to keep her mind on the instructions while the beauty of the grounds entranced her. Great boughs of flowering branches encased the walkway, and birds twittered from the treetops. The scent of life filled her lungs, that intoxicating mixture of soil, blossoms, and all manner of growing things.

The dower house came into view at the top of the next hill, and it captured Tabby's heart immediately. The gray stone building had a flare of the Tudor about it, and it was nestled into the landscape in a way that made Tabby think it was an original building rather than a modern revival.

"I feel I should warn you once more that Graham has been a bit disagreeable," said Mrs. Kingsley, pulling Tabby to a stop on the doorstep. "He is a good man and a wonderful brother, but he has been brought low by this ordeal. Please do not judge him too harshly, and try not to take his behavior to heart."

That sounded quite ominous, but Tabby was unafraid. If she could handle Joshua during one of his drunken tirades, she was certain that a sick seaman was easily conquerable.

Mrs. Kingsley led them inside, and a footman took their bonnets and spencers.

"Where is Captain Ashbrook?" asked Mrs. Kingsley.

"In the sitting room, ma'am," said the footman, motioning to the front parlor, but when the ladies entered, they found the gentleman lying on the sofa.

"Graham?" Mrs. Kingsley came to his side and pressed a hand to his head. The man swiped at it and grumbled a few crude words. Gentleman, indeed.

Captain Ashbrook bore little resemblance to his sister, though that had more to do with the obvious differences in their coloring. Where her hair was dark, his held a touch of blonde, no doubt from years of being out in the sunshine during his time in the navy. But there was something in the shape of their face and nose that held a familial bond.

"Dearest, you are burning up," she said, looking to Tabby for assistance.

Joining her new mistress, Tabby reached for Graham's forehead and found it feverish and damp. His blue-gray eyes turned to her, though they remained unfixed.

"Mina?" he mumbled.

"I am here," his sister whispered, taking his hand.

"My head is splitting."

Mrs. Kingsley looked to Tabby, and she knew it was time for action.

"We need to get him in bed," said Tabby.

The footman stepped forward and between the two of them, they were able to get Captain Ashbrook on his feet. The man was broad-chested and bulky, and far more difficult to support than Joshua was with his lithe frame, but the footman had enough heft and Captain Ashbrook had enough clarity to give them some assistance on the stairs.

"I do not need help, Mina," he grumbled in Tabby's ear, his voice so weak she barely caught the words.

"Of course, sir," said Tabby. "Anyone can see that you are perfectly capable of managing things yourself."

She grunted as he listed to the side, but the footman steadied him.

"I am a grown man," he whispered.

"And men of all ages get sick," said Tabby.

Mrs. Kingsley hurried around them to open the bedchamber door. She pulled back the bedcovers, and they got the captain horizontal once more.

"We need fever powder and water," said Tabby to the footman, and he hurried out the door.

Tabby set to work stripping off the man's boots. In other circumstances, she would be quite scandalized by it, but the situation was far too serious for such sensibilities. They had to get Captain Ashbrook comfortable and being in full clothing would not do. Between her and Mrs. Kingsley, they were able to get him reasonably disrobed and resting.

Pressing her hand to his forehead, Tabby felt the blazing fever that had grown fiercer in just minutes. The room was stifling, and she opened the window to let in a cool breeze. Grabbing a pitcher of water on his side table, Tabby doused the fire. The footman returned with the water and medicine, and together they were able to prop up the gentleman enough to get some of it down his throat.

Mrs. Kingsley stood, wide-eyed and wringing her hands, looking desperate for something to do but unsure of what.

"I need rags and cool water. The colder the better," said Tabby. "Ice, if you can manage. We need to lower his temperature."

"James, run to the main house and fetch a crate of ice," said Mrs. Kingsley before she went in search of the other items.

Tabby pulled her handkerchief from her reticule and dabbed at the sweat gathering on the gentleman's forehead. There was nothing more to do in that moment, so she sat beside him and pressed the cloth to his face while she hummed a tune. She'd never known if her mother heard it when she had done so for her, but it was instinctual. She could only hope it soothed his fevered mind. He may be caught somewhere between consciousness and delirium, but Tabby prayed he would hear it and know there were friends nearby.

Mrs. Kingsley returned with several rags and a bowl of water, and Tabby set to work bathing his face and neck. His skin burned so much that the cloth was warm when she pulled it away, so she cooled it in the water once more.

"I sent for the physician," said Mrs. Kingsley. "But who knows when he will arrive."

"Do not fret," said Tabby. "It's far too early to tell which way this will go, so there is no use in worrying yet."

"Easier said than done," said Mrs. Kingsley, coming around to the other side of the bed. Sitting beside him, she reached for her brother's hand and held it tight.

Chapter 3

Tabby arched her back, feeling it pop and crack as the muscles stretched. Her body ached, and her mind was a veritable mush; luckily, her feet knew the path, allowing her to march mindlessly home. It had taken several hours, but the captain was now resting comfortably after her and Dr. Clarke's ministrations.

What an odd day. A long one, too. But rewarding.

Employment. Income. Unusual though the lady may be, Tabby liked her new employer. The Russells would settle in Bristow; their life would not be what it once was, but as long as they did not starve and Phillip was happy, Tabby could accept that. There was no point in crying over what was lost. Not anymore. Now that she was formally employed, there was no returning to the past. Her reputation was gone. Genteel no longer.

Her tiny home came into view, and though the one room hovel was crumbling and decrepit, Tabby adored it because it was theirs. No more begrudging charity from sneering people; they were living on their own terms, and that was worth a great deal more than mere status.

Phillip watched from the window, beaming when he saw her approaching. He disappeared for a moment before the front door crashed open.

"Mama!" he cried, running to her.

Her aches and pains evaporated as Tabby scooped him up, reveling in his affection.

"I missed you, Mama," he said into her neck, and that brought a pang of disappointment. Though triumphant at finding gainful employment, it was equally difficult to accept that she would be forced to spend her days away from her Phillip.

"I missed you, too, my little man," she said, planting a kiss on her favorite spot of his cheek.

"Papa and I have been playing the quiet game," said Phillip, pressing a finger to his lips.

"Ah," said Tabby. "And have you been winning?"

Phillip gave her a nod and then wriggled out of her arms. Taking her by the hand, he led her inside, and Tabby was thrilled for the chance to sit by the warm hearth with her son and a bit of supper. Stepping through the doorway, Tabby's eyes adjusted to the dim interior to see her husband seated beside the dying fire, his eyes closed and head tilted back; the faint buzz of his snores was the only indication that he was alive.

Closing the door behind them, Tabby stepped around Joshua's outstretched legs and dropped a log into the flames. With the clouds hanging heavy in the sky, there was an unseasonable chill to the summer air and they would likely need the warmth.

Taking off her cloak and bonnet, she placed them on the hook by the door.

"Is it time for supper?" asked Phillip. "Papa said that you'd make it."

Tabby stiffened. She should not have been surprised. Such a menial task would require Joshua to stir himself, and the only thing Tabby could be assured of him doing was nothing. The bed in the loft begged her to lie down and rest, but now was not the time for it.

"Certainly, darling," said Tabby, casting her eyes around for options. Though she had stoked the fire, it would take time for it to be warm enough to cook with. Perhaps a hunk of bread and cheese would do the trick. Gathering it up, she placed it on the table before Phillip.

"I don't think Papa wants any," said Phillip. "He's been sick all day."

Tabby ran her hand over Phillip's chestnut hair. "I'm certain he's been very sick."

"But I was really good," said Phillip between mouthfuls of bread. "I played with my soldiers in the corner and kept very quiet."

Closing her eyes against the frustration, Tabby allowed one morsel of sadness to take hold of her. This was not the life she desired for her or her son, but it was what they had. She needed to be strong. Especially when faced with a future where she would not be present on a daily basis to ensure Phillip was properly cared for. Perhaps one of the neighbors would be willing to watch over Phillip during the day, and then Tabby could be at ease. Her position with the Kingsleys was better paid than she had expected, so they should have a little extra to lay aside for that.

Tabby looked at Joshua. She desperately needed to sit, but if she did so now, she doubted she would rise again until morning, and there was still much to do. Her exhausted body wanted to leave Joshua there, but she knew from hard experience that he would wake in the night and attempt to come to bed on his own, which would disturb her and Phillip.

Breathing deep, Tabby summoned her remaining strength, pulled Joshua's arm over her shoulder, and hoisted him up. He was lanky and thin, but any dead weight was heavy and difficult to manage, and this was not the first insensible person she'd had to drag about today. Tabby staggered with his weight but got him moving towards the loft. With some jostling, she was able to rouse him enough to climb the stairs that were so steep and narrow they were nearly a ladder. Gravity did the rest, and Joshua fell onto the pallet that served as their family bed; with a few more grunts and pushes, she got him onto his corner of it.

Tabby wiped at the sweat on her brow and found Phillip watching her from the stairs, his cheese and bread clutched in his hands. He studied his father with fascination but little comprehension, and Tabby hoped the lad did not fully appreciate how far gone his dear papa was.

Legs quivering, Tabby allowed herself to sit on the top stair. She needed to pack, but she needed a moment to rest more. The instant her lap was available, Phillip climbed onto it and shoved his bread at her mouth. Tabby chuckled and pushed it away.

"No, dearest, that is yours," she said. "I will get some later."

"How long do we have to stay here?" asked Phillip, glancing up at her.

"This is our home now, little man," said Tabby, kissing the top of his head and wrapping her arms around him.

"But I miss Kelland. And all my toys. And my pony," said Phillip. "Can I get a new pony?"

"No, dearest," Tabby said with a sigh. "We cannot afford it."

"But—"

"Rather than wish for all the things we cannot have, we must think of things we like about our new house," said Tabby. That exercise had helped lighten her own heart in such melancholy moments, perhaps it might help her son as well.

Phillip's forehead crinkled, and Tabby rocked the boy.

"It's cozier here," she said. When Phillip gave her a questioning look, she explained, "We are all together. No more enormous, empty rooms."

He nodded, biting into his cheese. "No more stuffy clothes," he added, holding up his arms and throwing back his head to show the utter lack of jacket or lace collar.

That brought a bigger smile, and Tabby searched for other things. "No more boring tea parties and morning visits with uppity ladies."

"I get to play in the mud!" said Phillip.

And so it went. It took some creativity, but they managed a suitably long list of things they adored about their new life and did not miss about the old one. Their life was hard, but there was much to be grateful for, and Tabby simply needed to focus on those good things. She had a position near her son. They had income. They had a home. Casting a glance at her dozing husband, Tabby wondered how long her strength would last, but for now, she clung to the little victories.

However, such good thoughts were beyond her when the next morning arrived and she was forced to bid farewell to her little Phillip.

"Dearest, please," said Tabby, peeling Phillip's hands from her skirts. "I will return in three days, and we will spend a whole evening together. Won't that be fun?"

"Mama, please!" he sobbed, tugging at her. "Don't leave me!"

Tears filled Tabby's eyes, but she forced them away. Falling to pieces would only make things worse. She could not allow herself to get distracted from her goals: a roof over his head, clothes on his back, and food in his belly were foremost, closely followed by saving for his schooling and preparing for his future. None of that would be possible if Tabby stayed.

Joshua pulled the boy away, lifting him into his arms. "Mama has to go."

"Why?" cried Phillip.

Joshua held the boy close, resting Phillip's head on his shoulder as the lad sobbed for Tabby. The sight of it tore at her heart. She wanted to care for her son, but their family needed the money. Staring at Joshua, a dark part of her soul hated that her husband had forced her into this heartrending situation. The multitude of positions available for a man with his connections guaranteed he'd need not work away from home. Not so for Tabby.

"I shall return soon," she promised before hoisting her portmanteau. Tabby had to leave. She had done the best she could for her son. Mrs. Allen had agreed to keep watch over Phillip. They had a home. They had food. Now, Tabby had to make certain that did not change.

Chapter 4

The devil take him. Graham stared at the bedroom ceiling, cursing the French for injuring him, his body for not healing properly, and the entirety of the medical profession who were incapable of doing a thing about it. A relapse. That was what Dr. Clarke had called it. A little word for a monumentally frustrating ordeal. This would set his recovery back again. Delay the next round of treatments. More time in this bloody bed like some skulking layabout.

Graham gritted his teeth as a stab of pain struck his thigh. When it passed, he let out a heavy grunt.

"Are you in pain?" asked a woman as she pushed open the bedroom door with the corner of a breakfast tray.

Something about her was familiar. It was an itching recognition that Graham could not name; she was pretty enough that he was certain he'd remember her if they had been introduced. She stared at him with brown eyes that were framed with delicate blonde eyebrows. Quite pretty, in fact.

"Who are you?" he asked.

The woman raised those eyebrows, though he had no idea why she should be surprised at such a simple question.

"I am Mrs. Russell, the new housekeeper. We met yesterday. I'm surprised you have no memory of it. You were incoherent at points, but I was with you most of the day."

Her accent surprised him. It was authentically genteel with none of the practiced elocution of the upper servants mimicking their masters.

She brought over the tray, and Graham held in a groan as he sat himself upright. His right arm supported him for a quick moment before giving out—accursed relapse. Placing the tray before him, Mrs. Russell reached over to lay a napkin across his lap, but he grabbed her wrist, and her eyebrows shot upwards yet again.

"I can manage that," he said.

"You could have said so."

Graham grunted and grabbed the spoon. His fingers were stiff, and it took greater effort than he wished to admit to get them around the utensil. But he did it. He supposed he should be grateful. After all, he was able to accomplish what any tot could do with a fraction of the effort. A day for celebration.

And that was when he noticed that Mrs. Russell was still in his bedchamber. Rather than disappearing the moment she had delivered the tray, the lady drew open the curtains and straightened a few incidentals.

Ignoring her, Graham focused on the spoon. He should use his left hand, but Graham would not concede defeat so easily. The soup sloshed, but the utensil inched towards his lips. He leaned forward to keep the mess above the bowl, but his muscles protested, and he splattered it on his front, letting loose a string of words that would've made his mother blush.

"Allow me," said Mrs. Russell, and Graham found himself, once again, at the mercies of a fluttering female.

"I am capable of doing it myself," he insisted, snatching the napkin to dab at the mess.

"I did not say otherwise," said Mrs. Russell. "I am standing here and am able to help, so I am."

Graham grunted again and refused to look at her. Until her

hand came to his forehead. Graham jerked away, but she hushed him and forced her touch on him once more.

"What are you doing, madam?" he demanded.

"I would think it obvious," she replied.

"You are overstepping your duties, Mrs. Russell. You are the housekeeper, not my nursemaid." He leaned away from her, but Mrs. Russell changed tactics and came at him from a different angle.

"After all the time I spent nursing you back from the brink of death yesterday," she said, "it would be a shame for the fever to return."

"You were there?"

"I already said as much."

Hazy recollections came to Graham, and the oddest of memories came into his mind. Her face watching over him. Broken bits of a comforting song.

"I was not on the brink of death," he grumbled but stopped fighting. The woman was too persistent for a man to mount much of a resistance.

"Hmmm," she said with a raised eyebrow and then leaned back when she found what she was hunting for. "Your temperature is what it should be."

"Is that your expert opinion?" he asked, reaching for the spoon once more.

"Allow me," she said, but Graham growled at her.

"I can feed myself and require no further help. You are excused."

Graham shifted the spoon to his good hand and ignored the housekeeper as she gave a disgruntled curtsy and retreated.

The devil take stubborn men. Tabby could not abide swearing, but the phrase came to mind without thought as she had heard the words from Joshua and his set on many an occasion. Regardless, they fit her mood to perfection. She had only been offering a bit of help, and the man behaved as though she was unraveling the very fabric of morality.

Pride. That word made Tabby seethe. She had seen pride do enough damage in her life, and she would not allow it any more control. Employer or not, Tabby would not be browbeaten.

Mrs. Bunting was rolling out dough on the kitchen table as Tabby entered. The woman took one look at her and offered up a tray of sweet biscuits. "You look as though you could use one of these."

"That man is insufferable," she said, taking the treat and biting into the bit of heaven. It was a mix of honey, cinnamon, and a dozen other things Tabby could not identify. Another blessing of this new life. Mrs. Bunting was not a fancy cook, but the simple fare she made was better than any elegant meal Tabby had ever tasted.

"He's a good man," said Mrs. Bunting, returning to her baking. "He's just been in a bit of a foul mood of late."

"Forgive me, but I do not find such assurances reassuring. It is never a good sign that others must vouch for a man's character because his behavior has demonstrated the opposite," said Tabby, taking another bite. "I have yet to hear a kind word from him."

"Captain Ashbrook has been visiting Avebury Park every shore leave since his sister became Mrs. Kingsley," she said, working the rolling pin. "He can be a bit gruff at times, as is often the case with those naval men, but he's uncommonly kind and generous."

"That man is a bit more than gruff."

"He's hurting," said Mrs. Bunting.

"That comes with being injured," said Tabby.

"Not just that," she replied, retrieving a circular cutter and pressing it into the dough. "In one quick moment he lost his entire life and livelihood. That'd be enough to bring any of us low."

Tabby munched on the biscuit and tried not to think of how similar her situation was to the captain's. "That does not excuse his behavior. One cannot sit around moaning about things one cannot change."

Mrs. Bunting nodded and gave Tabby a considering smile. "True, but it should allow him a bit of leeway, don't you think?"

If it were not for the wink that accompanied that statement, Tabby would feel thoroughly ashamed and set in her place. She still felt a bit of both, but Mrs. Bunting handed her another treat, and that helped soothe her feelings.

...

That afternoon Graham awoke to a hand on his forehead. Again. At least this time, he did not jerk away like a startled pup, but he found himself no more happy with the interruption than he had the last few times it had happened.

"It is time for your medicine," said Mrs. Russell.

"I do not want any more of that foul stuff," said Graham.

"That may be, but Dr. Clarke ordered that you take it for one more day." Mrs. Russell stood at his bedside, uncorking a bottle.

"No," said Graham.

Mrs. Russell ignored him and filled a spoon with the medicine.

"I feel perfectly fine," he insisted. "I do not need it."

Mrs. Russell stared at him with tight lips. She may have the bearing and accent of a fine lady, but she had none of the soft-spoken gentility one would expect. Graham was hard pressed to picture Mrs. Russell as a demure society lady flitting about a ballroom, for she had an air about her that would make even the roughest admirals turn tail and run. But Graham was not one to retreat. Crossing his arms, he met her eyes. He was master here, and it was he who would decide whether or not to take his medicine.

And then she struck, snatching his nose and pinching it tight.

Graham's eyebrows drew together at the oddity. He leaned away, but his right side screamed at him, and the lady's fingers were like a vice. The moment he opened his mouth to breathe, Mrs. Russell had the spoon in his mouth and the medicine down his throat before he could do a single thing about it.

"What are you doing, madam!" he sputtered.

"Taking care of you, though you are making it monumentally difficult," she said, stoppering the bottle.

Graham froze. "Taking care of me? You are the housekeeper."

"Of course I am," she said, gathering the spoon. "I take care of the house, and you are in the house, so I am taking care of you."

Mrs. Russell tried to hide the truth, but the woman was as successful as a child insisting he had not eaten a biscuit while crumbs littered his shirt.

"I do not need a nursemaid," he said, crossing his arms and ignoring the fact that his right arm did not wish to bend in that manner.

"The fact that you can hardly sit upright would beg to differ," said Mrs. Russell. Graham glowered at her, but at least she was no longer denying the truth. "Or the fact that just yesterday you were so delirious that the footman and I had to haul you into bed."

Graham could not believe her insolence. Mrs. Russell and his sister had been plotting, and Mrs. Russell was acting as though it were his fault. Mina was the one all tied in knots over his treatments. For all her talk of giving him independence and his own space, nothing had changed.

He would not stand for it.

"Women!" He bellowed the word like a curse. "I do not need some deuced woman fluttering about me. I am not an invalid. I am not a child. I may have been ill yesterday, but I am healthy now. So, your services are no longer required."

Mrs. Russell set down the medicine and crossed her own arms, staring at him. "Are you sacking me?"

Graham matched her gaze and gave her a nod.

"You did not hire me, so you cannot sack me," she said. "I am here at Mrs. Kingsley's behest, and I will not go until she tells me to leave—no matter how petulant you become."

She scooped up the medicine bottle and stormed towards the door, stopping when she reached the threshold to send a parting shot. "Perhaps if men were not so stubborn and pig-headed, women would not need to fret and worry about them. Perhaps if men thought of anyone other than themselves for one moment, they would see that women are only trying to help! Even children will stop fussing after a time, but men go to their graves bellyaching!"

Graham seethed. On his ship, such insubordination would be dealt with quickly and efficiently, yet he was stuck here, unable to do more than bark orders.

"Get me my sister. Now!" If Mrs. Russell refused to listen, Graham had no choice but to make Mina do so. He would not be mollycoddled.

Chapter 5

Now she had done it. Tabby paced the entryway, her feet moving as she awaited her executioner. She should have held her tongue. She should have smiled and nodded. She should have done anything except what she did. But Captain Ashbrook was so insufferable and deserved a good tongue lashing for his behavior.

Except that it may cost Tabby her position.

Leaning against the narrow hallway, Tabby covered her face. She had no idea how she would manage; being terminated within twenty-four hours guaranteed she would not find another position in a Bristow household, and they had no funds to move towns.

Tabby stood there, picturing the horrible things to come the moment Mrs. Kingsley arrived. James had surely delivered the message to the main house by now, and Tabby could not imagine Mrs. Kingsley siding against her brother.

Taking a breath, Tabby cleared her mind and sought out the good things that might come from this situation. But there was nothing. At best, she would not have to see Captain Ashbrook again. And perhaps she'd find a position where she could spend her evenings at home with Phillip, though that was unlikely. But neither made up for the fact that any new position would pay far less.

A hand on the doorknob had Tabby straightening as James stepped through the front door. However, she was greeted not by Mrs. Kingsley but by her husband.

"You must be Mrs. Russell," said Mr. Kingsley. "My wife was otherwise occupied when James came in search of her, and I thought it best that I manage the situation."

"Mr. Kingsley," said Tabby with a curtsy. "I am terribly sorry to inconvenience you, but Captain Ashbrook was quite insistent. Sir."

"I am certain he was," said Mr. Kingsley, handing his hat and gloves to James. "Where is the scoundrel?"

...

Graham stared at the ceiling, certain that it had been hours since his nursemaid had left with her tail tucked between her legs, yet Mina had not arrived. This whole situation was intolerable. Insupportable. Beyond the pale. Such a silly ruse. Had Mina truly thought he would not notice that his housekeeper was a nurse in disguise? Apparently, he was not only an invalid but a halfwit as well.

Hearing steps on the stairs, Graham leaned up to see his door open. But it was Simon.

"Good afternoon, Graham," he said, sitting on a chair that had been left beside the bed. "I understand you are upset about Mrs. Russell."

"Where is Mina?" asked Graham.

"She is not coming," said Simon, crossing his arms. "I intercepted James before he found her, and I thought it was time for us to talk."

From the look on Simon's face, Graham suspected it would

not be a pleasant one. Sitting before him was not the man with whom Graham had become acquainted. Simon was a congenial fellow, a doting husband, and a thoroughly enjoyable gentleman, but none of that was reflected in his expression at that moment. He looked far too disapproving for Graham's tastes, and since he and Simon had not shared many one-on-one discussions before, it was a tad disconcerting.

"You wish to sack Mrs. Russell?" asked Simon.

"I do not need a nursemaid," said Graham. "I am a grown man, and more than capable of caring for myself. I do not need Mina hovering over me."

Simon nodded. "And that is why your sister and I thought this would be a good arrangement. Mina does have a tendency to overdo it when nursing her loved ones, but you cannot be left alone if you are determined to keep going under the knife."

Graham began to argue, but Simon raised a hand.

"Mina has begged me to allow her to handle things," said Simon. "Out of respect for her, I have kept quiet, but I refuse to stand by and watch your behavior in silence any longer."

"My—?" But Graham fell silent with a sharp look from Simon.

"You've been a brute," said Simon. "Your surliness has been directed at every member of my staff. You have upset the entire household. We all know that you have been dealt a horrible blow, but it has reached a point where you must stop making everyone pay for it. Now."

Graham stared at Simon. "You cannot be serious. You are blaming me for the row with Mrs. Russell?"

"I am not talking only about Mrs. Russell," said Simon. "I don't even know all the circumstances of what has passed between you two. I am speaking of your conduct as a whole. Every day you snip and bark at anyone who comes close to you."

"Simon—"

"You have reduced your sister to tears on numerous occasions," said Simon, his voice growing harder. His jaw tightened, and Graham could swear he heard the man's teeth grinding.

"For the first time in months—months, Graham— she has been able to sleep because she knows you are being cared for and she no longer has to fret over every little thing she says or does, for she never knows what might set off your temper."

Graham wanted to argue, but he knew Mina well enough to know that Simon's assessment was likely true.

"I gave my word that I would not interfere," said Simon. "I hate to go back on it, but I cannot watch things unravel any further. I know you love your sister, but almost everything out of your mouth is rude, crude, or both. You are taking your frustrations out on her, and it is not right."

Graham's head fell onto the pillow. "You make it sound as though I've been the most inexcusable bully."

There was silence for a moment before Simon replied, "You have."

His head snapped up. Or tried to. Aches and pains kept him from moving too fast, but Graham got his head upright once more.

"We don't know each other well," said Simon. "With you being at sea, we have not had the opportunity, but you have spent every shore leave at Avebury Park, and I feel like I know your character well enough to know you are a good man. But in the months since you moved here, you have been unbearable."

Graham opened his mouth, but Simon gave him another silencing hand.

"I know you've had a rough time of it," said Simon. "Otherwise, we would have had this conversation a long time ago. But it has reached a point where you are no longer the man that I respect. You berate everyone around you. You lash out morning, noon, and night. You know as well as I that Mina does not need a direct cut to feel the pain. Simply being upset is enough to hurt her."

"Perhaps I should leave and stay somewhere else," said Graham, his eyes falling to the bedcovers.

Simon gave a huff. "Don't be an imbecile. That would make

matters worse. What would have happened if you had been living on your own when that fever struck yesterday?"

"It was not that bad—"

"It was," said Simon, drawing Graham's gaze to his own. Simon's eyes were ferocious. "If Mina and Mrs. Russell had not found you and been so swift in treating you, you would not be here. You pulled out of it quickly, yes, but the direction you were headed would have landed you in an early grave. Do you know what that would do to Mina if that had happened? To your family?"

"So, I am forced to stay here?"

"If you care about your health and your sister's wellbeing, yes."

Graham's eyes traced the damask patterns woven into the linens, his mind picking apart Simon's words. It couldn't possibly be as bad as his brother-in-law was claiming. Graham would be the first to admit that he had not been the perfect houseguest, but it was not as though he went about intentionally destroying the happiness of those around him.

Simon interrupted Graham's mulling by adding, "It is easy to justify and rationalize our behavior, Graham. It is so easy to believe that you are not truly hurting or harming others, but I beg you to avoid being as obtuse as I once was."

Graham sent Simon a questioning look, and the man sighed.

"When Mina and I were first married, I blinded myself to my behavior," said Simon. "And I am ashamed to think of how I acted then. I convinced myself that I was being the epitome of a perfect husband, but in the end I hurt the one person I love most in the world. Do not make my mistake."

That certainly gave Graham a lot to think about, but then Simon went one step further.

"Mina is with child," he said.

The sudden discovery brought a shift in emotion. Such joyful news. Mina had never admitted it, but Graham knew how much she longed for children with Simon. For five years, he'd been hoping to hear those glad tidings, but the look on Simon's face was not quite as happy as Graham would have expected.

"This is good news, isn't it?" asked Graham.

Simon let a smile grow on his face. "Of course. It is everything we have hoped for, but it brings a lot of anxiety with it. After what happened with your mother, Mina is understandably nervous. Once the initial surprise faded, she has been increasingly anxious about what will happen with her and the babe."

Memories of losing their dear mother and baby sister dimmed the felicity of the moment. Graham could still hear the cries from the night baby Catherine was born and died. First from their mother. Then the weak squawks of the babe. But then they grew silent and it was their own tears that filled the house. Father's bloodshot eyes as he clutched mother's limp hand. Mina gathering the boys close to say their final goodbyes. Too many ladies perished bringing their babes into the world for Graham to feel calm at the prospect of his sister facing it. He could only imagine how worried Simon must be, too.

"Mina has enough to fret about," said Graham. "And I am adding to it."

Simon nodded. "Until you are on your feet, she needs you nearby or she will worry incessantly about whether or not you are healthy and happy. However, she cannot bear the strain of watching your pain as you convalesce."

It had been a long time since Graham had eaten such an enormous slice of humble pie. It was difficult to take, and Graham wanted to protest the heaping spoonfuls that Simon was forcing down his throat, but if there was even a chance that what Simon had said was true (and he suspected that far too much of it was), Graham needed to be a better brother. After all Mina had done for him and the heartache she had suffered in her life, she deserved happiness. If staying at Gladwell House and suffering Mrs. Russell's nursing brought her peace, it was the least he could do.

"Fine," said Graham. "I will stay and keep Mrs. Russell on

until I return to sea."

Simon raised his eyebrows.

"And I will be more pleasant to others," said Graham.

A small smile quirked at the side of Simon's mouth. "Your tone fills me with such confidence."

Graham narrowed his eyes, but Simon stood and patted Graham on his shoulder.

"Do not let this hardship define who you are, Graham. You are a better man than your words and actions have shown of late," said Simon.

His brother-in-law turned to leave but paused. "And do not make your sister cry again. Frederick Voss taught me a vicious right-hook, and I am not afraid to use it." Simon moved to shut the door but added one final thing. "And don't tell her I talked with you, or she will pummel us both."

The door shut behind him, and Graham stared at the ceiling. In normal circumstances, there was no way Mr. Simon Kingsley would best Captain Graham Ashbrook in fisticuffs. But these were not normal circumstances, and Graham had to admit that in his current position, Simon would be more than a match for him.

That realization stung, though accepting that he may deserve such a beating pained him even more. Graham did not want to think that he had allowed himself to become the mean-spirited, cruel man Simon described, but there was enough ring of truth to his brother-in-law's words to leave Graham pondering it for a good, long while.

Chapter 6

Eavesdropping was not what a lady of sense should be doing, but too much of her future depended on the conversation happening in Captain Ashbrook's bedchamber, which is how Tabby found herself skulking outside his door. A grown woman hovering at a keyhole.

The conversation was infuriating. Her official acquaintance with Mrs. Kingsley was hardly twenty-four hours old, yet Tabby already liked her immensely. The lady was kind and genuine in a way that was unique among their class. Or rather, Mrs. Kingsley's class, as Tabby was no longer one of them.

Hearing Mr. Kingsley recount his wife's turmoil made Tabby wish to give Captain Ashbrook a thorough scolding. A grown man wallowing in self-pity. He was not the first nor the last to shoulder hardship. Plenty of others had, were, and would, yet he carried on as though he were the sole sufferer. Listening to his grumbling and groaning reminded Tabby far too much of Joshua and his constant moaning.

As she realized that truth, Tabby was forced to acknowledge that perhaps a touch of her own temper had stemmed from her feelings towards her husband. Perhaps she'd not been completely innocent in their exchange.

But then the conversation shifted. Listening to it, Tabby was shocked to hear Captain Ashbrook sound penitent. Not as much as he should be, but the fact that he accepted his guilt to any degree and promised to change was shocking. Elating. In her experience, wringing contrition from men with battered pride was a herculean effort. Nigh on impossible.

Tabby was so surprised at the turn that she nearly missed Mr. Kingsley's approach. Pushing away from the door, she hurried down the hall and pulled a rag from her apron pocket, wiping at invisible dust on a picture frame.

"Mrs. Russell."

"Yes?" asked Tabby, turning to meet him before tacking on a hurried curtsy and, "Sir."

"I hope there will be no more issues with your working here," said Mr. Kingsley. "But if there are, please come to me directly. In fact, anything that may upset Mrs. Kingsley should come to me, and I shall handle it."

Tabby smiled. "Yes, sir. And I would like to apologize again for bothering you. Mrs. Kingsley had wished me to keep the true nature of my position from Captain Ashbrook, but he worked it out."

"I have no idea why she thought you could keep it hidden," he said with a chuckle. "It is better out in the open, so do not trouble yourself. She is elated you are here and has every confidence that you will be able to handle the situation."

"I apologize for upsetting him," said Tabby. "I—"

Mr. Kingsley waved it away. "I have a feeling that the best thing for my brother-in-law is a firm hand. Sometimes it is the only way to sort stubborn men out."

"You sound as though you are speaking from personal experience," said Tabby, her smile growing.

"Unfortunately," he said just before Captain Ashbrook called out for her.

"I will leave you to it," said Mr. Kingsley with a nod as he headed down the stairs to show himself out.

Having the support of her employers and feeling a touch

more secure about her position, Tabby squared her shoulders. Speaking to him was not something Tabby relished, but it needed to be done. Better to face the brute head-on.

"Yes?" she called, pushing open the chamber door.

Captain Ashbrook lay exactly where she had seen him last, but his face turned to greet her. For all his earlier contrition with his brother-in-law, Tabby knew what was coming. No man cares to be put in a position of subservience to a woman, and as his keeper, Tabby suspected Captain Ashbrook would see it as nothing less.

Stepping into the room, Tabby straightened her already straight spine. She would not be browbeaten. Her position was not in jeopardy. Not yet, at any rate. And income or not, Tabby would not allow herself or any of the staff to be badgered by this man.

He raised a hand and beckoned for her to come closer. Tabby drew to his bedside, but did not sit in the chair Mr. Kingsley had occupied.

"I feel I should apologize," he said.

And that was when Tabby sat.

"My brother-in-law has informed me that I have been a bit of a brute as of late, and I know that I was unkind to you earlier."

Tabby watched for any sign of duplicity, but honesty shone in his eyes. At least, Tabby thought it was genuine, though it was hard to tell with a gentleman she had known for less than a day.

"I apologize for sacking you," he said, "and I hope we can put this behind us as it appears I am stuck with you."

"Stuck with me?" Tabby's eyebrows shot up. She needed to keep a better hold on her tongue, but the words were so vexing that she could not stop herself.

Captain Ashbrook let out a curse as his head fell onto the pillow. "Not stuck. That is not what I mean."

"It is what you said."

"I did, but I did not mean it."

"Hastily said words are often the most honest," said Tabby.

"And what about fever addled ones?" Captain Ashbrook sent her a pleading look, but Tabby placed her hand on his forehead.

"No fever."

The captain let out a chuckle, and then Tabby saw a tightening of the muscles in his face. He was trying to hide it, but she saw the pain. She had witnessed enough of his injuries the day before to surmise that such aches were likely his constant companion.

"Will you, Mrs. Russell, please do me the honor of staying on as my housekeeper and nursemaid?" The last word was filled with distaste but enough humor that Tabby actually smiled at the man. He was an oddity.

Tabby was going to twit him about being in his sister's employ, but she recognized the peace offering for what it was and decided it was time to accept it graciously. "I would love to. Sir."

The captain nodded and held out his hand. "Perhaps it is time we were properly introduced. I am Captain Ashbrook."

Tabby took it and replied, "Mrs. Russell, at your service."

Captain Ashbrook gave another nod, released her hand, and then said something that nearly knocked Tabby off her chair. "Now, with all that done and sorted, is there any chance I could get some more of your medicine? I have to admit it did wonders for my head."

A slight pink drew across his cheeks, and Tabby realized that the man was embarrassed. She knew she should ignore it, but the impulse to tease him was too strong. Such familiarity with her charge could be problematic, but Tabby's instincts told her he needed it. "You shan't fight me this time? I am a master at getting medicine down uncooperative throats."

Captain Ashbrook let out another laugh tinged with hidden aches, and though Tabby hated the thought of having caused it, the captain's spirits looked better for it.

"Your skills are quite impressive," he said. "I never stood a chance, but I give my word of honor, madam. No more fighting."

Chapter 7

Bent over on her hands and knees, Tabby attacked the stained floor of her cottage. Scrubbing the frayed brush against the wood, she scoured the dirt. The water came away filthy, and she dunked it in the bucket beside her and returned to work. Whenever her mind drifted to how unpleasant this chore was, Tabby tried to remind herself that having a floor was better than having none at all; their home may be small and poor, but she had seen others with nothing but dirt. Unfortunately, it was little consolation when she had to clean the same spot six times.

Her back begged for a rest and her knees were numb, but Tabby kept going. She was determined to turn this hovel into a home. It was not how she wished to spend her evening off, but since she'd not had the time to tackle the chore before, it must be done now. Joshua certainly had not seen fit to take care of it. Or the laundry. Or dinner. Or any of the other numerous tasks that needed doing.

The cottage filled with the aroma of cooking soup, and Tabby was pleased that it smelled so appetizing. She had no idea if it would be edible, but it was warm, and at the moment she was hungry enough to eat her bonnet. Perhaps she could get

Mrs. Bunting to give her a few cooking lessons when she returned to Gladwell House. Tabby did not know the woman well, but it was clear that food preparation in any form was the cook's passion, and Tabby imagined Mrs. Bunting would enjoy sharing that love with others, so she made note to ask when she returned.

How things had changed in a sennight. Captain Ashbrook was still prickly, but he had stopped fighting Tabby's efforts to nurse him. He was far from an ideal patient, but he was making strides. At the very least, his repentance was genuine enough for him to keep trying.

A sudden weight dropped onto Tabby's back, and she barely kept herself from collapsing as Phillip wrapped his arms around her neck.

"Phillip, no!" Tabby barked, and the weight disappeared as quickly as it came. Looking behind her, she saw her little man standing in the corner, staring at her with teary eyes. Tabby's anger still burned while her body ached from Phillip's well-meaning attack, but she took a breath and calmed her nerves. Phillip did not need another parent shouting at him.

"I'm sorry, Mama," he said, wiping at his cheeks.

"Oh, sweetheart," said Tabby, scooting closer to pull him into her arms. "I apologize. Mama is very tired and you are getting so very big now. Almost too big to jump on Mama like that."

Phillip clung to her. "I'm too big?"

Tabby kissed the top of his head. "So big."

He leaned back and smiled. "I'm a big boy."

Tabby smiled. "Yes, dearest. My little gentleman."

Phillip's stomach gave a mighty growl, and his eyes widened.

"I think it is time for dinner," said Tabby, leaning forward to buss Phillip's sweet face. He may be getting bigger, but his cheeks still held that infantine chubbiness that was so delectable.

Tabby slowly got to her feet. It was disturbing how difficult it was to straighten, but as she stared at the cleaner patch of floor, it felt well worth the effort. There was still much to do, but Tabby was making progress.

"Is Papa going to eat with us?" asked Phillip.

As Tabby had no idea where Joshua had disappeared to, she couldn't very well fetch him for dinner. "Not tonight, darling."

Phillip nodded and climbed onto a chair. Wrapping a rag around her hand, Tabby reached for the pot over the fire and placed it on the table. The aroma was heavenly, though that could be due to her own grumbling stomach. Lifting the lid, Tabby found a thick brown sludge. That was the only way to describe it. It looked horrid, even if it smelled good enough. Ladling some into a bowl, Tabby blew on it for a few moments while Phillip clamored for his meal.

"It's hot," she warned, placing it before him.

Tabby dug into her own bowl and found the veggies crunchy, the meat stringy, and the taste to be one step above bland. But it was hot and it was food, so Tabby tucked in. She truly needed to talk to Mrs. Bunting about cooking lessons. Tabby was certain she could find time away from her duties to learn the basics.

She ate another spoonful. Perhaps more than basics.

Glancing behind her, Tabby checked the window. A tiny bit of light colored the sky, so she still had some time before she needed to return to work.

"Are you going?" asked Phillip, poking his soup.

"Not yet."

Phillip dropped his spoon onto the table and slouched. "I don't want you to leave."

"I know, but I must," said Tabby before prompting him to eat again. "I will return in three days, and we will have a whole half day together."

That did not bring a smile to Phillip's face.

"Perhaps we can do something special together then," said Tabby.

Phillip straightened at that. "Like what?"

Tabby took another bite of the soup while she grabbed at any idea that might entice him. "We could have a picnic by the pond and see the ducks."

Phillip's eyes widened. "Can we feed them?"

Tabby nodded. "And perhaps there might be some cake left from Captain Ashbrook's tea that I could bring." Mrs. Bunting always had some sweets or treats lying around that Tabby would be allowed to procure for their picnic.

"Cake?" Phillip beamed.

Tears came to Tabby's eyes, but she blinked them away. Phillip was thrilled over a simple picnic and the hope of some cake. It was dispiriting to see how far they had fallen, but Tabby brushed aside the melancholy to grasp at the gratitude she felt at bringing a bit of joy to her son's life—however small.

As Phillip finished his meal, Tabby spun more stories of what they would do together, filling his head with dreams she hoped she could recreate.

...

Tabby stood at the window, staring out at the darkness. Joshua was still not home. She paced, desperate to make a decision but unsure of what to do. Phillip was already asleep in the loft, and she needed to return to work. Tabby could not leave her son alone, but she had no idea where her husband had gotten to. With only a quick word of goodbye, he had slunk out the door moments after Tabby had arrived. She could only wonder where he had disappeared to, and none of her wonderings were encouraging. Joshua knew she needed to leave, yet night was moving quickly to morning, and Joshua was nowhere to be seen.

There was nothing to be done but throw herself on the mercy of her neighbor.

Tabby slipped on her spencer and grabbed her reticule—

M.A. Nichols

and paused. Lifting the small pouch, Tabby realized it was lighter than when she had arrived. Ripping open the drawstrings, she found it empty. Every last coin was gone.

Several of Captain Ashbrook's more colorful curses came to mind as she wished her husband to the infernal pits of hell. That money was meant to care for their son, and he was likely spending it all on drink and cards. If it were not for the coins she kept hidden at Gladwell House, every last penny of theirs would be gone. That was meant to be the beginnings of their savings, but it would be their lifeline now.

How she wanted to shout and rail against the man for his selfishness, but Tabby was standing alone with an empty reticule, a sleeping son, and no time to waste. Shoving such thoughts aside, Tabby needed to move forward. There was no point in dwelling on Joshua's faults at present. She needed to return to Gladwell House or their family would have nothing. Putting on her bonnet, Tabby crept up the stairs and lifted Phillip onto her shoulder; her exhausted body staggered under his dead weight.

Tabby carried Phillip out of the cottage and towards Mrs. Allen's home. For a few coins, the woman had watched over the boy while Joshua was frequently indisposed; Tabby could only hope that she would be able to do so again.

"Mrs. Russell?" answered Mrs. Allen when Tabby knocked on her door.

"I hate to bother you, but I came to beg your assistance," said Tabby. She took a quick moment to rein in her emotions before explaining the situation. Mrs. Allen was already well aware of the issues the Russells were facing, but it was a new low to have to plead for help when Phillip's own father should be here. And to do so without compensation to offer up was doubly shaming.

"I can't be taking in all the neighborhood strays," said Mrs. Allen, crossing her arms.

"I realize this is an imposition," said Tabby, "but I don't know what else to do."

Heaving a sigh that conveyed just how enormous a burden Tabby was asking her to bear, Mrs. Allen took Phillip into her arms. The child stirred at the jostling, but she hushed him. "I'll take him, but you best pay me double next time."

"Double?"

"For the imposition," she said, closing the door behind her.

Tabby's head dropped. She hated the thought of leaving her son with such a sour person, but there was no choice. She tried to reassure herself that leaving him with Mrs. Allen was better than him being alone, but it was not much of a comfort. He should be with his father at home, but that was not possible at present, and Tabby had no other recourse than to accept the reality before her as she turned away from the forlorn cottages and began the trek to Gladwell House.

Chapter 8

Graham drew back his covers and pointed his toes. His right side was finally improving after the fever, while the left was stiff from disuse. Shifting his legs, he tested them and found nothing but a dull ache. It had been a fortnight since the fever, and there were no signs of another recurrence and no reason not to attempt walking. Fortune favors the bold, and all that.

Twisting, he dropped his feet to the floor and leaned forward. His right arm would not take much weight, but using his left side, he was able to get to his feet. It was thrilling, which was in turn demoralizing; he was only standing, yet it seemed like a monumental accomplishment. He had not felt this good in months. Though weakened by bedrest, Graham could feel a new vitality coursing through him. His cane sat beside the bed, but he ignored it. He might have needed it before the last procedure, but his leg felt stronger now.

Taking a step forward, Graham was elated when his legs kept him upright. His right had a pulsing ache, and he was wobbling and unsteady, but they held him. It was a far cry from what was needed in order to stand on a heaving, wave-tossed ship, but he was better than he had been in weeks. Progress.

Another step forward, and Graham drew closer to the door. The muscles in his right leg spasmed, clenching in excruciating pain before giving way. Graham toppled to the floor, landing on his bad arm, which sent more stabs of agony through him.

...

"You should cut them smaller," said Mrs. Bunting, picking up a piece of Tabby's vegetables. "Larger pieces, longer cook time."

Tabby looked at her cutting board and her pile of sliced potatoes. It had seemed right to her, but glancing over at the cook's own board, Tabby saw that they were at least twice the size of Mrs. Bunting's. Nodding, she set about recutting her ingredients. Cooking was not as easy as it seemed at first glance. It took more skill than throwing ingredients into a pot, but Tabby found herself enjoying the process. There was something so satisfying about taking all these random bits and making them into something delicious.

A loud thump sounded on the ceiling, followed by a bellowing shout so excruciating that Tabby felt a sympathetic pain. Abandoning her cooking, Tabby rushed for the stairs and hurried into Captain Ashbrook's bedchamber. He was collapsed on the floor, his jaw gritted as sweat gathered on his red face. After the initial shout, he was silent, but Tabby could see that it was because of his own force of will and not because he was unharmed.

"Sir!" She crouched beside him, uncertain of what to do. He needed to be moved back into bed, but after such a fall, he would need a moment to regain himself before she attempted it. She turned her head to call for James, but Captain Ashbrook grabbed her hand with his good one and shook his head.

Kneeling beside him, Tabby held his trembling hand; his

nightshirt was drenched with sweat by the time his grip loosened. She held her breath until he relaxed, his head resting against the floor as his lungs heaved.

Sensing it was time, Tabby helped him upright and with some effort they were able to get him off the ground and into his bed. Once he was settled, Tabby's irritation grew until she could contain it no longer.

"What were you thinking?" she asked, standing over him with hands on her hips. "You could have done yourself serious harm!"

"It seemed a good idea at the time," said Captain Ashbrook with a shaky voice. "If I wish to make progress, I must take risks."

Tabby grabbed a clean rag on the nightstand and wiped his brow clean. "Being assertive is one thing, and being foolhardy is another. What if I hadn't heard you fall? Or if you had cracked your head on the bedpost or nightstand? You should have called me, and I could have been here to help keep you from hurting yourself further. Let me get you some medicine."

She moved for the door, but Captain Ashbrook growled, "I do not need medicine. I need to get better."

Crossing her arms, she turned to him. "Medicine is how you get better." Captain Ashbrook gave her a dark scowl, but she only raised her eyebrows. "You are being disagreeable again."

His scowl deepened for a moment before it shifted, turning inward. With a sigh, he let his head fall onto his pillow. "I apologize. I need to get better, and this slow pace is so infuriating. It is so infernally boring being confined to bed all day long."

At that, Tabby had a brilliant upon brilliant idea. One that she should have thought of sooner. Lifting a single finger, she went in search of entertainment.

Disagreeable. Graham could not believe that this was what he had become. Surly. Ill-tempered. Snipping at everyone. Graham had never shied away from being stern or strict—it was paramount on a ship—but that was different from cruel or mean-spirited. But Graham did not know how to contain the frustration and helplessness he felt at being run aground and surrounded by people who did not understand his desperation to get himself afloat once more.

He must heal and return to the sea. It was his life. His heart and soul belonged there. To be ashore for so long was torturous, and he did not know how much more of it he could bear.

Simon may lecture him on his behavior, but Graham knew the fellow would not be so passive if Avebury Park and the life he had built were threatened. With each sennight and month, Graham's life at sea was floating farther away. A man cannot lose something so important and be expected to smile and spout pleasantries.

Graham needed to get better, and that fall had done more than bruise his body. For all his elation at the first few steps, it came crashing down in a trice. And not in a metaphorical sense. His body was still broken, and his dreams were far out of reach.

The door opened again and Mrs. Russell crossed to the bed, carrying a deck of cards. Graham sighed and laid his head on the pillows. An afternoon of playing a bunch of ladies' games was not at all what he wanted or needed. Pulling a chair close to his side, Mrs. Russell smoothed out a section of the bedcover, nudging Graham's legs to facilitate the cards.

"What is your game?" she asked.

Graham raised his eyebrows. "You propose spending an afternoon playing cribbage?"

Mrs. Russell fanned out the cards with one hand while dropping a small purse onto his lap with the other. "I was thinking more along the lines of ecarte or piquet. Perhaps vingt-et-un."

Graham gave a huff of laughter. "And what would you know of such things?"

Mrs. Russell looked at him with her mahogany eyes, her lids lowering while her spine straightened. "I know plenty about such things. I was taught well."

"Yes, because all ladies are taught dance, embroidery, and how to fleece young men in gaming clubs."

Mrs. Russell turned the cards in her hands, her fingers cutting the deck and shuffling them together with a dexterity and skill Graham had seldom seen. "My husband spent a lot of time in such places and taught me well, sir, and for all your mockery, you have not answered my question. Soldiers and sailors are notorious for gambling away the hours, so which game do you favor?"

"You wish to lose your wages to me?" he asked.

A smile crept across Mrs. Russell's lips. "You are assuming that you will win. Do you wish to test your mettle against a lady?"

Graham reached for the purse with his right hand, but stopped when his bicep pinched. Mrs. Russell saw it, but bless the woman, she said nothing. Graham switched tacks and reached with his left hand. Inside was a mound of pennies, and he smiled.

"Penny stakes?"

Mrs. Russell gave him an arched eyebrow. "I do not wish to beggar you, sir."

Graham actually felt like chuckling. And he did. A little moment of mirth that the residual pains from his fall did not care for, but it warmed Graham's soul. Even for someone labeled disagreeable.

"All right, madam," he said, dumping out the purse. "Let us start with piquet and work from there."

Mrs. Russell organized her own pile of coins on her portion of the bedspread and dealt their hands. Graham moved slowly, struggling to hold the cards, place his wagers, and play.

"Try holding them with your right," said Mrs. Russell. "It does not require dexterity to do so, and it could be a good exercise for that side."

Graham did as she bid and found she was correct. It was a struggle to get his damaged hand to keep hold of them, but with a few softly spoken prompts, Mrs. Russell had him sorted out to the point where he could play.

And then she trounced him. Soundly.

Every time Graham thought he had the upper hand, she out-maneuvered him, and his pile of pennies shriveled and died while hers grew healthy and stout. It would be infuriating if she weren't so amusing as she did so. Mrs. Russell had a dry wit, making just the right remarks about the card play to set him smiling. He could see her jests coming by the way her dimples peeked out at him. They were faint little things. Hardly noticeable at first glance and quickly overshadowed when the laughter reached her eyes and wrinkled her nose.

Graham watched the lady, speculating over the turn of fate that had driven her to become the caretaker for a dour invalid. It was clear she was a lady of breeding. Her accent and deportment were evidence of that. Yet, here she was in service. As all housekeepers were called Mrs., the title was not a clear sign of her marital status, but Mrs. Russell had mentioned a husband, so she had been married at one time or other.

A penniless widow. A genteel lady beggared upon her husband's death. Such things happened, and it would certainly explain Mrs. Russell's reduced circumstances.

It was beyond Graham's comprehension that a husband could leave his wife so unprotected and desperate. Setting aside a contingency in case of death was the first thing a responsible gentleman did after his marriage. To provide was a husband's premier responsibility, and Graham could not understand the arrogance behind not planning for his wife's future. No one lives forever, and it was foolish to assume one would always be around to do one's duty.

Mr. Russell had perished, leaving Mrs. Russell to fend for herself, and the genteel lady had been forced to surrender her former life and status to become a drudge. That bothered Graham. It would be difficult enough to lose one's spouse, but to have one's life so upended must be grueling. Only to be made worse by her unpleasant patient.

"Why are you so determined to continue injuring yourself?"

she asked, glancing from her cards as she played yet another killing blow.

"Pardon?" Graham placed his own card, though he knew this hand was a lost cause.

"The surgeries." Mrs. Russell sifted through her cards and spoke with a tone that was neither demanding nor accusatory.

Graham clenched his jaw. "That is none of your concern."

Mrs. Russell nodded and played another card. They continued on in silence for a few minutes while Graham waited for her to push the matter, but she did not. She was neither perturbed by his temper nor did she demand answers. In many ways, it was more effective than if she had pestered him; such an invasion into his privacy would have allowed Graham to hold onto his righteous indignation. Instead, he found himself confused and mildly curious.

"What, no retort?" he asked.

Mrs. Russell looked up from her cards. "Do you wish for one?"

"Not particularly, but after our last clash of wills, I expected more of a reaction."

"That was about keeping you healthy and maintaining my position," said Mrs. Russell. "This is simply curiosity. I asked because I wish to understand your situation so that I might better help you. However, it is your prerogative to tell me, and I can fulfill my duties without your answer."

The way she spoke was distant, and Graham missed the camaraderie that had blossomed between them. A grown man in need of a friend. How pitiful. But true nonetheless. He loved his sister and brother-in-law, but they were occupied with their own lives. They spent spare moments with him, but most of their days were taken up with their duties at Avebury Park and now with becoming parents. He spent his days in bed, healing. He could not even hold a book for long or write letters. His time was spent in quiet solitude.

But as Graham thought on that, he realized it was his own fault. In the beginning, Mina and Simon had spent a fair bit of time with him. And Nicholas and Louisa-Margaretta had brought their children for visits. Even Ambrose had torn himself away from London on several occasions. There were people who wished to help him, but he had driven them away with his foul moods. And now, he was doing the same with Mrs. Russell.

Graham sighed and put down the cards. Mrs. Russell watched him with questioning eyes but said nothing.

"I'm being a boor again, aren't I?"

Mrs. Russell's eyes widened, her lips twisting into a smile. "Truthfully?"

"I suppose that is my answer." Graham took a breath. "I apologize. Once again."

Mrs. Russell gathered her cards into a stack and held them in her hands. "In less than a sennight, I have received not one but two apologies from a gentleman. I must consult the Book of Revelations, for I believe that may be one of the signs of the Last Days."

"That is not a kind assessment of my sex," said Graham.

Mrs. Russell's gaze broke from his, turning to her cards. "It is not in the nature of men to admit their shortcomings."

Nothing changed in her posture, but little cues—the tightening of her shoulders and the pursing of her lips—made Graham suspect that there was a world of emotion behind those few words, which made Graham feel for her. No, it was not fair for him to add to her burden.

"I suppose that depends on the man," said Graham, "but I hope that I am not that intractable. And I do hope you will accept my apology. Or rather, apologies."

Mrs. Russell's tension faded, and she fanned out her cards once again. "I suppose that depends on whether or not you intend to do better. An apology implies penitence, and unless it is paired with action it is nothing more than lip service."

"So you accept my apology but with conditions?" asked Graham, retrieving the cards from his lap. It took a bit of work, but he got them into his right hand. "That seems a bit unjust."

"So is blaming others for that which is neither their fault

nor in their control."

"Touché."

Mrs. Russell added a few more pennies to her wager. "But if you work on your shortcoming, perhaps I can, too."

Graham chuckled. "It is a deal, madam. And I think it is time to abandon piquet and try my luck at ecarte."

Mrs. Russell gave a low chuckle as she gathered the cards, her dimples making an appearance. At his questioning glance, she replied, "I am even better at ecarte."

"I have been warned," he said with an answering grin. "Deal the cards."

Chapter 9

"**D**o you feel the texture? It's time to add the water," said Mrs. Bunting as Tabby dug her fingers into the mixing bowl.

Tabby had flour all over her arms and apron, and likely on her face, too, though she could not see the damage for herself. Slowly, she added the water to the crumbly mixture until it formed the dough for her crust.

Her mother would be mortified to see her daughter doing such menial labor, but Tabby adored cooking. It was slow progress, but with each lesson, she gained more knowledge and skill, and Tabby had managed to make not one but two deliciously edible meals. The next time she was home, Tabby would make Phillip a pork pie. It was his favorite and something that had been beyond their pocketbook for some time, but a homemade one was an affordable treat for the lad. Tabby could hardly wait.

Life was far from perfect, but it rarely was. However, at this moment, Tabby felt quite content with her lot. If Phillip could be with her, it would be perfect, but beyond that, Tabby had little reason to complain. There were aspects of being on a lower rung of society that Tabby found preferable to her previous position; she was learning new skills and talents that had previously been denied her, and Tabby reveled in the silver lining this cloud had produced.

But then the calm morning air was broken by the maid's sobs. Flying into the kitchen, Jillian dropped the breakfast tray onto the table and covered her mouth to stifle the noises, but Tabby saw fat tears rolling down her cheeks. Wiping the flour off her hands, Tabby ushered the girl to the table while Mrs. Bunting produced a sweet to calm her nerves.

Then Tabby went "once more unto the breach" as her father was fond of saying.

Captain Ashbrook was in a foul mood again. It had been a fortnight without a spark of temper, but the lull was over, and Tabby knew it was time to do battle once more. Cleaning off the flour as well as she could, Tabby scooped up the tray Jillian had abandoned and went straight to the captain's bedchamber. When she opened the door, she found him in bed, his eyes staring at the ceiling.

"Someone is being a bear this morning," she said, placing the tray on the table next to the bed and taking the seat beside him. Perhaps it was a bit too informal for a housekeeper to sit without being asked, but with as much time as she spent with the captain, it felt foolish to stand on ceremony.

"Bear?" Captain Ashbrook straightened and furrowed his brow. "What is your meaning?"

"Are you claiming that Jillian burst into tears for no reason?" Tabby crossed her arms, but Captain Ashbrook looked positively perplexed.

"She came in with the tray and placed it on my lap, but I asked her to move it there," he said, motioning to a side table.

Tabby tried to hide her smile, but from the narrowing of his eyes, she hadn't done a good job of it. "Did you ask or bark?"

"It was a normal statement with no meanness of spirit to it," he said. "She must be a sensitive soul, but if she took offense, that is her concern, not mine."

Tabby pictured what Captain Ashbrook's "statement" had been. She had been on the receiving end of such commands many times since coming to work at Gladwell House, and there was a definite harshness to them. "You have been at sea too long, sir. On land, we do not need to raise our voices to be heard above the roar of the waves or to keep an unruly crew in place."

"I am not as bad as all that."

"Jillian would beg to differ," said Tabby.

Captain Ashbrook's face pulled into a scowl, and she braced herself for the forthcoming argument. But then his narrowed eyes widened and his shoulders straightened, and Tabby saw the ill-tempered expression shift into awareness. The next moment, the frown was safely tucked away, and all was right once more.

It took no more than a few seconds, yet that display of self-control was a sight to behold. In her experience men did not change. Either they were born good tempered, like her father, or they were unable to rid themselves of their bad qualities, like her husband. They may manage a short-term alteration, but their true natures always won out. After years of learning that lesson in the most difficult of circumstances, Tabby had begun to accept that fact.

Yet here Captain Ashbrook was making a concerted effort to change. Certainly, Tabby had witnessed a similar metamorphosis in Joshua when he had been wooing her, but it had been nothing more than an attempt to gain her favor and disappeared as easily as her father had warned her it would. But Captain Ashbrook was not trying to impress her or anyone else.

And now she was gathering wool. It would not do to sit here, silently staring at the man.

Reaching for the stack of letters on the tray, Tabby offered them to Captain Ashbrook. "You have quite a pile of post today."

But the captain simply dropped them on the growing paper mountain beside his bed.

"Perhaps that is the custom of sailors," said Tabby, glancing at it, "but on land, we tend to open our letters, read them, and then write out a reply."

Captain Ashbrook raised his eyebrows. "Strange custom, that."

Tabby fought back another smile. "True. We are an odd bunch, but when in Rome, do as the Romans do, as they say," she replied with a shrug.

Captain Ashbrook snickered, a smile teasing his lips. "If you must know, there is no point in reading them as I have no ability to respond."

"That is odd logic," said Tabby. "You have no interest in knowing what is being sent you?"

The captain fidgeted, shifting in his bed, and avoided her gaze, but Tabby recognized the signs. He was embarrassed. And frustrated, too, if she had to guess. No one appreciated having their shortcomings shoved in their face, and that was exactly what these pieces of paper did to him. Pursing her lips, she glanced at the letters and for a brief moment, pictured what it would be like to receive correspondence from people she'd known in her former life. Hearing about things she longed to do but couldn't.

Clearly, it would be painful for Captain Ashbrook to face his missives, but avoiding such things never helped hardships. However, Tabby allowed her previous question to lapse and addressed the concern he was willing to admit aloud.

"Have you considered using your left hand?" asked Tabby. "It is more than capable of holding a quill. With a little training, I am certain you could master it." Her first instinct was to offer to act as his scribe, but a man in Captain Ashbrook's position needed some semblance of independence. In this small way, he would be able to have a touch of freedom.

"My left?" he asked, turning that hand to examine it. "I have never tried it. Do you think it possible?"

"Why not?" she asked. "There are those who favor their left hand and are trained to use their right, so why not the other way around?"

Captain Ashbrook raised his eyebrows, glancing at Tabby,

and she saw a faint light of hope in his gaze. "I have missed writing. I've kept a journal as long as I can remember, but I have not been able to add to it since…a while."

Tabby allowed his pause to pass without comment, knowing full well to what he was referring. "I think we should get you out and about today. You have been cooped up far too long, and it would do you a world of good. I can fetch you some paper with which to practice, and you can start training your left hand out in the beauty of the garden."

"Were you not cautioning me a fortnight ago to be more careful?"

"I am not suggesting you run into town," said Tabby. "It is a lovely morning, and you could have your breakfast outside."

"Outside?" Captain Ashbrook's face looked remarkably like that of a society matron who had spilled tea on her dress during a morning call, but Tabby hid her smile far better this time.

"For being so foolhardy before, you are being surprisingly reticent now," she said.

"I do not wish to repeat my previous mistake," he said, a frown on his lips. "Besides, you should be celebrating that I am doing as everyone wishes."

Before the gentleman could say another word, Tabby threw aside his bed covers. He reached for them, but she slapped his hands and retrieved his dressing gown. The captain sputtered and fought her, but he should have learned his lesson by now; Tabby would not be cast aside.

"Faint heart and all that," said Tabby, maneuvering his legs and helping him upright. "Take courage, dear Captain. The garden is not as frightening as all that."

Captain Ashbrook glared, but there was too much humor in his eyes to be particularly effective. "It is not the garden I fear."

No it wasn't. Tabby knew his fear, but she would not say it aloud for she had learned her lesson with Joshua. Support and help, but do not shove; it was better to allow him to come to his own conclusions. Granted, Tabby was doing a fair amount of shoving to get him off the bed and into his dressing gown, but she sensed this was what he wanted and needed.

With his cane in his left hand, and Tabby gently supporting his right side, they stood together, allowing him a moment to get his equilibrium.

"You..." Captain Ashbrook's voice faltered and a faint blush stole across his cheek.

"I shan't let you fall, sir," said Tabby.

The captain nodded, and Tabby knew she had guessed that particular worry correctly. She nodded in return and together they took a step. Captain Ashbrook made a tiny noise, which she suspected was a hidden groan, but he kept moving. Slow and rickety, they walked to the bedchamber door.

"Where all have you traveled?" asked Tabby.

Captain Ashbrook glanced at her from the corner of his eye as they stepped into the hallway.

"During your time in the navy. You must have seen a great many countries," she clarified. His brow furrowed, and Tabby clearly saw his confusion at the choice of topic, but it was the exact type of thing that could take his mind off the effort of moving.

"Most parts of Britain and Europe. The coast of America and Canada. The East and West Indies. Africa. Australia. About anywhere our sovereign has an interest and a port, I have visited."

The list was astonishing, yet he recited it with a casual tone as though traveling so extensively were a commonplace occurrence. When she told him such, he shrugged.

"It has been my life for almost fifteen years. It feels commonplace to me," he said.

They reached the top of the stairs, and Tabby halted them for a moment to allow the captain a rest.

"And which was your favorite?" she asked.

"India."

The answer came without thought and with such decisiveness that it drew Tabby's eyebrows upwards.

"Why is that?"

Captain Ashbrook's eyes drew off into the distance, as though he could see the place before him. "So many reasons, but primarily it is because the sights and wonders of that country are the greatest I have ever witnessed in my life. While there, I had the opportunity to visit what must be the grandest building in existence. White and gleaming, it stands above a river, surrounded by a series of red stone buildings so beautiful that they alone could rival many of the palaces of Europe. Yet they are nothing to compare to the structure they enclose."

Tabby hung on his every word as they crept down the stairs.

"It was made entirely of white marble. A bright spot on the landscape that gleams in the morning light. And when you draw closer, you see an intricate web of decorations formed from semi-precious stones set into the sides. That alone is enough to instill any visitor with awe, but when you go inside, every inch of the interior is embellished with similar inlays, filling the walls with flowers and vines as though you are stepping into an indoor garden fashioned from stone. It was overwhelming."

Tabby tried to imagine it, but her mind could not call up such pictures. As a child, she had spent a fair amount of time searching atlases, scouring for information on foreign lands, but none of them ever came close to holding her attention as Captain Ashbrook's words had.

"That sounds like a magnificent palace," she said.

"It was no palace," he replied. "It was a tomb for the favorite wife of a Mughal emperor."

Tabby gaped for a brief moment before asking another question. Step after step, she pulled from him a vast array of stories about his travels and experiences aboard his ships, which did as much to entertain her as it distracted him. The trip from bedchamber to garden took nearly an hour, yet it felt like only a few minutes passed as they talked.

Chapter 10

Graham did not know how Mrs. Russell managed it. Right when he had thought to dig in his heels and stay abed, she had him bundled up and out the door. He couldn't even be upset about the situation—except at his own weakness.

It burned his pride to admit that he had been avoiding testing out his limbs. After the last debacle, Graham found his determination wavering every time he had thought to, though pain had nothing to do with his reticence. It was fear alone that drove him to hide in his bedchamber; Graham could not face the possibility that his body might be worsening.

But then there was Mrs. Russell teasing and pushing him out the door and down the stairs, engaging him in such a lively conversation that Graham hardly noticed their journey to the garden. The lady was such a treat to talk to, and it was more than her ability to draw him from his melancholy. She made the world brighter, and Graham cherished his time with her.

He supposed he should be affronted at Mrs. Russell's heavy-handedness, but as it had already improved his mood considerably, he knew better than to criticize her for taking the initiative. He rather enjoyed seeing her get her dander up. Besides, her fussing was different from Mina's anxious fretting and far more agreeable.

Besides, the lady was right; it was a lovely morning and the sunshine felt good against his skin. It wasn't until he sat out in the open air that he realized how much of a toll being sequestered inside had taken. Such a simple thing that had such a great effect on his bedraggled spirits. It was as though he could finally breathe again.

Casting a look at his hands, Graham was sickened to realized that the tan he had acquired during his years at sea had faded until his skin was as fair as the fops in London.

Mere moments later, Mrs. Russell had a blanket on the chair beside him, a fresh tray of treats on the table before him, and a pile of writing implements all perfectly situated for him to enjoy a morning out in nature.

"Thank you," he said. Perhaps it was silly to thank a servant, but Mrs. Russell was more than that and deserved the acknowledgment.

The lady smiled, and something in Graham's stomach twisted. Not the fearful wrenching he had felt many times before a battle or during a storm, but an energetic, elating sort of thing. It filled him, and in an instant, he found himself staring at her lips and imagining things that he should not think. Graham felt his face heat, and he swallowed, turning his gaze away from the warm highlights in her chocolate eyes.

That was an avenue best left unexplored, for it was dangerous ground. Mrs. Russell was staff, and it was unwise to blur the boundaries. Besides, Graham would be at sea before long, and that was a poor life to give one's wife. Yes, most of his men and fellow officers were married, but having a wife and children one sees on rare occasions was not what Graham wanted. Two very good reasons why he could not allow himself to feel anything more than friendship for Mrs. Russell. She was an admirable woman, and he enjoyed her company, but there was no future between the two of them.

Even so, Graham found himself stopping her as she returned to the house.

"Did you need something else, sir?" she asked.

"You're going to run off and abandon me like that?" he asked with a single raised eyebrow. "Dump me in the garden and return to whatever you were doing before I bothered you?"

She matched his eyebrow and said, "Yes."

Graham laughed, and he flinched in anticipation of the various aches that had been paining him, but they did not come. Mrs. Russell came over to check on him, but he waved her off.

"I feel fine, truly," he said. "That is the first time it has not hurt to laugh in a very long time."

"That is what happens when you allow your body to heal rather than hacking it apart at every opportunity." Coming from anyone else, Graham would have taken offense to the words, but Mrs. Russell's tone held a touch of teasing that softened them.

"Please, sit with me," he said, gesturing to an empty seat at the table.

Mrs. Russell sat and studied him. Graham was not sure what she was looking for, but he waited for her to speak. The lady had a forthrightness to her that did not allow her to remain silent for very long; he only needed to be patient.

"May I ask you a question that may upset you?"

Graham's spine straightened, and his eyebrows rose. "That does sound ominous, but I will say yes if I am allowed to ask you a very personal and terribly gauche question first."

"Ominous, indeed. Ask away, sir," she said with a wide smile.

Graham folded his arms, watching Mrs. Russell carefully. "It is clear that you had a genteel upbringing, so how did you end up playing nursemaid to an ill-tempered naval captain?"

At Mrs. Russell's flushed cheeks, Graham both wished the question unasked and felt grateful for the opportunity to ask it; it bothered him far too much to be ignored.

She ran her hands along her skirt and fidgeted for a moment before she spoke. "Over the last few years, my financial situation has grown very precarious. Eventually, it became necessary to go into service."

Graham sensed a world of meaning beneath those words. There was far more to the story than she was telling, and what she had shared had not fully answered his question.

"Money is the reason anyone goes into service. That much was clear," said Graham. "But you do not strike me as a spendthrift."

Mrs. Russell's eyes refused to meet his. "I am not a spendthrift, but I married one. That was enough. After a decade of marriage, we had naught but a few pounds to our name. The house and everything of value was sold to pay the creditors."

Graham wanted to growl at the man. To beggar her like that was inexcusable. He wished he could pound the tar out of the late Mr. Russell and teach him how to be a proper gentleman who honors his responsibilities.

"You have no family or friends who might help you?" he asked. If Mina were in Mrs. Russell's shoes, she would be amply provided for by her brothers.

Mrs. Russell shook her head. "My parents passed a few years ago and I have no siblings. The family and friends I have left have done what they were willing to do, and I am no longer willing to beg for their charity. I would rather work for my living than be a drain on another."

Respect swelled in Graham's heart, bringing with it something deeper that he tried to ignore, but it was impossible when faced with such a lady. Not many would view such demeaning employment as preferable to begging from the higher social circle, and Graham admired her determination to be something better than a leech.

"Now you must answer my question, sir," she said, visibly pushing away her previous discomfort and meeting him face on. "Why are you so desperate to fix that which cannot be fixed?

With work, your leg and arm will be serviceable, but the physicians and surgeons all agree that you will not be fit to return to the sea. Yet, you persist in it."

Mrs. Russell had been right when she had predicted that he wouldn't like her question. Temper flared in his heart, burning through him, and if it were not for a concerted effort on his part, he would have bellowed at her with language that would be best left unheard by a lady.

Hearing it stated so baldly left him shaken. Others danced around it, but Mrs. Russell spoke with a directness that left no room for interpretation. Hearing his broken body described in such a manner struck him to his core. He was going to get better. He was going to be healed. With enough work he would return to his ship. Yet, here she declared with complete confidence that it would never happen—that he was holding onto a dream that would never become a reality.

"Madam," Graham said through gritted teeth, "I shall get better."

Mrs. Russell's gaze softened, her brow furrowing in concern. "A miracle may happen, yes, but Captain Ashbrook, it will not happen without divine intervention. Why are you insisting it will?"

"It must," he said.

"That is not an answer," she said. Lips pressed together, she spoke over him when he tried to rebut her. "I gave you an honest answer to your question, and I deserve an honest answer from you. Why are you so determined that you must get better?"

His eyes darted from her and scoured the garden, as if they would provide the answer. He wanted to pace, but he was stuck in this dratted chair. And Mrs. Russell waited. She did deserve an answer, but to admit the truth felt too vulnerable.

Graham sighed, his body slackening as he accepted the inevitable. He would not welsh on a promise.

"I feel like half a man," he said. "I have always been healthy and strong, and now I cannot go a few steps without someone half carrying me about. I cannot write or even read because I cannot hold the book and turn the pages at the same time. That alone would be enough, but there is more to it."

He took a breath, steeling himself to continue. "This injury has stolen away everything I love. The navy is more than my income. It is my life. My passion. Outside my family, the sea is the most important thing to me, and to accept that I cannot be healed is to accept that it is gone forever."

Graham's heart sunk in his chest with each word, and he rubbed at his face. He would not break. Things may be bleak, but Graham would not allow himself to fall to pieces. He may be a pathetic shell of a man who was of no use to anyone, but he could do that much.

Shifting in his chair, Graham had a vision of what his life would be if he stayed ashore. There were some who enjoyed idleness, but he could not face the idea of ending up like his brother, Ambrose, who lived for nothing more than frivolity. Though even that was unlikely to be Graham's future: Ambrose was a charming young buck, and Graham was a broken castoff. Even if he desired to fritter away his life in such a manner, he wouldn't be accepted into that sphere of society with his visible imperfections.

It was foolish to come out here. He should be in bed like the invalid he was. Shut away from the world.

"One moment my life was everything I wished it to be," he said. "And the next, it was ripped away from me. Do you know what it's like to have your life torn apart? Desperately wishing to piece it back together yet unable to do so?"

Graham met Mrs. Russell's gaze and saw tears and under-standing there. And that was when he realized that of all the people who had tried to talk sense into him, only she under-stood. The lady turned nursemaid. Graham had no doubt she had fought for her life, but it had been torn away from her just as cruelly as his.

"I know precisely how difficult it is," said Mrs. Russell, her voice quiet yet firm. "Life is far from perfect and rarely turns out the way we wish or plan." Her voice wavered, and she lowered her gaze for a moment. With another breath, she straightened once more and continued. "It is the nature of life, but that does not mean it must be unhappy."

Graham felt like groaning, but that would be terribly childish. He settled for a disappointed huff. "If you are going to start spouting off a bunch of empty proverbs about hope and optimism, I have no wish to hear it."

Mrs. Russell's gaze narrowed, her chin raising in challenge. "You may choose to ignore them, but there are always reasons to be happy just as there are always reasons to be miserable. I am not saying you need to be grateful for the hardships you are facing, but you can choose to see the goodness and blessings that come with it. Joy in life is a matter of choice, not circumstances."

Graham snorted at that tripe. It was not the most polite thing he had ever done, but it was far from the most impolite; goodness knows he had said things far worse in Mrs. Russell's hearing.

"And what wonderful blessings have come from your great misfortune?" he said with a touch of derision.

Mrs. Russell tensed, as though every muscle in her being was bursting with anger. "Do not mock me, sir. If you do not wish to believe me, that is your prerogative. You may wallow in misery all you wish, but do not speak to me as though I am nothing because I choose not to be so pitiful and rude."

Pitiful and rude? Graham took a breath and straightened in his chair. "How dare you, madam!"

But rather than quaking as most did when he gathered such fury about him, Mrs. Russell held his gaze, her own muscles tightening in response. And that forced Graham to recognize that he was being a boor yet again. It was not an easy moment for him to be trapped between wanting to give this servant a proper set-down and knowing it would be a mistake.

Sucking in another deep breath, Graham forced his temper to the background, straining to keep control of it. The heat of his anger ebbed, and with it came a dose of chagrin, which left a foul taste in his mouth. He had been having a tantrum. Again. For all his determination not to do so, it had snuck up on him.

Graham took another breath. And then another. When he had regained his composure, he spoke. "I apologize for being so disrespectful, Mrs. Russell. Though I would not say I am pitiful and rude, you were right to point out that I was behaving badly."

Mrs. Russell's brows drew together, and her head tilted to the side as she stared at him. Every time he apologized, she seemed so genuinely surprised that it made Graham wonder what in her life had taught her to disbelieve sincerely expressed remorse. Though he did not have to wonder long, as he guessed it was simply another reason to despise the late Mr. Russell.

"My sister and brother-in-law are fond of telling me to look for the good among the bad, and I find I am not fond of hearing it," said Graham.

Having regained her own composure, the lady nodded. "It sounds trite when coming from those who do not understand."

"But you are not like that."

"No, I am not," she agreed. "And I promise that if you will look for it, you may find blessings that come from your hardships. I have."

"Such as?"

"Cooking," she said with a smile. "My mother would be mortified, but I quite adore it. Mrs. Bunting has been giving me lessons, and I look forward to it every day."

The image of Mrs. Russell elbow deep in flour was surprisingly enticing; it hung in his mind for a good minute before Graham realized his thoughts had wandered into dangerous territory. Shoving it aside, he cleared his throat.

"So, you wish me to learn to cook?" He hoped the tone came off lighthearted, but it sounded more nervous.

Mrs. Russell laughed, which brought a smile to his lips.

"No, Captain Ashbrook. Not cooking, precisely," she said. "The first step is to recapture what you can." She pointed to the paper and quill. "Adjust to your current capability, and then explore new passions and pursuits. It would do you good. You must decide—"

But her words were cut short when Simon came hurrying through the back door. The look on his face sent a shiver of fear running along Graham's spine. He tried to stand, but he had exhausted his strength getting into the garden. Mrs. Russell sent him a look that kept him from trying again.

"Mrs. Russell," said Simon, his breath heaving. "Please, come...Mina."

At that, Graham tried in earnest to stand. "What has happened?"

"The baby..." Simon's face paled. "Something is wrong, but I cannot find a physician, midwife, or anyone else who can help."

Mrs. Russell's hand came to her mouth.

"Please," said Simon, turning to her, "you have some experience with medicine and healing, and you have been through childbirth yourself. Would you please—"

"Of course," she said. "I don't know how much help I can be, but I shall try."

Graham moved to follow them, but Mrs. Russell shoved him onto the chair.

"Sit!" she commanded.

"But..." Graham stared into her eyes, pleading for her to bring him along. He would be of no help whatsoever, but the thought of anything happening to his sister filled him with such dread. He needed to be there with her.

"Promise me you will stay put," she said. "Hurting yourself will do your sister no good. I will send you news as soon as possible."

Graham saw the logic and reason, though his heart wished to protest. Giving his word, he watched Simon lead Mrs. Russell away, praying that all would be right with Mina and her babe.

Chapter 11

Tabby was winded by the time they arrived at Avebury Park. Tearing off her bonnet and spencer, she cast them to the butler before scurrying to catch Mr. Kingsley, who was already moving up the stairs to find his wife. Her muscles burned, but she forced herself to keep up. They wound their way through the halls of Avebury Park, and then the gentleman ushered Tabby into a bedchamber.

Mrs. Kingsley lay on the bed, her body shaking with great sobs. Mr. Kingsley hurried to her side, sitting in a vacant chair beside the bed to hold her hands.

"What has happened?" asked Tabby.

Mrs. Kingsley tried to answer, but her words came out so broken that it was beyond indecipherable. Taking a jerking breath, she managed, "The baby."

Tabby knew that feeling all too well. The panic. The heartache. The anguish. She had experienced it many times before, and her heart broke for any woman having to suffer like that. Sitting on the edge of the bed beside Mrs. Kingsley, Tabby looked to Mr. Kingsley for permission and the gentleman relinquished one of his wife's hands, allowing Tabby to take it in hers.

"I know how frightening this is," she said, her voice soft and soothing, though tears filled her eyes as memories flooded her mind. "I know how lost you are in this moment. But I must ask you to do something for me."

Mrs. Kingsley stilled and watched Tabby with questioning eyes.

"Take a breath," said Tabby. Doing it alongside the lady, Tabby took several deep breaths, the tension easing from Mrs. Kingsley with each one.

"Good," she said, rubbing Mrs. Kingsley's hand and continuing the exercise until the lady calmed.

"Now, tell me what is the matter," said Tabby.

Mrs. Kingsley shuddered, her eyes widening, but Tabby kept her tone soothing and had Mrs. Kingsley breathe through it.

"Cramping," she said, taking another jerking breath. "And bleeding. Something is wrong. I know it."

Tabby kept her hands gentle, though her chest tightened, and she needed a breath or two for herself. "That can happen, and I know it is alarming, especially with your first child, but we need to keep calm."

Mrs. Kingsley nodded. Beside her, Mr. Kingsley looked as harried as his wife. Though his feelings were bottled inside, his eyes were red and held a glimmer of tears, telling Tabby just how fragile his own heart was at present. Transferring the lady's hand to her husband, Tabby mouthed the word, "calm" to him. He nodded and continued Tabby's efforts to lull his wife.

"Do you have paper and a pencil?" she asked, while sorting through her memories to recall the exact ingredients of the tisane she had taken in such instances. A maid standing off to the side stepped forward with both in hand, and Tabby scribbled out the recipe. As she wrote, it crystalized in her mind, and she handed it to the maid, who hurried to fetch it.

Tabby sat beside the pair, and Mr. Kingsley kissed his wife's hand, his eyes never leaving hers. Tabby shifted to move away, but Mrs. Kingsley gave her such a pleading look that Tabby remained where she was. A little discomfort on her part was worth it if it helped Mrs. Kingsley.

"Will they be fine?" asked Mr. Kingsley.

Tabby wanted to give all the reassurances the couple wished for, but she knew well enough that false promises hurt worse than a gentle truth. "This could be nothing. It is not uncommon for such things to happen, but it could be the sign of something worse. I don't know for certain."

Mrs. Kingsley tensed, and Tabby placed her hand on the lady's knee, speaking in soothing tones. "It is too early for us to worry about the worst possible outcomes. I am certain the physician will be here soon, but until then, we must hope for the best. This truly could be nothing out of the ordinary."

The lady looked fairly calm, but Tabby knew the best medicine at this time would be distraction, and she scoured for something to pull Mrs. Kingsley's thoughts away from her fears.

"I forced Captain Ashbrook outside today," said Tabby.

Both Kingsleys stared at her, but Tabby saw understanding dawning in Mr. Kingsley's eyes because he jumped right in with, "That's right. He was sitting in the garden."

"Truly?" Mrs. Kingsley's voice wobbled, but it came out in one word, which was most satisfying.

"What did you do to him?" asked Mr. Kingsley. "Toss him over your shoulder and carry him out like a sack of flour?"

A chuckle. An actual chuckle came from Mrs. Kingsley, and Tabby wanted to hug Mr. Kingsley. From the strain around his eyes and mouth, Tabby knew he was not as diverted as his tone implied, but as it was helping Mrs. Kingsley, he appeared willing to aid things with a bit of humor.

"Not quite," said Tabby, and she began telling them about her battles with the gallant Captain Ashbrook. Lacing it with as much wit as she could muster, Tabby had Mrs. Kingsley smiling at various points, though the tension in Mr. Kingsley's posture never lessened.

The maid interrupted at one point with a tray, and Tabby

helped Mrs. Kingsley drink a cup of the tisane, praying that it would work, all while keeping her patient distracted as they waited for someone more qualified to arrive.

...

Mrs. Kingsley lay on her bed, her face turned towards Tabby as tears rolled down her cheek and soaked her pillow. Sitting on the chair beside her, Tabby clutched Mrs. Kingsley's hand, running her thumbs over it as she hummed a soothing tune. On more than one occasion, her mama had done the exact same thing for Tabby, but in those cases, she had been sobbing over the loss of her child. How grateful she was that these were tears of relief.

"All is well, Mrs. Kingsley," said Tabby. "Doctor Clarke said it was nothing but a scare."

There was a watery chuckle. "You have spent most of the day at my bedside, holding my hand and comforting me. I think you have earned the right to call me Mina."

Tabby wanted to accept. On her part, she already thought of Mrs. Kingsley as a friend, but in truth, she was Tabby's employer, and one did not take such liberties with one's employer. "I appreciate the gesture, madam, but I could not presume—"

"I know it is not strictly proper, but over the last month, I feel that we have grown quite close."

New tears gathered in the lady's eyes, and Tabby knew how emotional—even irrational—a woman can be when increasing. And after the scare she had suffered, Tabby thought she deserved that little indulgence.

"Fine, then. Mina. But only if you return the favor," she said with a smile.

"As you wish. Tabby," replied Mina.

The two women sat together in silence, and Tabby continued to hum and hold Mina's hand. It was the least she could do, and Tabby appreciated the opportunity to ease the lady's burden.

"I am so frightened, Tabby," said Mina, her voice barely above a whisper. "My mother and baby sister died in childbirth. What if that happens to us?"

"It is natural for you to worry after having seen the dangers firsthand," said Tabby, squeezing her hand. "But that does not mean it will happen to you. My mother's mother passed in childbirth, but neither my mother nor I came close to that. The physician has assured you that everything is as it should be. It is best if you hold onto that rather than make yourself anxious over what might never happen."

Mina nodded, her eyelids drooping. The poor lady had been a wreck most of the day, and she needed her rest. Tabby hummed her a lullaby, hoping it would do the trick. Within moments, her breathing grew deeper and her muscles slackened. Carefully, Tabby released Mina's hand and stood, stretching her back.

Looking at the window, Tabby was surprised to see that the sun was setting. The whole day was gone, but she knew it had been time well spent. In truth, she had not done much, but both of the Kingsleys had been calmer with her there, and that was no little thing. At such a time, peace was a precious commodity.

Crossing to the door, Tabby stepped out into the hall and found Mr. Kingsley leaning against the wall, facing her. The man looked as though he had been dragged behind a horse, and it was clear that though she had calmed his wife, he was far from it.

"Thank you for your help today," he said. "You were miraculous with Mina. She has been a ball of nerves ever since she realized her condition."

"And I imagine you have been on edge as well," said Tabby.

Mr. Kingsley's gaze fell to the floor. "We hoped for a child for so many years, but I never thought about how frightening bringing one into the world is until I was faced with my wife putting her life in harm's way to do so. In the abstract it had been an exciting thing."

"She and the babe are fine."

"For now," he replied. "But we have several more months of this before we know for certain."

"And then you have years of illnesses and accidents awaiting you," said Tabby. "There is never an end to worrying about what may go wrong. Life is fleeting, and spending your time fretting about what could be is only going to waste it, and make you miserable in the process."

"But—"

"No," said Tabby, and his eyes snapped to hers. Perhaps her tone was a bit harsh, but Mr. Kingsley needed to understand. "No buts. There is no excuse. Life is filled with heartache. There is no avoiding it. Your wife may lose your child. It happens. With no rhyme or reason, it does. Far too often. But do you know what happens then?"

Mr. Kingsley shook his head.

"You hold your wife close. You comfort each other. And then you try again. Or you let it tear you two apart. Destroy the joy you have built together," said Tabby. Her words hitched as thoughts of her own marriage came to mind. "It is your choice, Mr. Kingsley. Embrace a chance for happiness or live a life in fear."

Mr. Kingsley watched her, one side of his mouth slowly quirking upwards. "I see how you have made such strides with my brother-in-law, Mrs. Russell. You are not a blindly optimistic person, but you have such a glow of it about you. It is hard to stay in the doldrums with you around."

Tabby's face colored, and she gave a bob in acknowledgment of the compliment.

Mr. Kingsley pushed off the wall and nodded as he stepped into the bedchamber.

"One more thing, Mr. Kingsley," said Tabby, turning to face him again.

The gentleman gave her his attention and nodded for her to continue.

"It appears as though she has spent a fair amount of time resting over the past weeks," said Tabby. "From what I have seen of her and her brother, that is the last thing she needs. They are people who have to be occupied or they end up lost and emotional. She should take her rest as Doctor Clarke directed, but he said there is no reason she cannot go about her life in a day or two. You must encourage her to do so. A little exertion shan't hurt her or the baby, but sitting about fretting will."

Straightening, Mr. Kingsley gave Tabby a bow. A proper gentlemanly bow. The kind she had not received in a very long time. She returned it with a curtsy, and he walked away to join his wife at her bedside. Taking the chair Tabby had vacated, he held Mina's hand, placing yet another kiss on it. Mina's eyes opened a fraction, followed by a broad grin at the sight of her husband.

Tabby's heart warmed at the tender moment, but the scene brought memories to mind that made her chest tighten. Joshua had not greeted her in such a fashion when she had awoken after losing their first child. Or the others. Joshua had sought his refuge in a bottle.

No. This would not do. She was getting too maudlin. After all her lectures on hope, Tabby would not allow herself to get sucked into such melancholia. Two stillborn children and countless false starts, but it had given her Phillip in the end, and he was most certainly worth all that hardship. And all that Joshua continued to put her through.

Turning away, Tabby found a footman waiting to lead her to the main entrance. Following him, she allowed her mind to wander over the good in her life. A son she loved. A position, which was becoming more and more pleasant with each passing week. An employer whom Tabby could count as a friend; the first true friend she'd had in years, for Tabby knew Mina would not abandon their friendship so quickly as others had when her fortunes had failed her.

Thinking through the list, Tabby's heart lightened, chasing

away the darkness that had been creeping in.

At the door, the butler handed over her bonnet and helped her with her spencer, giving her a rare smile that most haughty butlers would be ashamed to have displayed. Tabby thought it a perfect representation of the Kingsley household. Proper while yet flouting convention in small ways.

"Thank you, Mrs. Russell," he said. "Mrs. Kingsley is resting much easier because of you."

"It was nothing..."

"Jennings," he supplied.

"It was nothing, Jennings. I am happy to help," she said, adding this moment to her list of blessings. She had done some good today, and that was no small thing.

Chapter 12

Graham wanted to pace. Needed to. It was a desperate itch he could not scratch. He had spent hours prowling the deck of his ship when his mind was filled with thoughts and questions that needed working out. It cleared his head and focused the chaos until he saw clearly once more. But now, he was stuck sitting on a sofa that was more decorative than durable, his eyes affixed to the windows facing the front of the house.

A clock in the room ticked the hours away, and the sun slowly sunk behind the horizon, yet there was no word. That long stretch of silence was not a good sign. If all were well, a messenger would have sent word, or Mrs. Russell would have returned.

Mina could not lose her child; Graham could not stand the thought of it. His sister had spent most of her adult life accepting that marriage and motherhood would not happen for her, embracing her broken dream with a courage and strength that Graham envied. Yet, here it was finally within her grasp, which would make the loss that much greater.

It was in those long hours of waiting that Graham realized how greatly he underestimated his sister. Not that he had overtly, but thinking about her hopes and dreams, Graham realized how much stronger she was than he. Spending years of her life wishing for a husband and family, yet never allowing herself to wallow in it or lash out at others. Graham had no doubt that there were times when her heart cried out in sorrow over it, yet she never allowed it to control her.

Unlike him.

For the first time since he had awoken as this broken creature, Graham prayed for something other than the return of his health. Though he doubted deals with the Almighty ever worked, Graham would gladly accept his crippled body and transfer his long-awaited miracle to Mina. Heal her and save her babe.

Mina.

His dear sister.

And that was when Graham caught sight of Mrs. Russell walking the path towards him. In the dimming light, it was difficult to see her expression, so he had no clue whether her spirits were high or low. Gripping his cane, he hefted himself off the couch. His right leg moved easier than it had this morning, but it was still a monumental effort to get across the room in time to meet Mrs. Russell at the door.

"Captain Ashbrook," she said in surprise, pulling off her bonnet. "What—"

"What news?" he asked, snatching it from her hand and tossing it onto a peg beside the door. "Mina and the child?"

"They are fine," she said, her brows pinching together. "Mr. Kingsley was supposed to send word. I asked him to send a footman."

"Are you certain?" he insisted.

"Yes," said Mrs. Russell, taking off her spencer and hanging it next to the bonnet. "Quite certain. The physician insisted it was only a scare. I would have returned sooner, but she desperately needed the company."

Turning her attention on him, her eyes grew worried. "You poor man! To be so worried while we have known the truth for hours. I could thrash Mr. Kingsley," she said, herding Graham into the sitting room.

"Simon can be a bit focused when it comes to Mina," said Graham, taking his previous seat on the sofa. "I should have known that he would forget to send word while his attentions were on his wife. I would be angry over his thoughtlessness if it weren't a byproduct of his devotion to my sister."

Calling to the maid, Mrs. Russell ordered some tea and dinner be brought. Graham wanted to say it was unnecessary, but at that moment, his stomach reminded him that he had not eaten since that morning. Any time Mrs. Bunting or Jillian had tried to tempt him, he had shrugged them away, but now his hunger was returning in force.

"Luckily, it was nothing serious," said Mrs. Russell, sitting in an armchair beside him. "Anything out of the ordinary can be terrifying for expectant parents, and I was glad to ease her fears a bit."

"Yes, Simon mentioned you were a mother," said Graham, and he was quite impressed with the nonchalance in his tone. The only thing that had taken his mind off of Mina was thoughts of Mrs. Russell and the mysterious children Simon mentioned. And he had spent a fair amount of time pondering over them. In their time together, Mrs. Russell had never mentioned them, though Graham supposed that was likely due to the fact that he rarely asked her any personal questions. They had chatted and talked about shared interests and such, but he could not think of anything—outside of their discussion that morning—that had been particularly personal.

Mrs. Russell nodded, staring at her lap while she smoothed her skirts.

"How many children do you have?" he asked. And where were they? How were they coping with their mother leaving after having lost their father? From what Graham surmised, Mr. Russell had not been much of a husband, but it was still devastating to lose a parent. There were a lot of questions he wished to ask, though he was conscious that most of them were highly inappropriate and thus could not be voiced aloud.

"One boy. Phillip," she said, her gaze turning upwards with a smile. "He is four, and the sweetest little man in all creation. He's staying in a cottage near town where I can visit him in my free time. Are you musical?"

The question was unexpected, to say the least, and Graham found himself frantically grasping to understand where it had come from.

"Am I musical?" he asked, as if restating her question would somehow illuminate his confused mind.

"Yes. Either playing or singing or even attending musicales," said Mrs. Russell, leaning forward as if his answer was something she eagerly awaited.

"No," he said. "Most instruments do not fit neatly in the tight confines of a ship."

Mrs. Russell nodded. "So your musicales were rather forlorn events, I suppose."

"We did not..." but Graham caught himself before he went any further. "You are teasing me."

Mrs. Russell's lips hinted at the smile lurking beneath the calm facade. "Just a little, sir. Outside of your naval life, have you shown any interest in music?"

Graham shook his head. "Mina is the musical one in the family. I like listening to it as much as any person but have no desire to create it myself. But I'm at a loss as to why you would ask it."

"Hobbies," said Mrs. Russell, giving him a smile that Graham knew many a man would willingly risk life and limb to receive. It would not be nearly so enticing if the lady had any awareness of its power, but it was artless and genuine. "From our earlier conversation."

Graham's brow furrowed, as he scoured his mind for any memory that might clarify her enigmatic words.

"New things to occupy your time," she said. "Training your left hand to write shall be our first project, but you need others."

Graham had enough to occupy his time. Healing and getting stronger. Salvaging his life took enough of his time and focus.

"Do not turn your nose up at it," said Mrs. Russell, her eyes narrowing, and Graham raised his eyebrows. "I can see what is going on in your head. You think me a fool, but you need to find new passions. You need something else to love."

"Now that the sea is beyond my reach?" Graham fought to keep the growl from his voice.

Mrs. Russell straightened, and Graham relaxed the tension in his shoulders. His dashed temper was going to cause more problems if he wasn't careful.

"Now that your life has changed," she clarified.

Graham wanted to glower and grumble at that, but Mrs. Russell did not deserve to be on the receiving end of his ill-humor. More than that, Graham knew that he was not being the type of man he wished to be. He had never been a bully or cruel and did not wish to develop such characteristics. Unclenching his jaw, Graham took a moment to compose himself before speaking.

"And you believe picking up an instrument will fix everything?" he asked.

Mrs. Russell watched him for a moment before speaking carefully. "I think carrying on as you have is guaranteed to make things worse. Finding new things to enjoy will brighten your world."

Graham drummed his fingers along the arm of the sofa, staring out the front window. Brighten his world. No matter what Mrs. Russell thought, simply taking on a few new hobbies would not be enough to replace the sea. However, there was sense in what she said. If nothing else, it would help stave off boredom until he was healed enough to return to his ship and his men.

"Fine," he said. "But please, no instruments. There must be something a bit more gentlemanly for me to do."

Mrs. Russell chuckled. "Unless you wish to spend your days

chasing debutants, drinking, and gambling, I'm afraid you might have to stray from 'gentlemanly' pursuits. By their very definition, gentlemen are not known for their industry. Besides," she added, her face remaining angelic with the exception of the devilish glint in her gaze, "since when does a naval man care about what's gentlemanly? I thought you live by your own code—the code of the sea."

The touch of melodrama in her tone combined with the acidic and apt description of his dull peers set Graham laughing, and he knew that whatever else may happen, spending time with Mrs. Russell would be diverting.

Chapter 13

This was her lot in life. Tabby forced herself to remember that and not allow herself to be overwrought by such things. It was only an entrance. The servants' entrance of Avebury Park was far humbler than the main entrance, naturally, and it was fitting for her to use it. Doing so was no cause for distress, but her position with Captain Ashbrook felt more like a companion and friend than servant, and it was getting difficult to remember her fallen place in the world.

Knocking on the door, Tabby waited a moment before a young maid opened it and ushered her inside.

Each time she came to visit Avebury Park, Tabby found herself enchanted with it. Being far more modern than Kelland Hall, it had great windows and open spaces to give a lightness that was quite different from the heavy dreariness of the Russell estate. And there was an understated yet elegant feel to the decorations. A mixture of simplicity and grandeur that seemed a perfect representation of its master and mistress. Yes, Tabby greatly admired Avebury Park.

However, there was one aspect in which the Park could never hope to outshine the Hall. This newer building had not seen enough centuries to have accumulated the stories that filled every cranny of Kelland. When speaking of its past, it was impossible to distinguish myth from fact, but that only made Tabby love its history all the more. There was the armchair that was said to have been Queen Bess's favored seat when she had passed the night there. And the ghost of the poor maid who had died in the fire of 1638 who haunted the restored portion of the eastern wing. And every piece of armament decorating the walls laid claim to some prestigious war, leading all the way back to the Battle of Hastings. There was so much life that had happened there.

Coming to a stop before a door, the maid said, "Please wait here, ma'am."

Tabby did so, and the girl went into the room, leaving Tabby alone in the hall, though she could hear everything going on inside.

"Mrs. Russell is here to see you, ma'am," said the maid.

"Wonderful," said Mrs. Kingsley. "Send her in."

The maid returned to the hallway and ushered Tabby into the large sitting room. To one side, Mrs. Kingsley stood by a table with a mountain of flowers scattered around a vase. With a snip of her shears, Mrs. Kingsley cut off a stem and slid the blossom into the pot.

The maid disappeared, leaving the two of them alone.

"Do come in, Tabby," said Mrs. Kingsley. "I hope you don't mind if I keep working on my arrangement. I need to get these in water or they shall wilt."

"Certainly, madam," said Tabby with a curtsy.

Mrs. Kingsley paused and leveled a look at Tabby. "Madam? I thought we agreed to use Christian names when it was only the two of us. Or did you hope I had forgotten that in a fit of emotion?"

Tabby hesitated for a moment before answering truthfully. "Yes, I'm afraid so. I don't think it wise for me to be so informal with my employer."

Mrs. Kingsley turned her attention to the budding arrangement, placing in a few more flowers before she spoke again. "It must be difficult to find yourself in such an altered position."

"I make do."

Mrs. Kingsley glanced at Tabby before working another stem into the vase. "I am certain you do. We may be fairly new acquaintances, but I have a feeling you are not one to shrink under such a burden."

Tabby had no words to respond to that and decided to forge ahead with the business at hand. "I came to see how you are faring. I wanted to come sooner, but Captain Ashbrook has kept me busy the last few days."

Mrs. Kingsley smiled while shifting the blossoms around in the vase. "I am certain he does. My brother may be a grown man, but I am certain you would agree that he can be as demanding as any child when he wishes to be."

Tabby laughed. "It would be unkind of me to admit it."

"But it could be construed as unkind if you disagree with me." Mrs. Kingsley's eyes held a hint of mischief in them.

"Then I must beg to be excused from making any statement about my charge's behavior."

The pair of them laughed, and Tabby watched the lady add flowers here and there to the arrangement. Having tried her hand at that skill, Tabby appreciated seeing someone who had a talent for it. Moving efficiently and with little hesitation, Mrs. Kingsley's vase filled with a rainbow hue of blossoms, and Tabby knew she could never match the lady's skill.

"I'm doing much better," she said. "I can never thank you enough for your kindness."

"It was nothing—" began Tabby, but Mrs. Kingsley interrupted.

"It was not nothing," she insisted, giving Tabby an uncompromising look. "It meant the world to us. Both Simon and I are faring much better after your help and words. He even suggested I return to my usual duties, which has helped enormously, though I would not have agreed to do so if you had not set my heart at ease."

Tabby nibbled on her lip, pleased to hear such things. Her

soul warmed at the thought of Mr. Kingsley heeding her advice, and she could see with her own eyes that Mrs. Kingsley had improved because of it.

"It is better to be active than sit around fretting about that which you cannot change," said Tabby. "It is harder to give in to despair when you are occupied."

Mrs. Kingsley glanced from the flowers and studied Tabby. "I think I have discovered the source of Simon's change of heart. He went from wishing to bundle me in blankets until the baby was born to insisting that I need to do something with myself. Of course, I was as eager as he to languish in bed for the next few months. Thank you for talking sense into us."

"It is easy to allow fears and heartache to dictate our emotions," said Tabby. "I am pleased I could help."

"You did. Enormously," she said, placing one last stem in the vase and turning. Glancing at it from every angle, Mrs. Kingsley scrutinized her work. "Is it right, you think?"

"Gorgeous," said Tabby without even a modicum of embellishment.

Mrs. Kingsley glanced at Tabby. "Truly?"

"Of course," she replied, confused that the lady had no idea how lovely the arrangement was. "I have no talent for flowers, but the hours I spent attempting it gave me an appreciation for what should be admired and what needs to be tossed in the trash bin."

Mrs. Kingsley's cheeks flushed, and Tabby smiled at the artlessness of it. Leaving the flowers on the table, she ushered Tabby over to the sofa and sat with a sigh. "I may have more energy than when I was lying around all day, but I still find myself quite exhausted at times. But what news of my brother?"

"Captain Ashbrook is doing much better," said Tabby. "He spends less time abed and goes outside every day."

"You are a miracle worker," said Mrs. Kingsley.

"I came to see if I might borrow some art implements," said Tabby, choosing to ignore the praise and dive right into the heart of things. "He needs something to do other than sit around and think about what he has lost, but he is not fit to do anything strenuous. I thought we might try his hand at painting or drawing."

"Of course," said Mrs. Kingsley. "I have enough to equip an army of artists, and I would love to donate some to the cause. If it suits him, we can get him his own. Though he has never shown the slightest bit of interest in it before, perhaps he will grow to love it."

"I would welcome any further ideas," said Tabby. "With time, I am hopeful that we can get him walking and riding, but in the meantime, he is an active man being confined to the house. It is a struggle to find things engaging enough to keep his attention. I have already read him most of his books, and he needs more."

"Absolutely," said Mrs. Kingsley. "I know his taste in literature. I will have a mountain of them shipped to Gladwell House immediately. And perhaps I can send—"

At that moment, Mr. Kingsley strode into the room. "I heard Mrs. Russell was visiting, and I wanted to come and see how things were faring with my irascible brother-in-law."

"Not so much irascible as bored," said Tabby.

"You must help us invent ways to entertain Graham," said Mrs. Kingsley, reaching for his hand.

"Anything," he said as he joined her on the sofa. "What are you looking for?"

Mrs. Kingsley slipped her arm through his in a manner that was so commonplace it should not have been remarkable. There was nothing exceptionally romantic about the gesture, and Tabby had indulged in far more glaring displays of affection when she and Joshua had been first married, but the simplicity could not hide the sentiment beneath it. All of her and Joshua's passionate exhibitions held not a fraction of the comfort, tenderness, and closeness that Mrs. Kingsley's understated movement conveyed.

Mr. Kingsley held his wife's gaze for a moment, and though it wasn't heated, Tabby was witnessing something far more deep and meaningful; a look of true love. One based on friendship and respect, which ran far deeper than anything Tabby had ever felt for her husband—even at their best of moments. With that realization, Tabby was struck by a longing as intense as she had ever felt. A desperate melancholy that swallowed her heart whole, for she had run headlong into marriage with a man unlikely to ever give her such a look.

"Pardon?" asked Tabby when she realized that Mrs. Kingsley had been speaking.

"Could you please tell us a little more of what you are looking for?" she repeated.

With a nod, Tabby launched into a recounting of her discussions with and observations of Captain Ashbrook. It was a difficult path to walk, as she was uncertain how much to divulge. The Kingsleys may be his family, but there were things she knew he would not wish them to know. Skimming over anything that felt too personal, Tabby laid out her plans with the Kingsleys when a sudden thought entered her head.

"Perhaps you can show him around the estate. Demonstrate what you do," she said. "He needs a new profession, and though I do not think he has a penchant for working the land, he just may find he has a liking for it."

"That is a capital plan," said Mr. Kingsley. "As soon as he is up to traveling the estate, I can show him some more, but in the meantime, there is not much I can do for him. Mr. Thorne handles most of the bookkeeping and at home business. But perhaps there are other options."

And so, the three began plotting for Captain Ashbrook's future.

Chapter 14

The delicate paintbrush felt liable to snap between Graham's massive fingers, which wasn't what he needed to be thinking about at the moment. Studying the clump of blossoms on the garden table, he dipped the bristles in a dash of blue and touched it to his paper. The pigment flew from the brush, spidering across the painting haphazardly. With a curse, he dropped the brush and reached for a rag, bumping his cup, which fell to its side and sent a shower of dirty water flying. Mrs. Russell abandoned her paints and rushed to mop up the mess.

"Don't bother," he grumbled. "The bloody thing is ruined already. None of the blasted colors go where I wish them to."

Mrs. Russell dabbed at it with her rag. "I need to start penalizing you every time you use such language, sir. With the carelessness in which you speak such foul words, you are liable to teach your future niece or nephew a few colorful phrases that will make your sister blush."

Graham shoved the half-finished painting away. It was pointless to pick the thing up again; there was no salvaging that mess. Resting his elbows on the arms of the chair, he stared at the sky. It was another beautiful day, and he adored being out in the garden, but this was a sad waste of time. Watercolor painting was far too infuriating. The colors had a mind of their own, and Graham did not have the patience to master it.

"Surrendering so easily?" said Mrs. Russell. "I thought you were made of sterner stuff."

He looked up to find her standing there with a smile and a sopping rag in her hand. The sunlight cast a shimmer of gold in her hair, giving it more contrast than usual. It was such a unique color, alternating between various shades of blonde and even the occasional hint of brunette. Graham found it quite entrancing to see it all pinned up, the light and dark gathered together.

"I fear it has conquered me," he replied with a matching smile.

"Painting is a fearsome foe," she said with a mockingly serious glance before returning to her seat. Retrieving a sketchbook, Mrs. Russell handed it over along with a few pencils. "Perhaps you should try sketching. Graphite is far more orderly than watercolor."

Lifting the pencil, he flipped open the book, finding a pristine page. The infuriating painting sat abandoned next to it, and Graham stared at the blue streak marring his meager efforts. He had spent an hour on the thing, and one misstep had ruined it all. However, it did not warrant his reaction.

Though spoken in jest, Mrs. Russell's comment made him think about the state of his language. Truly, he had not thought himself so foul mouthed as all that, yet one small mistake and he had let out a string of words that he should not have said. He hadn't even thought to speak the words; they'd simply sprung free without his bidding.

Some might argue that he wasn't in the presence of a lady and need not worry about such things. Mrs. Russell was a servant, after all. But she was more than that to Graham, and whether or not she was forced into employment, she was a lady of the highest quality and didn't deserve to have her ears befouled by such language.

And there was truth to her warning. He'd thought himself

able to rein in his tongue while in mixed company, but the longer he remained ashore, the more he realized that wasn't true. For short periods, he could manage it, but doing so on a permanent basis was more challenging than he had expected. It was a blessing he had not spoken thusly in front of Mina, for she would give his mouth a good scrubbing with a generous supply of soap if she had.

"You are right," he said.

Mrs. Russell glanced up from her painting. "I usually am, and I am glad you have finally accepted the state of things. It makes life so much simpler to acknowledge reality for what it is. Does that mean you shall stop fighting me over each little thing?"

Graham chose to ignore that and the cheeky twinkle in her eye and clarified his statement. "You are right about my language. I have developed a habit of cursing. A byproduct of my life at sea, though that is no excuse," he said, rolling the pencil between his fingers. "It has been pure luck that I've not said something in front of Mina. She would box my ears if she ever heard a single one of the words with which I assailed you."

Her eyes widened, and she straightened in her seat. "Pardon?"

"I wish to break my bad habit, but often, I don't realize I have said anything amiss until after the fact," he said. "Perhaps you could point it out when I have misspoken. As a boy, Mina would flick my ear to get my attention when I misbehaved. Perhaps you could do the same." Graham smiled at Mrs. Russell, but she only stared back at him.

"Are you all right?" he asked when she appeared unable to do more than blink.

"Are you in earnest?"

"Certainly," he said.

The lady blinked some more and then nodded. "I...ah, yes, sir. I would love to help you."

"I even promise not to get cranky when both my ears end up bruised and throbbing," he said, and Mrs. Russell gave him the laugh he had been fishing for.

"You should not make promises you cannot keep," she said with a sly smile.

Graham grabbed at his chest and said with more than a touch of melodrama, "You wound me, madam. Deeply."

The expression on Mrs. Russell's face shifted, bringing a warmth to it that Graham rarely saw. Not to say that she was unkind, but it was clear that she was weighed down by troubles. Yet in that moment, she looked at peace.

"I think it is wonderful that you wish to better yourself, and I will do whatever I can to help you," she said. Her voice was soft, blending in with the sound of the bees and birds singing around them. She dropped her gaze to her painting and retrieved her brush, dipping it into a bit of color and gently pulling it across the page.

Graham reached for the sketchpad, pulling it onto his lap to get a better angle, but he held the pencil in his hand as he watched Mrs. Russell. Tabby. Mina had called her that once, and the name suited her. The lady was regal enough for Tabitha, but her heart was a Tabby.

Watching her, Graham wondered for the first time what it would be like if he were to stay ashore—with her.

To allow himself such thoughts was straying into dangerous territory. She was his sister's servant. Not that it was a question of class, for Graham knew Mrs. Russell had ample amounts of it, but they lived under the same roof. Even if he wished to ignore the social taboo of courting a servant, doing so while they were so often sequestered alone would destroy Mrs. Russell's reputation. There was no good that could come of brushing up against such conventions. They existed for a reason. And he was not one of those gentlemen who viewed the servant class as prime plucking for a bit of fun. Mrs. Russell deserved better.

Besides, Graham would return to sea, and if he were to marry, he could not imagine leaving the lady behind. And children need their father. It wasn't in his nature to live such a separate life from his wife and children, which is why he had never pursued matrimony in the past. So there was no need to think of Mrs. Russell as anything more than his caretaker.

Then why did the thought of leaving her behind make him uneasy?

Giving her a sly glance, Graham saw the surface beauty that would entice many a man to alter the course of his life in order to secure her as his wife. Yet, it wasn't her fine features that had his conviction wavering. It was her. The life and light in her eyes, the passion and kindness that formed her very core. In only a few weeks, she had become a central figure in his life. Every hour was touched by her presence. Their conversations filled his days, and the realization that he was going to lose all of that left him feeling hollow.

Smoothing his hand over the paper, Graham knew better than to speculate about such things, but it still hung there in the corner of his mind. Mrs. Russell's smile. Her laugh. Her company. With a few strokes of the pencil, he began to sketch out the blossoms on the table, though his eyes strayed to his companion more often than they did to his subject.

This would not do. Graham forced himself to concentrate. With more lines, the image began to take shape, and Graham found himself smiling at the crude drawing. This was much better than watercolor.

Chapter 15

Tabby twirled a daisy between her fingers as she strolled along the country lane. The sun was setting, the ripening wheat catching the dying rays, making it look as though the fields were ablaze. The walk from the estate to her home was the most beautiful part of Bristow, and if it weren't for the fact that she was desperate to see sweet Phillip again, she would happily spend a few moments wading through the fields and listening to the birdsong.

As she walked along, she reached into her reticule, retrieving Captain Ashbrook's latest drawing. He had deemed it worthy of the trash bin, but Tabby had rescued it from that heartless destruction. Rough though it was, the drawing held promise. Captain Ashbrook's talent was quickly outstripping Tabby's own meager abilities, and she was anxious to see him improve.

The gray lines came together into a picture of a faraway beach. Tabby always struggled to imagine the distant lands he described in his tales and had begged him to draw it for her. Though he claimed it did not do the place justice, it was entrancing. Tabby beamed at the drawing before tucking it away once more. Watercolor had not been the right choice, but sketching most certainly was.

Her feet knew the path to her son and followed it without any prompting, allowing her mind to wander over the past weeks. It had been an age since she had spent time with someone so enjoyable as Captain Ashbrook. His life was one grand adventure roving the seas, and Tabby never tired of his stories.

Captain Ashbrook. The man puzzled her deeply. He was such a contradiction of terms. Domineering and demanding, yet introspective and open to criticism. Tabby had never met a man who was so strong willed yet willing to admit he was wrong. Thinking on their conversation about his language, Tabby could not believe that a simple off-hand comment had inspired a change in him.

Even at his best, Joshua had needed strong prodding to do anything. It pained Tabby to remember their courtship and how she had lauded his every improvement, offering them up as proof of Joshua's worthiness to her father when in fact, they had all originated from her. It hadn't been his idea to attend church services. He had gone happily, eager to please her, but he had never initiated it. She had asked him to refrain from drink, and he had done so willingly, but not of his choice.

Yet Captain Ashbrook was taking pains to address his shortcoming of his own volition. Her remarks might have inspired him, but the ensuing efforts were made independent of her.

It had been a sennight since Captain Ashbrook had made the resolution, and he was far from perfect, but he never harried her when she reminded him or snapped when Tabby brought an unconscious uttering to his notice. In fact, he appeared to appreciate it. Tabby struggled to believe it was in earnest, yet every time she corrected him, Captain Ashbrook thanked her and tried again.

Following the curve of the road, Tabby saw her home just ahead. Her heart swelled at the sight of her poor, pathetic little cottage. It looked cruder and more dilapidated than she remembered, but seeing Phillip's nose pressed to the front window made it a most welcome sight. Hitching her skirts, Tabby allowed herself to run the rest of the way, and Phillip broke into a smile as wide as hers. Then the door was flung open, and Tabby scooped him up from the doorstep, burying kisses into his neck.

"Oh, my sweet boy!" Tabby squeezed him until he was certain to burst and then nibbled on his chubby cheeks.

"Mama!" He said the word with half excitement, half frustration at the flood of affection in which she drowned him. Of course, Tabby ignored his hands that went from hugging to pushing for a moment longer, reveling in the feel of having her dear child in her arms again, but eventually, she set him on his feet.

And that was when she noticed the strangers inside her house, watching the whole scene.

Joshua sat at the table, looking far more worn and gaunt than when she'd seen him three days ago. His eyes were red and the skin beneath was purpling—clear signs that he'd only just dragged himself out of a bottle. Behind him stood a man, though "man" was too small a word for what he was. Tabby had heard many described as barrel-chested, but never had the descriptor been so aptly applied. Broad and brawny, his arms were as big around as Tabby's waist. And though his eyes held something of an appreciative glint to them as they perused her person, Tabby felt chilled at its underlying malice.

"You must be Mrs. Russell," said another, drawing Tabby's attention away from the brute looming over Joshua.

The second fellow was middle-aged and well dressed; not the top tiers of fashion, but high quality and fastidiously put together. Shipshape and Bristol fashion, as Captain Ashbrook would say. He offered her a proper bow, and Tabby gave him a curtsy while grabbing Phillip's hand to pull him close. The man's manner was everything courteous, but a prickling at the back of her neck had Tabby stepping between him and her son.

"I've been looking forward to making your acquaintance,"

he said, a warm smile on his lips, though his eyes held none of it. "Your husband speaks so highly of you."

Tabby glanced at Joshua, but his eyes were trained on the floor.

"My name is Mr. Crauford, and this is my associate, Mr. Gibbons." The man spoke as though they were standing in a grand ballroom and not a dingy hovel. "And your husband insisted that you might be of assistance."

"Crauford, please..." said Joshua with a pleading whine.

Mr. Crauford gave both of the Russells a smile and then motioned for Joshua to speak. Her husband stood, keeping a weather eye on Mr. Gibbons, who had yet to move or speak. Coming to Tabby's side, Joshua pulled her into a corner, which had the greatest amount of privacy they could hope to find.

"I need your pay," he said without preamble, holding out his hand as though she would simply give it over without further comment.

"No," she said, pulling away from him. Phillip stood beside her, his eyes bouncing between his parents. Tabby did not wish for him to witness what was certain to become a scene, but she would not allow him to wander while those men were here.

"Now, Tabby," said Joshua. "I need it."

"But we need it to live."

Joshua huffed. "We owe these men money, and if we don't pay things will get far worse for us than going to bed hungry."

"We owe them money?" said Tabby. "How?"

"It was from before," he said, his eyes darting to the men. "I thought I'd taken care of it all, but I overlooked one of our loans."

"You said you took care of it all, Joshua," Tabby said through clenched teeth. She glared at him, but he avoided her eyes. "You said it was over. Done. You promised me that we were starting afresh."

"I thought—"

"Do not give me excuses, Joshua," said Tabby. "Give me a way to feed our child. Give me some hope that you are being honest with me." *Give me back the husband I loved and the life you promised us.* As much as Tabby wanted to say the words, she withheld them. Not so much because Joshua deserved to be sheltered from her hostility, but because of the two little ears listening to the words she spoke.

"Of course I am being honest, Tabby," he said, his jaw clenching, though he wouldn't meet her eyes for more than a second. "How dare you suggest otherwise! Now, give me the money so we can be done with this."

"But we need this for food and rent, Joshua!"

"Do you know what these men will do to us if we don't give it to them?"

Tabby's eyes shot to Mr. Crauford and Mr. Gibbons. The massive man sat there, impassive and staring off at nothing in particular while the smaller watched them with cool detachment. For all of Mr. Gibbons' strength and size, it was Mr. Crauford that terrified Tabby. Gibbons might be the weapon, but it was Crauford who took aim.

Pulling open her reticule, she dropped her coins into Joshua's waiting hand.

"This is all we have," said Joshua, passing it over to Mr. Crauford. "Is it enough for now?"

For now? Tabby's heart sunk at the thought that there was more to come. More debts. More payments. That was supposed to be over. Finished. The point of selling every last possession and living in squalor was that they would be able to break free of their financial burden and begin anew, but Joshua had ruined even that.

Mr. Crauford nodded, and Mr. Gibbons moved to open the door.

"Until next time," said Mr. Crauford with a courtly bow, but Tabby ignored it. That made the man smile, a genuine one that touched his eyes and sent a cold shiver along her spine.

All of the Russells watched as Mr. Crauford and his associate stepped through the door, closing it behind them. It was silent for a full three seconds and then Joshua reached to take

Tabby into his arms. Before he could fully close them around her, she pushed away and crossed to the other side of the room.

"Mama?" said Phillip.

"Go play with your soldiers, dearest," she said, keeping her back to Joshua.

Holding a hand over her mouth, Tabby closed her eyes. She'd hardly put anything aside after the last time Joshua had eradicated their savings, but she had a few hidden coins with which to feed Phillip and pay the rent. She hoped it would be enough now that the rest of her wages were in Mr. Crauford's pocket.

Joshua's hands came down on her shoulders, and Tabby stiffened as he rubbed her arms. "Don't fret. It will be fine. I promise." The last bit was whispered, and she felt his breath tickling her neck before his lips met her skin. Tabby stepped away, but Joshua pulled her close.

"I have missed you," he murmured, pressing another kiss to her neck. "Between your absence and our lack of privacy here, it's been a while since we've had time alone just the pair of us." Another wet kiss crawled up her neck.

Tabby bent her head away from the invading lips, twisting out of Joshua's hold to face him. "How can you possibly believe that I would wish for you to touch me after what just occurred?"

He crossed his arms, his brow raised. "It is done. Over. And now I was hoping to have some intimate time with my wife."

"How much?" asked Tabby, crossing her own arms and steeling herself for what she knew was going to be a grim discussion.

Joshua's lips pulled into a sultry smile that had once made Tabby's heart sigh. "Should I be explicit?"

"How much do we owe them? They said what we gave them was good enough 'for now.' That means more is owed, so how much is it?"

With smooth practice, Joshua drew closer, his hands coming to rub Tabby's arms. "Don't bother yourself with those details. I am handling it."

Tabby pulled free of his touch. "How much, Joshua?"

He stepped away with a curse. "Let it go, Tabby. I am handling it."

"How?" she snapped. Tabby cast a quick glance at Phillip, but he was busy playing with his pair of soldiers—the only toys the boy had left because of how his father handled things. "I am bringing in the only income this family has, so how are you 'handling' anything?"

"It is none of your concern," he said in a low growl.

At those words, Tabby's heart throbbed in her chest, sending a surge of heat into her veins. It coursed through her, tightening her muscles until she felt so taut she could snap.

"None of my concern?" She felt as though she were burning alive, but her words were steady and hard as steel. "You have beggared us and driven us into this dire situation, and you say it is none of my concern?"

He opened his mouth to interrupt, but Tabby spoke over him, her voice rising. "Now, how much do we owe them?"

"Leave it, Tabby!" he replied with equal volume.

"Tell me, Joshua! How much do we owe those men?" Tabby was nearly screaming. She could not think of another time in her adult life when she had raised her voice so, but she could not concern herself with what the neighbors heard, if her tone hurt Joshua's feelings, or even if Phillip were bothered by it. She needed to know, and she would not let it go until she had her answer.

"It's nothing," he said, matching her tone. "A trifling, so let it go."

Coming in close, Tabby let her rage burn through her gaze as she stared into his eyes. "How much is it?"

Joshua's eyes blazed, too, but he could not match her stubbornness. Not now and not over this. Tabby would not relent until she knew the truth of the matter in its entirety. Too much of Phillip's future depended on it.

"Thirty pounds," he muttered.

Tabby's breath froze in her lungs, her hands flying to her

mouth. Thirty pounds. Stepping over to the table, she slid onto the chair, her legs no longer able to hold her upright. Thirty pounds.

"Thirty pounds?" she whispered, her eyes staring sightlessly at the wall. There had been a time when such a sum would've been naught but a trifling to Tabby, but that time had long passed. Now even thirty shillings was no small thing.

When she met his eyes again, she found Joshua standing there, devil-may-care, as if he weren't living in a hovel, wearing threadbare clothes, and without a penny to his name. "Thirty pounds is more than I make in a year, Joshua. How are we ever to pay them back?"

"I am taking—"

Tabby slammed a fist on the table, making him jump. "Don't you dare say you are taking care of it, Joshua Russell."

More than anything else that had happened, that sobered Joshua. His cheeks paled, his bleary eyes widening. Taking a breath, he nodded. "I have a plan. A brilliant plan," he said, coming to sit beside Tabby. "I know a man who will lend us the money to pay off Mr. Crauford."

Tabby sighed and closed her eyes. "And how will we pay off this new debt?"

Joshua reached over to take her hands in his, and she opened her eyes to see him smiling at her as if everything were right in the world. "That's just it. We pay what we can, but when the debt comes due, we borrow from another source. And then another and another. As many as we need. We will be able to keep ourselves afloat for years doing that, giving us plenty of time to pay it off."

Pulling her hands from his, Tabby stood, turning away from her husband and pinching the bridge of her nose. "Are you mad? Borrowing on top of borrowing on top of borrowing. We will never dig ourselves out from under it."

Joshua snorted. "Why is it that my plans are always mad? It was your decision to bring us out here in the first place. If we had stayed put we would be—"

"Living off the charity of others!" Tabby whirled on him. "Living off the scraps they threw us. Do you have no self-respect? No sense of honor? Or duty? Our family is drowning in debt, and you are acting as though nothing is amiss."

"And you are making a fuss over nothing," he replied. "Half the gentry live off borrowed funds—"

"Look at where we live, Joshua!" Tabby screamed, unable to contain the burst of furious energy. "Look at our lives! We are not gentry anymore, we—"

"I am a gentleman," Joshua shouted over the top of her words. "No matter how you choose to debase yourself, I am a gentleman!"

Tabby's heart pounded in her ears as she glared at her husband. Debased? He spoke as though she were nothing more than muck under his boot.

"How dare you..." she ground out, but stifled sobs cut off her words. Just over Joshua's shoulder, Tabby saw Phillip sitting in the corner, his soldiers abandoned as he held his hands over his ears, tears streaming down his cheeks.

"Dearest," she said, shouldering past Joshua to reach her son. "Oh, darling," she crooned, scooping him into her arms. Phillip wrapped around her, burying his wet nose into her neck. Tabby held him and felt tears gathering in her own eyes as his little body shook in her embrace.

Joshua watched with dull eyes, though Tabby read his thoughts well enough. It was that ever-present resentment lurking beneath all of the man's thoughts and actions. Tabby had sensed it far before Joshua had ever admitted it aloud, and now he trotted it out in almost every conversation.

"I sacrificed everything for you," he said.

Tabby's jaw tightened, and she wanted to rail against the stubborn, selfish oaf, but it would accomplish nothing, and she would not upset Phillip further. Taking a breath, she allowed her love for her son to calm her. The peace that came from holding her dear little man in her arms washed over her, leaving her shaking from the aftermath of the confrontation.

Staring into Joshua's eyes, Tabby felt so very exhausted. "That is the difference between us, Joshua. You are not the only one who sacrificed for this marriage, but at least I acknowledge that it was my decision to marry you. Mine. And I have accepted the consequences that came from it."

Her husband's eyes narrowed on her for a long moment before he stomped out the door, slamming it shut behind him. Phillip flinched at it, and Tabby rubbed his back as she rocked him.

"Everything is all right, dearest," she whispered, carrying him over to the table. "No need to be upset." That was the only lie she would allow herself. She wished to say more to calm his frightened soul, but Tabby could not tell her son that it had been nothing more than a bit of talking. It never was with Joshua.

"Would you like to help me make some dinner?" she asked, hoping a distraction might be the solution. "I have a new recipe I am longing to make for you."

Phillip sniffled, and he shook his head while keeping it buried in Tabby's neck.

"Aren't you hungry?"

Yet another shake of his head.

Tabby leaned into him, her cheek resting against him. "That is probably for the best. It has cabbage, and I know how much you hate cabbage. Disgusting thing."

"I love cabbage," he whispered.

Tabby shook her head in mock distress. "Oh, no. That cannot be right. You hate cabbage."

Leaning away to meet her eyes, Phillip rubbed a hand across his cheeks, shaking his head. "I love it."

"No, I am positive that you hate it more than anything in the world."

Little wet hands grabbed her cheeks, pulling her face to stare directly into his. "I love it," he said with such an earnestness that Tabby was hard pressed not to laugh. Her dear little man.

"And carrots?" she asked. "Surely you cannot like those,

too."

Phillip nodded. "And carrots."

"No," said Tabby, shaking her head. "That doesn't sound like my little man. What have you done with him?"

Straddling her lap, Phillip put his hands on his hips and narrowed his eyes, giving a rather good impression of his former nanny. "You're being silly."

"Not I," she replied, and before he could say another word, Tabby attacked his tummy, tickling it in all the spots guaranteed to get her a good squeal of laughter. Phillip wriggled, and he was getting big enough that it took some maneuvering to keep him on her lap.

"Stop!" he gasped between giggles, but Tabby probed his prime spot, and he could not get out another word until Tabby released her prisoner.

Phillip went limp for a moment to catch his breath, and then shot off her lap, running to the farthest part of the cottage and out of reach of his tormentor.

"Will you help me make dinner?" she asked, standing and brushing off her skirts, but that was when she noticed there was no fire in the hearth. Tabby sighed. It would take time to build the proper heat, meaning dinner would take even longer. There was no point in dwelling on that frustration for it was far from the most important in her life at present, so Tabby got to work. Only a short while ago, starting a fire had been daunting, but now Tabby started it with ease, getting all the components into place.

"All right, Phillip," she said, straightening and going to the cupboard. "We will need cabbage, carrots, onions..." But Tabby's voice drifted off as she opened the door to find the pantry bare. It was not as though it had been filled to bursting before, but there had been a fair amount of food when Tabby had last inspected it only a few days before. Now, there was nothing but a tiny, withered potato sitting alone in the corner.

Staring into the void, Tabby battled between seething rage and hopeless despair. A few of Captain Ashbrook's less than choice words sprang to mind as she thought about her husband. With it being Sunday, the market would be closed, and she could not face the thought of begging her neighbors for help. No doubt, they already knew too much about the Russells' hardships, and Tabby could not bear the humiliation of revealing that she had no food to feed her child.

But Tabby could not let Phillip go hungry.

"Are we going to make the soup, Mama?" asked Phillip as he dragged a chair over from the table so that he could see into the upper shelves of the cupboard.

"Not now, Phillip." She grabbed him off the chair, placing him on the ground, but Phillip immediately climbed up it again.

Gladwell House. The thought popped into Tabby's head, and she shied away from it. But it was the only option. The staff were gone for the rest of the day, and Captain Ashbrook would be in his room. The house would be mostly empty. Tabby could sneak in, fetch something from the pantry, and replace it later using the meager savings hidden in her room. No need to explain to anyone. No one would be the wiser.

Gathering their things, Tabby led Phillip out into the summer evening. The air was warm, the insects buzzing lazily in the sky, and much of the walk was as beautiful as it had been only a scant half-hour before, yet Tabby's bruised soul struggled to find any enjoyment in it. Even hearing Phillip chatter on about all the important events of the last few days was not enough to raise her spirits; it only reminded her that she was missing so much of his life. Visiting for a few hours a week did not make up for all that lost time, especially when most of her trips home were a frenzied torrent of chores to be done while Joshua lazed about and watched her toil.

It was best not to think of that man right now. Tabby's heart couldn't bear it.

Pulling free of Tabby's grasp, Phillip dropped to the ground, kneeling beside a grasshopper. He poked at the insect, and it leapt into the air, making the boy flinch and topple backwards. And then he let out a laugh. Scrambling to his feet, he chased after it.

"Sweetheart!" called Tabby, torn between frustration at the delay and amusement at his childish delight in such small things. Eventually, she had him in hand and going the right direction.

"Now, Phillip," she said as they approached the front gates, "I need you to be very quiet when we go inside. Not a word."

Phillip nodded, though his attention was on the world around him and not at all on her.

"Phillip," she repeated, forcing him to focus. "What did I say?"

He shrugged.

"Not a sound when we go inside," she reiterated, and he nodded.

Going around to the back door, Tabby led Phillip into the kitchen. Her stomach twisted as she stepped across the threshold. It was not as though she were stealing. Tabby fully intended to pay for every last bit of food they took, but the flutterings in her heart made it hard to believe herself anything but a thief. However, it was better than facing the others and admitting her dire circumstances.

Phillip started to speak, but Tabby put a finger to her lips, making her feel even more abominable.

Leading him to the pantry, Tabby took a basket and began filling it with the bare necessities. Nothing fancy. Nothing more than she could afford. She kept a running tally in her head as she placed each item into her basket.

"What are you up to?"

Tabby jumped, whirling around to see Mrs. Bunting standing in the doorway.

"I..." But Tabby had no idea how to finish that statement. Unfortunately, Phillip decided to do it for her.

"We are getting dinner," he said.

Tabby's head slumped with a sigh, her shoulders falling. "We were not stealing, I promise, Mrs. Bunting."

"Of course not. The thought never crossed my mind," said

Mrs. Bunting, looking at the boy. "And this little fellow must be Phillip. Your mama speaks of you often. Do you like biscuits?"

His eyes widened, and he gave a solemn nod.

Beckoning for him to follow, Mrs. Bunting soon had the pair of them gathered at the table and plied with sweets.

"What are you doing here?" asked Tabby. "I thought you were going to spend the evening with your daughter."

"Her youngest has a fever, and I didn't want to impose while they had their hands full," said Mrs. Bunting, prepping a pot of tea before seating herself across from Tabby. "But might I ask what you are up to?"

Tabby blushed, her eyes falling to the tabletop. With succinct words, she described her pitiful situation, artfully avoiding the horrid scene with her husband that precipitated it. But judging from the look in Mrs. Bunting's eyes, she knew there was more to the story than Tabby was sharing.

"I would've asked my neighbors for help, but I had nothing on hand to pay them, and I hate to impose on them any further," said Tabby, picking at a biscuit. "When my husband is unavailable, they help with Phillip, and—"

"Husband?" asked Mrs. Bunting. "You're married?"

Tabby's eyes widened, her mouth gaping, but before she could speak, Mrs. Bunting continued. "No, of course you *were* married," she said, glancing at Phillip. "I assumed you were widowed. You never speak of your husband."

Tabby shifted in her seat, avoiding Mrs. Bunting's gaze. She did not know what to say. It was true that she never spoke of Joshua. Tabby preferred it that way, for it allowed her to avoid uncomfortable questions about her private life. When she met the cook's eyes, she found understanding staring back at her.

"Not all husbands are worth discussing, are they?" said Mrs. Bunting.

Tabby glanced to Phillip, but his sole focus was on devouring the tasty treat before him. "No, they are not."

Mrs. Bunting tapped her hand against the table and got to her feet. "Well, this calls for a bit of supper. I have a few lovely meat pies left over from Captain Ashbrook's dinner. That should do the trick."

"I did not mean to impose," said Tabby.

"Imposition, nothing," said Mrs. Bunting, bustling to the pantry and retrieving a few bits of this and a few pieces of that. "I'd count it as a blessing if you'd keep me company."

Tabby's heart warmed and she gave the woman a smile, filling it with all the gratitude she felt inside, and Mrs. Bunting waved it off, though there was a sympathetic glimmer in her eye.

"Now, Phillip," she said. "Do you prefer beef or venison?"

"I think he would rather have hedgehog," said Tabby.

Phillip squealed, wrinkling his nose, and Mrs. Bunting—bless the woman—jumped right into it.

"Oh, I do have some lovely hedgehog," said Mrs. Bunting. "Badger, too. With a side of moss and rotten potatoes? How does that tickle your fancy?"

Phillip covered his mouth, stifling a giggle. "That's disgusting!"

"It's true, Mrs. Bunting," said Tabby with a sparkle in her eye. "Phillip eats only moldy bread and raw trout."

Phillip squealed again, but the sound of Captain Ashbrook's footsteps had Tabby shushing him.

"Mrs. Russell?" he called.

Tabby sent a look to Mrs. Bunting, and the woman waved away Tabby's concerns, placing a slab of pie on a plate and handing it to Phillip. "I'll watch him."

Hurrying from the kitchen, Tabby rushed to meet Captain Ashbrook. The last thing she needed was for her employer to discover Phillip eating his food. Not that she thought the captain would dismiss her over such an infraction, but it was best not to tempt fate. Phillip would be gone soon, and it was best if Captain Ashbrook remained ignorant of the visit and why it was necessary in the first place.

"Yes, Captain Ashbrook?" she replied, meeting him at the top of the stairs. The fact that he had made it from his room on his own was a bit of an accomplishment, but stairs were beyond his ability at the moment.

"I heard your voice and was wondering if you had arrived earlier than planned," he said with a smile. "We might read a bit more of that novel we started this afternoon."

A definite Phillip sound came from the kitchen, catching Tabby's attention, but the captain appeared not to notice.

"I'm afraid I cannot at the moment, sir," she said with a quick bob, "but perhaps in an hour or so." That would give her enough time to return Phillip home.

Captain Ashbrook watched her silently, and Tabby worried for a quick moment that he had heard the little boy's laughter.

"Is something the matter?" he asked.

"No, sir," she said with another sketch of a curtsy. "Only busy."

"Then I shan't keep you," he said.

Tabby stepped forward to help him to his room, but he waved her off. "I can manage, Mrs. Russell, though I shall need your assistance tomorrow. My brother Ambrose has decided to visit, and Mina wishes for us to dine together."

Tabby gave him all the necessary assurances that she would be there to help him. It was thrilling to see the captain moving about under his own power, and that he was willing to go all the way to the Park was a miracle on its own. With all that had happened today, Tabby needed this little victory. The captain was making progress, and though it did not erase all the pain this evening had brought her, it gave Tabby a lighter step as she returned to the kitchen.

Chapter 16

I t had been too long since Tabby had ridden in a proper carriage. There'd been a time when she thought them a most uncomfortable means of transportation, but after spending so many months on foot, she reveled in the rocking, bumping motion as it conveyed her and Captain Ashbrook to the main house; it may be a short distance but it was one that her charge would be unable to make under his own power.

However, as much as Tabby enjoyed the convenience, she could not help feeling discomforted. Everything about the moment made her keenly aware of how low her status had become. It was not as though Tabby were ignorant of the fact that she was no longer a grand lady, but at odd times, the difference in her station slapped her across the cheek, and sitting across from Captain Ashbrook in all his evening finery could not fail to highlight it.

Tabby may not be dining with the family, but she was not about to appear on their doorstep looking like a ragamuffin. She had dressed in her finest gown and taken extra time to arrange her coiffure with a touch more style than usual. There were no artfully dangling ringlets or delicate twists and braids, but it was as fine as she could manage in the circumstances. All in all, she looked pleasing—for an afternoon walk through the park.

There was no more dressing for dinner for Captain Ashbrook's poor caregiver. No grand evenings swathed in silk. No balls. No theatre. The destitute lady could not afford any of that, even if she received such invitations or had the time to spare for such frivolous events.

Tabby bit her lips, tightening her mouth to stave off the trembling of her chin. This would not do! She blinked several times, holding off the tickling in her eyes. She could not do this. Not now. Not ever. It was pointless to moan and mope about what had been. A useless expenditure of energy that Tabby would not indulge.

Her life was not a loss. She had many things to be grateful for. A position that allowed her time to see her son. And it was work that she enjoyed. Heaven knows, plenty of women in Tabby's situation were forced into far more dire employment to survive.

The carriage rolled to the front entrance of Avebury Park, and Tabby ran a hand along her muslin skirt. She was only there to accompany Captain Ashbrook into the house. She was there in an official capacity, and there was no need to work herself into such a state for being so plainly dressed. But years of habit and training pricked at her heart, making it clear that her appearance was unsuitable.

A footman handed her out of the carriage, and Tabby stood to the side to take the captain's arm the moment he stepped down. Helping him up the stairs and to the front door, Tabby felt a flush of satisfaction. To think that when she'd taken this position, the captain's attitude and health had been so poor that the thought of him going to the main house for dinner seemed an impossibility. Yet, now he was hobbling up the steps. Even if he was leaning heavily on his cane and herself, Captain Ashbrook was there.

Jennings had the door open for them when they approached, and before he could take their jackets, she heard Mina calling for them, which brought a grin to Tabby's face. The lady stood on the stairs, a hand resting atop the growing swell of her stomach. When Tabby had been in the family way, there had been none of the quintessential glow that many associate with expectant mothers. Being ill for months on end had made it impossible to feel the level of joy needed to radiate such contentment. But for all her fears about the child, Mina was alight with it, and it suited the lady more than Tabby could say.

"It is so good to see you both," said Mina, coming down the stairs to embrace her brother and Tabby, in turn. It surprised Tabby a touch, but then again, Mina had proved to be a most unusual sort of lady. One that Tabby was finding more and more difficult to think of as Mrs. Kingsley.

"Mina, dearest," said Mr. Kingsley. "Perhaps you should allow them a moment to breathe before you pounce."

But Mina ignored her husband. "I am overjoyed to have you at Avebury, and Ambrose, too. If Nicholas and his family were here it could be a full family gathering."

"Graham," greeted a new voice, and Tabby looked to find a gentleman leaning against the wall.

His dark locks were perfectly coiffed into the windswept fashion so many gentlemen adored; the type that had all the appearance of being careless and easy, as though he had just come in from a rigorous ride but, in truth, had taken more time to arrange than Tabby had spent on her own hair. From the top of his head to the tip of his boots, he was the picture of a wealthy gentleman who toed the fashion mark without stepping over into foppish.

Tabby knew that such gentlemen followed one of two approaches to society. Either they adopted a constant state of ennui and haughty disapproval of everything and everyone about them or turned into the frivolous flirt that flattered their way into everyone's good graces. Joshua had been the latter, and with only one look, Tabby could tell that Mr. Ambrose Ashbrook would be right at home with Joshua's set.

"Ambrose," said the captain. "I am surprised you pulled yourself from London."

Mr. Ashbrook pushed away from the wall, sauntering over to the group. "I thought it might be nice to take a break from Nicholas and Louisa-Margaretta's noisy brood."

Captain Ashbrook chuckled, though Tabby could not find the humor in the flippant remark concerning his own kin. Everything about the gentleman's expression, from the carefully crafted sparkle in his eyes to the smirk on his lips, set her on edge. Such people had no concern for anything but their own pleasure, and Tabby had no more patience for that selfish, self-centered, egotistical crowd.

How she wanted to glare at him and show him how little his demeanor impressed her, but giving the cut direct to her employer's family would not be the wisest decision. Tabby contented herself with wild imaginings of how she would have done so, reliving all the things she wished she had said during the endless evenings in which she'd been forced to hold her tongue around Joshua's dearest friends.

"Dinner is served," Jennings announced, and Tabby helped Captain Ashbrook into the dining room. Once he was settled, she gave a bob and turned to leave.

"Where are you going?" asked Mina from her place at the foot of the table.

"Madam?" responded Tabby.

Mina's eyes narrowed at the honorific but said nothing. She motioned towards an unoccupied place setting beside Captain Ashbrook.

Tabby's eyes widened and shook her head. "I cannot possibly do that. I'm not dressed to dine with you."

"But Graham will need your assistance," said Mina.

"Graham does not need assistance to eat," interjected Captain Ashbrook, but he closed his mouth at the scowl Mina gave him.

"Of course, I shall stay to assist with the journey home," said Tabby, "but Captain Ashbrook is more than capable of handling the evening without my assistance. I should be more comfortable in the servants' hall until he has need of me."

"But the invitation was for both of you," said Mina. "And it does not matter how you are dressed."

"Yes, madam," said Mr. Ashbrook. "You are quite welcome, no matter your attire."

The words were innocent enough, but the gaze that accompanied it was anything but. That quirk of his lips and innuendo in his eyes as he perused her figure made her feel as though she were nothing more than a light-skirt for his enjoyment. A familiar sickness wafted over her, one that she had felt many times when Joshua's lewd friends made such slight comments. Tabby found a bit of comfort in knowing that she need not fend off more flirtations as she would not be spending the evening in Mr. Ashbrook's company. Though Joshua's friends had taught her many ways in which a lady may protect herself, Tabby preferred not to endure such scenes, even if it would be ever so enjoyable to impale the gentleman with an obliging fork. Wretched man.

"That might be," said Tabby, "but it is not appropriate for me to dine with your family."

"But..." Mina began, her voice quivering. At that, the entire group tensed, watching with growing alarm as the lady's eyes glistened. "I wished for you to dine with us."

"And I am most grateful." Tabby nearly let Mina's Christian name slip out, but it would not do to be so informal in mixed company no matter how unconventional the lady may be. However, Tabby also knew that using Mina's proper title would only cause more distress, so Tabby omitted any names or honorifics in their entirety. It was better that way.

"You are too kind, and I would love to visit you tomorrow if the captain does not need me," insisted Tabby, dropping her voice in hopes that only Mina would hear the next bit, though Tabby suspected it would do no good. "But joining you is uncomfortable for me. I am your servant, and I am grateful for your friendship, but dining *en famille* crosses a line that should not be crossed."

She hated saying it and even more that it caused Mina's un-happiness; most of the lady's reaction was due to her increasing state, but some of it stemmed from the part of her soul that was disturbed by Tabby drawing such a distinction. But she had to do it. It was too painful, too difficult to be so close to her former life and remember that it was not hers anymore. If she were to take that place at the table, it would be all the more difficult to accept her current status when the dinner was over and Tabby returned to the role of servant once more.

"Dearest," said Mr. Kingsley, coming around to join his wife.

Mina waved off his concern. "I am fine. I am only disap-pointed, but I cannot seem to keep control of my emotions of late. Truly, I am not so distraught that I should be on the verge of tears."

Tabby gave Mina a commiserating smile. "With my Phillip, I once cried for an entire evening because I broke a teacup. The thing was not special or sentimental. It was a plain, ordinary, easily replaceable piece. I cannot even remember why it af-fected me so, but I wept continually the entire time, no matter how anyone tried to comfort me."

"I apologize that I have made you uncomfortable," said Mina, brushing away all signs of distress and taking a breath. "Of course you should go if you feel you must, but know that you shall be missed."

She called for a footman, and the young man appeared, prompting Tabby to follow.

They disappeared down the hall, and she would not allow herself to look back. It broke Tabby's heart to do so. Regardless of her official capacity, Mina had become a friend, and Tabby wanted nothing more than to spend the evening with her. But Tabby's situation was far too precarious. Her heart too fragile. Too much of Phillip's future and wellbeing relied on this posi-tion. Tabby could not undo her feelings for her odd and endear-ing employer, but she could keep a bit of distance.

Tabby did not think Mina the type of lady to dismiss her

over a petty disagreement between friends, but it was best not to risk it. More than that, Tabby struggled with the constant flipping between friend and servant. Equal one moment and lesser the next. And each time she flitted between them, the more difficult it was to accept that she was no longer part of the elite.

Life was different now and would never return to what it had been. There was no magic inheritance to come, no sudden turn in fortune. She was a penniless servant, and that would not change. Tabby had accepted that fact, but flouting the proper order and rules of her station made it all the more difficult to remember it. Though she knew Mina meant well, pretending she was a guest only emphasized just how much she had lost, and there was only so much Tabby's heart could take.

An arm snaked around her shoulders, and the footman pulled Tabby close. "Hello there, you pretty thing."

Tabby gaped at him, shoving against his hold. "How dare you!"

"Come on," he said, leering at her. "Just a little something for my troubles."

With a strategic elbow, Tabby wrenched herself free of him. Putting distance between them, she glanced at the empty hallway.

"There's no one here to see," he said, waggling his eyebrows as if that would somehow entice her to fall right into his embrace.

"Not on your life." Without waiting for him, she continued down the hall, but he took a parting grope of her backside and Tabby whirled, using the momentum to add to the force of her slap. It connected with his face with a satisfying crack that echoed in the halls.

"What, because I'm not one of those swells, you won't give me the time of day?" he asked, rubbing at his reddening cheek. "You'll hand out your favors to the captain, but not some lowly footman?"

"Duncan!" Jennings barked, and Tabby glanced behind her

to see the butler hurrying towards them. "Return to your post!"

The footman glowered at Tabby when Jennings came up beside her, but the lad said nothing more as he stormed away.

"And we will be discussing your behavior later," added Jennings. Duncan's steps faltered before continuing on his path back to the dining room.

"Are you all right?" he asked. Tabby nodded, unable to say the words aloud. She was physically unharmed, but the sickness in her stomach would not dissipate so easily.

"I apologize for that," said the butler. "Duncan is a bit too sure of himself and was indulged too often in his last position. Though I've been working with him, some of his habits have been harder to break. Not that I am excusing him, but I hope you do not believe I would ever condone such behavior."

"Of course not," said Tabby.

From the look on his face, she saw that the man was no more mollified with the words than she felt at speaking them, but he held out an arm to her. "May I escort you to the servants' hall, madam?"

The little bit of courtly behavior helped settle Tabby's ruffled spirits, and she took it. "Do you escort all the servants?"

"Only the ones I'm especially fond of," said Jennings with a smile.

Tabby stiffened for a moment at the implications. After what she had endured, Tabby could not face another scene.

"Oh, not in that sense, madam," said Jennings, patting her arm as they walked along. "I have been happily married for over forty years, and I fear no woman can ever compare to my dear Sarah."

"She is a lucky lady to have such devotion," said Tabby with a touch more earnestness than she had meant to convey. She kept herself from wallowing in the longing she felt, but she could not stop the swell of it that seized her heart. What would it be like to hear her spouse say such things?

Tabby shook herself free of such musings and turned her thoughts to his earlier statement. "But I am at a loss, sir. How did I earn such a distinction?"

"I am not one to gossip about my master or mistress," said Jennings, "but I will say that Mrs. Kingsley was a godsend to Avebury Park. She is a true lady and the best mistress a butler could hope for, and you have been exceptionally kind to her."

Jennings stopped at a door, and from the noise behind it, Tabby suspected they had reached their destination. Facing her, Jennings continued. "Mrs. Kingsley has not been blessed with many friends and has few confidants."

That surprised Tabby. Mina had such a kind heart that it was difficult to believe she was in want of companionship. On the other hand, Tabby was no stranger to the fickle nature of society, and Mina was too unique to fit well into the tight mould required for acceptance among the gentry.

"Besides helping her brother, you have given Mrs. Kingsley much comfort during this emotional time. For that, you have my undying thanks," he said, giving her a bow.

Another blessing. It may seem a small thing to an outsider's perspective, but the words and gesture warmed Tabby's heart. Income and stability for Phillip may be her premier motivation, but knowing that she had accomplished some further good buoyed her spirit. A prickle of tears came to her eyes, but Tabby brushed them off. Giving the butler an equally deferential curtsy, she smiled at the man.

Motioning for her to proceed him, Jennings opened the door and ushered her into the servants' hall.

Every word and movement ceased the moment she crossed the threshold, as though she were a hound that had stumbled into a fox's burrow.

"Molly," said Jennings to one of the maids, "would you please fetch a plate for Mrs. Russell?"

"I don't wish to be a bother," said Tabby. "I'm certain the kitchen staff are busy with dinner. I can wait until I return to Gladwell House to dine."

Jennings leveled an impatient look at Tabby. "You must be famished, and it'll be no trouble. There's always meat pies on hand, and as Mrs. Kingsley had planned on you dining with them, there's a fair bit of food laying around."

"A slice of pie would be fine," said Tabby, glancing at the unwelcoming stares of the servants. They were not hostile per se, but there was no warmth to them, either. Jennings pulled out a chair for her, and Tabby's face flamed as she sat. The butler's behavior was very kind, but it was not helping the situation.

As uncomfortable as Tabby had felt about dining with Mina and her family, she could see that being here would not be much better. Her manners were too fine for her to pass for a servant, and her purse too light to pass for a lady. Neither side would ever welcome her fully. This was Tabby's life. Her future. Neither fish nor fowl, as they say.

But filled with the warmth of Jenning's kindness, Tabby would not allow it to pull her down. There was still plenty of good in her life.

Chapter 17

G raham propped his leg on an ottoman, sighing at the relief it gave him; with only Simon and Ambrose there for company, Graham allowed himself that uncouth indulgence. Each day he was getting stronger, but he still had far to go.

Ambrose sat low in the armchair, swirling a snifter of brandy in his hand, and Simon sat as far away from the youngest Ashbrook as the room would allow. He doubted Simon was consciously aware of it, but Graham chuckled at the manifestation of his brother-in-law's hidden frustrations with Ambrose. With Mina having retired early, it left an even larger, silent gap between the two gentlemen.

"How are you feeling, Graham?" asked Simon. "You seem to be doing better."

Graham nodded. "Much better, but I have a long way to go yet. I think I might be well enough to start the next round of treatments."

"Next round? I thought you were done with that."

"Of course not," said Graham. "There are options to pursue."

"What options?" Simon gaped like a carp.

"There are hundreds of physicians and surgeons in our fair country," he replied. "You don't think I would give in after only a small handful have deemed it a lost cause, do you?"

Simon's shoulders tightened, his face pinching into a scowl, but when he opened his mouth to speak, Ambrose broke in with a chuckle.

"Out with it, brother. You're simply looking for any reason to keep that delicious nurse of yours around," he said before gulping down the brandy faster than any sailor.

"Pardon?" asked Graham.

Ambrose waved at the footman to refill his glass. "You have that gorgeous creature waiting on you hand and foot. You cannot tell me that you don't enjoy that. You two together. Alone." And at that, Ambrose raised his eyebrows suggestively.

"That's not amusing, Ambrose," said Simon.

"It was not meant to be amusing. It was meant to be insinuating," replied Ambrose. "You cannot honestly say that you would be upset at having such a pretty little thing like Mrs. Russell at your beck and call. You may be married, but you have two eyes."

Simon's jaw tightened, and Graham could almost hear his teeth grinding from across the room, but Ambrose was more focused on his drink and did not seem to notice. Or maybe he did and did not care. It was difficult for Graham to tell anymore.

Simon rose to his feet to glare down his brother-in-law. "Ambrose, I will tell you this once and only once. I do have eyes, but they only see Mina. Now, if you will excuse me, I am going to join my wife. I am certain you two can entertain yourselves on your own."

Graham watched his brother-in-law escape and felt for the man. Though Graham loved his brother, even he struggled to enjoy Ambrose's company, and Simon did not have years of pleasant associations to help ease the frustration rife in any conversation that revolved around Ambrose. This facetious fribble with a penchant for causing contention in the family was not the lighthearted lad Graham had known. Ambrose had been the family jester. The one to tease them out of their doldrums. The one that helped them find laughter and happiness in their darkest times. Graham could only hope that one day that kindhearted lad would return to them.

"So when do you plan on starting the next round of treatments?" asked Ambrose, his eyes locked on the amber liquor swirling in his glass.

"You're not going to try and talk me out of it?" asked Graham.

"Why would I?"

"Everyone else has attempted to do so."

Ambrose shrugged. "Why would you stop fighting if there is a chance you can win?"

Graham stared at Ambrose. For all his man-about-town demeanor, he appeared to be the only member of the family who understood.

"Every man needs a purpose, and it is only right that you fight for yours," said Ambrose, gulping the rest of his brandy and staring into the empty glass.

For the first time in years, Graham truly examined his brother, and he found himself wondering if Ambrose enjoyed his gad-about life as much as he claimed. Or perhaps it was nothing but a jovial facade.

"Why did you come to visit?" asked Graham. "London must be growing quieter with the Season coming to a close, but I am certain there is plenty to occupy your time. And I doubt your visit has anything to do with escaping Nicholas's family." Graham watched him for a moment, and a sudden thought entered his head. "It wouldn't have anything to do with Mina's scare last month, would it?"

Ambrose met Graham's gaze, his eyebrows raised. "Yes, I rushed all the way here because I was worried about my sister and future niece or nephew."

His tone was everything one expected of a flippant young buck, but there was something beneath it that made Graham doubt Ambrose's obnoxious veneer.

"If you must know," said Ambrose, "things were getting tense in London. A friend of mine landed in a bit of hot water after a gentleman discovered that his wife had a special understanding with my friend. I thought it best to decamp for a bit rather than get swept up in that madness."

Ambrose signaled for another drink, and Graham shook his head at his own silliness. It was pointless to imagine something deeper in Ambrose's shallow mind.

"Perhaps you need better friends," said Graham.

Ambrose snorted, downed the refreshed drink, and stood. "When my family starts sermonizing about my life, I know it is time to leave. Good night, Graham. I shall send in that luscious nursemaid of yours to 'escort' you home. And then, perhaps, your night will get even better."

"Ambrose!" Graham growled, but before he could give his brother a proper setdown for such filthy implications Ambrose abandoned his glass on the side table and strode from the room.

Mina had written of her concern for their baby brother, and Graham had thought it troubling but not overly concerning. Seeing Ambrose in all his boorish glory gave him a better understanding of what exactly their sister had meant, and Graham worried what would happen to his brother if he continued this aimless life of his.

And as surely as Graham could see the destined disaster, he saw his own life unfolding in such a manner. A pointless life with nothing to do but sit about. A gentleman of leisure. The thought of it sent a shiver down Graham's spine. Such things had never appealed to him, and after having experienced the joys of his navy life, a lazy life on land was inconceivable. Just the thought of passing his days in such a fashion filled Graham with dread.

He could not allow that to be his future. Not ever.

Chapter 18

And once again, Tabby found herself lurking at keyholes. This was what she had been reduced to. Hovering at the door, skulking about like some ne'er-do-well. But Captain Ashbrook had left her no choice. She had never heard mention of Mr. Davis before the man appeared on their doorstep, and now, the two of them had been in the captain's bedchamber for over an hour.

Kneeling on the floor, Tabby wondered how often other servants did the same. Perhaps they all crouched in the shadows, gleaning whatever gossip they could from their masters and mistresses. Of course, that would presume the gossip was worth overhearing. What was happening in Captain Ashbrook's bedchamber certainly fell into that category.

"It is impossible to tell from an external examination," said Mr. Davis. "It is clear that your wounds are causing you trouble, but without another surgery, it is difficult to know what is going on. Perhaps there are some splinters festering in there."

Tabby's hand flew to her mouth. Another surgery? The man could not be serious. Captain Ashbrook was doing better every day, and to perform another operation would set him back or even do more harm; to do so on nothing stronger than a "perhaps" was ludicrous.

"You think it possible?" asked the captain. "It took several tries before they got everything, but I believe I would know if there were some remnant splinters remaining, and it doesn't feel as though that is the case."

At least Captain Ashbrook appeared to have some common sense; Tabby was glad to hear that.

"Perhaps, but you would be amazed to know how often a fragment is overlooked," said the surgeon. "Sometimes all it takes is another set of eyes to find it."

The captain gave one of those masculine grunts that meant nothing and all things at the same time.

"Ma'am?"

Tabby jumped out of her skin, nearly bumping into the door, and she turned to see the footman standing behind her. Placing a finger to her lips, she hushed him. His eyebrows rose, but James followed her order, coming over to join her beside the door.

"What are you doing?" he whispered.

Raising a silencing hand, Tabby returned her attention to the door in time to hear Captain Ashbrook say, "When can you do it?"

"No!" Tabby hissed, but she slapped a hand over her own mouth. That fool! What was he thinking? Another operation? Surely, there were only so many times a body could undergo such torments, and Tabby wanted to shake the man for putting himself and his family through it.

"Is he mad?" whispered James. "Captain Ashbrook barely survived the last one."

The footman looked as worried as Tabby felt, but there was no time to dwell on it. The surgeon was coming towards the door, and Tabby jumped from her spot before the two servants scurried out of sight. Standing side-by-side, Tabby and James hid inside the adjacent room.

"Thank you, Mr. Davis," said Captain Ashbrook as the door

opened. "Until this afternoon."

Mr. Davis passed by the doorway where Tabby and James stood, and she nudged the footman forward to escort the surgeon out. Once they were gone, Tabby stormed into the captain's chamber.

Graham drummed his fingers against the grip of his cane and stared out the window. Another operation. Though he would never admit it aloud, it terrified him. Swallowing past the lump in his throat, Graham's mind filled with memories of the past tortures. The cutting. Slicing. Digging. The burning agony of fever. Sweat broke out on his forehead at the thought of enduring it all again. If there were any other option, Graham would gladly take it, but the medicinal remedies offered by the physicians and apothecaries had not helped enough.

"Another?" Mrs. Russell burst in through the bedchamber door, her brown eyes blazing. "After everything we have done to heal your body you would undergo yet another surgery?"

Her appearance was so startling that Graham stared at her for a full ten seconds before his brain allowed him to respond. "It is none of your concern."

Mrs. Russell heaved a sigh, crossing her arms. "Surely, you can do better than that. As the one who cares for your health, it is clearly my concern."

"But you do not get to make the decision for me."

"Though perhaps you could have mentioned it before the surgeon appeared."

Truth be told, he hadn't wanted to because he knew exactly how Mrs. Russell would react. "I'm doing what I must."

"What you must? I thought we discussed this already," said Mrs. Russell. "We have talked about this many times, and I thought you had decided to let go of this. Move on."

Graham tapped his cane against the floor, his jaw clenching. "Move on to what exactly? Being an invalid for the rest of my life? Quit the one thing that matters most to me? Do you truly think a bit of sketching would make up for what I have lost?"

"Of course not," said Mrs. Russell. "But there is much you can do, if you will open yourself up to the possibility. You could find a new vocation."

"What do you know of it?" bellowed Graham. "How could you possibly understand what I am going through?"

"Oh, of course," said Mrs. Russell, adopting a look of false contrition. "No one else could possibly understand what the great Captain Ashbrook is suffering. His burden is so heavy that no one else can hope to match it." Her expression darkened. "Do you ever think of anyone but yourself? Do you ever stop for one moment and think about what others are suffering?"

"I—"

"I am not finished!" she barked, glowering at him. "Do you think this is the life I chose? Do you think that as a child I dreamt of a time when I would be forced to wait on others? Do you think that I am overjoyed to have fallen from mistress to servant? Everyone suffers heartache and loss. Everyone has struggles and difficulties. Most plans do not turn out the way one intends, but that is life. It is not guaranteed to end perfectly, but that does not give you the right to act the fool."

Graham ground his teeth together. "Are you this vicious with everyone, or am I the only one to have the honor of feeling the slice of your tongue?"

Mrs. Russell's complexion reddened with fury, and her eyes narrowed on him. "I am tired of watching others make fool-hardy and ludicrous decisions. I am tired of watching people throw away the good they have simply because it isn't what they desired. I am tired of holding my tongue while mulish men make a muck of their lives!"

"Fiend seize it, woman!"

"Language, Captain Ashbrook!" Mrs. Russell shouted with a stomp.

At that, Graham let out a slew of curses in his mind. Heaven save him from meddlesome women who stick their noses where they do not belong. There were not curse words enough for all that he wished to unleash on the lady standing in front of him.

But that one thought doused his anger, bringing his thoughts and emotions up short when he realized where his temper had led him. What was he becoming? The sort of gentleman who hollers and curses at ladies? To belittle Mrs. Russell like a cad?

Graham scrubbed at his face, the fire fading from his soul, leaving him slumped in his chair.

"You have so many opportunities and possibilities within your grasp, yet you refuse to accept any of them because it's not the thing you wish," she said. "Yes, your life is not perfect, but it is far better than most in your circumstance. Stop squandering it!"

And with that, Mrs. Russell stormed out of the bedchamber, slamming the door behind her. The sound reverberated through the house, dissipating into heavy silence.

...

Standing at the kitchen table, Tabby sliced the onions and pretended the vapors were making her teary. Mrs. Bunting stood at the oven, opening the latch to check on the bread, and a muffled moan lingered in the air. Tabby's hands shook, and she paused as a scream followed it.

Tabby's stomach convulsed with each cry. She tried to block the sounds from her mind, but they broke through her defenses, stabbing at her heart. Looking at the knife in her hand, images filled her mind of the surgeon's tools that were slicing into Captain Ashbrook's broken body. Even with a floor between her and the makeshift operating chamber, Tabby could hear his whimpers. The kitchen knife clattered to the table, and she tore off her apron and rushed out into the garden.

But there was no respite to be found. Tabby felt each of the captain's cries, as if the butcher were cutting into her flesh. Dropping to the bench, she covered her face, hiding the tears that coursed down her cheeks. The pain was too much for her. Listening to anyone's agony would be tortuous, but with it being someone so dear to her, it was excruciating.

And he was very dear to her.

Though his family paid Tabby to attend him, she had grown fond of Captain Ashbrook. She had never considered a gentleman a friend before, but she could not deny that she thought of him as such. After all, she had spent more time with Captain Ashbrook in these short weeks than she had with anyone else in the past year. Hours of reading together, conversing. She may care for his physical needs, but they shared a bond that was greater than caretaker and charge.

Tabby could not stand the thought that he was in such pain at that very moment. That no matter how foolhardy she thought this plan, there was nothing she could do to stop that charlatan of a surgeon from going about his work.

Dropping her head, Tabby allowed the tears to flow for her friend and said a silent prayer on his behalf.

Captain Ashbrook let out a painful groan, the sound lingering in the air long after he'd gone silent. Getting to her feet, Tabby paced the garden, searching for any way to distance herself from the bloodshed happening inside the house. But she could not abandon her post, and there was no respite from the captain's pained cries.

Blast the stubborn man for putting them both through this torment.

...

Heat engulfed him, blazing through Graham's body. His eyes felt like they were boiling in his head. Sweat soaked his sheets, but he couldn't move to push them away. In the darkness, the sounds of shouts and splintering wood blasted his ears. Voices were speaking, but he couldn't make out their meaning. The room around him exploded, shards of wood stabbing into him, ripping his body to shreds.

"Lieutenant, make it stop!" wailed little Ian. He would recognize that voice anywhere. The young midshipman who'd been under his command back when Graham had been nothing but Lieutenant Ashbrook. Then the boy appeared, lying on that bloody table as the ship's surgeon hacked at his arm. Blood coated the table and floor, covering them all.

The boy thrashed and screamed, rolling off the table and crawling towards Graham. He bent to help, but when he turned the lad over, it was Lieutenant Willis's face, his mouth gaping as he fought for his last breath. But his features rearranged to form those of yet another poor soul he'd served with who had perished in the never-ending battles. Shifting and twisting, the distorted creature tugged at Graham's legs, and he screamed, kicking at it.

Rearing away, Graham ran through the darkness. The air pulsed with heat until he felt like he would melt into the floorboards. He slogged through the mist that wrapped around him, pulling at his limbs. Onward he fought, looking for any escape from those demons.

And then a light appeared from above, illuminating a bed that sat just feet from him. In the center lay his mother, her dark russet hair cascading across the pillows, the bedclothes pulled tight across her chest. Her skin was pale, tinged with blue, and her eyes stared sightless at the ceiling, her lifeless babe tucked into the crook of her arm.

"Mother?" he called for her, but before Graham reached the bedside, the ground opened up, swallowing it into the earth below. Dirt poured in, filling it as the bed sunk deeper. And then his mother's eyes opened.

"'Tis as it should be, Graham," she said, cradling her daughter as the dirt trickled in on top of her.

Moments later, there was no sign she had ever been there. Graham fell to his knees, digging at the ground frantically. His nails scraped the soil, cutting into his hands, but no matter how long he worked, the hole never deepened.

Sweat streamed down his skin, filling his eyes, and Graham swiped at it, but he couldn't see. His lungs sucked in a breath, but he couldn't breathe. His arms and legs shook, collapsing beneath him. Graham twitched, fighting to control his body, but it would not respond. And the ground began to sink. His eyes watched the edges of the hole deepen until he was surrounded by dirt walls. They tumbled inwards, covering his hands and feet.

Graham screamed, but his mouth would not open. His soul shrieked as he willed his arms to move, but not a single muscle twitched. There was nothing he could do as the soil inched up his body. He fought it, pushed himself, strained against it, but the dirt covered his face and swallowed him whole.

And then he heard the singing. A faint hum in the blackness that wrapped around his heart, calming it.

Tabby.

Cold hit his forehead, and rivulets of water ran down his temples. The feel of it made him sigh. It disappeared, and Graham turned his head to find it. But there was nothing. Nothing but burning emptiness.

Another tune wound its way through the air, soothing him, and another press of cool, damp cloth touched his forehead, resting for a moment before moving to his cheeks and neck. Everywhere it touched was a little piece of paradise. But it was the sound that brought Graham the most peace. Tabby was there.

"I'm sorry," he said. He needed her to know that. "I should have listened to you."

The dream tugged at him, pulling him back into its horrid embrace, but Graham fought against it. He could not return to those horrors.

"I'm just so afraid," he said. "I need to fix it."

"Why?" The question hovered there beyond his grasp, and Graham did not know if it was from the dream or reality. His fevered brain did not care.

"What am I without it?" He whispered the words as flashes of his nightmares flickered around him. "I have nothing."

"That is not true," she said. "And you know it."

Her words faded into music, her sweet notes cutting through the dark despair around him. The tune never wavered, never stopped. It simply shifted from one to another. It sounded like something a nursemaid would sing to her charge, and it only further lightened Graham's soul.

Something in her words pricked at Graham, tugging at his conscience. What did he have? What was he? The fever plagued his mind, making it impossible to formulate a coherent thought, but those questions lingered there in the background, caught with him between the waking world and the unconscious abyss.

"Thank you, Tabby," he whispered.

Chapter 19

Lifting the teacup to her lips, Tabby took a sip. It was cold but brought blessed relief to her dry throat. Savoring it for a moment, she set the cup on the nightstand and retrieved the book resting beside Captain Ashbrook. With her free hand, Tabby touched his forehead and cheeks, testing the temperature. She had done so countless times, and it was a welcome thrill to find his fever had broken.

"Now, where were we?" she asked. Not that she expected an answer. Captain Ashbrook had not spoken more than a few feverish words since the surgery, but Tabby found herself speaking to him as though nothing were amiss. It helped keep his sad words from haunting her. He thought he had nothing. At certain points during her vigil, Tabby wanted to shake him for such a foolish belief, but mostly, it tore at her soul. More than the words, it was his tone. The hopelessness in it.

Tabby batted away those thoughts and found her place on the page. They had read this novel before, but Tabby could not bring herself to open a new book. There was no indication that the captain heard any of it, and it felt wrong to begin something different if he was too incoherent to enjoy the story. Besides, she rather liked this one and did not mind rereading it, though she would never admit it aloud. After all the times the captain had teased her about her literary preferences, she was not about to give him the satisfaction of knowing he had successfully converted her to his tastes.

"'The behaviour of the huntsman struck Brown, although he had no recollection of his face, nor could conceive why he should...'" began Tabby, halting mid-sentence when she looked over the top of the book to see Captain Ashbrook watching her. Tossing it aside, Tabby leapt from her chair.

"Captain?" she asked, taking his hand. "Can you speak?"

He swallowed, his brow tightening, but his eyes remained focused on her.

"Here," she said, grabbing a glass of water. Carefully, she leaned him up enough to get him a few sips. Immediately, her hands checked his pulse and fever. Though she knew both would be as they were when she had checked them mere moments ago, it gave her such comfort that she could not stop herself from doing so once again.

His lips opened, though his voice was rough. "I do not need a woman fluttering over me," he croaked.

For a single, awful, infuriating moment, Tabby stared at him, but then she noticed the twinkle of humor in his eye. "Yes, you are a pillar of manly strength. A veritable Hercules ready to leap from his sickbed."

"How long?" he asked, and Tabby saw the pinch of his lips that she had come to recognize as a sign for thirst mixed with a stubbornness of not wishing to bother her. Without waiting for his express request, Tabby helped him drink a bit more.

"Three days," she said, laying him on his pillows. His eyes were fixed on hers as she stood so near him, and Tabby felt a blush creep across her face. "Your fever broke last night, and you have been in and out of consciousness since then."

She sat on her chair, but his gaze never left her. It held an intensity that left her wondering if a hint of the fever lingered in his mind.

"You look as though you could use some rest," said Captain

Ashbrook.

And for the first time in days, Tabby laughed. "It is very wrong of you to point out that a lady looks haggard and tired, especially when it is your fault that she is in such a state. I have been unable to rest since the surgeon arrived."

At that, the captain finally looked away, staring at the ceiling. They sat in silence for a few minutes, but Tabby could not stop herself from pressing the issue.

"You nearly died," she whispered, swallowing past the lump in her throat. Memories of those terrifying hours had worn Tabby thin until she felt fragile enough that the smallest bump would break her.

His gaze fell to her, and though he did not say a word, she read the disbelief in it. The stubborn, bull-headed fool. But Tabby did not have the strength to summon her righteous anger.

"Don't you dare look at me that way, Captain Ashbrook," she said, her voice quiet but steady. "There is no way you were coherent enough to know what was happening, so do not act as though I am exaggerating. Your sister called the vicar in to pray over you."

The memory of Mina's tears as her husband led her away echoed in Tabby's mind. The poor lady had been inconsolable, but Tabby couldn't bring herself to talk about that yet. That was Mina's story to tell, and though Captain Ashbrook deserved to know how much distress he had caused, she knew this was not the time for it.

Something shifted in the captain's eyes, and Tabby leaned forward to test his forehead once more, but his temperature remained healthy. Sitting so close, she saw the true cause of the change. The beginnings of tears shimmered in his eyes. Ignoring them, as she knew he would prefer her to, Tabby helped him take another drink.

"Why are you so determined to throw your life away?" she asked as he lay propped in her arms. Tabby had held the gentleman thus many a time before, but in that moment, there was something so familiar about it. Comfortable. Some part of her wished they could remain like that.

The thought startled her, and Tabby put him down and sat in her chair, giving herself some distance.

"The navy is my life," came the raspy reply.

And at that, Tabby knew it was time to steel herself to say the blunt truth he needed. "The navy is your past, Captain Ashbrook. No matter what treatments you pursue, there is no way you shall ever return to it. There is no undoing the damage done. This is your life. A landbound life. And if you do not accept it, I doubt you will survive the year."

The captain looked away from her, turning his head to stare at the wall, but Tabby saw the sheen of tears.

"But..." He stopped and cleared his throat but didn't turn to face her. "To accept that it is gone is to accept that I have lost everything."

Tabby dropped her head at the selfsame hopelessness that had been in his voice when he'd spoken those similar, fever-addled words. Resting her hands on the edge of the bed, Tabby gathered her thoughts, struggling for the words to say to him in this moment. Sending out a silent prayer, she hoped that she'd find the right ones.

"I know," she said, swallowing past the emotion gathering in her throat. Sucking on her lips, she allowed a few tears of her own to fall, knowing that restraint would not help her cause. "I know what it is like to feel that way."

Her breath hitched, and Tabby squeezed her eyes shut as memories best left undisturbed rose to the surface. "I felt it when the physician placed my lifeless babe in my arms."

Tabby could not speak for several moments, allowing the feeling of it to wash over her. Her sweet baby with his golden fluff of hair. His perfect little fingers and toes. She remembered the weight of him in her arms, the feel of his tiny body clutched to her breast. All the pain that swept over her as she realized that her dear child was stillborn. Months—years, even—of hoping and waiting for that blessed day to arrive, and it had ended with a hastily dug grave.

A touch returned Tabby to the present, and she opened her eyes to see Captain Ashbrook resting his hand atop her clasped ones.

"You lost a child?" His brow bunched, his clear eyes filling with sympathy.

"Two," she said. "Both stillborn."

He blinked away the tears forming in his eyes, and Tabby felt his heart reaching out to hers. Heaven help her, she reveled in the kindness and support as his hand entwined with hers.

"I know what it is to lose everything," she said. "Being a mother is such a part of who I am, yet I was childless for many years. Teased with the promise of babies of my own, only to lose so many of them. And that was only the beginning. Little in my life has unfolded as planned. So many of my hopes and dreams have rotted away, but I know allowing that heartache to define me would be my true downfall."

Like Joshua. Tabby did not say it aloud, for she did not wish him to be part of this conversation, but he lingered there in the back of her mind. That was what Joshua had done. Allowing the disappointments to become the focal point of his life until it had infected the whole of him, ruining the good along with the bad. Always searching for some way to consume happiness rather than generating it within himself. Searching for meaning in a bit of gin and whiskey and the flick of a face card.

Tabby squeezed the captain's hand, her wet eyes meeting his. "There is nothing wrong with mourning a loss, but you must move on. You must. Joy is not an accident. It comes from living one's life, finding the good among the bad, and moving forward. Until you accept it, you will never truly heal. Please, you—"

But she stopped short when the door opened and Jillian entered.

"Oh, sorry, ma'am," she said, blushing, and turned to leave, but Tabby stopped her.

"What is it?" Tabby asked, pulling her hand from Captain Ashbrook's to wipe at her eyes.

"Mrs. Bunting had a question about dinner, ma'am," she said.

"I shall be there directly."

Jillian bobbed and shut the door, leaving Tabby and Captain Ashbrook alone together. Folding her arms, she stared at the floor. In the moment, sharing such personal things had seemed wise, but the interruption had broken the spell between them, leaving her feeling flushed and fidgety as she thought about what had passed between them.

One does not speak of such things in polite society, but it had felt right to share her secret heartache.

"Please..." she whispered, a fresh tear crawling down her cheek. Not another lost life. Not again. Suffering her own heartache had been bad enough, but watching it tear apart her husband and destroy her marriage compounded that pain.

"Please, do not let this crush you. I cannot stand to watch it," she said before fleeing the room.

The door closed with a click, and Graham desperately wanted to call her back. Pull her into his arms. Give her the comfort she deserved. But Graham sensed she needed the distance. Truth be told, he could use it, too.

With his good hand, he rubbed at his head. Exhaustion pulled at him, his brain still fogged from the fever, yet his mind refused to stray from the scene that had just unfolded.

His heart was twisted from the pull of a dozen different emotions, and Graham could not sort through it all. He did not know what he should feel or what he wished to feel. It was a tangled mess, which was only further complicated by his sluggish thoughts and weary body.

But there was one prevalent sentiment that overtook it all. He was awed by Mrs. Russell's fortitude. It was not as though he were unaware that she had suffered in her life. She had shared bits of it before, but he'd had no true understanding of what the poor lady had been through. Her words dug into him like a surgeon's knife. All that pain. He wished there were some way he could have sheltered her from such hardships. Yet, it was clear that Mrs. Russell had soldiered on. More than that, she seemed a genuinely happy sort of person.

Graham wanted to be like her.

Acknowledging that made him realize how empty he felt. Perhaps it was simply the strength of his desperation that had sheltered it from recognition, but lying there, seeing the type of person he wished to be made him see the void inside himself for what it was. It was as though his soul had atrophied.

Tears gathered in his eyes, coming from that small sliver of himself that still lived. The part that recognized something he desperately desired. Graham wanted to be full of life and vitality like Mrs. Russell, not this shell of a man who wallowed in his misery. He wanted to be happy again, and he knew the first step to take.

Graham drew in a slow breath, holding it, though his right side twinged at the movement. He let it out in one long, shaky gust. Swallowing the knot in his throat, Graham steadied himself to speak aloud the words that needed to be said.

"I shan't be healed."

Blinking frantically, he sucked in another breath through his nose; his jaw clenched until it ached. He had made enough of a spectacle of himself; he would not allow himself to do so now as he cut from himself the last remnant of hope that he had kept safely buried in his heart.

"I shan't return to the navy." Speaking it made it real, bringing with it a new wave of agony. His lungs hitched, and there was nothing more to be done about the tears gathering in his eyes.

"This is my new life." The words were jagged and broken, but they came. Graham covered his eyes, his body shaking, and he allowed the emotions to swallow him whole, embracing the ensuing tears and sorrow that washed over him. And yet, he did not drown.

It took several long minutes before Graham regained control of himself. His face was flushed, his eyes burned, and he had not a single tear left in him, yet as he lay there, utterly spent, something lingered in his heart. A glimmer of something good. Not happy or contented, but welcome all the same. Graham lay there in silent contemplation as he sifted through the emotion.

Acceptance.

It made no sense that it should lift his soul. His drive to return to the sea had been a raging fire, carrying him through the long months of pain. Yet, now that it was gone, he was not left with the dark despair he had expected to find. No, it was as though a crippling weight had been lifted, leaving his heart lighter and freer. It did not paint his life in rosy hues and make him want to leap from his bed and dance off into the sunset, but it gave him peace. Calm.

A year of fighting, and he was done. There was nothing left to give, nothing left to do. This was his life. And that frantic desperation, which had been his constant companion these last months, was gone.

Mrs. Russell's words came to his mind. Graham was not alert enough to remember the exact wording, but he remembered the spirit of it. And she had been right. Accepting his lot brought a modicum of relief. A sense of ease, even. Facing the stark truth was not a happy thing, but it was better than hiding from it and allowing it to dictate his life. A lingering sadness still clung to his soul, but that all-consuming panic was gone. He could face this challenge head-on rather than running from it like the coward he had been.

And that left Graham wondering if Mrs. Russell had not been right about other things. The good among the bad. She had chastised him about that enough times that even his fever-addled brain could hear her voice clearly. It was easy to see all the bad that came from this change in his life, but Graham wondered if there were any good in it. Lying there for minutes on end, his mind wouldn't stray from the dark reality of what this would mean for him.

A cripple. Though Graham had not spent much time among society, he knew enough to know that it made him an outcast. Perhaps people would not openly snub him, but having such a defect made others uncomfortable, and when faced with discomfort, most tend to look away or stare in horror. Neither of which was appealing. Not that he truly cared about their reactions.

Graham felt the sway of the boat beneath him, smelled the salt breeze as it rushed past him. That was gone. His life. His passion. His purpose. If it weren't for the fact that he had no tears left, that thought would've brought on another round of them, but Graham stared dry-eyed at the ceiling, caught in the melancholy gripping his heart.

But then again, he would never have to eat hardtack ever again. Fresh bread was a luxury that those ashore took for granted and could be counted among Graham's favorite things, and there was no reason he would not be able to eat it with every meal for the rest of his life.

Or sauerkraut. No more sauerkraut. Just the thought of that briny mess made Graham's throat tighten. Vegetables were a precious commodity on a ship and most captains, Graham included, carried a large supply of the foul but easily stored foodstuff. In small doses, it was fine, but by the barrelful, it was disgusting.

And yet, there'd been plenty of times when Graham had thought hardtack and sauerkraut the most delicious feast imaginable. Those long stretches at sea when supplies were short and the victuals dwindled with each passing day. He'd not suffered through many such voyages, but Graham still remembered a stretch as a lowly midshipman when his ship had been cut off from supplies. The hunger had been a gnawing maggot, eating away at him until all he could think of was food. The crewmen withered away, several of them succumbing to scurvy and starvation. Graham remembered the haunted look in the sailors' eyes when the last rat had been killed and consumed.

No, Graham would not miss that.

Or the battles. For all that he was a naval man, the fighting had been a necessary unpleasantness for the opportunity to sail the seas. Of course, the strategy required for broadside battle was thrilling, but the bloodshed and death that surrounded it weighed on Graham's heart. The flash of swords. The screams as ships were torn to pieces. The gore littering the deck. Graham would never have to hear the dying moans of his sailors. Would never have to scrub his friends' blood from his hands and face. He would never have to kill. Flashes of his fevered nightmares sprang to mind, and Graham shook away the images.

As he churned over these thoughts, Graham realized that if ever there was something good that had come from this tragedy, it was spending this time with his sister and her husband. His relationship with both had strengthened greatly over the past year, and as much as he wished for his old life, Graham could not say with certainty that he would be willing to erase his memories of Mina and Simon during the past year even if it meant restoring his health.

That thought startled him, but it was true. The more Graham thought on it, the more he sensed its veracity. He cherished seeing his sister flush with the glow of motherhood. To witness her so happily settled with Simon. To become better acquainted with his brother-in-law. This was all a grand blessing that had come from his injury, and it made Graham ponder about all the other things he had missed while at sea; Mina's letters had been so plentiful and detailed that Graham hadn't thought much about the life he was missing ashore.

Regret lingered in his heart, but the warmth of that thought grew, filling Graham with a hope that had been sadly lacking in his life for many months. A true hope based on something more than a fantasy he had built in his head and an unwillingness to face reality.

And then a new thought struck him.

He could build a family of his own. Marriage had never been a priority to Graham. Not that he disliked the possibility, but being surrounded by sailors and having little contact with ladies hadn't been conducive to such musings. But now that his attention was forced away from that life, Graham wondered at the possibility. Truth be told, he wondered at a very specific possibility.

Tabby. If ever there was a blessing to be found in his injury, it was Tabitha Russell. Graham could say unequivocally that it had directly brought them together. That cannonball had thrown Tabby into his life, upending everything he had thought he wanted.

Graham flushed at the memory of her hand entwined with his. It had been terribly inappropriate, and Graham would love to blame it on his addled mind, but it had been no thoughtless gesture, and he would not regret it. It had been far more gentlemanly than sweeping her into his arms, which is precisely what he had wanted to do; not that he could manage that in his current state.

Exhaustion seeped into Graham. Regardless of how his mind spun, he felt his strength ebb. He shifted, fighting off the sleep that pulled at him. As he lay there, Graham's future shifted before him, and a new picture began to form. Not of his ship and his men sailing the world, but a far quieter yet similarly grand life. A home with a wife and children. But there was no fighting his body as it drifted into unconsciousness to fill his mind with dreams of Tabby.

Chapter 20

"You never did!" Tabby gasped, eyes wide as Captain Ashbrook laughed.

"I did," he said through a wide grin.

Tabby wiped away the tears of mirth. "The poor man."

"Poor, nothing. Bentley had to be one of the most arrogant, vainest men I ever sailed with, and he got everything he deserved. Besides, it was only a little henna I had picked up in India. It came off eventually."

Tabby shook her head, and though she wished to give him a good scowl for his wicked ways the image of the fop waking to find his face covered in blemishes was too delicious.

"Don't give me that look," said Captain Ashbrook. "I was locked on a ship with him for weeks at a time, forced to listen to his never-ending diatribes about hygiene. We once had to cut our water rations, and the man used his for washing rather than drinking."

Leaning into the chair, Tabby felt more lighthearted than she had in a good, long while. The sun came through the windows, giving the entire bedchamber a glow, but it paled in comparison to the lightness in the captain's expression. In the month since he had awoken from his delirium, Captain Ashbrook had become a different man. Something had changed in him. Gone was the brooding melancholy that the Gothic novel heroes would be hard-pressed to equal.

Tabby was no fool. She knew there would be hard moments ahead for him, but for the first time, Tabby truly thought he had turned the corner.

"You, sir, are incorrigible," she said, finally giving way to a laugh.

"Ah, but that is part of my charm," he said with a waggle of his eyebrows.

Tabby could not argue with that. In such spirits, the man was too charming by half.

"Have you thought about writing down your stories?" she asked.

The captain scratched at his jaw. "Why would I do that?"

"To preserve them," said Tabby with a shrug. "Or you could publish them. No, give it a thought," she said when he started to shake his head. "Besides being entertaining, you could be helping the next generation of sailors. You could share your experience and knowledge."

"There are books aplenty about sailing," he replied.

"All of which are certain to be incredibly dry," she said. "Yours could blend stories of the high seas with practical knowledge. If anything, you could give people a glimpse into the life of a naval officer. I am certain there would be those who would love to read such accounts."

"I do not—"

"And you enjoy writing," she said, cutting off whatever half-hearted argument he was going to pose. "Your sister told me about your letters, and I doubt there is a man alive who has spent so much time corresponding with his relatives."

The more she spoke, the more Tabby latched onto the idea. It would not be as grand as sailing the world, but it would give the gentleman a manner in which to use his passion.

"Captain—"

But Jillian knocked on the door, cutting off any further argument.

"Ma'am," she said with a curtsy, "may I speak with you a moment?"

Tabby stood, giving Captain Ashbrook a quick, "We shall continue this later," before following the maid out into the hall.

"There is someone here to see you, ma'am," was all Jillian said, refusing to speak further on the subject. Tabby followed her downstairs, but instead of the sitting room, the maid led her to the kitchen. Sitting at the slab table was Phillip.

"Sweetheart!" she said, rushing to him.

"He appeared on the doorstep a few minutes ago," said Mrs. Bunting.

Phillip grinned around a mouthful of biscuit, his mouth ringed in milk. He tried to speak, but crumbs went flying this way and that.

"What are you doing here?" Tabby asked as she swept the mess.

Taking a big swallow, Phillip tried again. "Mrs. Allen had to leave, so she left me at home, but Papa wasn't there. And I waited and waited and waited for him, and I was so hungry, so I came to the food house."

"Mrs. Allen left you alone?" asked Tabby, her heart stopping at that thought.

Phillip nodded. "Patience flew to wensa and needed her mama."

Tabby tried to interpret his words, but no matter how he rephrased the sentence, she could not decipher it. Not that it mattered, for it did not change the situation. Tabby's heart chilled at the thought of Phillip making the long journey from their cottage to Gladwell House and all the possible hazards he may have faced, and she swept him into her arms.

"Mama," groaned Phillip, pushing away from her.

Sitting him on his chair, Tabby's mind whirled at the problem that had landed in her lap.

"I can distract Captain Ashbrook while you take him home,

ma'am," offered Jillian.

"But there is no one at home to watch over him," said Tabby.

"Don't fret," said Mrs. Bunting. "We will figure something out."

...

Mrs. Russell was acting quite strangely. It was as though she could not sit still for more than a few minutes before she disappeared again. Graham knew something must be going on, but the lady deflected any questions he posed. He watched as she hurried out of the room for the fifth time in the last hour and knew it was time to do a bit of investigating.

Throwing off the covers, Graham gingerly brought his legs out and set his feet on the floor. Sliding them into the waiting slippers, he reached for his cane. Graham sat on the edge of the bed, preparing himself for the journey, and when he felt ready, he leaned forward, placing all his weight on his cane. His muscles ached and protested, but he got to his feet. And again, he waited. It was one thing to be upright and another to move about, and Graham knew better than to rush things. Of course, he knew better than to stand on his own, but with Mrs. Russell's evasiveness, he doubted she would help him.

His left leg was weakened from disuse but functional. His right was another matter. Pain shot through his thigh when he tried to lift it, so he slid it along the ground. That movement wasn't much better, but at that point, even a moderate improvement was something. His right arm throbbed in time with his heartbeat, but he could ignore it. The cane hit the ground with a snap, his right foot dragged along, and his left stomped with more noise than he wanted. There was no sneaking about with as much racket as he was making. Snap, drag, stomp. Snap, drag, stomp.

That cacophony aside, Graham was grateful that he made it out of the room and to the top of the stairs. His body was no better than it had been before the last failed surgery but no worse, either, which Graham now counted a blessing. Standing at the top of the stairs, he paused, giving himself a moment to rest before he tackled them. If he went slowly enough, Graham knew he could do it. In fact, this whole interlude surprised him on two fronts: first, that he was making as much headway, and second, that Mrs. Russell had not come running at the sound of his movements.

Graham glowered at the stairs, determined to make it down in one piece and without gravity doing all the work. Cautiously, he took the first and rested. Then the second. It took many long minutes as he inched to the ground floor. And still, Mrs. Russell had not swooped in. Something was definitely amiss.

Once he reached the final step, the rest of the journey felt like it took no time at all. Graham found the sitting room empty and followed the sounds of chaos coming from the kitchen. With the din it was no surprise that they had not heard him coming. Pushing open the kitchen door, he found it far removed from the clean and orderly fashion that Mrs. Bunting usually kept it in. Flour covered the table, sprinkled about like the first snow of winter.

"Phillip!" gasped Mrs. Russell, grabbing the flour sack from a small boy. The child was clearly the origin of the snowstorm as he was covered in the white powder, his blue eyes standing out among the mess.

"Hello!" he said, waving a hand at Graham, sending a shower of flour across the floor. "We're making fairy cakes."

Mrs. Russell's eyes widened as she saw Graham, and the other ladies froze like startled deer.

"Captain Ashbrook..." Mrs. Russell began, but her words trailed off.

"You must be Mrs. Russell's son," said Graham, dragging himself across the room, though he did not get more than a step before Mrs. Russell came to his side and helped him to the table.

"Phillip," the child said, sticking out his hand, but Mrs. Russell grabbed Phillip's wrist before he covered Graham in a fine dusting of flour; Graham simply ignored that and gave the child a hearty handshake.

"I apologize," said Mrs. Russell. "My neighbor watches him, but something happened and she is unable—"

"Your son is more than welcome here," said Graham. "Do you mind if I join you?"

"You want to make fairy cakes with us?" asked Phillip with a broad smile.

"It sounds delightful," said Graham, reaching over to brush off a seat.

"You don't have to—" began Mrs. Russell, but Graham interrupted.

"You have told me how much you enjoy cooking. Perhaps it is time I try my hand at it, too." Graham lowered himself onto the chair and groaned at the relief it brought. "What do we do?"

Mrs. Russell glanced at Phillip and Graham, over to Mrs. Bunting and Jillian, and then at Graham once more. He saw the thoughts spinning through her head, and he gave her a reassuring smile. A bit of the tension left her shoulders.

"First, I must take my messy boy outside for a good brushing. Then, we shall make some fairy cakes," said Mrs. Russell, leading the child out the back door.

Chapter 21

The kitchen was a mess, and Tabby was unsure who was more responsible for it—her son or her charge. There were more than a few splattered eggs surrounding Captain Ashbrook's seat, and Phillip would need a bath to rid the last remnants of batter and flour from his hair. But that afternoon had to be one of the most enjoyable Tabby had experienced in a long time.

Captain Ashbrook was unfailingly patient with Phillip's chattering and mistakes, laughing them off as he made his own. Phillip sat beside the gentleman, rambling on about all the intricate details of his young life, and the captain seemed genuinely pleased to listen. Seeing Phillip beam at the attention made Tabby's heart warm with gratitude, even though a part of her soul dimmed at the longing it brought to her heart.

This was the sort of scene she had wished for when she had married all those years ago. Joshua cuddled next to his son, giving him all the love and affection the boy craved. Phillip deserved a father who cared more for him than drink or card games. This was no feigned contentment from the captain. It was clear from his words and actions that he liked the boy, and Tabby blinked away the tears threatening to form.

This wasn't her life. This wasn't her family. Tabby had to remind herself of that. Her husband was off somewhere avoiding his responsibilities, forcing it all onto Tabby's tired shoulders. For good or ill, she had made her choice when she had spoken her marriage vows, and wishing it were different would not change that.

But then Captain Ashbrook leaned over. "You have a very sweet son," he whispered.

His nearness startled her, making her heart thump. But when she met his eyes, it wasn't fear that she was feeling. And then his smile softened, and Tabby's pulse quickened.

"Thank you," she said, standing to put some distance between them. This would not do! She had to control herself. She was not free to feel such things. Not that she was feeling anything. Captain Ashbrook was a good fellow, and it was naught but appreciation for his kindness towards her son. Meaningless. A passing fancy. A bit of nothing that would die off once she cleared her head.

Bustling over to the sink, Tabby retrieved a wet rag and began scrubbing at the table.

"Are they ready yet, Mama?" asked Phillip.

The little cakes rested on the clean end of the table to cool. Some had not come free of their teacups easily and sat in crumbling heaps. Others were simply misshapen. Overall, they were quite possibly the ugliest fairy cakes ever made, but they filled the kitchen with a smell so intoxicating that Tabby was tempted to pop one in her mouth.

"Only a few more minutes, dearest," she said. "We must wait or they shall burn your tongue."

"Are you certain?" asked Captain Ashbrook, his own face looking as eager as Phillip's. "Perhaps we should test one."

He reached over, but Mrs. Bunting slapped his hand away with a smile. "Patience, Captain Ashbrook!"

The captain retreated and sent Phillip a commiserating look, and the two sat side-by-side with their arms folded, their eyes locked on the cakes.

"Boys never grow up," mumbled Mrs. Bunting, and Tabby chuckled.

The kitchen door opened, and James poked his head inside. "Mr. and Mrs. Kingsley are here to see Captain Ashbrook."

"One moment," said Tabby, fetching Captain Ashbrook's cane. Handing it to him, she helped him to his feet.

"Perhaps we should present them with some of our fairy cakes," said the captain, ruffling Phillip's hair with his free hand.

"Can we, Mama?" Phillip bounced off the chair, rushing over to the sad, crumbling heaps.

"That may not be the best idea," she said. "You aren't supposed to be here, darling, and—"

"Nonsense," said the captain. "Surely, you do not think my sister and brother-in-law are going to be upset about him being here."

Tabby sighed. That was exactly the sort of naive thoughts she'd had during her privileged life, but Tabby hated taking advantage of her employer's generosity.

Captain Ashbrook smiled, his eyes softening. "It shall be fine. I promise." Turning to Phillip, he said, "I happen to know that my sister adores fairy cakes."

Phillip beamed and scrambled over to the treats. Tabby reached him just in time before he grabbed at them with his bare hands.

"Let's put them on a tray, shall we?" she said, leading Phillip to where the serving trays were kept. Handing one to her son, Phillip carried it to the table, and in short order, Tabby had the cakes, plates, and napkins gathered on it.

With a few brushes of her hands, she cleared off bits of flour and crumbs that were on his shirt, then scrubbed his face clean of any splatters of batter and tidied his hair. Perhaps this was a mistake, but Tabby would make certain Phillip looked as presentable as possible, given the circumstances. The thought of marching into that room with her son rattled her. It was not as though she expected Mina to be affronted at the audacity, but

Tabby had never thought to have her family and employers mixing.

Tabby moved to straighten the remnant mess on the table. "I apologize, Mrs. Bunting, for leaving things in such a state."

"Don't fret, dear," said the cook, shooing her away. "This has been the most fun I've had in ages. I can take care of this."

"Mama, look, I'm so strong!" said Phillip, and Tabby turned in time to see him lift the tray from the table. It tipped to the side, and Tabby lunged for it, but Phillip righted it before it clattered to the ground.

"Phillip," she said, reaching for it.

"I've got it, Mama," he insisted. His muscles were straining, but he kept it level.

Captain Ashbrook stood at the kitchen door, holding it open for Phillip, and motioned for Tabby to join them. As she stepped past him and the door shut, Tabby noticed a bit of flour on the captain's sleeve and brushed at it. With a few pats, she had it clean and did so with the other. When her hands moved to his chest, Tabby's eyes met his.

Her breath caught in her throat, and her heart paused for a brief moment. In the narrow hall, they were closer than she had realized. Her hand rested on his chest, and his eyes softened, warming Tabby through until she felt as though made of melted butter, and in that instant, Tabby wondered what it would feel like to have his arms around her.

A clatter of dishes snapped Tabby out of her thoughts and returned her to the present, bringing a wave of shame as she realized where her mind had led her. Stepping away from the captain, her heart pounded and her cheeks blazed. She still could not catch her breath, but it was for an entirely different and unpleasant reason. What was she thinking? She had no right to entertain such thoughts.

Pain twisted through her, chilling her heart under a wave of icy guilt. She was not free to feel such things. This was not her husband. This was her charge. Her duty. The way to feed her family. For her son, she had to keep herself in check. Tabby was in this house in order to provide for Phillip. Nothing more. And she would not allow herself to forget that.

Graham took a breath, tamping the urge to sweep Tabby into his arms and kiss her soundly. It was pointless trying to think of her as Mrs. Russell any longer. He may not take such liberties aloud, but in his thoughts, he could ignore the bounds of propriety and revel in the depths of his feelings for her.

The strength of the emotion surprised him, leaving him frozen in place as she bustled away to help Phillip navigate to the sitting room. It was not as though he'd been ignorant of those latent desires, but this afternoon had allowed it to take shape. He loved Tabby. It may have been a few short hours, but spending time like a proper family made him yearn for it to be a reality with this lady and her son.

There was no room for doubt any longer. Graham would court Tabby, but he needed to find a manner in which to do so without ruining her reputation. She was already in a compromising situation, and he needed to tread carefully.

Tabby opened the door to the sitting room, pulling Graham from his revelations, and he stepped forward to follow Phillip and her into the sitting room. Graham smiled at the boy as he carefully walked the tray over while his mother hovered to save it if the worst should happen.

Mina sat on the sofa, and Simon stood beside her, and it did Graham good to see her looking so well. The smile she gave him made him think that she had forgiven him for putting them all through that final scare. Luckily for him, his sister was a kindhearted sort unsuited to nursing grudges.

"It appears you are hiring footmen at a rather young age, Graham," said Simon as the group entered and Phillip placed the tray on a side table.

"I'm not a footman," said Phillip, wrinkling his nose. "I'm a boy."

"A young man, more like," said Mina. At that, Phillip puffed out his chest and gave a childish attempt at a regal nod.

Simon coughed to cover his chuckle, and Graham found himself doing the same. Glancing at Tabby, Graham noticed the tension pulling at her lips, and with a hand at her back, he ushered her to sit.

"All is well," he whispered to her as they took their seats before explaining to Mina and Simon. "This young man is Mrs. Russell's boy, Phillip. The woman who watches over him is unavailable at present, and he is going to be staying here at Gladwell House until she is free once more."

"To stay?" asked Tabby, her eyes widening. "Oh, I could not possibly impose—"

"Nonsense," Graham said. "You cannot send him home alone, and he is a pleasure to have around."

What Graham truly wanted was to offer him a permanent place in the house; mother and child deserved to live together, and Graham wanted to be able to give that to Tabby, but he was no fool. As much as he loved the idea, having Phillip stay even these few days would raise eyebrows—just as Mina's and Simon's were at that very moment. Of course, the townsfolk would appear less intrigued and more affronted than the Kingsleys. Graham attempted to look indifferent about the offer while his sister stared at him, but he could not fight the red tinge heating his cheeks. Mina's eyes darted between Graham and Tabby, a smile creeping across her face.

"Absolutely, Tabby," said Mina. "This young man cannot be left alone."

Tabby's brow furrowed, her shoulders rigid as she looked at her son, who was carefully handing Mina and Simon their fairy cakes. Slowly, the tension eased from her and she nodded, a hint of shine filling her eyes.

"Thank you," she whispered.

In that moment, Graham did not care that his sister was beaming at him like he was a courting buck or that Simon's gaze grew far too knowing for comfort. The gratitude in Tabby's expression wrapped around Graham's heart, making him wish he could do more for the dear lady. What he had offered was so small, yet it meant worlds to her, and Graham was grateful that he'd been able to bring her such joy.

...

Candlelight filled the sitting room, but Tabby struggled to see her stitches. It would be better for her eyes to put off the chore until daylight, but she needed to mend the ripped seam or Phillip would have nothing to wear tomorrow. All his clothes were in a terrible state for Tabby rarely had time to deal with such things, and Joshua had neither the ability nor inclination to lift a finger to help the situation.

Tabby set the mending down and rubbed her forehead. Such thoughts were not helpful. Not at all. But it was difficult to maintain her civility towards the man who had disappeared without a trace. Even when she had returned home to fetch more clothes for Phillip, Joshua was not there. Tabby hated the dark visions that entered her mind as she wondered where he was. Though she wished to think the best of him, she had known him far too long to indulge in such fantasy. At best, he was ensconced in some seedy pub, wrapped around a bottle of gin.

"Are you tired?" asked Graham. Captain Ashbrook. Tabby gave herself a mental shake for allowing such a slip. He was her charge. No matter how comfortable things felt, they were employer and employee. They were not friends or familiar enough to allow herself such liberties. As much as she wished to.

"I am fine," she said, retrieving her work and forcing her eyes away from the delightful scene in front of her.

Phillip lay cuddled into Captain Ashbrook's good side. The gentleman had a children's book open and was reading from it. Phillip had hardly allowed the poor captain a break since Mina had brought it by that evening, and yet Captain Ashbrook appeared to be enjoying it as much as Phillip. Her little man

A True Gentleman

looked so contented there, and the sight of it brought tears to Tabby's eyes. This was what she wanted for Phillip. A happy childhood. One where he was cherished and loved, not shoved aside and shouted at.

That was not fair of her. Tabby knew that. Joshua cared for Phillip. It may be buried deep in his heart, but it was there. During their good moments, Tabby could see it.

But Tabby was lying to herself. Or refusing to see the truth of the matter, at any rate. It wasn't the sight of Phillip so happy that made her heart light enough to float away. At least, not in its entirety. It was Captain Ashbrook.

He glanced at her, and she dropped her eyes, returning to her work, and a moment later, he continued with the story. His voice reminded her of a cello, low and melodious, murmuring the words in a gentle hum. Tabby had never thought that a speaking voice could be attractive, but Captain Ashbrook certainly had one.

No. This would not do. She could not allow herself such thoughts. Every moment spent dwelling on such things gave them more strength in her heart. Even the smallest of them latched onto her, infecting her soul, and she could not allow herself to be overpowered.

Tabby cast her thoughts to her husband, searching for those specks of good that helped her through the dark times. Sorting through her memories and feelings, Tabby hunted for anything to strengthen her resolve, but there was nothing. Not a single thing to which Tabby could cling. The only blessing that had come from Joshua Russell was Phillip.

Picturing the Joshua from their courtship, Tabby tried to summon a spark of feeling for him, but the only one that came to the surface was disgust. Her fingers moved the needle through the fabric, her hands going through the motions as anger filled her. There was no denying it. No hiding it once it had been discovered. There was nothing left of the young love she had once felt for him. Tabby despised her husband.

Dropping the mending on her lap, Tabby begged to be excused, rushing out of the room before Phillip or Captain Ashbrook could stop her. She hurried through the house, not stopping until she was safely hidden in her bedchamber. Tears ran down her cheeks as she mourned the decision she had made, cursing the blind naiveté that had tied her to such a useless man.

Knowing that Joshua had given her Phillip had helped to keep the resentment from growing into this ugly thing twisting her heart, but it was impossible to rein in any longer. And Tabby could not feign ignorance as to the origin of the shift.

Graham. Tabby allowed his name to sit in her mind, unchallenged. Just for this moment. Graham had changed everything.

Tabby had feelings for him. She refused to consider any word that signified something deeper than that. To step over such a line would be her ruin, but it was foolish to deny the truth. She cared for Graham. Deeply. She had spent nearly every hour of the last few months at his side, and though he was frustrating at times, he was such a good man. The type Tabby had hoped Joshua would be.

The hopelessness of her situation weighed on her heart until it threatened to rip in two. Married to one man, yet wishing it were another.

Tabby swiped at the tears. No. She could not even think such a thing. What was done was done, and allowing herself to believe otherwise for even a moment would only bring more pain.

Standing in the middle of her room, Tabby fought her feelings. Her heart ached to run to Graham, to wish that all could be different. But there was no changing her circumstances, and she could not allow herself to fantasize about a future with Captain Ashbrook.

Tabby took several deep breaths. Her feelings may be pulling her one way, but there was no doubt in her mind that she could not give in to them. She was no animal to be driven by her emotions and instincts. No matter how terrible Joshua may be, he was her husband. She may have been an impetuous young miss when she'd spoken her wedding vows, but that did not diminish the fact that she had said the words of her own free will. The promise she had made had not been contingent on Joshua keeping his, and his actions did not diminish the fact that she was bound to him.

For good or bad, Tabby had chosen Joshua Russell, and there was no undoing it.

And Tabby knew what needed to be done. Stepping to her desk, she pulled out paper and wrote a letter to the Wilton Servant Registry. No matter how good her pay, it was not worth the potential cost. There was only so much temptation she could withstand, and Tabby refused to test her limits any further. The sooner she was able to find a new position, the better.

Chapter 22

Humming, Tabby shifted the basket in her arms, moving it so she could see the stairs as she descended to the ground floor.

"James?" she called, and the footman appeared before her foot hit the last step. "Please take this to the main house," she said, handing the laundry over. With a nod, he took it and hurried out the front door, leaving Tabby to follow the sounds of Phillip's giggles.

Pushing open the kitchen door, Tabby found yet another mess. With each bake, the captain and Phillip were getting better at containing the disaster, but they were a long way from being clean.

"Mama!" cried Phillip, a smear of batter covering his forehead. "We are making lemon maddylines."

Grabbing a towel from the table, Tabby scrubbed Phillip's face. "Is that so?"

"Mrs. Bunting got the recipe from the cook at Avebury Park," said Captain Ashbrook. "They are the best I've ever had, and we wanted to try our hand at making them."

Tabby glanced over at the captain and nearly laughed at the boyish glee on his face and the flour across his cheeks that matched Phillip's. She reached to wipe it away but caught herself and covered it by wiping at Phillip's face again.

"Ugh! Let me go!" he squealed.

Her face felt aflame at that impulse. Locking it far away, deep in her mind, Tabby composed herself. "And where is Mrs. Bunting?"

"We wanted to do it on our own," answered Phillip.

"Mrs. Bunting is getting a well-earned rest," said Captain Ashbrook.

"Ah," said Tabby as she glanced at the mountain of dirty bowls and spoons and drips of batter coating the table and floor. Perhaps the poor woman was not going to get much of a rest in the end.

Captain Ashbrook held a bowl in the crook of his arm. "I must admit you were right, Mrs. Russell. When you mentioned cooking, I couldn't understand what you found so enjoyable about it, but it's quite gratifying. It is an odd combination of exactness and instinct."

The smile he gave her unsettled Tabby's heart, and she took a breath, forcing her mind away from thoughts best left alone. "Well, I'm certain you've been having fun, Phillip, but we need to go into town to purchase some things. I am afraid you shan't be able to stay until your madeleines are done."

Phillip's smile died an instant death, his eyes getting big and watery. "But Mama, I want to stay."

"Dearest, that isn't possible," said Tabby, pulling a mixing spoon from his hand.

"Mama..."

"He can stay, if you wish," said Captain Ashbrook.

Phillip's spirits lightened at that, and he nodded his head, reaching for the spoon. She moved it out of his reach.

"That is not the best idea," said Tabby.

"But you shan't be long," insisted the captain. "You can take Mina's carriage and return in a trice. Surely, not having Phillip along will make the errands go quicker, and we can have fresh madeleines ready for you when you return."

Staring at the lumpy mixture in the captain's bowl, Tabby was certain that whatever came out of the oven would not be appetizing.

"I hadn't planned on taking the carriage," said Tabby. "And I do not wish to impose."

"Please, Mama." Phillip clasped his hands, his eyes echoing that plea.

"Your errands are part of your duties, so it is no stretch to think it proper for you to use the carriage for them." Captain Ashbrook set down the bowl, leaning towards Tabby. "And having your son around is not an imposition." His tone dropped into a lull, his eyes warming in a way that made Tabby wonder what was going on in the man's head. If it weren't for the fact that she was married, she would suspect that he harbored romantic feelings for her, but Captain Ashbrook was too honorable a gentleman to make advances towards another man's wife.

"I would hate to spoil your fun," said Tabby when she regained the ability to speak.

Phillip beamed, yanking the mixing spoon from her hand and reaching for the bowl of batter.

"Belay that," said the captain, pulling the bowl out of Phillip's reach. "The recipe says to be careful how much we mix it." Motioning for Phillip to draw closer, the man wrapped one arm around the boy, allowing him to grip the spoon already in the bowl. "Now, slowly."

Phillip wrapped his fingers around the handle and looked at Captain Ashbrook with stark admiration, and it brought a shine of tears to Tabby's eyes. The child was so desperate for such attention, and seeing the captain heaping it on her son fractured her resolve.

"Go. We shall be fine," he mouthed to her as she watched them.

They may be fine, but Tabby was anything but and could only hope that she would receive a quick response to her inquiry for a new position. Tabby's heart was not strong enough to be battered about in such a fashion.

...

"And done," said Graham as he closed the oven door. He hoped they turned out, but at that point, a successful bake was secondary to the joy of being allowed time alone with Phillip. Though part of him had originally reached out to the boy for Tabby's sake, Phillip had quickly wormed his way into Graham's heart. It was hard not to adore a child that was so like his mama; the thoughtful lad stood beside him, holding his cane so that Graham could take it the moment his good hand was free.

"In a few minutes, our first batch should be done," he said. "Perhaps we should get some air until then." Graham certainly needed some. It made sense that the large oven would keep the kitchen warm, but the air was stifling, and after only an hour, he was ready to retreat. He wondered how Mrs. Bunting managed it all day long.

Graham took his cane from the boy, and Phillip took his right hand, making Graham wince at the twinge his muscles gave as the boy squeezed it. Regardless of the pain, Graham was not about to push the child away for it brought him far more joy than hurt.

Hobbling along, they moved to the back door. The garden was lovely, though the blooms were fading with the end of summer. Taking a deep breath of air, Graham could smell that fall was coming. The familiarity of that scent startled him. It had been a long time since he had been ashore during that shift from summer to fall, yet he recognized the subtle undertones wafting on the breeze that told him the change was coming.

With that came memories of autumns long past. Ones filled with harvest festivals and apple cider, dancing and games. Each merry possibility filled Graham with anticipation. As a child, he had loved the season and all the holiday festivities that quickly followed it. He had not thought about such things in many years as his time at sea had not allowed him to partake in all the revelries.

Phillip led him over to the garden table, and Graham sat as

another memory struck him. He had not thought of his first year at sea in ages. It was not the most pleasant of times in his life, and thus had been buried in the deep recesses of his mind, but Graham remembered the longing. The homesickness. The misery. The navy had been his choice, but the transition to the sea life had not been pleasant. There had been many nights when Graham had lain awake at night, wishing he were home. Graham huffed at the realization that he was feeling such things once more but in reverse. Life was a strange journey, indeed.

As Graham was lost in thought, Phillip leapt onto his lap, dropping his weight directly onto Graham's wounds. Little knees and elbows jabbed in all the worst spots, making Graham bellow in pain. It ripped from him, shoving past all common sense and decorum as the agony twisted his muscles. Words came to his mind, but Graham had just enough control to keep them locked away, though he wanted to curse until every last bit of his misery was gone.

Breathing through it, Graham waited until the throbbing reached a bearable level. But when he opened his eyes, the boy was gone.

"Phillip?" Graham struggled to keep his voice calm and steady. He winced as he twisted in his seat and then caught sight of him hiding in the bushes.

"Come here," he prompted, but the child did not move.

Graham wanted to go to him, but he knew better than to try his leg after such a shock. "Phillip, please."

Little eyes peeked at him through the foliage, and Graham's heart caught at the sight of tears.

"I am not angry," he said. That was not the entire truth. Graham had been plenty angry in the moment and he certainly wished the child had been more careful, but Graham knew better than to lay blame where it did not belong. Phillip had not meant any harm and was too young to understand. Even if a childish part of him wished to unleash his residual fury at the boy.

Phillip watched him for a moment, and Graham focused on

looking far calmer than he felt. The boy inched out of the shrubbery, inching closer.

"I'm sorry," Phillip whispered, his voice hitching with tears.

"It was an accident," Graham replied, reaching for the boy and helping him to climb onto the good side of his lap. Phillip's little arms went around his neck, and Graham felt tears against his neck.

"I'm sorry," he repeated.

"And I apologize for shouting," said Graham, rubbing a hand along the boy's back. "I didn't mean to scare you. You startled me is all."

Phillip would not look at Graham, but he felt the child nod. "People shout too much. I don't like it."

The tone of that simple statement sent chills through Graham, and he wanted to clutch the boy tighter. "Do people often shout at you?"

Another nod.

"Who?" Graham asked the question, though he feared he knew the answer.

Leaning away, Phillip wiped at his eyes. "Papa."

Graham stifled another surge of anger at the thought of anyone shouting at such a sweet child. Especially the boy's own father. "Was he often angry?"

Phillip's chin quivered, his face crumpling, and he grabbed Graham around the neck once again, burrowing in as though he could hide from the memories. And then there was another little nod of his head.

"I make too much blasted noise," he said with a quiver in his voice.

Hearing the curse come from Phillip's little voice shook Graham, but he suspected the lad was quoting his father, and it disgusted him. He now understood why Tabby despised foul language, for hearing it repeated thusly was worse than what Graham's coarsest sailors had let loose. Though he'd made progress with improving his language, this cemented his determination to never let such words leave his lips again. Graham refused to teach such crude behavior and language to innocents.

"That is not true," said Graham. "You are never too noisy here."

Phillip sat upright again to look Graham in the eyes. "Truly?"

The hope in that one word twisted Graham's heart in two. Phillip was too young to worry about such things. He was a child and deserved to live as a child ought, and Graham found himself hating the man who had mistreated this sweet boy. The more he heard about Mr. Russell, the more Graham was certain he had been no gentleman—regardless of his social status.

Graham wished he could let things lie, but a question niggled at him, refusing to allow him to let the moment pass. "Did your papa ever hurt you?"

His little brow wrinkled, and he gave Graham a shake of his head, allowing Graham to breathe a sigh of relief. He had seen enough captains who thought extensive corporal punishment the only way to instill obedience, and Graham knew that such attitudes were not exclusive to those at sea. It was not something he would wish for little Phillip.

"What about your mama? Did he hurt her?" Graham hated to voice the concern aloud, but he had to know.

Phillip shook his head again.

There were so many things Graham wished to ask, but his guilt at digging into Tabby's secrets kept him from doing so. With time, he would be able to ask her himself, but at present, questioning her son would be an invasion and was best left alone.

Hearing what little he had, Graham felt his resolve crystalize, and he knew that whatever else he did in this life, he would make certain Tabby and Phillip had a happy home and a comfortable life. It was a silent vow made only to himself, but Graham knew he would do everything to keep it.

Phillip relaxed, leaning into him, and Graham's arm pulled him tighter. How he adored this little boy. In such a short time, the lad had wrapped him so firmly around his finger that Graham doubted he would ever be free. Not that he wanted to. It was too late for Graham Ashbrook. He could not explain how he had gotten himself so thoroughly tangled in such a short time, but his heart was lost to this child and his beguiling mother.

"Do you think the maddylines are done?" Phillip asked, all thoughts of the previous conversation gone.

Graham looked at his pocket watch. "Just about."

...

Gladwell House had never seemed very close to the heart of Bristow, but then again, Tabby had never taken a carriage into town, either. As much as she hated the idea of being so informal with the Kingsleys, it was a blessing to be able to travel there and back in so little a time, which would allow her a minute to peruse the lending library shelves. Tabby had already selected a few titles for Captain Ashbrook, but there were a few others Tabby was curious about. Running her fingers along the spines, she scoured the bookshelves, but her search was fruitless.

Taking her books to the counter, she greeted Mr. Sims. He gave her a nod and began noting her selections in his ledger without another word.

"And how are you and Mrs. Sims?" she asked.

"We are in good health."

Tabby blinked at the abrupt answer. In all the other times she had been here, the man had never been reticent, yet Tabby could not pull more than a few short words from him. Perhaps if he were busy, she would understand the behavior, but there were only two other ladies in the shop, and they were whispering in the corner.

"Is there any chance you will be getting *The Excursion*? I have been meaning to read it but have not seen it here."

"No." The reply was terse, and the man refused to glance from his ledger.

"It is indecent," came a harsh whisper from one of the ladies. "Positively immoral!"

Tabby turned to look at them, and when she caught their eye, the ladies blushed and put their heads closer together, though they continued to speak loud enough for Tabby to hear.

"I hear they have become quite close," said the other with a tone that announced to anyone listening that they were speaking of a scandal.

"Thrown together in such a manner, it is no wonder," said the first. "And with such a husband..."

"But to behave in such a wanton manner," gasped the second.

Mr. Sims deigned to look at Tabby, and she saw the accusation in his eyes. The whispered conversation became ever more clear when the man slid the books across the counter to her, as though touching her would taint him. Tabby's face blazed, her mouth opening as though to explain, but she had no words to offer. Her head grew light, and Tabby escaped the confines of the shop.

The bright sun blinded her for a moment, and Tabby felt adrift, unsure of where she was headed or what she was doing. Those caustic words bounced around her thoughts, her shame giving strength to their accusations. She may not be explicitly guilty of the offenses leveled at her, but in her heart, Tabby knew she had been unfaithful. Tabby yearned for Graham, not her husband. She cringed. Captain Ashbrook. Not Graham.

Stumbling along the road, she hurried to the carriage.

"Tabby!"

Halting, she closed her eyes at the sound of her husband's voice, dreading that he was there to see her in such agitation. His hand clamped around her arm, jerking her into an alley. Tabby tried to wrench free, but his fingers dug into her flesh.

"So, you've resurfaced," he said, spittle flicking across Tabby's cheek.

"I have resurfaced?" she said, throwing her weight to yank her arm, but he just held her tighter. "Where have you been? Phillip was abandoned at home, alone, and you were nowhere to be found."

"My business is my own," he said, though his bloodshot eyes told her exactly what his business had been. "I need money."

Tabby jerked her arm again. "You cannot be serious."

"You have enough to spare, or is Captain Ashbrook not generous with his lady-birds?"

Tabby's vision blurred, and her chin wobbled. "You think so ill of me?"

"I don't care who you lift your skirts for," he growled, and more spittle flew into her face. "Service every man in Bristow, for all I care, but you'd better give me a bit of the profits."

The blood rushed from Tabby's face, her mouth gaping. Her hand flew before she knew it was moving, striking Joshua's cheek with a crack. He reared away, but his hand did not release her arm. Joshua blinked at her, as though the hit had knocked his senses straight again. The fire in his eyes faded and his face crumpled as he released his hold on her. Tabby clutched her books to her chest, wrapping her other arm around herself.

"I apologize," he said, his head dropping low. "I don't know what came over me. I cannot..." his voice faltered. "I need money, Tabby."

"And Phillip needs to eat."

He nodded, his gaze remaining locked on the ground. The muscles in his jaw tensed. "Perhaps I should come by Avebury Park and ask Mrs. Kingsley for a bit of help to tide us over. I know she is inordinately fond of you. Or I could speak to Captain Ashbrook directly."

Tabby tensed, and she moved to step around him, but he blocked her path.

"I wish there were no need to be so harsh about it," he said, reaching to touch her, but Tabby pulled away. "You do not understand the weighty matters I am dealing with. I need the money, and if you are unwilling to give it, I will have to take other steps."

Tabby dabbed at her gathering tears and tried to summon her strength to keep the tremors in her body from growing. There was nothing more to do. With a tug of her reticule, Tabby pulled out a few coins and dropped them in Joshua's outstretched hand. He picked through each one, his lips tightening.

"Isn't there more?" He ran a hand through his mussed hair.

"That's all I have."

Joshua barked a curse and kicked the wall beside Tabby. She flinched, but the next moment he stormed away. Covering her mouth to hold back her cries, Tabby leaned against the bricks. The world around her tightened, making it difficult to breathe, but Tabby would not allow herself to crumble.

Movement at the mouth of the alley reminded her that there were others in the streets of Bristow. Others with wagging tongues, and Tabby had supplied enough fodder for the gossip-mongers today. Gathering her residual strength, Tabby escaped to the waiting carriage, not stopping until she was safely ensconced inside. Only then did she allow the tears to trickle down her cheeks.

Chapter 23

"Mama! Are you watching?" Phillip shouted as the pony trotted past her. Tabby leaned against the fence, watching her son bounce around the stableyard. Phillip beamed and whooped, and though he nudged his mighty steed, the groom kept him at a walk.

Tabby felt Captain Ashbrook approaching long before she heard his distinctive footsteps, and then he was standing there beside her, sharing her bit of the fence.

"Phillip is enjoying himself," he said.

They were four short words, yet they undid all of Tabby's hard-earned control over her emotions. There was no denying the yearning she felt for the man, which only strengthened with each passing hour. Being around him was like scenting a heavenly meal on an empty stomach, but she knew she could not partake. And it was only getting harder to remember why she mustn't.

"Yes," replied Tabby, her voice rough. She cleared her throat. "He has always adored horses and ponies."

"Then I am glad he is able to have this opportunity." That low and gentle voice of his wrapped around her, unraveling her hard-fought self-control.

"Thank you for it," she managed to say. Tabby did not look at the captain, but she sensed his smile.

"I would do anything for Phillip," he said.

Tabby had no ability to guard her heart from such kindness. She swallowed back the emotions, blinking away the prickles of tears.

"And for you..." His words came out as little more than a whisper, so soft that she hardly knew if they were real or the imaginings of her muddled heart.

Straightening, Tabby raised her hand to Phillip. "You are doing splendidly!" she called, allowing the diversion to put some distance between them. The man had no idea how appealing he was, but Tabby needed to keep her wits about her.

"I have been thinking," he said. "Perhaps it would be best if Phillip moved into Gladwell House. I have not spoken with Mina about it, but I doubt she would object. A boy needs his mother."

Tabby turned to stare at Graham. He leaned against the gate, watching her with that half-smile of his on his lips. She should not have looked directly at him for it set her heart aflutter. Tabby wished she could shake some sense into her mudded head; she was no simpering debutante to be so affected by a gentleman's attentions.

"To stay?" she replied. "You cannot be serious."

Graham's head cocked to the side. "And why not? He is a delightful child, and we both adore having him around."

"It is unseemly, Captain Ashbrook," she said, as though speaking his proper name would somehow allow her to gain control over her erratic heartbeat. "There would be talk."

The man seemed to consider it, but he shook it away. "Perhaps, but certainly people would understand that it would be better than leaving the child alone. That neighbor you hired cannot be trusted with him."

Tabby could not argue with that. There was no chance she would ever entrust Phillip with Mrs. Allen again, but before she could speak, Captain Ashbrook continued.

"Who else would watch him but you?"

Tabby's knees felt weak, but there was no place to sit. Surely, he could not mean...

Her mind grasped for calm, but understanding dawned, and for the first time in her life, Tabby felt liable to faint. He did not realize she was still married. How could that be? She understood Mrs. Bunting's misapprehension, but Tabby had spoken with Captain Ashbrook about her husband. She scoured her memory for what had been shared, and she could not recall if there had been anything explicitly stated.

But it was pointless. Clearly, Captain Ashbrook thought her a widow, and he would not think so if she had said anything to the contrary.

Holding back a groan, Tabby thought of all the time they had shared together. A dozen different moments came to mind, and she saw them all anew. His words, his gestures, his gazes. Knowing that he thought her free to welcome such attentions shed a different light on them.

Graham cared for her.

The sun blazed in the sky above, but a cold shiver spread through her. Turning away from the gentleman, Tabby closed her eyes as her own behavior surged to the fore of her thoughts. Every kindness had been meant innocently, but now knowing what she did, Tabby saw how they might lead him to believe she was open to his affections.

The thought of it set her insides twisting and reeling, and Tabby wished she could disappear into oblivion. It was one thing to risk her own heart, but knowing she had led him on—however unintentionally—stung. There was no way to undo this. Not without bringing great pain to him.

"Mrs. Russell?" His voice was close behind her, and Tabby felt him at her back. His hand brushed her arm, and Tabby closed her eyes at the feel of it, allowing herself one moment of weakness.

A horse whinnied from inside the stables, the sound coming out like a great trumpet, and Tabby whirled around to see

Phillip's pony skitter. The groom kept the beast under control, but Phillip swayed in the saddle. He wrenched the pony's mane, and it shrieked, knocking him clear off.

"Phillip!"

Using his one free arm, the groom caught her son while holding firm to the pony's lead. Tabby rushed around the fence and into the yard, hurrying over to her boy. With a great gasp, Phillip let loose a wail, which made the pony yank at the groom.

Tabby scooped Phillip into her arms, and he buried his face into her neck, his nose and cheeks wetting her skin.

"He's fine, ma'am," said the groom. "Only a bit of a scare."

Rubbing her little man's back, she sighed. "I know. A bit of a scare for both of us. Thank you for catching him."

The groom gave her a nod. "Sorry about that. Buttercup doesn't spook easily, but Black Devil has been in a mood today," he said, nodding over to the stable where the horse that had started the trouble gave another agitated whinny, batting against its stall.

"Is he hurt?" asked Captain Ashbrook. Even with his sore leg, he was only a few steps behind her.

"No," said Tabby, though Phillip had not released her. "Though perhaps it would be best if I took him home."

Captain Ashbrook nodded, reaching over to pat Phillip's back. "I shall have the carriage readied."

Tabby shook her head. "I shan't trouble you. I can walk."

"Don't be silly."

The last thing she needed was to be in closer proximity to Captain Ashbrook. "It was time for us to leave anyway, and you are set for dinner with your sister and brother-in-law. I am certain it must be nearly time for you to join them."

"Mrs. Russell," said the captain, his eyebrows raised. "Surely, you understood that you and Phillip were included in the invitation."

Phillip's cries had never been a pleasant sound for Tabby, but at that moment, she was beyond grateful that he was sobbing. "I think it best if I get him someplace quiet. Perhaps another time," she said, though she knew another time would not come.

"At least allow me to escort you," he said, offering her his arm.

Tabby shook her head. "It would push you beyond your limits, and I could make the journey on foot faster than they can ready the carriage."

Captain Ashbrook drew closer, and Tabby's breath caught. Focusing on Phillip, she was able to keep her hands from shaking.

"I would like to be of assistance," he said, his eyes pleading with her.

"We are fine. Truly."

Disappointment clouded his gaze, but he stepped away. Without a backwards glance, Tabby marched out of the stableyard and headed towards the path to Gladwell House. By the time she was out of sight, Phillip's cries had calmed and he was quiet against her shoulder.

And that was when Tabby realized she had not corrected the captain's misunderstanding. The thought of having to do so did horrid things to her heart, but she knew she must admit the truth. To allow things to stand as they were would only cause greater pain to both of them. Perhaps it was early enough that his heart would not be bruised.

Hopefully, she would find a new position soon. They would part and never meet again. A weight settled in her heart, pulling at Tabby until it was a struggle to put one foot in front of the other. It was for the best, even if it did not feel so. Tabby must stay until she had a new position; they could not afford for her to leave now. For Phillip, she would bury her feelings for Captain Ashbrook, though she longed to pack her bags and disappear that instant.

Thank heavens tonight was her evening off. She could take Phillip home and deal with this awful mess tomorrow.

Chapter 24

Flexing his fingers around the handle of his cane, Graham stood outside Simon's study. In his thoughts, this step had been an easy one, but standing on the precipice was daunting. In the hours and days he had been thinking about this very moment, not once had Graham expected to be nervous. But there it was, that tickle in his stomach. Not that Graham doubted what should happen, but that Simon might not approve. And not that Simon's disapproval would sway him, but Graham liked the gentleman and feared the possibility of a rift.

A gentleman and a servant. Graham may not be well-versed in the ways of society, but he knew enough to know that such a breach of social divides would not go unchallenged. Especially when the couple lived under the same roof.

But Tabby was worth it.

Rapping his knuckles against the wood, Graham waited for Simon's call and stepped into the room. Having never been inside before, it startled Graham how much it looked like his father's study. But then again, Graham didn't have much experience with gentlemen's studies. Perhaps they all looked vaguely the same with their mounds of books stacked along the walls, dark woods, and massive desks sitting before even more massive windows.

"Graham," Simon said in greeting and motioned for him to take a seat. "What brings you here?"

"I wanted to speak with you about my future." Graham knew he should have begun the conversation with some polite inanities, but he had no inclinations towards the inane.

"Your future," Simon said with raised eyebrows. Leaning into his wingback chair, Simon regarded Graham. "If it weren't for the smile on your face, that would sound very ominous."

At that, Graham's smile grew. "Yes, well, I have never had much of a head for finances, and I was hoping you would help me navigate it."

"I would love to," he said. "Though in truth, Mina asked me to take a look at your accounts months ago, and you are in a good situation."

Why that revelation was surprising, Graham did not know. That was so like Mina to go quietly about ensuring that those she loved were cared for. A mother hen through and through.

"Enough to purchase a home?" asked Graham.

Simon's eyes widened. "You are looking to settle? Ashore?"

Graham squeezed the head of his cane and then drummed his fingers against it. A small part of him hurt at the thought of his lost past, even though he knew moving forward with his life was the best option. The only one. Fighting for his naval career had occupied so much of his thoughts and efforts that it was difficult to adjust to this change in course—even if it had the promise of being a far better future.

"I have already written to my superiors to tell them that I am unable to continue my duties," he said. "Though I have not yet received a reply, I don't anticipate any trouble on that front. With any luck, the whole thing should be settled fairly quickly, and I will be a retired naval captain."

Simon stared at Graham. "Is it wrong for me to be glad you have come to your senses?"

Graham huffed, though he smiled in return: the relief on

Simon's face was too humorous to do otherwise. "I have been a bit of a fool."

"It happens to the best of us."

"Yes, well, I'm ready to move forward, and that includes finding a home."

"There is no need for you to move out of Gladwell House," said Simon. "I know it may not be an ideal situation, but do not feel as though you need to leave the moment you are able."

Graham shifted in his seat, leaning his cane against the chair beside him. "It is a fine spot for a bachelor brother, but as I am on the mend and hope not to be so..." Graham struggled to say the word and felt a blush creep across his cheeks, "unattached much longer, I believe it time for me to secure more permanent lodging."

Simon grinned like a fool. "Unattached? And might I ask the name of the lady?"

Graham crossed his arms, but Simon gave him a steady gaze. He could not believe his brother-in-law was going to force him to say it aloud. Not that he minded saying it aloud. Any time he was able to speak of Tabby was a blessed event, but Simon was only tormenting him.

"Tabby Russell," he mumbled.

"Congratulations!" said Simon. "I should send for Mina, and we can celebrate."

Graham raised a hand. "I haven't spoken to the lady yet. At this point, I am simply assessing what is to be done for our future."

"'Our future,' eh?"

Graham wanted to growl at the triumph in Simon's face, but it was difficult to do when his mouth kept pulling itself into a silly grin. "Yes, our future. We haven't spoken explicitly as I cannot press my suit while we are living under the same roof, but I have every reason to believe she is receptive."

"'Receptive,' eh?" chuckled Simon.

Sighing, Graham pinched the bridge of his nose.

Simon raised his hands. "I apologize, but it is impossible to pass on the opportunity to tease you." Leaning forward, Simon rested on his elbows. "In all seriousness, I like your Mrs. Russell, and if you wish to start a life with her, we must alter your present arrangement. You courting a member of staff will raise enough eyebrows without you two being in such close quarters. We don't want to add fuel to the fire."

"She is not staff," he bristled.

Simon raised placating hands again. "You may not think of her that way, and heaven knows Mina does not, but to everyone else, she is. I am not suggesting that you need to revise your plans, but you must be careful. I have seen how much damage rumors can cause, and for both your sakes and that of her boy, we must proceed with caution."

Graham nodded, not liking the stark reality but accepting it all the same. His eyes drifted to Simon's desk, mindlessly tracing over the knick-knacks cluttering it. Graham would hate for Tabby to be hurt by such malicious things, and if there was any way for him to protect her from it, he would do his part.

"I am happy for you," said Simon, drawing Graham's gaze back to him. His fingers tapped the desk, and Simon's own eyes drifted away. "To find someone with whom you wish to spend your life is an incredible thing."

Tabby and Phillip entered Graham's thoughts, and he could picture their future together. The image filled his heart until it was ready to burst, though a flicker of fear lurked in the shadowy edges of that glorious future. "She has not yet accepted me. As I said, I haven't spoken with her, and she may not feel the same."

Simon grunted and nodded. "That is a terrifying place to be in—loving someone and unsure of whether they reciprocate— but the risk is worth it. As one who has been in your shoes, I will attest that finding the right woman can make your life heaven on earth and losing her brings on the agony of hell."

"That is not comforting."

Simon shrugged, his gaze turning to a vase of lilies displayed on a pedestal against the wall. "The greatest blessings often come with the biggest risks. I cannot begin to tell you how terrified I was to prostrate myself before Mina and beg her to forgive me. Not because of my pride but because I was certain she despised me."

Graham straightened, staring at Simon. "What did you do that was so terrible?"

Shaking himself out of his thoughts, Simon straightened and swallowed, though his gaze did not return to Graham's. "I would prefer not to dredge up that bit of my past." Simon ground his teeth together. "It does not reflect well on me, and though years have passed, it is still painful to recall. But the point is that securing your Lady Love may not be easy, but it is worth it, and if there is one thing that Mina has taught me, it is to hold onto hope."

Graham chuckled. "That sounds like Mina."

Simon's expression softened as it usually did when he was thinking about his wife. It was filled with love and contentment, the kind which Graham hoped to find with Tabby. The kind he knew was possible with her. The kind that nestled into his heart and warmed him like the sun, turning his frigid world into a summer's day.

"Well, we shall need to formulate a plan to get Mrs. Russell out of service and Gladwell House," said Simon. "But if we are to do so, it would be best to include Mina in this discussion. My brilliant wife can find a solution far faster than either of us."

Standing, Simon led Graham out of the study, and the two men made their way through the house.

"I know she will not accept charity," said Graham, his cane tapping along with his dragging steps. "She despises being a drain on others."

"And I like her all the more for it, though it presents a bit of a challenge," Simon replied. "Perhaps with you nearly able to live on your own, we can offer her a position as Mina's companion. I would feel better having someone around to assist her during the last months before our child is born. My steward is taking over more of my duties as we get closer to the arrival so that I may be free to watch over my wife. Perhaps we could pose Mrs. Russell as a similar sort of helper. Mrs. Witmore does a fine job with the household, but Mina has a myriad of other duties with which she could use some help."

"That could work," said Graham as they reached Mina's private sitting room.

"Dearest," said Simon, pushing open the door. "Mina?" Simon disappeared into the room, hurrying to his wife's side. Graham hobbled in to find Mina bent over, leaning on the sofa arm, one of her hands wrapped around the swell of her belly.

"What is the matter?" asked Simon, helping her to sit.

Her face was pinched, and she eased out a breath. "Only a bit of pain, Simon," she said, when she could speak. "Dr. Clarke assured us it was normal to feel such things from time to time."

Simon crouched before her, taking her hand in his. "That does not look like 'only a bit of pain,' Mina."

"It is gone now," she said with a tired smile. "Truly, I am fine."

"Perhaps, but I would feel better if we sent for Dr. Clarke," said Simon.

Graham came up beside him. "He is right, Mina. It's best not to risk it."

"You two," said Mina. "It scared me the first time it happened, but Tabby assured me that all expectant mothers feel such things at times. They are only a bit uncomfortable, that's all. Nothing to worry about as long as they do not happen frequently."

"It is better to be safe than sorry, Mina," Simon said, echoing Graham, and he nodded at Graham to call for a servant.

"Honestly," Mina said, crossing her arms. "I know I've had scares, but this is not one of them. There's no need to bother anyone."

Graham ignored his sister and tugged on the bellpull. Mina complained louder, but he stared at the door, awaiting a servant to answer. Moments later, a footman stepped inside.

"Fetch Dr. Clarke," said Simon, just as Mina repeated,

"There is nothing wrong."

"Sorry, sir," the footman said with a bow, "but there's been a nasty outbreak of influenza that has Dr. Clarke and the rest of the physicking folk in Bristow busy. Even if I could find him, I doubt he'd be available."

"Perfect," said Mina, and Simon and Graham darted glances at her. Her cheeks pinked. "Not the influenza, of course, but there is no need to bother Dr. Clarke with such things. It is only a little cramp, and it's already gone. I feel fine."

"Then fetch Mrs. Russell," said Simon. "She has helped before."

Graham nodded. "It is her evening off, and she took her son home."

Simon stood and gave the footman orders to send the carriage, all while Mina began protesting in earnest.

"Simon, you cannot think to bother the poor lady when she is at home," said Mina. "This is silly."

Kneeling before her, Simon took her hands in his once more, and Graham turned away from the couple, giving them a bit of privacy.

"Please," Simon whispered. "I know you think it is nothing, but I shan't be easy until someone looks at you."

There was a quiet moment before Graham chanced a look at them—only to turn away at the sight of his sister kissing her husband soundly. Graham's cheeks burned, and he cursed the fact that he could not overcome his family's tendency towards blushing. It wasn't as though he were unaware of the deep affection between the couple, but at times it was a bit more enthusiastic than he cared to witness. The footman stood not far from Graham with a far more passive expression, though Graham recognized a similar awkwardness lurking in the young man's eyes.

It was a good moment later before Simon finally spoke. "Send the coachman to fetch Mrs. Russell."

Chapter 25

Phillip poked his soup, the look on his face stating clearly how little he cared for their dinner. Likely, the boy was still moping about leaving Gladwell House, but Tabby knew it was best not to think about that place or the people inside it.

"This is delicious," mumbled Joshua without looking at her. "Thank you for making it."

Tabby's eyebrows shot up at that, her spoon freezing halfway to her mouth. Joshua chanced a glance at her, and then his eyes returned to his bowl, his shoulders slumping.

"I suppose I have not said that much of late," he said.

"Ever" would be a more accurate assessment, but Tabby wasn't about to browbeat the man. For once, he was sober and polite, and she was in no mood to stir up trouble.

"I've missed having you two around," he said. "The cottage was so empty without you here."

Bringing his free hand around, he rested it beside his bowl. Easing it forward, he reached for her hand. Tabby watched his fingers wrapping around hers, but his touch felt as foreign as any stranger's.

"My position doesn't allow me home very often. I wish it

were different, but as is, I have no choice in the matter," said Tabby, her tone implying much, and Joshua's hand retreated. She watched him, hoping for any sign that he wished to do his duty, but he dug into his soup as though she hadn't spoken.

A knock broke the silence, and Tabby looked to Joshua, but he continued to eat. Sighing, Tabby stood and walked to the door to find the Kingsley's coachman on her doorstep.

"Evening, ma'am," he said with a nod. "I've been sent to fetch you. Mrs. Kingsley's had another scare, and they were hoping you'd take a look at her since the physician is unavailable."

"Of course, one moment," she said, and he gave her a nod before returning to the horses.

Tabby moved to fetch her bonnet and spencer but halted at the somber look on Joshua's face.

"Do you have to leave?" he asked.

"You've never minded my absence before," she said. Perhaps she wasn't entirely opposed to needling him tonight.

"Perhaps I've never showed it, but that does not mean I haven't minded." His gaze fell to the floor before he returned to his meal. The dejection in his posture pricked Tabby's conscience. Heaven knows, she had every right to be haughty and cold, but being openly hostile brought her no peace. Drawing near, she touched his shoulder, drawing his eyes to hers.

"Mrs. Kingsley is a good woman, and if I can bring her a bit of comfort, then I feel I should go," said Tabby. "But Phillip..."

When she turned her attention to her son, she found him asleep, his head resting on the table.

"The poor mite is exhausted," said Tabby, walking over to crouch beside him. She ran her hand through his hair, but Phillip did not stir. "I hate to wake him."

"Then leave him be," said Joshua, turning his attention to his dinner once again.

Tabby nibbled her lip. It made sense to leave him home, but she hesitated.

"I can be trusted to watch over my own son, Tabby," said

Joshua. He did not look at her, but his whole body tightened.

"Can you?" Tabby replied, unable to stop the words from coming.

Joshua's eyes narrowed, and he nodded towards the door.

Tabby stroked Phillip's head, worrying for a brief moment that she was making a mistake, but no matter how disjointed things may lay between her and her husband, Tabby did not believe Joshua would abandon their son. And as there were no spirits in the house, Joshua would remain sober while she was gone, so there was no reason to worry.

Besides, Mina needed her. Tabby could not bear the thought of abandoning her at such a moment.

Placing a kiss on Phillip's head, Tabby fetched her things and hurried out the door.

...

Steeling herself for what was to come, Tabby burst into the sitting room and found nothing of what she had expected. At least, not in its entirety. The first surprise was seeing Captain Ashbrook scrambling to his feet; her steps faltered for a brief moment before Tabby forced her attention away from him, though she could not stop her heart from stuttering. The second was that Mina looked more put-upon than overwrought.

"Mrs. Russell," said Mr. Kingsley, standing, though he would not move from his wife's side. "Thank goodness you have come."

Mina sighed, shifting on the couch, and mouthed "my apologies" to Tabby.

The captain stepped towards her, ushering Tabby to Mina's side.

"What is the matter?" she asked.

"A bit of discomfort," said Mina. "That is all."

"It looked a bit more than discomfortable," Mr. Kingsley

insisted. "You were doubled over."

"How do you feel now?" asked Tabby.

"Perfect. They walked in right as the pain struck, but it went away mere seconds later, as you said it would, and there have been no signs of trouble since."

Tabby came to sit on the sofa before Mina, unsure of what to say or do. The lady looked out of sorts, but no more than a woman in her condition would be, and far more comfortable than Tabby felt at Captain Ashbrook taking the seat beside her.

"And the babe?" asked Tabby.

"As active as he ever is," she replied as her husband returned to his seat beside her.

"She," corrected Mr. Kingsley, lacing Mina's arm through his, his other hand resting on hers.

"You are going to feel quite foolish when the day arrives and you are greeted with a son," said Mina.

Mr. Kingsley beamed, moving his hand to lay on the swell where their child rested, and Mina's hand joined his. For a brief moment, the two of them sat together as though she and Captain Ashbrook were not there. It was such a small thing, an innocent scene that many a couple shared together, yet the sight of it brought a deep longing that threatened to swallow Tabby whole.

She did not fault Mina for her happiness. On the contrary, it gladdened her heart to see the lady find it, but it brought memories Tabby preferred left undisturbed.

Disappointment. That is what Tabby remembered most. The unfulfilled hope of sharing such a scene with Joshua. He had been as pleased as any father at the announcement, but it was nothing to compare to Mr. Kingsley's tender joy.

And then there was the horrific moment when that bright future had been ripped from them. There were no comforting looks or words. Only more of her joy stolen away when Joshua reached for a bottle instead of her.

Tabby gave herself a mental shake, forcing such thoughts from her head. No wallowing. No dreaming of things that could not be. It did no good.

Mr. Kingsley smiled and whispered something to his wife. It was not a particularly overt display of affection, but the intimacy with which they spoke and gazed at each other made Tabby blush and avert her own gaze to give them some privacy. Her eyes caught Captain Ashbrook's, who looked equally uncomfortable and yet amused at the display. For a quick second, Tabby was swept into a silent moment with the gentleman, their eyes shining and cheeks pinking.

But then Tabby remembered that such moments were not for the pair of them, and she turned away.

"If the babe is moving and there have been no more pains, then there is little to fret about," said Tabby.

"Are you certain?" asked Mr. Kingsley. "Perhaps she has been doing too much of late. If the babe were to come too early—"

Mina's eyes widened, and Tabby interjected, "Such pains often plague expectant mothers. As long as it is not happening on a regular basis or getting worse, it is nothing out of the ordinary."

"Calm yourself, Simon," said Mina, patting his hand. "We are fine."

"Perhaps you need some rest?" asked Mr. Kingsley. "Or are you hungry? Would you like some tea and cakes?"

Mina looked at Tabby, sending her a silent plea.

"You are right, Mr. Kingsley," said Tabby, giving Mina a secret wink. "A little rest will set her to rights again, so perhaps it would be best if you two give her some time alone. I promise to watch over her."

Tabby stood, forcing the gentlemen to their feet, and she began herding the nervous father-to-be out the door.

"But I should be here with her," said Mr. Kingsley, but Captain Ashbrook interjected.

"I am positive Mrs. Russell knows what to do," he said, sending Tabby a conspiratorial look. "A little peace and quiet will do Mina a world of good. Besides, I would love to finish our conversation."

His tone held too much significance to be ignored, even if Tabby did not understand the underlying meaning. For a moment, her eyes connected with his, and in it, she could see more than he likely meant to share. There had been moments when she had wondered where Captain Ashbrook's feelings lay, but there was no mistaking the depth of his regard in that moment.

Mr. Kingsley gave a mild protest, but in the end, he stood in the hall with Captain Ashbrook, giving Tabby strict instructions to send word if Mina needed him. Captain Ashbrook's eyes sparkled with mirth as he led his brother-in-law away.

Shutting the doors, Tabby stared at the wood. Captain Ashbrook had feelings for her. Tabby would not allow herself to think in terms of love, but she knew he felt something for her that was significant enough to warm her heart and sicken her stomach. The look in his eye was exactly what a woman hoped to see. But he was not her husband.

Tears came to her eyes as she pictured that lovely gentleman. However unknowingly, she had raised his hopes, and now, she would be forced to crush them. Closing her eyes, Tabby steeled herself for what needed to be done.

"Oh, you are a dear," said Mina with a sigh as Tabby joined her on the sofa. "Simon is being so sweet, but I was feeling a bit overwhelmed with his hovering."

"You seem rather calm," said Tabby, forcing the despair from her voice. "I expected to find you both in a dither."

Mina smiled, waving Tabby's worry away before resting her hands on her stomach. "We have fallen into a pattern—an unspoken agreement, of sorts. Only one of us is allowed to worry at a time. As long as one of us keeps a clear head, things never go too askew, and today is Simon's day for fretting. I am certain in a day or two, it will be me falling to pieces and him holding me together, but for today, I am at peace with it all."

Tabby nodded, her thoughts far from Mina's words.

"Thank you for rescuing me," said Mina. "I do love Simon, but I fear I do not have the energy today to handle his fretting.

I know he means well, but neither he nor my dear brother would listen to a word I said. I apologize for them dragging you here on your evening off. I am certain you would rather spend it with your dear little Phillip."

Again, Tabby nodded, swallowing and turning her eyes away to hide her tears. Blinking, she forced her heart to calm.

"I am afraid I have some rather sudden news," said Tabby without preamble. Perhaps she could have thought of a kinder way to phrase this, but in her present state, it was difficult enough to form the necessary words. "But I must give my notice."

Mina straightened, her face paling. "Notice?"

Tabby swallowed and forged ahead. She had money enough to pay next month's rent and could work as a washerwoman to make ends meet until she found another position. Though Tabby hated leaving the financial security behind, she had to before the situation got any worse. Tabby would find some other way to provide for Phillip.

"Yes," said Tabby, unsure of what more to say. The platitudes filling her head were nothing more than lies she could not utter.

"But I don't understand," said Mina, leaning forward. "Graham...but he..." The lady straightened again, and something in her eyes shifted. "Of course, Graham is getting better, and he shan't need assistance for much longer. While we were awaiting your arrival, we spoke about it, and I thought it a splendid idea if you were to become my companion. With the baby coming, I shall need some assistance with matters of the estate that Mrs. Witmore is unable to attend to. You could serve as my steward, so to speak—"

Tabby raised her hand, cutting off Mina. "I appreciate your generous offer, but I must decline. It is best for me to leave Avebury Park altogether."

"Have you two quarrelled?" she asked. "I am certain that Graham—"

"Graham—Captain Ashbrook," Tabby corrected herself, "is

not the problem." She rubbed her head. "Yes, he is, but not in the way you think. He is a good man..." But Tabby could not continue down that path. Tears blurred her vision. Biting her lips, Tabby turned her gaze towards anything other than Mina's pleading eyes.

The sofa shifted, and Mina moved to sit beside Tabby, taking her hand in hers. "Please, tell me what is the matter. I know that something is troubling you, and it pains me to see it. Perhaps there is something I might do to help."

Tabby shook her head, clinging to Mina's hands as though they were a lifeline. "There is nothing to be done to resolve this in a happy fashion."

Shaking her head, Tabby avoided looking at Mina. Tears rolled down her cheeks, and Tabby knew that as much as she wished to keep her shame buried, this good lady deserved the truth.

"I am married," said Tabby, meeting Mina's eyes once more.

Mina froze as though the world had paused. "'Am,' as in presently? As in not widowed?"

Tabby's chin quivered as she nodded. With little prompting, Tabby exposed the entire tale to Mina. From the moment she met Joshua to the present, she poured out her heart, aches and all. With each word, more came with it, pulling the truth from her—even the bits she had not planned to reveal. Mina sat quietly and absorbed it all. The minutes ticked away, but Tabby had no real sense of its passage as she sat there, unraveling her story. Mina drew her arm around Tabby's shoulder, holding her together when she felt like falling apart.

"I never meant to mislead anyone," said Tabby, turning to catch Mina's eye. Hoping her gaze expressed the utter earnestness in her heart, she pleaded with Mina. "I swear I never said I was widowed, and I had no idea that you all believed differently until this afternoon."

"Of course not," said Mina. "We all made assumptions."

"And you did not guess that my husband was a good-for-nothing whose selfishness drove me to seek employment rather than fulfilling his duty himself?" asked Tabby. Though the question was not particularly humorous, there was something about it and the situation that drew a chuckle from her, though it bordered more on hysterical than humorous.

Mina kept an arm around Tabby, but her free hand rose to her temple, rubbing it. "Oh, you poor thing. You have not had an easy time of it, have you?"

"And as much as I would love to stay, I cannot," said Tabby. "I sent out inquiries about another position, but it is clear that Captain Ashbrook..." She swallowed past the lump in her throat. "That he is developing feelings for me."

"There is no developing, Tabby," whispered Mina, closing her eyes and shaking her head. "He is in love with you. Just before you arrived, he was speaking of his plans to marry you."

Tabby's stomach felt as though someone had dropped a lead weight into it, and she covered her mouth with her hands. She could picture it. See it all in vivid detail. That quirk of a smile of his on his lips. The sparkle in his eyes. But more than that, Tabby saw it all vanish when he discovered the truth of her situation.

She would give anything to undo the past, to erase it all so that he would not be crushed by this. If only she had been more vocal about her husband. If only she had been more forthright. If only she had never come to Avebury Park. But even as she wished it, pain pricked her soul at the thought of never having met this incredible man. And buried under all that self-loathing, there was the barest hint of delight at the knowledge that such a gentleman loved her.

Nausea wafted through her, churning the few bites of dinner she'd eaten. How could she possibly feel that? How depraved was she to have caused so much pain, yet be happy to know that his feelings ran so deep?

Tears built in Tabby's eyes until she was blinded by them. Arms folded around her, and Tabby fell into Mina's embrace.

She tried to fight the sobs, but it was no use. Her life was nothing but disappointment. Nothing but the wreckage of what it should be. And it was all her fault. Her fault for marrying Joshua. Her fault for taking this position. Her fault for becoming so familiar with Graham.

Mina held her as she cried, and Tabby welcomed the support. It had been so long since anyone in her life had been there to hold her up that Tabby did not care that she was making a spectacle of herself. She mourned the broken dreams that filled her life.

It took many long minutes before Tabby was able to rein in her emotions enough to speak. Leaning away from Mina, Tabby wiped at her eyes.

"It is all my fault," said Tabby.

Mina shook her head. "No, it isn't."

Tabby bit her lip. "It was my choices that led me here and hurt so many others in the process."

Squeezing Tabby's hand, Mina held her gaze. "There are too many people who have made wrong decisions in this scenario for you to shoulder all the blame, Tabby. So, do not try to do so. If your husband had not forced you into this situation, if Graham had not been so stubborn about returning to sea and forced us to hire you, or if any one of us had bothered to ask you directly rather than making assumptions, things would be different."

Mina paused for a moment, her lips pursing. "Though, I will say that your husband bears the largest portion of guilt. For goodness' sake! How do you stand it?"

Tabby sniffled, her eyelids drooping. "You suppose I have a choice, but I gave it up the moment I married him, and now I am bound to him for the rest of our lives. If I were to leave him, I would have to leave Phillip, and I would never do that. Whatever has passed between my husband and me, I assure you he cares for his son and will not let him go, and the law is on his side."

"Of course," said Mina. "But there must be a way around it.

Something I might do to help you, for your husband has proved that he cannot be trusted."

"There is nothing—" began Tabby, but Mina straightened.

"Rosewood Cottage," she said. "It's a small enough property that most do not realize I own, and it is in a tiny village in Herefordshire called Farrow. You could stay there as long as you need. Anything to keep you from having to live with that man—"

Both ladies jumped when the door swung open.

"Dearest, what is the matter? We were passing by, and you sounded agitated," said Mr. Kingsley.

Tabby swiped at her face, turning away from the intruders as her heart thumped at the sound of Captain Ashbrook.

"Mrs. Russell, are you unwell?" he asked, drawing up beside her, but Tabby could not meet his eyes.

Standing, Tabby stepped away from Mina and her brother, turning to the door. "I'm afraid I must be going," she said. Tabby was unsure of when or how to tell him the truth, and though every part of her heart and soul shuddered at the thought of it, she knew she must. And soon.

"What is the matter?" asked Captain Ashbrook.

Mina shifted, and her husband helped her to her feet. "Graham, please leave it be," she said.

But he would not be deterred. Tabby felt him move closer, though she did not look up from the floor. Her body tensed as his feet came into view, stopping before her.

"Please," he said, lowering his voice to a hush. "Tell me what is troubling you."

Tabby cheeks burned, her throat tightening, and she knew she must do this. For both their sakes, she had to be direct. Meeting his eyes, Tabby fought back the tremors.

"I appreciate your concern, Captain Ashbrook," she said. She had to be strong, though she nearly lost her nerve when she cast a quick glance at Mina. The lady's face was ashen, her eyes red. "But I must get home. Phillip and my husband are waiting for me," she said, her voice cracking.

Those little words cast a spell over the room, holding them in place as they silently stared at Tabby.

"Husband?" asked Mr. Kingsley, but Mina hushed him.

Captain Ashbrook did not move. His eyes were locked with hers, and Tabby was swallowed up in them.

"You are not a widow?" His question came out as a murmur, little more than a whisper. Captain Ashbrook swallowed, his jaw tightening, though his gaze did not waver.

Tabby shook her head, for she could not form words. Captain Ashbrook turned away, his eyes blinking in rapid succession. During their months together, Tabby had seen the captain suffer through surgery, fevers, and a myriad of losses that had brought the poor gentleman low, but in that one, brief look, Tabby saw a pain burning in his gaze that was far brighter than all that combined.

Reaching forward, Tabby grabbed his sleeve.

"I am sorry," she breathed. "I did not...I cannot..."

He stared at where her hand rested, his lips twitching. They both paused there for a moment before Captain Ashbrook pulled away, striding to the door. Holding her hands to her mouth, Tabby watched him retreat. Her lungs jerked, but she stifled it, knowing that it would do neither of them any good for her to break, but when the door clanged shut behind him, there was no strength left in her limbs.

Mina's arms came around Tabby, and for the second time that day, she allowed herself to be held and to mourn what could not be.

Chapter 26

The carriage pulled away from Avebury Park, rocking as it traveled along the gravel drive. The strain of the day had drained her, leaving Tabby nothing more than a husk. She had no more tears or regrets. There was not enough of her soul left to feel such things. It was silly for her to return home when she was expected back at her post shortly, but Tabby needed to ground herself in reality. She needed a few moments with her true family. With Phillip.

Looking out the window, Tabby saw the pathway leading to Gladwell House. The house was obscured by the trees and garden, but she saw a glimmer of candlelight coming from Captain Ashbrook's room. Turning away from it, Tabby covered her face. What had she done? Unintentional or not, she had crushed the heart of a good man, destroying her own in the process.

Taking a deep breath, she straightened her spine and dropped her hands. This needed to stop. Tabby could not do this anymore. Her guilt may not be an easy thing to wave away, but Tabby knew she needed to let go of the rest of it. There was no future for her and Captain Ashbrook.

Their cottage lay ahead, and Tabby felt like leaping from the carriage and running the rest of the way on foot. Hardly waiting for it to stop, she threw open the door and hurried into her home. It was dark inside, with only the wavering light from the hearth illuminating the single room. Beside it, Joshua was slumped over in his chair, fast asleep.

Tabby sighed. This was not the reception she needed, but standing there, staring at her husband, Tabby found herself thinking over the years. With his face relaxed, Joshua almost looked like the man she'd married, though wrinkles framed his eyes and lips.

Touching his shoulder, she nudged him awake.

Bleary eyes opened to meet hers. "You've returned," he said, scrubbing at his face, and Tabby couldn't help remembering a time when seeing each other had warranted more than a perfunctory statement.

"How is Phillip?" she asked.

"Perfectly fine," he said, scratching at his head. "I put him to bed after you left, and he hasn't stirred since."

Having not checked the time, Tabby had no idea how late it truly was, but she was surprised to find that Phillip had been sleeping the entire time. The poor thing must have been tuckered out from all the excitement of the day.

Turning away from Joshua, she climbed the stairs to the loft and crawled up next to Phillip. There was barely enough candlelight to see his little face; his lips were puckered together, his brow furrowed. The sight of him was enough to ease a bit of the burden weighing down her heart. He was so sweet and precious to her that Tabby was hard-pressed to regret her life with Joshua. Though his father left much to be desired, Phillip was about the most perfect child that had ever graced the earth, and Tabby would never wish him undone.

Leaning forward, Tabby placed a kiss on his forehead but jerked away when her lips met fevered skin. Tabby pressed her hands to his cheeks and forehead, and he was ablaze. The blanket tucked around him was damp with sweat, and pulling it away, Tabby found Phillip's clothing drenched.

"Joshua!"

At the urgency in her voice, he came running. "What?"

"Phillip is burning up," she said. "How long has he been like this? Bring me a clean nightshirt."

"I have no idea," he said as he fetched it.

"Did you look in on him?" she asked, stripping off Phillip's clothing, but as she did so, his little limbs began to shake. Speaking soft promises to her little man, she moved as quickly as she dared to get him into clean clothes, though it did little good as his nightshirt was quickly wetting against his skin.

"Did you?" she prompted, shooting a glance at Joshua.

He shrugged. "He was asleep, and I didn't want to disturb him. He was coughing a bit here and there, but nothing to worry about. It's naught but a little cold. "

"Coughing?" asked Tabby, changing out Phillip's sopping blanket for hers. Reaching over into the corner where Phillip's soldier had been abandoned, she stood it next to him; perhaps he would sleep better with the toy guarding over him.

Joshua nodded but offered nothing more.

"You must fetch the physician," said Tabby.

"It is nothing but a trifling cold, and we do not have the funds to fetch anyone."

Tabby shook her head, smoothing the blankets and checking his temperature, though she knew it was silly to think it had altered in mere seconds. "The servants have all been talking about a bout of influenza in the village, and it is no trifling thing. There have been a few deaths already." The word choked Tabby, and Joshua's face fell.

Getting to her feet, she pushed past her husband, hurrying to where her reticule hung beside the door. Emptying the coins into her hand, she counted them out. They were far from enough to pay for a physician.

"Take this," she said, hurrying to Joshua and shoving the coins into his hands. "You must fetch the apothecary. He should be able to do something."

Joshua stared at the money, and Tabby closed his fingers around it. "I am trusting you, Joshua," she said, pulling his eyes to hers and putting all the fierceness she could muster into them. "I would go myself, but I must stay with Phillip. Please do this."

"You think I cannot be trusted to fetch help for my son?" Joshua's hand clenched the coins, a muscle in his cheek twitching.

"You have drunk away the money intended to feed your son, so do not act affronted, Joshua Russell," said Tabby.

His gaze fell away, and in the firelight it looked as though he were blushing.

Swallowing, he whispered, "I never meant to do that. I know you don't believe me, but I have to say it."

"Then prove it. Fetch us the help we need."

Nodding, Joshua moved towards the door but stopped, climbing into the loft to give Phillip a kiss goodbye before hurrying off into the night. Sending out a silent prayer, Tabby hoped she had done the right thing.

...

Married. His Tabby was married. The words taunted Graham as he paced his bedchamber. With his cane and limp, it was an uneasy movement, but his mind would not allow him to sit still. Married.

Graham's eyes ached, and the feel of his lids closing on them brought a combination of pain and relief. His body begged him to sleep, but his mind could not rest. Tabby was gone. Out of his reach. Yet again, the life he wanted was ripped from him.

Dropping onto his bed, Graham rubbed his face. Pinching the bridge of his nose, he lowered his head. As much as he wanted to blame someone—anyone—for the way his heart twisted in his chest, Graham knew the guilt lay with his own soppy self and his assumptions. His lips trembled, and he fought to keep his breathing steady. His Tabby.

It was hard enough knowing they could not be together, but Graham could not accept that she was still bound to the man he'd despised for so long. The man who had ruined her fortunes and forced her into service. The man whose temper and boorish behavior had his boy cowering at a raised voice. Thinking back on every horrid thing he had learned about Mr. Russell made the pain all the more acute.

With a growl, he surged to his feet. Laying hold of the first thing he saw, Graham hurled the teacup against the wall with a string of words he had not used in a long while. Not caring if he woke everyone within a five mile radius, he let loose his anger. And yet, he did not feel any better. If possible, it made him feel worse, for Tabby's voice came into his head, teasing him for such childish behavior, and he could feel the tweak of his ear to remind him to watch his language.

Not that it mattered anymore. Tabby would never be his. So why bother?

And yet, even as he thought it, shame filled Graham. He had not thought he could reach deeper depths of despair, yet here he was. Whether or not Tabby was part of his life, did he wish to return to that sour, crass person?

Glancing over to the window, Graham noticed the growing sunlight. He could not believe it was morning already. The night had passed quickly as he vacillated between anger, disbelief, and sorrow. Scrubbing his face, Graham yawned, his body sagging beneath his exhaustion. Hours of thinking, yet he had no clear answers or comfort, and Graham suspected it would be a long time before he found either.

Below him, he heard the servants stirring. Only yesterday, it had been Tabby bustling around, and the sound had pulled him from bed far earlier than was natural for him so that they might spend more time together. But Graham knew it would not be Tabby downstairs. After what had passed between them, Mina would certainly move her to Avebury Park.

That thought gave Graham a start. Tabby would not be sacked, but what would happen to the lady? It would do no good for them to be under the same roof, and even if Mina moved ahead with making Tabby her companion, it would keep her in regular contact with him. Avoiding Tabby would be impossible.

Tabby would be forced to leave.

That should not bother him, for Tabby was not his to protect and care for, though Graham didn't know who he was trying to convince with such a ludicrous thought. Regardless of whether Tabby could be his, he loved the lady. His feelings were not her fault, and the thought of her losing her position sent a stab of guilt slicing through him. Tabby already had a good-for-nothing husband, and Graham would not add to her burdens.

Standing, Graham resumed his pacing. With his body on the mend, there was no reason he had to stay at Avebury Park. Surely, he would come to visit his sister, but being there once or twice a year should not cause undue distress to Tabby—Mrs. Russell. Graham knew it would likely cause all sorts of distress to his heart, but for her sake, he would manage it. Propriety wouldn't allow him to do more for the lady, but Graham could do that.

However, he had no idea where he would go. He could not move forward with his plan to purchase a home. Not now. Just the thought of moving into the place he had hoped to live with Tabby and Phillip pained him. No, perhaps there was another option. Perhaps he should look into bachelor lodgings like Ambrose had in London. That filthy, blighted city.

But the details did not matter at the moment. What mattered was for Tabby to know her future at Avebury Park was secure. As much as it pained him to think of facing her again, Graham needed to tell her she was free to stay. Needed to explain it. Needed for her to understand.

For it was the only thing he could do for her.

...

Wracking coughs shook Phillip, and Tabby stroked his head as he fought through it. With each wheezing breath, Tabby's own felt stifled in her lungs. Rocking him side to side, Tabby hummed a tune, hoping it would calm him.

"Shhh..." He felt so tiny in her arms, so thin, so frail. Leaning her head down, she pressed another kiss to his scorching forehead.

"Hold on, sweetheart," she said. "Papa is getting you some medicine."

Phillip's eyes opened, but there was nothing coherent in them. Sliding closed again, he took a rattling breath, the air tripping and catching.

Hours. Without a clock, Tabby could not know for certain, but she felt them pass as she sat there with her sweet little boy fighting for each breath. Through the curtains, she could see the first rays of sunshine stretching across the world, yet Joshua had not returned.

Tabby had made many mistakes in her life, but for Phillip's sake, she hoped she had not misplaced her trust in her husband. Whatever his faults, Joshua loved his son. Tabby clung to that belief.

There was nothing for her to do. No balm or medicine she could give Phillip, only the wordless tune she hummed as she cradled him in her arms. He may not know what was happening, but Tabby wanted to make sure that Phillip knew his mama was watching over him. That he wasn't alone.

"Mama loves you so," she whispered between his breaths. "Yes, she does. So very much."

Never in her life had she felt so helpless. So useless. There was nothing for her to do. Nothing she could do. There was no more money for her to lure help to her home, and even if there were, Tabby could not abandon Phillip to fetch someone. Not while he fought for each breath.

With every passing minute, it grew worse, and Tabby sat there rocking and singing, praying that each noise outside the cottage was Joshua. But it never was.

And then the silence stretched out. A long, deathly stillness. No wheezing. No coughing. Nothing.

Tabby shifted Phillip upright, laying him over her shoulder to thump on his back.

"Breathe, darling," she said, but he lay unmoving in her arms.

Her hand struck his back harder, hoping it might help. That somehow it might clear his lungs. Draw in a breath. Anything. For there was nothing else she could do,

"Breathe," she said, her hands shaking. "Please breathe."

Tears filled her eyes as the silent seconds wore on.

"Breathe for Mama, Phillip!" she begged while sending out a litany of prayers for even the tiniest of movements from her son.

"Please…" she said, closing her eyes. She could not face this. Not this. Not her Phillip.

A crackle of sound came from his lungs, and Tabby's eyes shot open. Pounding on his back, she crooned to him. Phillip coughed as though his lungs were ripping apart, but he took a great sucking breath, and Tabby felt as though she could breathe once more.

"Oh, my little man, thank you," she whispered as she rocked him.

On and on, Tabby hummed and clutched Phillip, nursing him through each agonizing breath, praying that it was not his last. And that someone would come to help her.

Chapter 27

G raham's eyes scoured the roadside for any sign of Tabby as the carriage rumbled towards her home. She should have returned to the Park hours ago, yet there was no sign of her. Though Mina and Simon cautioned him, Graham could not stop himself from calling a carriage. If Tabby had not sent word, there must be something wrong.

"We're here, sir," said the coachman as the horses pulled to a stop in front of a series of cottages that were more hovels than homes. Sickness twisted his stomach as he looked at the dilapidated wreck that housed Tabby and Phillip. Graham's cramped berth as a midshipman had been more inviting than this.

Not allowing himself to dwell on it a moment longer, Graham alighted from the carriage and knocked on the front door. Scant moments later, it flew open, and Tabby stood there, eyes wide and red.

"What is the matter?" asked Graham, staring at her tangled mess of hair and the clear streaks of tears on her cheeks.

"Phillip is sick," she said, and Graham heard a rasping cough inside the cottage that was so strong it made his own lungs hurt. "Joshua went for the apothecary, but he has not returned, and I don't know what to do." Her words grew frantic, her breath hitching with each one.

Another barking cough came from the loft, and Tabby hurried away and up the stairs. Graham followed after her, though his ruined leg could not handle the steep steps. Holding onto a rung, he watched Tabby tend to Phillip, lifting the limp child and rubbing his back. Her eyes met his, tears falling down her cheeks, and Graham wanted nothing more than to bundle them up and take them home, where they would be watched over and cared for. But Graham knew he could not do that.

"I'll fetch the physician," said Graham.

"We cannot afford him," whispered Tabby, clutching her son.

But Graham refused to acknowledge her words as he hobbled out the door. If there was any chance that medicine could heal Phillip, Graham would make certain he got it. Climbing into the carriage, he bellowed his directions to the coachman.

...

Holding Phillip in her arms, Tabby had no room in her mind to think of anything else. She had not thought as to why Captain Ashbrook had appeared on her doorstep, but she was grateful for any help. And she had no doubts that he would return with it in all haste.

But the knock on the door came far speedier than she had anticipated. It was as though it had been only minutes since he left, yet there was Dr. Clarke hurrying through her home and up the stairs to Phillip. Moving away, Tabby stood at the bottom of the steps to give the physician all the space he needed.

"How long has he been like this?" he asked while pulling open his medical bag.

"He was feeling tired yesterday, but I thought nothing of it," said Tabby, wringing her hands. "I had to leave last night for a few hours, and when I returned he was burning up."

Taking a deep breath, Tabby tried to calm herself as she recounted the events of the evening, but tears poured down her cheeks as she described the details. The physician asked a few more questions, and someone squeezed her fingers. Looking down, Tabby was shocked to see herself clasping Captain Ashbrook's hand. She had no idea when she had reached for him, but she allowed herself a brief moment of comfort before she released him.

His eyes glimmered as he held her gaze. "It'll be all right," he whispered.

"Will it?" asked Tabby, too aware that nothing in her life was all right at the moment.

Motioning her to the table, Captain Ashbrook opened the cupboard door. For a brief moment the captain's control slipped, and Tabby saw the dark glower he gave the near empty pantry. But then it was gone, hidden beneath a calm facade as he pulled out a loaf of bread and brick of cheese. With easy movements, he sliced some up and placed it on the table before her.

"You need to eat something," he prompted when she stared at it. "It won't do either of you any good if you faint because you neglect yourself."

"Thank you," she whispered.

Captain Ashbrook reached over and gave her hand another quick squeeze, his eyes telling her more than any words he might speak. The strength of it was terrifying and elating all at once, and everything that Tabby could've ever wished to see.

Picking up the bread, she bit into the tasteless food, watching as he readied a kettle on the hearth. The minutes ticked by as Captain Ashbrook forced food and drink upon her. Listening to the physician's movements, Tabby felt her heart breaking. She could not lose her son. Could not. He had to get better. Tabby sent out a silent prayer, begging for any sort of divine intervention.

Eventually, Dr. Clarke came down and set his bag on the table. "It is influenza," he said, fiddling with the clasp. "And a serious case at that since it has traveled into his lungs. However, he is a strong lad with a good constitution, and it looks as though he made it through the worst of it, so I am optimistic that he will pull through. The medicine I gave him should ease his cough and let him rest a bit."

Retrieving a few small bottles, Dr. Clarke gave Tabby instructions on how to administer each tonic and powder. Pausing, he studied her a moment and then pulled out pencil and paper to write down the detailed instructions.

"You look ready to collapse yourself, Mrs. Russell," he said, handing it to her. "You must rest, or you will fall ill, too. There is not much more I can do here, though you can send for me if—"

The front door swung open, and Joshua staggered into the room, bumping into Dr. Clarke before collapsing onto a chair. Tabby stared at him for a brief moment before ushering the physician out of the room with all the proper gratitude and goodbyes. Through design or accident, Tabby did not know, but Joshua did not speak until the door was firmly shut behind Dr. Clarke.

"What is he doing here?" he asked, glaring at Captain Ashbrook.

Seeing his bloodshot eyes and hearing his slurred words, Tabby's heart pounded in her chest. "He is doing what you—Phillip's father—wouldn't do!"

Joshua's jaw slackened, his eyes widening. "I tried, Tabby! I went to the apothecary's house and his shop, but he wasn't around. I waited for hours out in the dark and cold, but he never returned."

Tabby loomed over him, her hands shaking. "Then where is the money I gave you? The money that we need for food and medicine for your son?"

Joshua's eyes drifted and his jaw tensed, and she recognized the signs of falsehoods being strung together. "I was worried about the boy. I couldn't stand the waiting and needed something to ease my mind."

Tabby banged her fist against the table, making Joshua jump. "Get out. Now!" she barked.

"This is my house!"

"And I have a child to nurse," she said, grabbing the medicines and marching to the door to yank it open for him.

"Are you truly upset about a few drinks?" he asked. "This is ridiculous, Tabby!"

"Ridiculous?" Tabby fairly hissed the words, and she stomped to his side, leaning over until her nose nearly touched his. "Phillip stopped breathing. I held him in my arms as he struggled to stay alive. Do you know what that is like? Holding your dying child and being unable to do anything about it? Of course you don't because you were out drinking away the money for his medicine. Phillip was fighting for his life while you were getting drunk."

Joshua gaped at her, his eyes showing the first honest bit of concern and guilt she'd seen in many a year, but it did not matter to her in that moment. Phillip was her sole focus, and she had no more time to deal with his sniveling father.

"Now, get out!" she said, pointing to the door.

Phillip gave a wet, rattling cough, and Joshua looked to the loft, though he could not see the child from where he sat. Glancing at Tabby, he nodded and struggled to his feet, stumbling outside.

"Perhaps I should go, too," said Captain Ashbrook, and Tabby flinched. In her anger, she had forgotten the gentleman was standing there, and if she had less on her mind and more energy, she would be embarrassed, but she was too exhausted to care that he had witnessed such a scene.

Captain Ashbrook shuffled to the door, stopping for a brief moment to look at her. "Please keep us apprised of Phillip's condition," he said, his hand clutching his cane in a white knuckle grip. "And if you should need anything further, do not hesitate to ask."

Tabby held his gaze for a scant moment and saw his whole heart in his eyes. And she had not the strength to hide her own.

Not now. Standing there in silence, their souls spoke out as clearly as words, confessing the depths of their affections and speaking the words they could not give voice to. It was a look that held a world of wishes and hopes and all the agony that went with each impossibility.

"Thank you for your assistance, Captain Ashbrook," said Tabby when she finally found her voice again. "But I must attend to Phillip."

"Of course," he said with a deep bow. The remnants of her broken heart shattered at the shine of tears in his eyes. And then he stepped through the door and out of her life forever.

Tabby's eyes slid closed, her hand coming to her lips. It felt as though her heart had been torn from her chest, but there was nothing to be done. She had made her choice all those years ago, and it was no use to wallow in regrets. That had been Tabby's guiding principle throughout these unbearable years, but until now, it had been only she who had suffered the consequences of that impetuous decision to marry Joshua. Hearing Phillip's ragged breaths above and Captain Ashbrook's faltering footsteps outside, Tabby knew she was not the only one paying for her mistakes anymore.

Turning away from the door and such useless thoughts, Tabby climbed the stairs and curled up next to Phillip. Brushing her fingers across his clammy forehead, Tabby watched her little man sleep.

Graham was no stranger to helplessness. After the last year, he had become well acquainted with the feeling. Being immobile had given him a new sense of weakness that he had never known before, but standing on Tabby's doorstep, Graham knew he had never understood what it meant to be powerless. He could do nothing more for Tabby or Phillip. He could not comfort them or provide for them any more than he had already. Paying for the physician had already crossed the line of propriety. Not that Graham cared. With Phillip's life on the line, he would have done far more than merely throw aside convention.

Gritting his teeth, Graham breathed through the tightness in his chest and swallowed the lump in his throat. As Tabby often said, "There is no undoing the past." Graham only wished it were possible to ease the heartache that came from it, but time was the only remedy.

Stepping away from the cottage, Graham ambled to the carriage but halted at the sight of Tabby's husband collapsed in the ditch. Graham's heart pounded in his chest, a flash of heat consuming him as he marched over to the disgusting lump of a man. With a quick poke of his cane, Russell's eyes opened, staring up from the mud.

"You," he grumbled, struggling to get that one syllable out. The look on his face made it clear he had meant to shout it, but the man was too far gone. Rolling over, he jerked to his feet, slipping and falling on his face a few times before he got his balance.

"You are poaching my woman." This came out with more force, and Russell shook his fist at Graham before lunging. Even with his injuries, Graham easily dodged the sloppy punch, and Russell stumbled, falling onto his backside.

"I have done no such thing, you pathetic excuse for a man," said Graham, glowering at him.

"Poaching..." he mumbled. "She's mine. Not yours."

"Then act like it, Russell!" Graham growled, forcing himself to rein in the less than choice words he would rather say to the man. No matter how much he wanted to let loose those foul words, Graham held onto his control, for he would not stoop to Russell's level.

"What is wrong with you?" asked Graham, jabbing him hard enough to leave a bruise. "You have that incredible woman and child in your life, yet you treat them like garbage!"

"But I love them..." he slurred.

Graham leaned over him, his teeth grinding together as he let his unadulterated fury burn in his eyes. "Then stop treating her like a drudge. Stop wasting your money on drink and cards, and take care of your family. I am no cad and would never blacken her virtue, but I would have no compunction in doing everything in my power to provide her the life she deserves if she ever left you."

"She cannot," said Joshua. "Phillip is my boy and she's my wife. The law says they belong to me."

Graham's teeth creaked under the pressure of his jaw as he scowled. "There are ways and means, sirrah, so do not test me. If I had to spend every last farthing to make Tabby and Phillip safe from you, I would do it. If she merely hinted she wished to be free of her sniveling worm of a husband, I would beggar myself to do it."

"What?" Russell's eyes widened, his jaw slackening.

"Though I would never have to go that far," said Graham, his voice lowering until it was little more than a growl. "There are always ships in need of a crew, and with little more than a word, I could have you pressed into service on a vessel so vile that you would beg to be cast overboard and drowned in the sea."

Russell lay there in the mud, trembling, but Graham knew there was one more thing left to say. "And so help me, if you ever give your son reason to cower again, I will find you and acquaint you with true pain and fear," he said. The look in his eyes promised violent retribution, and Graham stabbed the cane at Russell's chest one final time. "Do we understand each other?"

Russell nodded, his eyes filling with tears. Turning to the carriage, Graham left the man blubbering in the mud.

Chapter 28

Something brushed Tabby's cheek, and her dreams faded. She had no idea when she had fallen asleep, but as the blackness cleared and her eyes cracked open to the hazy room, Tabby realized she must have. And that was when she saw Phillip's blue eyes staring at her.

"Darling!" she gasped, shooting upright to test his temperature. A flush of fever remained in his cheeks, but his skin was dry, which was a blessing from heaven as she had no more clean sheets or nightshirts to put him in. After two days of agonized watching and waiting, Tabby breathed a sigh of relief. Phillip was truly on the mend.

"Oh, sweetheart," she said, kissing his forehead. "You had Mama very worried."

His brow furrowed, but he gave her a faint smile. It was one of the greatest things Tabby had seen in a good long while.

"Where's Papa?" he asked, glancing around the loft.

Smoothing his blankets, Tabby smiled. "He had some important business that took him away, but I am certain he will return soon." Heaven forgive her for the lies, but there was no power on earth that would force her to tell her son the truth: Tabby had no idea where Joshua was.

"Let me get you something to eat," she said.

"Cake?" asked Phillip with a tired smile.

"No, darling. We don't have any cake, but it would not be what you should eat if we did. I have some soup," she said, making her way down the stairs. "And perhaps a little bit of bread."

"With butter?"

She paused on the final step, looking at his precious face for a brief moment. "Yes, with butter."

Bustling about the cottage, Tabby opened the cupboard. Though there was precious little in there, they had enough to make a decent soup. Pulling out vegetables, Tabby laid them on the table, freezing when she spied the remnants of the food Captain Ashbrook had served her. It was such a small thing, but her heart melted at the memory. It was enough that he had saved her son by fetching a physician as quickly as he had, but he had then waited on her, caring for her in the only way he could. It was perhaps one of the dearest acts of kindness she had ever received.

Brushing away a tear and clearing a spot, Tabby went to work chopping and dicing. Phillip's breaths rattled in the background from time to time, but there was nothing desperate in the sound. He was getting better. No doubt it would be days before he returned to his usual self, but knowing that he was past danger allowed Tabby's nerves to calm. Popping bits of this and that into the pot, Tabby readied the meal, stoked the fire, and set the soup to cook, feeling a hint of normalcy in the movements.

But when she turned, she caught sight of someone through the window. At first glance, she thought him a vagrant sitting in front of the cottage. It was not a terribly unusual sight, but the way he watched her was unsettling. It wasn't until she got a good look that she realized that it was her husband beneath the grime. That moment of peace evaporated in a trice, burning up in the anger flaring in her chest.

Stepping into the loft, she checked on Phillip, grateful that her voice remained calm as she told him, "I am going outside for a moment, love." He blinked heavily and nodded before cuddling into the blankets and closing his eyes.

With a few quick steps, Tabby strode out of the cottage and towards Joshua.

"Drunk again?" she asked, forcing herself not to shout. She no longer cared if her neighbors heard, but Phillip did not need to know the extent of his father's depravity. "Your son is sick and you go gallivanting around town? Have you no shame?"

"How is Phillip?" asked Joshua, jumping to his feet.

"Don't pretend you care. You made it perfectly clear how little he matters to you."

"Tabby, I am sorry—" he began.

"Don't you dare, Joshua Russell," she said with a stomp. "Don't you dare stand there, telling me you are sorry. You do not know the meaning of that word. You use it over and over again, and it means nothing to you!"

Giving her tongue free rein, Tabby unleashed every heartache and pain she felt, listing all his sins from the first moment they had met until the present, laying it all at his feet without caring one jot about his feelings on the matter. Joshua stood before her, shoulders slumped, as she unburdened her heavy heart.

Tabby swiped at her cheeks, but tears poured down them. "He nearly died, Joshua. Died! All because you were too selfish to do what you were supposed to. If Captain Ashbrook had not arrived, we might be burying Phillip today."

Joshua sagged, his gaze falling to the ground. "I know," he whispered, his voice thick. "I am a pathetic husband and father."

Tabby stared at him as he covered his face, his shoulders shaking.

"I don't understand what happened," he said, his voice thick with tears. Swiping his nose on his sleeve, Joshua's red eyes met hers. "I went to fetch the apothecary. I swear I did, Tabby. And I waited there, like I said, but it took so long. I stood there forever, and he never came. The pub was next door, and I went in for a pint. Only one pint. I was so worried about Phillip and needed something to calm my nerves. I don't understand what happened. It was one pint and then suddenly it wasn't."

Joshua's face crumpled, and he slid to the ground, plopping down to cry in the mud. Staring at the sight, Tabby found herself wondering how she had ever fallen in love with such a man.

"I am useless, Tabby," he bawled. "I know it. I wanted to do the right thing, and I do not understand what happened. One moment it was a little drink, and the next I was stumbling drunk. And Phillip...poor little Phillip...my son..." His breaths tore up his words, coming out in jagged gasps.

"I do not deserve you, Tabby," he said, wiping at his eyes. "I know it. The moment I saw Captain Ashbrook come to your aid, I knew it. And then he said..." Joshua gulped, his brow twisting. "It does not matter what he said, but it was all true. I have been an awful husband and father. I do not deserve you and Phillip. I have ruined you both."

Tabby stared at the sniveling man, and a part of her pitied the pathetic picture he made, but she steeled her heart. Such displays had worked in the past, and Tabby would not allow herself to be taken in by it again. Turning away, she stepped towards the cottage, but Joshua grabbed her skirt.

"Please do not leave me, Tabby," he begged. "I apologize for everything I have done to you and Phillip. I know I do not deserve a second chance, but please let me try to make it right."

Tabby yanked her dress free. "This is not your second chance, Joshua. It is not your third or fourth. I have given you so many of them, and you never make it right."

Joshua climbed to his feet and grabbed her hands. "But if there is a possibility that we can make things better between us, do you truly wish to throw it away without trying?" he asked, his eyes pleading with her. "Ever since you tossed me out, I have been sitting here, hoping to talk to you. Please do not give up on us. I know I have done nothing to earn your trust—"

"You took the money intended to keep Phillip alive and

drank it away," Tabby said, fighting to keep her voice from rising. "I don't know if there is enough mercy in the world to forgive such selfishness!"

"Please, Tabby," he begged. "I know I have been a worthless excuse for a man, but you made me a good one once. You can do it again."

Tabby groaned, pulling her hands out of his grip. "So, it is *my* responsibility to make you better? I cannot make you anything, Joshua. If you wish to change, you must do so yourself. No one can do it for you."

His expression crumpled again, and he hung his head. "I know that it is not up to you, and I know I have not done my share, but I know that I cannot do it without you, either. I need you, Tabby. I need your strength and conviction. With you at my side, it feels possible to exorcise these demons from my life," he said, stepping closer and reaching for her hands once more.

Tabby stared at their entwined fingers, feeling lost and confused. She had heard such words from him before, and every time a part of her hoped that he would mean it—that this time, his desire to change would last.

"I despise the man I have become," he said, his Adam's apple bobbing. "I have sat here and thought about my life, and there is not a single aspect of it that I like. What sort of man behaves the way I have? What sort of husband forces his wife into such a position? I want to start anew. Begin again. Start over and have a proper family with you and Phillip."

"Why?" she asked. "What does it matter to you?"

"Because I love you both," he said, his chin trembling. "I know I have done an awful job of showing it, but I do. I have sat here and thought about everything, and I give you my word of honor that I am going to change. I swear never to touch a drop of alcohol again."

Tabby stepped away, freeing her hands. "I have heard such things before, Joshua. You beg my forgiveness, promise to stay sober, yet it always ends with you deep in a bottle."

But Joshua stepped closer, his eyes shining with an earnestness that she had not seen since their courtship.

"I have not been the man you deserve, Tabby," he said, grabbing for her hands again and clutching them to his chest. "I know that. I wish I could change the past, but all I can do is offer my word—though I know it means little to you—that I shall do better. I cannot begin to tell you how much it hurts me to know that in my family's darkest moment, it was not I who mended things. I will not allow that to happen again."

He swallowed, his jaw tensing. "I want us to be a family. A proper family. While you were tending Phillip, I wrote to Cousin Maurice to beg him to take me on as a clerk."

"A clerk?"

Joshua nodded, his cheeks burning. "He offered me the position shortly after we sold Kelland Hall, and I turned him down, but you have suffered too much because of my pride. I am certain he will accept. We could move to London, start afresh. Things will be perfect again. Like they were when we first married."

Reaching up, Joshua played with a lock of her hair, reminding Tabby so much of when he was courting her. He wrapped it around his finger, that small smile on his lips, and it was as though the years melted away. The feeling startled Tabby, shaking her to her core. It had been so long since she had allowed herself to hope for such a thing that seeing it standing before her left her breathless. A new beginning.

If it were only empty promises, Tabby would never believe him, but for Joshua to choose of his own volition to relinquish his status as gentleman—however inapt the descriptor was for his lifestyle—and take on a lowly profession said more to Tabby than his words. For once, Joshua was truly trying because he wished to. More than any other time, this moment held a spark of possibility.

A family.

Tabby searched her heart and found little trust there for the man standing before her, but there was a glimmer of hope. If there were a true chance of recapturing the beauty and splendor that their marriage had once held, perhaps she needed to try. Phillip deserved a loving family. He deserved to live in a home where his parents loved and cherished each other.

"Can we begin again?" asked Joshua.

Her mouth went dry and her heart fluttered in her chest in a way that was entirely unpleasant. Tabby felt on the edge of a precipice, daring to jump off into the wide unknown on nothing more than the promise of a possibly reformed scoundrel.

But if it worked—if he did get better—Tabby would have everything she had dreamed of for so many years.

Swallowing past the lump, she nodded.

Joshua broke out in a grin. "Truly?"

"Yes," she squeaked.

With a triumphant shout, Joshua scooped her into his arms and spun her around, crushing her to his chest. When they stopped, his hands came up, framing her face in his strong fingers, and he leaned into her, but Tabby leaned away.

"I am willing to try again, Joshua, but I am not ready for that," she said.

Joshua nodded, his throat clenching. Loosening his grip, he gave her space, his head lowered. "Of course."

Carefully, he reached for her hand, raising it to his lips. The look in his eyes begged permission, and she did not stop him as he pressed a kiss to her hand. Stroking the spot with his thumbs, he smiled, his eyes softening. Tabby wished she felt something in return.

Chapter 29

Standing in the doorway to Mina's sitting room, Graham froze at a sound he had never thought to hear from his sister. A giggle. Mina Ashbrook was not the type of girl to giggle, but it appeared Mina Kingsley was. The sound was so foreign that Graham had not recognized it for what it was until he was at the threshold, and then he was certain that he did not want to go into that room.

And that was when the floorboard beneath him creaked.

"Hello?" she called.

He held still, but then she followed with, "Graham?" And he knew it was best to forge ahead.

"I thought I would come by for a visit," he said, striding into the room.

Mina's cheeks flushed red as she straightened, her hands smoothing her skirts and patting at her hair. Beside her, Simon sighed and leaned away from his wife to fold his arms and glower at Graham.

"What are you doing here?" she asked, her eyes avoiding Graham as she grew redder until her face could heat a pot of tea.

Standing before her, Graham looked at her with raised eyebrows. "Would you prefer I leave?"

"Of course not," she said at the same moment Simon replied, "Yes."

Mina gave her husband a stern look, though he only replied with a smile that left Graham wishing he hadn't come to Avebury Park. Flexing his fingers around his cane handle, he cleared his throat, and Mina returned her attention to Graham.

"Of course, we want you to stay," she said. "I hadn't expected you to be venturing out at present..."

She turned to Simon, who remained slumped against the couch, his face showing no hint of embarrassment, though a fair touch of frustration. "And certainly not at this exact moment," he mumbled.

Mina swatted his arm, and Simon sighed and straightened before prompting Graham to sit. Giving a quick kiss on Mina's cheek, Graham took a seat on the sofa opposite.

"Would you like something to eat? Or a cup of tea?" asked Mina.

"The cakes are especially delicious," said Simon as he smirked at his wife, drawing another flash of pink across Mina's cheeks.

"Behave," she whispered, giving her husband a stern look as she tucked a wayward lock of hair behind her ear.

Graham cleared his throat and tried to loosen the lump that had formed there. "No, thank you. I am not hungry or thirsty at present." The thought of eating such things brought a putrid turn to his stomach, followed by a stab of pain over his memories of baking with Phillip and Tabby.

Mina's hands fidgeted in her lap, and Graham watched her squeeze them until her knuckles were white. The silence in the air was of the awkward variety, but he had no idea what to say. Graham had not come to visit for any reason other than to escape the ghosts that haunted Gladwell House. He had no thoughts to offer, as the only things on his mind at present were best left unsaid.

"It is good to see you out and about. I have been worried that..." Mina halted, her gaze slipping to the side.

"I would lock myself away and revert to behaving like a brute?" asked Graham with a dry tone. Mina did not need to know how tempting that course of action had been. And still was. It was a constant struggle to keep himself from climbing into bed and hiding from the world until his body withered as surely as his soul.

Mina's right shoulder nudged upward in a half-shrug, her eyes dimming. "It is not easy to suffer such a blow, Graham. Losing the one you love can break even the strongest of souls."

Simon pulled Mina's arm through his and rested his other hand on it.

The truth of her words weighed heavy on his heart, and Graham felt that darkness stalking him, waiting for him to embrace the hopelessness of his situation. It was so much easier to surrender; the relief it promised to bring was almost too tantalizing, but Graham knew it would cost him dearly.

The first days, Graham had welcomed the despair, embracing it with his whole heart. Alone and mourning, he had locked himself away. But he could not go on like that. As much as he wanted Tabby, he did not want to be that man. The man he had been. Tabby had opened his eyes to the truth of his behavior, and there was no returning to his former ignorance.

"Mina thinks Margueritte is a terrible name for our girl, but I adore it," blurted Simon, startling Graham out of his thoughts.

And that was when Graham noticed Mina's brows drawn tight together, her lips more a grimace than a smile. It may be his heart that was broken, but hers ached alongside his.

"I have to agree with Mina," said Graham, taking the hint in Simon's eyes. "It is too close to Louisa-Margaretta."

"Then perhaps we could name her Amelia, after my mother," Simon said with a face that was too innocent to be anything other than teasing.

"Do not even jest about that, Simon Kingsley," said Mina, glaring at him. "Though I am warming to Helena."

"Truly?" said Simon with a smile. "And Frances?"

Mina scrunched her face, shaking her head. "It's a name that belongs to a dour old governess. Besides, I have told you that he will be a boy."

They went back and forth with Graham adding the odd comment. His spirits were too low to do much more than feign a smile from time to time. Speaking required too much pretense, but between his acting and Simon's distractions, they were able to coax Mina away from fretting over his broken heart at present. There was nothing to do about the situation, so it did no good for Mina to dwell on it. Graham did enough of that for them both.

But then the door opened.

"Message for you, madam," said Jennings with a bow.

Mina smiled and motioned for him to bring it, but her expression faltered when she unfolded the paper to see the signature at the bottom.

"It is from Tabby," she said, and Graham's breath caught. There had been no word since Dr. Clarke's visit, and he would not breathe easy until he knew for certain that Phillip was well. Easing forward in his seat, Graham tensed and fought to keep himself from snatching the letter from Mina's hand, watching as her eyes sped over the words. With each sentence, her face crumpled.

"Is it Phillip?" he asked, unable to wait a moment longer.

Mina's gaze jerked to his, and she shook her head. "He is awake and on the mend."

And Graham could breathe again. Leaning into the sofa, he allowed the knowledge to calm his frantic heart.

"They are leaving Bristow," said Mina. "Her husband has accepted a position in London, and they are moving there as soon as Phillip is well enough to travel."

"Then that is good news, darling," said Simon. "He is finally shouldering his responsibility."

"But I worry about her. That husband of hers is a lout, and I fear for her and Phillip." Mina's voice grew weaker with each word. She stood, and Simon tried to coax her back down, but she shook her head and made excuses about needing a moment alone before slipping out of the room.

Simon slouched onto the couch with a grunt, his head thumping against the seatback. "She has been on edge ever since Tabby told her the truth. I had finally managed to distract her from her fretting when you and that letter arrived. No offense intended, Graham, but you and Mrs. Russell have awful timing."

"I apologize that our problems have inconvenienced you," said Graham through gritted teeth.

Simon's head jerked upright to meet Graham's gaze. It took only a brief look at Graham's expression before he sighed. "My apologies. I didn't mean to be so callous."

Unable to speak, Graham simply nodded, his thoughts returning to Tabby's letter.

She and Phillip were leaving. Graham wasn't certain if he was relieved or devastated at the prospect. Perhaps if he hadn't met Joshua Russell, Graham would be able to accept it as readily as Simon, but Graham's heart froze at the thought of her being so far away from any form of support, completely at the mercy of that...Graham could not think of words strong enough to describe such a creature that was more worm than man.

Graham rubbed his thumb along the handle of his cane, his jaw tightening. He wanted nothing but the best for Tabby and her son. If her husband would finally provide that, then Graham would wish them joy, but it was impossible for him to believe Russell would change so completely. And if he regressed, Tabby would be left alone to fend for herself and Phillip. Again.

An image came unbidden into his mind. Tabby and Phillip in their own little home. Graham could do that for them. He had told her husband as much. He could tuck them away someplace where they would be safe and happy.

With him.

As soon as he thought that, a myriad of scenes played out in his mind. Sharing his life with Tabby. She did not deserve to be bound to such a contemptible man as her husband. She deserved to be cherished and loved. Graham could give that to her and so much more. Plenty of others went where their desires drove them; why couldn't he? Society was filled with those who sought for love and affection outside the bonds of marriage. Could it truly be so bad to entertain such an arrangement for the two of them?

But even as those thoughts crept into his mind, sour dread landed in his stomach, bringing with it a stronger question. Could he live like that? Make Tabby and Phillip outcasts? Bywords? Even if he could live with sinning against God and Tabby's marriage vows, Graham knew he would never forgive himself for making them pariahs. There were already rumors circulating around Bristow about their relationship, and each one pained him. Even contemplating living as pretend husband and wife was enough to twist his conscience into such knots that even the best sailor would be unable to unravel them.

No.

As much it pained him, Graham knew it was best to have distance between them. For her to leave. To never see them again. No matter how strong his resolution, there was only so much temptation one could bear. Eventually, it would override his morals, and then all three of them would suffer for it. There was nothing more he could do for them. The only thing left was to hope and pray that for once in his miserable life, Joshua Russell would act honorably.

And if for any reason Tabby needed his help, Graham would freely give it. But at a distance.

"How are you?"

Graham jerked out of his thoughts, having completely forgotten his brother-in-law sitting before him. "Pardon?"

"I suppose that answers my question," said Simon, and Graham glanced away from the sympathy in the man's eyes; he refused to lose the tenuous control he had over his emotions. "I am truly sorry for you and her, Graham. I know what it feels like to lose the woman you love, and I would not wish that on anyone."

"What?" The peculiarity of that statement was enough to grab Graham's entire attention.

Simon sighed, sitting upright to fiddle with the buttons on his waistcoat. "Mina left me once."

Graham had nothing to say to that, so he sat, silently gaping at Simon.

Clearing his throat, he continued. "It was in the first months of our marriage. I was feckless and treated her shabbily. Unintentionally, of course, but that does not lessen my crimes. My behavior gave her no choice but to leave, and I cannot describe how..." Simon's gaze grew distant, and he shook his head, as though unsure of how to word it. "...devastating it was. Though I am grateful she did it because it forced me to acknowledge how badly I was acting."

Simon drifted off into silence for a moment, his eyes dimming. "Those days when I thought I had destroyed our marriage were the worst of my life. It has been nearly six years, yet I am still plagued with the occasional nightmare that Mina is gone—either because I'd been unable to repair the damage I had caused or bungled it again and lost her once more."

He swallowed, dropping his gaze to the floor and shifting in his seat. "The point is that I know how hard it is, and I am very sorry that you have to go through it, but I hope..." Simon cleared his throat again. "I know it is hard, but please do not abandon all hope and lock yourself away again."

The muscles in Graham's jaw ached, and he forced himself to relax it. As much as it pained him to hear it stated aloud, he needed the emotional reinforcement. He would not regress to what he was. He would not.

"Are you still planning on leaving Avebury Park?"

Graham shrugged. "It makes no sense to buy a home for myself, but I do not relish the thought of living at Gladwell House indefinitely." Or at all. It held too many reminders of her.

"Mina and I would love for you to stay in the neighborhood," said Simon. "Or you could move into Avebury Park again. Now that things are settled with your health."

Graham gave a faint grunt and a nod.

"I should go check on Mina," said Simon, standing and straightening his jacket. "She is taking this turn of events quite hard, though I am not certain who she hurts for more—you or Tabby."

The next moment, Graham was alone. Dropping his head, he sighed, wishing it were easy to pick oneself up and move on. Simply make the choice and be done with it. But he knew it would be a long road before he would be able to forget the incredible woman who had healed more than his ailing body.

...

"I can do it myself, Mama," whined Phillip, reaching for the spoon in her hand.

Tabby evaded his grasp, keeping the dinner from making a mess all over their bedding. "I need you to be careful," she said.

"But I can do it."

With a sigh, Tabby handed over the spoon but kept a tight hold on the bowl, though Phillip tried to grab it. "Let me hold the bowl so that it doesn't spill."

If the past week had not been so utterly exhausting, seeing him have enough energy to pout and complain would be something to celebrate, but in her current state, Tabby had only enough strength to hold herself upright.

"Careful, Phillip," she said as he scooped up a spoonful. Droplets of broth fell onto the blankets, and Tabby sighed, accepting that she would need to wash them again. At least Phillip was strong enough that tomorrow he might be able to eat at the table.

The door below opened, and Tabby heard Joshua's footsteps approach the stairs to the loft.

"I've got it, Mama," said Phillip when she tried to adjust the bowl to catch a bit of carrot dangling from the edge of the spoon.

"Phillip, watch the spoon."

"But Mama—"

"Listen to your mother, Phillip," came Joshua's voice moments before he came into view.

"Papa!" Phillip fidgeted, upsetting the bowl, and Tabby barely saved it from splattering soup across their pallet.

"Well, hello there, my boy," said Joshua, chucking him on the chin. "It appears as though I was missed," he said, his gaze meeting Tabby's. She read the question there, and she gave him an encouraging smile. Joshua's grin dimmed at the hesitancy she could not hide.

"I have a surprise for you two," said Joshua. Reaching out of sight, he pulled out a bundle. Tabby smelled the goodies before he unwrapped the handkerchief covering them. Two perfectly thick slices of cake lay on his palm, and Joshua offered them up.

"Not before you finish your soup," she said, intervening before Phillip bit into it.

"Right," said Joshua, wrapping it up once more. "I shall keep it until you are finished."

Phillip launched himself at the soup, digging into it with the fervor of a man dying of starvation, and Tabby gave up on trying to keep the mess at bay. It was a lost cause.

"And what about you, Tabby?" asked Joshua, holding out the second slice.

"Where did you get it?" she asked.

Joshua's eyes dimmed, and he looked away from her. "Does it matter?"

"You know it does," she whispered, though it was impossible to keep Phillip from overhearing.

With a nod, he replied, "I did some odd jobs for the baker in trade."

Tabby stilled. "You did?"

He nodded again. "I wanted to bring you both a treat."

"Thank you, Papa," said Phillip, gobbling his piece the moment he was free to do so.

For a brief moment, she and her husband watched each other, and then Tabby leaned forward and placed a light kiss on his cheek. "Thank you," she whispered.

Joshua smiled and handed her the cake, and Tabby took a bite. Spice cake was not her favorite and heaven knows that they could have used something more practical, like a loaf of bread, but Tabby was not about to turn away Joshua's offering.

"There is a stage that passes through to London every morning," said Joshua. "And Cousin Maurice assures me he has rooms above his office we can rent, and they shall be ready upon our arrival. I think it shall be just the thing."

"A new start," she said, leaving the rest of her treat on her lap.

Phillip smiled around a mouthful of cake, and Tabby wished with all her heart that this would be the answer she had been seeking. Sliding over, Tabby made room for Joshua to join them, and she looked at her little family, hoping this would last. Phillip regaled them with his stories, making both Tabby and Joshua smile.

A knock at the door startled her out of her reverie. Joshua moved to answer it, but Tabby insisted he stay; Phillip so rarely got such attention from his papa that she was loathe to interrupt it. Climbing down the stairs, Tabby opened the front door to find the footman, James, standing on her doorstep.

"Message for you, ma'am," he said, handing over an envelope.

Tabby could feel Joshua's eyes on her back, and her limbs grew weak. The only thing that kept her upright was seeing that the handwriting belonged to Mina. Tabby had not the strength to read even a single word from Captain Ashbrook.

Glancing over her shoulder, James shot Joshua a hard look before giving Tabby a deferential nod. "We shall miss you at the

Park, but good luck," he said and gave her a quick wink before turning round to stroll down the lane.

Standing in the doorway, Tabby looked at Joshua's dark expression.

"It is from Mrs. Kingsley," she explained. "Perhaps a letter of recommendation."

The fire in his eyes died, and Joshua nodded, turning to Phillip, but Tabby knew she could not read it there. Stepping outside, she closed the door behind her. Regardless if it were nothing more than a sterile letter from her former employer, Tabby could not read it in front of her husband.

Stepping around the cottage until she was out of sight, Tabby cracked the seal. The wind caught the edges of the banknote wrapped inside the envelope, and Tabby nearly lost it to the elements. Catching it tight, Tabby's breath caught when she saw that it was worth ten pounds. Holding that small fortune set Tabby's heart racing, and she stared at it for a good several moments before reading the attached letter.

Dear Tabby,

I know you must do what is best for you and your son, but I cannot be easy unless I do something for you, my dear friend. I hope that your new life in London is everything you wish, but if it is not, I want you to know that you have a safe haven to run to. No matter what has happened between you and my brother, we care about you and Phillip and wish only the best for you, my dear friend.

Please keep this money in case the worst happens. I pray that all shall be right for you, but if it is not, please use it to find me.

Your friend,
Mina

P.S. And Rosewood Cottage is <u>always</u> at your disposal. Simply tell Mrs. Engle that I have sent you, and she will take care of you.

Tabby could hardly make out the last words as her eyes misted over. That dear, sweet woman. There was no conceivable way for her to need such a sum to make the journey, but Tabby knew it was more than that. Mina was giving her a safeguard.

"Tabby?" called Joshua.

Crumpling the banknote and letter together, Tabby shoved them into her bodice, tucking them out of sight.

"Coming," she replied while she checked to make sure they were safely hidden. If Tabby had not known her mind before, she knew it now. Mina had given her a means of escape, and as much as Tabby wanted to believe that her life with Joshua would be different from now on, too many years of married life had taught her not to trust Joshua's change of heart. Not fully, at any rate.

For her sake, and most especially Phillip's, Tabby needed to keep it hidden. For now.

Chapter 30

London
Nine Months Later

Having spent much time in London before her marriage, Tabby had known the city to be a noisy place, but their tiny rooms in the middle of a commercial thoroughfare had no respite from the sounds of the street below. An unending cacophony of movement. Tabby wondered if she would ever acclimate to it and tried not to think of the country sounds she missed so dearly.

With quick movements, Tabby worked her needle through the fabric, mending the tear in Phillip's new trousers. Halting between stitches, she arched her back and stretched her neck. She'd been hunched over the mending for hours. In Bristow, much of the family's laundry had been ignored as she'd not had the time for it. Now, it occupied her days. Between washing and repairs, keeping her family in clean clothes was a monumental task, for there was a never-ending stream of dirty garments needing her attention.

"When is Papa coming home?" asked Phillip.

Tabby glanced out the window. The sun had not yet set, but the evening was wearing on and Joshua should have arrived by now.

"Soon, sweetheart," she said. "Sometimes Papa has to work late."

Nibbling on her lip, Tabby wondered if she and Phillip should eat dinner without him. The last few weeks had seen quite a few of these long days for Joshua, and Tabby had no notion of when he might return. However, she did not wish to give up on dining as a family.

Tabby watched Phillip play on the floor, his soldiers scattered around him. Every time she saw those little figures that were multiplying at an alarming rate, Tabby wanted to smile. His clothes were clean, his belly full, and he had actual toys with which to play. Though they all may be far simpler versions of what they'd enjoyed at Kelland Hall, they were far grander than what they'd had in Bristow, and Tabby counted their blessings.

Setting to work, Tabby finished patching the trouser knees and started darning a pair of Joshua's socks. With fall, winter, and spring gone, the nights were growing warm enough that such articles were unnecessary and could await their repairs, but they were the last of her pile, and she was desperate for it to be empty. For once.

Footsteps echoed on the stairs, and Phillip perked up at the sound of it while Tabby put a quick finishing stitch in the sock before clearing it away. Phillip abandoned his toys and rushed to the door as it opened. Joshua grunted as Phillip launched himself at his father, but rather than picking up the child, Joshua patted him on the head and brushed past with a mumbled greeting. One look was all it took to tell Tabby that today had not been a good day for Joshua; even his hair and cravat were drooping. Going over, Tabby wrapped her arms around him, hoping to give him some bit of comfort.

"And suddenly, my day has gotten a bit brighter," said Joshua, giving her a squeeze.

She smiled and leaned in to give him a kiss. But then she caught a faint whiff of something on his breath that she had not smelled in nine months.

"You've been drinking," she said, jerking away.

Joshua huffed and pulled off his jacket, hanging it on the post. "I needed something to help me through the drudgery of my job. Do you know how soul crushing it is to do something you despise day in and out? It was only a pint. Something to relax me. That is it."

"We discussed this."

"No, you decided it," he replied. "I have had a long, hard day working to support my family, and I deserve a bit of refreshment. Not all of us are allowed the luxury to sit around all day."

Tabby's nostrils flared, and she sucked in a breath to calm her burst of temper. "Just because you never did housework does not mean that those at home have nothing to do." Tabby crossed her arms and narrowed her eyes. "And it is never only a bit of refreshment to you. It never stops at one drink, Joshua."

"It did today, and all the other times I've enjoyed a pint over the last few weeks, so stop complaining," he said, brushing past her to sit at the table.

Blinking, she stared at him. "You have been lying to me?"

"That would suppose I told you I was abstaining," he said with a huff. "I never did."

"You gave your word that you would give up spirits," she said. "When you were sitting there in the mud, begging me to forgive you, you gave your word of honor that you would abstain."

"Ale is hardly spirits, Tabby. I need something to get me through the day!" he growled, fixing a hard eye on her. "Do you have any idea how much of a sacrifice it is for me to work as a clerk to a lowly solicitor? I despise it and all the legal profession, yet I go every day to provide for you, and then I arrive home and you immediately harp at me about a single drink. Now, are we going to eat dinner or would you rather stand around criticizing me?"

Taking a breath, Tabby allowed it to bring a shaky calm over her. It took at least three more before she was able to usher Phillip to sit and dish up their bowls. Phillip glanced between his parents with a scrunched brow as he ate, but Joshua stared at his food. Tabby poked the chunks of beef and vegetables, her appetite gone.

Perhaps it was a touch of an overreaction to a single drink. For any other man, Tabby would not begrudge him something so small, and Joshua had certainly been working hard to provide everything they needed and more. So much of his behavior had been commendable that a part of Tabby felt guilty for denying him such a seemingly small thing. Except, it was no small thing. It may be to any other man, but Joshua was not well-acquainted with moderation.

"Joshua—" she began.

"I do not want to talk about this," he said, thumping his fist on the table. "I have done everything you have asked. Everything. I have been a model husband and father for months now. I deserve an occasional ale to help me through the absolute tedium that makes up my days."

"But you gave your word," she said, reaching over to place a calming hand on his arm.

"I apologize that I am not as good a man as your sainted Captain Ashbrook," he said through clenched teeth. His eyes locked with hers, and Tabby saw the anger burning in them, but it did not compare to the fury she felt at having Joshua invoke the captain's name during a disagreement yet again.

"Stop that," she snapped.

Phillip stared wide-eyed at them, and Tabby sucked in a deep breath before continuing.

"I have never once brought up his name since we left Bristow," she said, dropping her voice to a whisper. "Not once. Now, would you please stop mentioning him?"

"Why whisper, Tabby?" asked Joshua. "The boy already knows. Everyone with eyes knows that you fell in love with that man. Our marriage would be fine if you did not insist on clinging to your feelings for him." Shoving his bowl aside, Joshua stood and stomped to the door.

"Where are you going?" she asked as he yanked on his

jacket.

"Out where I can get a bit of peace and quiet. For once." And before she could say another word, he was gone, the door slamming behind him.

Tabby gaped, listening to his footsteps tromping down the stairs. Nine months was all it had taken for their marriage to revert to what it had been. Not in its entirety, but Tabby sensed it coming. She had been down this path often enough to see the signs. This may have been Joshua's longest period of contrition, but it had ended as disastrously as the others.

And yet, this time was different. Sitting there, blinking at the door, Tabby waited for the ache and anguish that always accompanied this familiar battle, but there was nothing. She was hollow inside. There was nothing left to salvage between her and Joshua. They had tried, but there was no returning to what they once were and no hope of building something new with Joshua clinging to his destructive behavior; she could never love such a man.

But perhaps he had been correct. Tabby had tried, but her heart would not let go of Captain Ashbrook. Though she never allowed herself to dwell on thoughts of him, he still lurked there in the hidden recesses. The captain had become an integral part of her life during her time at Gladwell House, and Tabby missed him. Their conversations. Their friendship. At times, the longing for him overwhelmed her.

Even at their best, Joshua had been more lover than companion, and Tabby could not think of a single conversation in which they had spoken of anything meaningful. Her young mind had believed that they shared some deep connection, but it was nothing more than a fantasy dreamed up by a lovelorn child. Joshua was handsome, to be sure, and his manner pleasing. Engaging even. He'd had a way of making her feel like the center of his universe, and what girl could withstand such an allure?

Perhaps it was not so surprising that things had fallen apart between them. Phillip was the only thing they shared in common. Not a one of their interests or goals in life were aligned. For a brief time, Joshua had molded himself into the gentleman Tabby wished him to be, but it had been no more real than the garden follies that littered the British landscape.

Not like what she shared with Graham. Tabby shoved away the errant thought.

Little arms wrapped around her waist, pulling Tabby from her thoughts. Giving Phillip a kiss on the head, she helped him onto her lap, though he was getting too big for it now.

"Sorry, dearest," she said, rocking him. Placing another kiss at his temple, she hummed a tune as he relaxed.

Happy thoughts. Those little blessings. Tabby's mind turned to those and began listing off all the things she loved about their life in London. There were plenty of things she missed, but they had a good roof over their heads. Though Joshua grumbled about it, he had a good position that provided far better for their family than Tabby could. Things were not easy for them, but even with this regress, they were better off than they had been.

And that was enough for her.

...

Courting was no easy thing. Quite daunting, in fact. And doing so in front of an audience made it all the more difficult. But there was no helping the matter, so Graham sat on a sofa at an appropriate distance from Miss Amy Ingalls as her mother and his sister made polite conversation while pretending not to watch their every move. If it weren't for his discomfort, it might even be humorous to see both matrons feigning aloofness while pinning all their hopes on this brief afternoon tea.

Graham watched Miss Amy. She was a handsome young lady. A man would have to be blind not to notice such things.

M.A. Nichols

Her hair was the color of ripened wheat, gathered in an elaborate style that highlighted her natural curls. Her eyes were the color of cornflowers, and they sparkled as she spoke. Her figure was everything a man could want. Her complexion fair. Her lips so perfectly formed that they practically begged to be kissed. All in all, Miss Amy was about as close to perfection as one could wish for.

If only Graham had an inkling of interest in the girl.

"Do you care to hunt, Captain Ashbrook?" she asked with a sweet smile.

"It is Mr. Ashbrook, Miss Amy," he replied. "And I fear I never developed a taste for hunting."

The girl gave him a demure smile, batting her eyelashes with a titter. "You may no longer have claim to that illustrious title, sir, but I fear you shall always be Captain Ashbrook to me. It is far too dashing a name, and I insist on using it."

Graham's lips twisted into something approximating a smile. Miss Amy needed more practice at flirting before she would achieve a natural air to it, and Graham feared he would be forced to give her that experience. Mina caught his eye, and they shared a silent laugh before returning their attention to their guests.

"As you wish," he conceded.

"Though it is very disappointing that you do not hunt," said Miss Amy. "The forests around our home have quite the best game in the area, and I am certain Papa would love to invite you to join him."

"He is too kind, but I must decline."

Miss Amy reached forward, placing her hand on his forearm. "Oh, dear. I fear I may have offended you, sir. I did not intend to call attention to your special circumstances."

Even her blush was lovely to behold, though it was wasted on Graham. He said nothing in return for it was far more polite to allow her to believe his refusal stemmed from physical incapacity rather than disinterest; though his leg had not the strength for such demanding sport, it was not the reason he had

256

declined.

Graham's fingers tapped along his knee as he struggled for a topic of conversation. In the few visits they had shared, it had become clear to him that they had little in common, though it did not deter Miss Amy and her mother. Luckily, the girl was keen on conversation and produced it in great volumes with little prompting on his part.

And like it did every time he found himself in such situations where little was required of his attention, Graham's mind wandered towards topics best left alone. Or rather, a single topic. A topic with eyes so dark and rich that a man could lose himself in them. And hair that held every shade of blonde, the hues blending together in a lovely array. A smile that so often held a hint of humor, especially when she was guaranteed to trounce him at a hand of cards.

He fought for impassivity, but thoughts of Tabby filled him, and Graham found himself lost in answerless questions about where she was and what she was doing. His jaw tightened as he wondered if she was safe. If her husband was treating her the way she deserved.

And Phillip. Graham couldn't count the number of times he had awoken in the night with memories of the boy's confessions about his father. The way the child had cowered away from a raised voice. One did not develop such instincts in a peaceful household.

"It is so good of you to have called on us," said Mina with an emphasis that pulled Graham out of his thoughts. She gave him a pointed look, and Graham returned to the conversation.

"Yes, ladies," he said, getting to his feet before they rose. "It is always a pleasure."

With a proper bow and a few more pleasantries exchanged, Mina ushered them to the doorway where Jennings awaited to escort them out.

The moment the door was closed, Graham limped over to the window, staring out at the garden to distract himself with thoughts of how he might capture it on paper. The shadows and highlights. The curve of the tree branches. However, that drew his mind to sitting in Gladwell's garden with Tabby. Graham could not be free of the memories. Everywhere he went, he carried her with him. And yet, Graham was uncertain as to whether he wanted to be rid of her.

"It shall get easier, Graham," said Mina, coming up beside him and taking his arm. She squeezed it and gazed out at the garden.

"Promise?"

Mina turned her eyes to him and nodded. Her eyes held understanding, and Graham welcomed it. It did not make things better, but her borrowed strength allowed him to bear it up. Then her expression shifted, a smile tickled her lips and her eyes sparkled. "And in the meantime, you are giving Miss Amy some much needed practice with her flirting."

Graham chuckled. "It is painful to watch her exuberant batting of her eyes."

"Ah, but she is young. With time, she shall be as skilled as the rest of her set," said Mina. "Now, come with me to the nursery and spend some time with Baby Oliver. In my experience, many of life's ills can be forgotten when cuddling an infant."

Chapter 31

Keeping a wary eye on the passing traffic, Tabby led Phillip along the busy streets. He tugged on her hand, desperate to move faster, but she kept him at a steady pace and away from the carriages rolling past.

"Can we stop at the market and get a treat?" asked Phillip, yanking Tabby towards the store windows.

"Phillip, stop!" she said, pulling him out of the path of the passersby he was intent on ignoring. "You must watch where you are going."

The lad stood before her, kicking at the ground as he looked up with all the repentance he could muster. "Sorry, Mama."

"Perhaps we might stop in," she said as they continued along. "I could use a bit of licorice. What do you think?"

Phillip's grin was so wide, Tabby felt certain his cheeks would burst, and she squeezed his hand. Walking side-by-side, it astonished her how big he was getting. Those bright cheeks were showing less and less of his baby sweetness, and he was slowly morphing from her sweet child into a proper boy.

But then something caught Tabby's eye in the bookshop that froze her in place. Someone collided with her, and she gave mumbled apologies before tugging Phillip towards the storefront.

"Careful, Mama!" he cried as she nearly crashed into a passing couple.

"Apologies," she mumbled, her eyes honing in on the fresh display of black leather books in the windows. One sat open among the stack, displaying the cover page and an illustration of a ship pulling into an exotic port. *My Life at Sea* by Graham Ashbrook. Tabby touched the glass and leaned closer, her eyes tracing the sketch that was so clearly one of his own.

Her breath hitched as she stared at it. Tabby bit her lips, but it did not stop the tears from gathering in her eyes. He had done it.

"Are you interested in a copy?" asked the bookseller, stepping in front of his store to adjust the sign hanging on the door.

Her voice caught, but she managed a quiet, "No."

That one word was the most blatant lie Tabby had ever told. She wanted nothing more than to dump out the coins in her reticule and purchase a copy. Tabby longed to read his words and see his drawings captured inside, but she could not allow herself such an indulgence. She might be able to spare the money, but she could not afford the emotional toll.

No, it was enough to know that he was moving forward with his life. No matter what had passed between them, Graham had not allowed it to ruin him. A tear slipped down her cheek before she realized it was ready to fall, and she brushed it away and cleared her throat.

"No, thank you," she said again, firmer. "I was only looking."

"If you are interested in such tales, the author himself is coming to Town to do a few lectures," said the proprietor.

Tabby smiled and gave a polite goodbye before walking away. Her steps came lighter than before. As much as it hurt to know she would never see him again, she was filled with a sense of peace. Graham Ashbrook was seeking his joy, and Tabby said a silent prayer that he would find every last bit of it that he deserved. And more.

"What about the licorice?" asked Phillip, pulling Tabby back to the present.

"Of course, my little man," she said, leading him through the crowds. Turning down a few streets, the bustle and noise faded behind them, and Tabby was grateful for a bit of quiet. This muted section of the neighborhood had to be Tabby's favorite corner of London. Though there were plenty of markets and shops closer to home, spending a few minutes in this haven from the chaos and commotion made the out-of-the-way journey worthwhile.

"Would you rather have a licorice, marzipan, or chocolate?" asked Tabby, leading Phillip around a puddle.

"Chocolate," he blurted.

"Well, I believe I shall get a bit of licorice," said Tabby. "Though I do love Mr. Porter's marzipan."

"I like—"

Hands jerked Tabby, lifting her off the ground and shoving her into an alleyway. She screamed, but a meaty hand clamped over her mouth while another man emerged from the shadows to snatch Phillip from her. Sinking her teeth into the massive fingers, Tabby bit down, tearing into his skin. Blood trickled into her mouth, mixing with the taste of the sweat and filth on his hand, but she would not release, kicking and swinging behind her.

The man bellowed, throwing her into the side of the building. Sucking in a deep breath, Tabby let loose another scream and lurched to her feet, but the man's fist swung into her face, cracking against her cheek. The force of it threw her into the wall, her head slamming against the brick.

Tabby collapsed to the ground, her mind struggling for coherency. Her limbs twitched as she tried to get them under her. Phillip cried out, and Tabby straightened, pushing through the haze engulfing her thoughts, but another blow threw her to the ground once more. Both sides of her face ached, throbbing in time with her heart, and a pain drove into her head where it had hit the bricks and cobblestones.

"Leave it, Mr. Gibbons," said a man, though Tabby's addled mind could not tell where or who he was.

Rough hands yanked her to her feet, and Tabby hung limp in the giant's arms. Her stomach churned as the world spun around her, and when the image cleared, Tabby saw a man whom she had hoped never to see again.

"Mrs. Russell," said Mr. Crauford, his hand holding Phillip by the collar.

"Leave him be," said Tabby, her voice coming out more a whimper than command. She tried to scream, but she could not get enough breath in her lungs.

"Mama!" Phillip squealed and kicked at Mr. Crauford, but the man shook the child like a rag doll.

"Stop it!" Tabby fought against the massive limbs holding her still, but they did not budge.

"Your husband owes me an awful lot of money, Mrs. Russell," said Mr. Crauford. "As he insists on avoiding me, I thought it best to approach you directly and explain the situation. We are old acquaintances, after all." His smile bespoke of everything refined and elegant, even as his hands circled Phillip's neck, his fingers indenting the skin.

"We have made our payments as agreed," she said. "What more can you possibly want?"

The hands holding her shifted until the one at her waist caressed her hip. Mr. Gibbons leaned down, and Tabby squirmed, but he buried his nose into her neck, breathing in with a low sigh that tickled her skin. Tabby's limbs shook, her stomach twisting in knots as nausea washed over her.

"Behave, Mr. Gibbons," said Mr. Crauford. Keeping a firm hold on Phillip, the man drew closer to her.

Tabby tried to swallow, but her mouth and throat were as dusty as a desert. "Please, there must be some misunderstanding."

Mr. Crauford tsked, pursing his lips. "Now, Mrs. Russell,

do not insult my intelligence."

"I swear to you," she said, her voice trembling. "We put aside the funds every sennight."

"Ah, but Mr. Russell has not made a payment in the past month," he said, reaching forward to brush aside a lock of her hair that had fallen free of her bun. "And I just received word that he has racked up debts with nearly every one of my competitors in town. Not to mention the string of those you left behind in Bristow. I am beginning to worry that he does not intend to honor our contract."

The world around her froze, sealing Tabby away in the shock of that moment. She could hardly breathe and her thoughts swam.

"That cannot be," she whispered with wide eyes. Her lips quivered as she shook her head.

Mr. Crauford watched her and squeezed Phillip's neck for a brief moment. "Please deliver a message to your husband for me: I want my money by the end of the month, and if he does not deliver, I shall have to take more drastic steps to recover it."

Tabby flinched away from Mr. Gibbons as he nuzzled her hair.

"Patience, Mr. Gibbons," warned Mr. Crauford. "They have until the end of the month."

Releasing Phillip, he turned away, and the bruising arms around her disappeared. Tabby's knees buckled, and she fell to the cobblestones, the edges of the uneven stones digging into her knees and hands. Phillip rushed to her, and Tabby tugged him behind her and away from those devils.

Mr. Gibbons lumbered after his boss, but Mr. Crauford paused at the edge of the alleyway to give her a deep bow. A smile stretched across his lips as he said, "For your sake, I hope our paths do not cross again."

And then they were gone.

It began with minor trembles, but they spread through Tabby and grew until she quaked. Kneeling there on the wet and muddy pavers, there was nothing she could do to stop them as she panted. Her heart pounded in her chest, the sound of it thumping in her ears, but above that, she heard Phillip's sobs.

Pulling him into her embrace, her own tremors subsided as she focused on calming her son. Tabby crooned to him, rocking him there in the alley. There was no way he could understand what had happened, but he understood the danger.

It took several moments, but Tabby's strength returned to her, and she was able to stand. Lifting Phillip onto her shoulder, Tabby hurried out of the alley and through the maze of streets until she was once again engulfed in the crowds. For the first time since moving to London, the noise and bodies milling around her brought a sense of calm.

Phillip was getting too heavy for her to carry, so she put him down and led him along the street, making as direct a path as she could to Joshua. He could not have done this to them. It was not possible. It was one thing for him to regress now, but for him to have taken out so much debt meant something far more sinister.

Tabby burst into the solicitor's office, her eyes scanning for her husband.

"Cousin Tabitha," said Cousin Maurice, striding towards her with a massive tome in his hands.

"I need to see—"

"I appreciate your plight," he said. "I truly do, but it is extremely inappropriate for you to come here in such a fashion. I gave you to the end of the month, which is more than generous, considering the circumstances—" But then he stopped when he looked her in the face. "Good heavens, what has happened to you?"

His tone and posture changed in an instant. Ushering her over to a chair, he gave orders to his clerk, though Tabby could not concentrate on those unimportant details as she pulled Phillip onto her lap.

"Where is Joshua?" she asked, pushing aside his proffered handkerchief. She hadn't even noticed the drops of blood splattering her bodice. Touching her forehead, she felt a trickle seeping from a gash; the skin around it was already swollen and warm to the touch.

"What do you mean?" asked Maurice, ignoring her protestations to press the cloth to the wound. "I sacked him last month. He may be my cousin, but it was a mistake to ever take him on."

"Sacked?" Tabby knew she was parroting the gentleman, but she could not believe her ears.

"I know this is a blow to you and Phillip," he said, dabbing at her face, studiously avoiding her startled gaze, "and I am truly sorry for any heartache it will cause you two, but I feel I was more than generous to let you stay in my rooms until the end of the month. You are family, and I can overlook his utter uselessness as an employee, but I cannot overlook embezzling."

Tabby grabbed Maurice's hands, pulling him away from his ministrations and seizing his full attention. "He stole from you? And you sacked him?"

Maurice stood up, staring at her. "You don't know any of this, do you?" He did not bother to wait for her answer for it was clear enough. "Did he do this to you?"

"No," said Tabby.

Not directly, at any rate.

Ignoring Maurice's protestations, Tabby nudged Phillip from her lap and led him out of the office. Shrugging the gentleman off, Tabby hurried out the door and into the street. She had to find her husband.

...

Tabby sat in the armchair as Phillip played quietly on the floor. He hardly made a sound as he moved his toys across their parlor floor, no doubt sensing Tabby's dark mood. She hated that it was leaching into him, but there was too much in her heart for her to pretend all was well. Her foot tapped against the ground as she watched the front door, awaiting Joshua's return.

With all of London as his hiding ground, it hadn't taken long for her to abandon the search. There was no getting around it. Tabby had to wait until Joshua deigned to return home. The sun inched across the sky, making the shadows crawl across the floor as she waited.

All those foul words that Joshua insisted on using came to her thoughts, polluting her mind in the flood of her anger. How could she have been so blind? How had she fallen into this trap again? Debts in Bristow. Crauford had said there were debts there, too. Even as he had made all his golden promises, Joshua had been lying to her. What a fool she'd been! Tabby berated herself for ever believing him. Believing his blatant lies and manipulation. Believing he had changed. Believing he was a man and not a weasel.

Her jaw tightened, her toes rapping a rapid beat against the floor. Tabby's heart hardened, blackening towards the man who had brought her so much anguish. She could imagine what his response would be. More lies. More promises. More begging for forgiveness. Just the thought of it brought tears to her eyes. Tabby could not do this again. Not again. The verbal parry. The dancing around the truth of the matter.

Joshua loved them. On some level, Tabby knew it. When things were perfect in the world and the stars aligned, Joshua was as loving and attentive as any wife and mother could wish for. But life rarely had such moments. There were always bumps in the road, and when it came down to it, Joshua loved himself and his own pleasures more.

Phillip froze at the sound of Joshua's footsteps on the stairs. His usual excitement dimmed as he clutched his soldiers to his chest. The door opened, and Joshua came in, acting as though all was right in the world. Until he saw Tabby's face.

She flinched at the curse that flew from his lips when he hurried over to her.

"What happened to you?" he said, tugging her to her feet

and lifting her chin to examine both sides of her face. His eyes darkened as he saw it. "Who did this? So help me, I shall kill them."

Tabby pulled free of him, crossing her arms. "Mr. Crauford paid a visit and asked me to give you a message."

In a flash, everything in Joshua shifted. The fury in his eyes evaporated into pure terror, the flush of his cheeks paling until he was gray.

She relaxed her jaw, loosening the tight muscles before continuing. "As you have taken out loans from every money-lender he knows, he is calling in your debt and demands it in full by the end of the month."

With each word, Joshua's eyes widened, his complexion growing more ashen.

"He threatened us, Joshua," she said. "His thug grabbed Phillip and me off the street and hit me. Do you have any idea how terrified we were? And then Cousin Maurice told us you were sacked for stealing, Joshua. Stealing!"

Despite her protests, Joshua pulled her into his arms. Tabby squirmed and shoved at him, forcing him away.

"I trusted you," she spat as she wrenched free.

"I know," he said, reaching for her hands. "And I failed you, but I promise it shall be fine. I shall get the money to pay him off. My luck has been a bit faulty as of late, but it is about to change. I feel it."

"Mama?" called Phillip.

"All is well, dearest," she said with a fragile calm that was as false as her husband. "Why don't you take your toys into the other room?"

The couple stared at each other as Phillip gathered his soldiers and shut himself in their bedchamber, his eyes never leaving his parents as the door closed behind him.

"Your luck?" Tabby forced herself not to scream at him. "You had a good position. A good future. What were you thinking?"

"A gentleman can make more at the tables in one evening

than I can make in a year!" he said. "Would you rather I languish in some dingy office for the rest of my life?"

"I would rather have a steady income and a life where I do not have to be afraid of being assaulted by ruffians because my husband is so far in debt that we cannot ever hope to be clear of it!"

"But Tabby, all will be fine," he said, placing placating hands on her arms, but she shrugged him off. "The last few weeks have not been kind to me, but we can start anew somewhere else. New names, if need be. The moneylenders will never find us. We could go to the North Country. Yorkshire, perhaps." His eyes and grin grew wider. "Or the continent! You have always wanted to see Italy. We could buy a little villa in the countryside."

Tabby gaped at him. "Are you listening to yourself, Joshua? Are you truly listening? What are you thinking?"

Joshua raised his hands. "All will be well. I promise." He inched towards the door. "I shall scrounge up some funds, and when I return we can decide where to go."

Wide-eyed, Tabby watched him scurry out the door. It was as though he were blind to the utter nonsense he was spewing. A villa in Italy?

Tabby's hands flew to her mouth, and she slumped onto a chair, her body trembling and heart thumping as though she were in that alleyway once again. Joshua was going to get them all hurt. Thoughts of Mr. Gibbons' hands on her sent a shudder through her, knotting her stomach. Or worse. Much worse.

This was no longer a matter of simple comfort. This was her son's life on the line. Again. The realization startled her. Twice, her husband had put her son in danger. Neither was intentional, but in some ways that was all the more terrifying. Joshua's misguided intentions were going to ruin them all, and Tabby would not let that happen.

Getting to her feet, she rushed to the bedroom. Phillip sat cross-legged on the bed and watched as she burst in.

She grabbed their only working piece of luggage. The portmanteau was dinged and barely holding together, but it would do. Speeding around the bedroom, she gathered their clothing, scooping up everything the two of them would need.

"What are you doing?" asked Phillip

"Packing," she said with a brittle smile. "You and I are going to go on a trip."

"Where?"

Dropping to her knees, Tabby pried up a loose floorboard, snatching out the dusty envelope hidden inside it.

"Herefordshire," she said, brushing off the paper and shoving Mina's letter and banknote into her bodice.

Chapter 32

"Darling, please stop," said Tabby, as Phillip tugged on her arm. Her joints felt like they had been rattled right out of their sockets, and her muscles were cramped, but at last they had arrived at Farrow. The rocks on the road dug into Tabby's boots, and the portmanteau weighed down her left side, but there was something so invigorating about being in the country again.

Beside her, Phillip jabbered on about the birds in the trees beside the road, the passengers they had traveled with, the place they were going, the bug that had landed on his arm, the cow in the pasture, and every other thought that popped into his mind. He rarely needed anything more than a nod and an occasional affirmation, leaving Tabby's mind free to wander.

Coming to Rosewood Cottage had been the clear option when they had set out from London, but as their destination drew closer, worry nibbled at Tabby. Perhaps she was overstepping her bounds. Mina may have offered help, but that had been months ago. Tabby supposed it did no good to fret about it now. Of all the concerns in her life, imposing on someone's hospitality was a trivial issue that would not stop her from doing what needed to be done. Now that the necessary step had been taken and Joshua was behind her, social niceties would not keep her from providing for Phillip. With a few pounds left over from Mina's bank note, they would have funds enough for food, but needed a haven while Tabby decided what was to be done with their future.

Following the bend in the road, Tabby caught sight of Mina's cottage. Or at least, she hoped it was the place. After such a distance, she was desperate for a proper rest.

Sitting on a little hill, Rosewood Cottage was surrounded by rolling grasslands. Tabby wondered why such a place had been so inappropriately named, but she was instantly taken with the simple beauty of the building. It was as though it glowed, a shining beacon calling to her, and Tabby understood why Mina was fond of the place. It had an aura that promised a warm hearth and cozy chairs. Seeing it was such a blessed relief that Tabby felt the beginning of tears come to her eyes.

Phillip broke free of her grasp and ran ahead, exploding through the gate to rap on the front door, and Tabby had to scurry to catch him. The door opened as she arrived on the doorstep, and a middle aged woman grinned out at them.

"Good afternoon, ma'am," said the lady, wiping her hands off on her apron.

"Good afternoon, Mrs. Engle," said Tabby. "I'm a friend of Mrs. Kingsley, and she told me to stop by if I should have need of a place to stay."

Mrs. Engle blinked at her for a moment before her eyebrows rose. "You must be Mrs. Russell," she said, quickly gathering her inside. Upon getting a closer look at Tabby's face, Mrs. Engle gasped, grabbing Tabby's chin to turn her face to the left and right. The woman's brow drew tight together.

"Oh, you poor thing!" she said.

Tabby had not glimpsed her face since her encounter with Mr. Gibbons, but seeing the expressions on her traveling companions had painted a clear picture, and the tears in Mrs. Engle's eyes only confirmed what the stiffness and painful throbs in her body were telling her.

"Mrs. Kingsley mentioned you might arrive," she said, bustling Tabby into the parlor and divesting her of her cloak and luggage in a trice. With equal efficiency, she soon had Phillip herded into the garden to explore and Tabby wrapped in a quilt on the sofa with a spread of tea and cakes around her. The whole thing happened so quickly, and Tabby was so tired, that she simply watched as the woman fluttered about like a mother hen, making certain that the pair of them were both comfortable.

Finally, the woman sat beside Tabby, extending a teacup to her. "Drink up, dear."

But the whirlwind of hospitality ravaged Tabby's last bit of reserve, leaving her heart unguarded and unchecked. A sob burst from her, and Tabby covered her mouth to hold it in, but Mrs. Engle set aside the teacup and drew her into her arms.

"There, there. Let it out," she crooned, holding Tabby as she wept. "You are safe now."

...

There had been a time when Graham had thought the crash of the waves hitting the side of his ship was the greatest sound to be heard, but it was nothing compared to an infant's laugh. A full-bodied squeal of joy rung through the Park's hallways, and Graham picked up his pace as he hurried to the sitting room. Pushing through the door, he caught sight of Simon and Mina sitting side-by-side on the sofa.

Mina leaned into her husband, beaming at her son who lay across her lap as Simon tickled the little belly. Oliver let loose another peal, his limbs flailing and back arching.

"Graham!" Mina's face lit at the sight of him, and Graham faltered at the vision she made. There was no doubt that his sister did not hold true to the conventional standard of beauty, but there was something within her that shone with far more power than mere beauty. It was the look of a lady so utterly content and pleased with her world that there was no hiding the brightness of her soul.

Coming over, he bent to kiss her cheek. "You look radiant, Mina."

A flush filled her cheeks, and Mina ducked her face, but Simon nudged her chin upwards and whispered, "You do."

"Oh, you two," she said, her face reddening further as she gave a tiny roll of her eyes and a shake of her head. "It's good of you to visit, Graham," she said, motioning for him to sit. "It's always a wonderful surprise."

"Ah, but I must be honest," said Graham, scooping the babe off his mama's lap, "I came to visit young Master Oliver." The child swung his little fist, smacking Graham in the face. And then giggled.

"You think that funny?" asked Graham, but Oliver's fingers reached for his mouth, grabbing Graham's lip. Tiny fingernails dug in, and Graham tried to pull away, but Oliver gripped tighter, a low chuckle building into a hoot of laughter.

"Darling, be gentle," said Mina, standing to extricate Graham's mouth from the onslaught.

Once his lips were free, Graham handed Oliver back to his mama, who was better at dodging the clenching fingers. However, a stray lock of her hair made its way into his grasp, and it was Graham's turn to assist her.

"Actually, I did come with news," said Graham as they took their seats on the sofas. "It may come as a shock, but I have decided to move to Portsmouth."

Simon's eyebrows raised. "And what is in Portsmouth?" he asked as Mina gaped and asked, "When?"

Graham smiled. "I have already begun to pack my things, and I plan on going straight there after my trip to London next week. The Royal Naval Academy has invited me to lecture there while I am working on my next book."

Mina's face was a comical mix of pleasure and pain. "How wonderful for you. That is a great opportunity, though I wish it were not so far away."

"It is not permanent," he said. "I shall likely settle in Bristow at some point, but for now, I feel in need of a change."

Glancing at Oliver in his mama's arms, Graham already felt homesick for his life at Avebury Park. It may not be his proper home, but he had passed the last two years here, which was greater than the entirety of his time spent at his ancestral home since he had left it to join the navy.

"I am going to miss your little man," said Graham, the endearment coming out without a second thought. His heart twisted at the memory of Tabby's endearment, but Graham shoved it aside as he did every time life brought such things to mind.

"He does love his Uncle Graham," said Mina, kissing his little cheeks.

"I shall visit as often as I can," he promised.

"You don't have to leave, you know," said Mina, but Simon gave a disapproving grunt.

"Leave him be," said Simon.

"I am simply giving him options."

"He knows the options and has made his choice."

"And he shan't be gone forever," added Graham. "And he shan't miss being discussed as though he weren't sitting in front of you."

"And what of Miss Amy?" she asked, making Graham sigh. He had known she would, but Graham hadn't wanted to discuss this aspect of his life.

"She is a sweet enough girl, but I have no interest in courting her," said Graham, squirming beneath Mina's examination. "I am not ready for thoughts of marriage, and it would be cruel to raise the lady's hopes."

Mina nodded, though she could not hide her disappointment. "I understand, but I had hoped that as some months have passed since..." Her words faltered, but she was saved from having to complete that thought when the door opened and Jennings entered with a bow.

"Urgent message from Mrs. Engle, madam," he said, offering up the missive before bowing out of the room.

"Urgent?" Mina mused. "What could possibly be urgent at Rosewood Cottage?"

Graham's eyebrows rose. "You still have that little property?"

"Of course," said Mina. "I could not bear to part with it."

"We both love it," said Simon, giving his wife a warm smile. "We have very fond memories of the place."

Laying Oliver on her lap, Mina turned the letter over and broke the seal. Her eyes darted across the page as Simon read the words over her shoulder.

"What is the matter?" Graham asked when his sister's eyes widened.

"Oh, dear," she said, handing Oliver to Simon. "I must write back at once."

"Of course," said Simon as Mina begged Graham's forgiveness and rushed out of the room.

"What has happened?" asked Graham.

Simon laid his son across his thighs and offered up his fingers for Oliver to grab. "There are a few issues that need Mina's attention. Nothing for you to worry about." Though the look on Simon's face was not as convincing as the words he spoke, the gentleman would not say another word on the subject.

Smiling at the baby, Simon lifted one of the tiny fists to his mouth and nibbled at it, making Oliver chuckle.

"Portsmouth?" he asked before switching to Oliver's other hand.

Graham shrugged. "It feels as though it is the right thing to do for now."

"It sounds like an escape," said Simon. "Changing venues will not erase your feelings for Mrs. Russell."

There were times when his brother-in-law was a touch too interfering. Especially about courtship.

"Perhaps not," said Graham. "But staying in a place where

everything reminds me of her is not helping, either. In Portsmouth, I may even manage to go an hour without thinking about her."

Simon nodded. "I know it shall take time, but I hope you will move on. Trust me when I tell you that clinging to the past never brings anything but pain."

"I am not clinging," said Graham. "It has only been a few months."

"Over nine. You two have been apart longer than you were together," said Simon, glancing at Graham. "I am not saying that you need to engage yourself to the first lady you meet, but from the manner in which you spoke last year, it seems as though marriage and a family are what you desire. If that is still the case, you need to let go of Mrs. Russell. Find someone else."

"Just like that," Graham said with a heavy dose of sarcasm.

Simon shrugged. "It worked for me, and now I have a wife who is the most incredible and lovely woman I have ever met, and far better than I could've hoped for." Simon's smile warmed as he spoke, and his eyes turned to his son, making his grin broaden. "And a perfect little son."

Scrunching his nose, Simon kissed Oliver's tiny fingers. "He truly is the most wonderful baby, isn't he?"

Chapter 33

Putting her weight behind it, Tabby leaned into the bread dough, kneading it against the wooden table. Mrs. Engle worked opposite her, stirring a pot of stew over the hearthfire. She had only spent some three months at Gladwell House, yet cooking with Mrs. Bunting had become so second nature that Tabby had missed having another woman in the kitchen. Working with Mrs. Engle filled Tabby with a peace that she had not felt in many months.

"That's a lovely tune," said Mrs. Engle.

"Hmm?" Tabby looked up from her dough.

"You hum when you work, and it is lovely," she said. "Are you certain you wouldn't rather sit and have a cup of tea? I can manage on my own, and you are a guest."

Tabby grinned a natural, full-faced grin that lightened her heart even more. "You are kindness itself, Mrs. Engle, but I adore cooking, and unless you feel I am a bother in the kitchen, I would prefer to roll up my sleeves and help than sit around watching you do all the work yourself."

"Of course, you sweet girl," said Mrs. Engle.

"I don't like feeling as though I am a burden," said Tabby. "I had hoped to find a position in the area, but it is clear that

Farrow is too small for me to find anything suitable."

"There's no need for you to be rushing off," said Mrs. Engle, turning to point her messy spoon at Tabby with a hard look. "I know you wish to make your own way, but Mrs. Kingsley insisted you stay as long as you need to get your feet under you. There is no shame in taking a bit of help when you need it, and you truly need it."

Mrs. Engle returned to her pots, leaving Tabby to struggle against Rosewood Cottage's intoxicating allure. Tabby wished it were possible for them to stay. It had only been a few days, but Tabby already felt at home with the Engles. There was something about the house and those lovely caretakers that called out to Tabby's lonely soul, bewitching her with promises of a happier life. But to give into it would be to accept Joshua's original plan to live off the charity of others. No matter how good Mina's intentions and enticing the situation, Tabby could not allow herself to be lulled into it. Accepting a bit of assistance was one thing, but becoming dependent on someone to whom she had no claim of dependency was beyond what her pride would allow.

Tabby heard Phillip laugh in the sitting room as he sent his soldiers into battle against Mr. Engle. The resultant crashes and mock massacre made the two women smile.

"It is wonderful having you here," she said. "It gets awfully quiet with only the pair of us. The Kingsleys do come for a visit from time to time, but it's nice to have a child around. Though, I suppose they shall bring their little one for a visit."

"Then Mrs. Kingsley had the baby?" Tabby paused in her work to look at Mrs. Engle.

"Aye," she said, stirring the pot. "A boy. Oliver."

It did Tabby good to hear such news, and she gave the dough one last knead before placing it in a bowl to rise.

"Mrs. Engle!" hollered a boy as he burst through the kitchen door. The lad had to be nine or ten years old, though it was hard to tell beneath the grime covering his face. "Pa sent me to warn you. Said there's a Bow Street Runner poking around the village, asking about a lady and her son who went missing."

Tabby's heart caught in her throat, flour smearing across her face as her hands flew to her mouth. Joshua had done it. He'd called the authorities on her.

"He's going to take Phillip!" said Tabby, wringing her hands. "He shall take my boy, and there is nothing I can do about it."

"My thanks to you and your pa, Jimmy," said Mrs. Engle, sending the boy on his way with a few sweet rolls in his pockets.

Tabby stripped off her apron, hurrying into the sitting room to see the evidence of Phillip's battle strewn across the floor. There was nowhere for them to go on such short notice. Nowhere to run.

"Don't fret," said Mrs. Engle, following behind her. "We shall find a way to deal with this."

"But if Joshua pushes the issue, there is nothing to be done," said Tabby, staring at her son, who watched her with wide eyes. "The law sides with the father, and I cannot allow Joshua to take him. Phillip would never be safe living in such conditions!"

"What's happened?" asked Mr. Engle, getting to his feet.

"Jimmy came to warn us that a Bow Street Runner is on his way," said Mrs. Engle.

Scooping up the soldiers, Tabby stuffed them into their sack, and as she did so, her thoughts coalesced into a definitive decision. She would not allow Phillip to live in Joshua's care. Not anymore. Joshua was not merely self-destructive; his actions were bound to destroy them all, and Tabby would not sit by and watch her son be swept up in it.

"Mr. Engle," said Tabby, grabbing the man by the arm. "Would you take Phillip to the neighbors? Keep him out of the way for now. The law may force me to return to my husband, but I shan't allow him to take my son. If I must leave, wait until we are gone and then take him to Mrs. Kingsley." Though Tabby hated the thought of forcing such a responsibility on her friend, she knew Mina would accept it wholeheartedly. If Phillip had a happy home, that would be enough.

"Of course, I would do that for you, but I don't think it will solve your problem," said Mr. Engle. "No offense, ma'am, but the marks on your face are distinctive enough that you were likely easy to track. Whoever is coming has to know the boy is in the area, too. I doubt he'll leave without the both of you."

But the discussion was pulled to an abrupt halt when a fist pounded against the front door. Dropping the toys to the floor, Tabby grabbed Phillip's hand, pulling him close to her, and prayed this would not unravel the way she feared. Mrs. Engle came up beside Tabby, squeezing her arm as Mr. Engle went to open the door. Tabby's heart raced as the two men exchanged what amounted to pleasantries between men, and moments later they appeared in the sitting room.

"You must be Mrs. Russell," said the stranger.

Tabby pressed Phillip behind her, but the man did not even glance at the boy. "And who are you?"

"Mr. Rodger Down," he said. "I am a Principal Officer with the Bow Street Magistrates' Court, and I am here to ask you a few questions about your husband."

Tabby felt like stepping away from the man's unwavering gaze but held herself firm. "I cannot see why that is any of your business, Bow Street Runner or not."

"Principal Officer," he corrected. "And it became my business when Joshua Russell was beaten to death in an alleyway off Chartering Street."

"What?" Tabby's hands flew to her mouth, and the air caught in her lungs.

"He was murdered," said Mr. Down. "Late last Thursday."

At that, Mrs. Engle stepped forward and crouched next to Phillip. "How about we take your soldiers out into the garden, young man? We can build them some trenches in the flowerbeds."

Phillip glanced at his mother, and she tried to smile at him.

Tabby nudged him towards Mrs. Engle. "Go ahead, sweetheart."

The boy allowed himself to be led out, though he kept his eyes fixed firmly on his mother. No doubt, he was sensing the tension in the room, but Tabby prayed he did not fully understand what had been said.

Once the door was shut on the pair, Tabby returned her attention to the officer. "He is dead?"

"When was the last time you saw your husband?" he asked, standing with his hands in his pockets as though nothing were out of the ordinary. Tabby supposed it might not be for him.

"Last Thursday evening," answered Tabby.

Mr. Engle gave a grunt and scowled. "She arrived Sunday with a face the color of a plum and swollen so badly you could hardly tell it was her. Joshua Russell got everything he deserved."

"Did he beat you regularly?" asked Mr. Down.

Tabby shook her head. "Never. He had his faults—many of them— but he never raised a hand against me or Phillip. However, he owed a lot of money to unsavory people, and one of them wished to send him a message. I left because I knew it was no longer safe for my son to be with my husband as long as he insisted on spending money he did not have and drinking himself into oblivion."

Mr. Down stared at her face, examining the remnant marks, and Tabby tried not to cower beneath his gaze. It reminded her too much of Mr. Crauford's cool expression. Then he nodded and turned to leave.

"Is that it?" asked Tabby.

The man halted and turned to look at her with raised eyebrows. "Is there anything more you need to tell me?"

The question—the whole situation—had Tabby in such a state that she could not answer. It felt as though she had stepped into some dream and was trapped in a vise, her whole body seizing until she could not breathe.

"Your husband ran with a seedy crowd," said Mr. Down

when she did not speak. "From what we have pieced together, he tried to steal from the wrong person and got himself bludgeoned to death for his troubles. The only reason I dragged myself out to this backwater hamlet is because the man's wife and child went missing about the same time, and I had to be certain they hadn't met the same fate. Now that I have done that, I can return to civilization."

Mr. Engle ushered him towards the door, but Tabby stopped him with a single question.

"And are you certain he is dead?" she asked.

"He was buried after the coroner's inquest," said Mr. Down, a hint of a smile on his lips. "So, if he wasn't before, he is now."

"And you are certain it was him?" she asked.

"Maurice Russell identified him," said Mr. Down, his eyes narrowing. "But you would know all this if you had bothered to stay where you belonged."

And with that parting jab, he left.

"Never you mind him," said Mr. Engle, patting her on the shoulder. "You did right by your boy to get him out of that situation..."

But Tabby did not hear the rest of what he said. It was as though the world had halted in its turn, freezing everything around her. There was no sound, no movement, no time. It held Tabby there in that moment as it stretched into eternity.

Joshua was dead.

Just thinking the words broke the spell, and Tabby's hands flew to her mouth to hold back a jerking sob. Mr. Engle awkwardly patted her shoulder, saying some nonsense words, but Tabby turned away. She hurried to her room and slumped onto her bed, pulling her knees in tight as she lay down.

Tears poured from her eyes as a barrage of emotions battered her. There were too many for Tabby to know if she was crying for Joshua, Phillip, herself, all three or none of them. She simply embraced the emotions, allowing them to wash over her. She could make no more sense of what she was feeling than she could of this sudden turn of events, and the only thing she could do was to allow herself to feel it all. Her eyes burned, her breaths coming in jagged bursts as her pillow dampened. But as the minutes continued their march through the day, the shock began to fade.

Joshua was dead. Tabby closed her eyes and rubbed at her head. He was gone. Lying there, she could not believe it was true. No matter how she had wished for things to be different for her family, she had not wanted Joshua's life cut short.

And yet, Tabby felt a flash of relief. There was no denying it or the rush of thoughts and possibilities that came into her mind. It had been years since Tabby had found any sort of happiness with the man, and knowing that she and Phillip were free to build a new life for themselves sent a thrill of joy coursing through her that made her stomach clench.

How could she think that? Tabby covered her face, scrunching into a tighter ball. What sort of woman felt relief at her husband's death? What sort of woman allowed herself to entertain thoughts of another man when her own husband was barely in his grave? But there he was, lurking in her thoughts, strong and gallant with promises of a golden future together. Captain Ashbrook. Graham.

Burying her head into her pillow, Tabby felt the torrent of emotions swell, drowning her in their depths, and she surrendered to it. There was nothing else to do until it calmed again.

Chapter 34

Flicking back the straps across the top of his case, Graham opened the lid and pulled out his clothes. Perhaps it was pointless to unpack when he was only staying in London for a sennight, but he preferred having everything laid out properly. A few days to explore the city and then his lecture at Helmsley Hall.

Just the thought of it had his palms sweating.

Sailing and naval life were comfortable topics, but speaking on them in front of a crowd was extremely discomforting. Everything was prepared and ready, but having never done something like this before, Graham was quite nervous at this new undertaking. But he would forge ahead, come what may.

As he paced the hotel room, he went through his plans for the coming days. It had been years since he'd visited Town, and though the city had never enticed him, Graham was looking forward to visiting a few favorite spots. He wondered if the shop on Lounton Street still served those eel pies he liked.

A knock at the door drew his attention, and he called for the visitor to enter.

"Message for you, sir," said a footman, holding up a silver tray.

"Finally," he said, retrieving the missive. He had written Ambrose weeks ago about this trip and had yet to get a response; he had hoped to see his errant brother before leaving for Portsmouth. Not that he expected anything other than a last minute note—if he received anything at all. Ambrose was not known for his fondness for writing. Assuming Graham's missive even made it into his brother's hands.

The footman bowed and left Graham to his letter, but he found Mina's handwriting on it. Flipping it over, he broke the seal and read through the scant lines. In a few short words, she laid waste to his self-control, and Graham's strength failed him. Sitting on the bed, he read and reread the letter, his heart quickening with each pass.

Tabby was free?

Graham sat there, dazed and startled at the news. It was everything he had hoped for and yet nothing of what he had expected. Tabby was free. The thought repeated in his mind for several moments before he shot to his feet, shouting for the footman to fetch him a carriage.

...

Closing her eyes, Tabby turned her face to the sun, reveling in the warmth. A breeze blew through the garden, making the leaves rustle around her, and the scent of blossoms filled her lungs. She couldn't remember the last time she'd felt so content. The fact that she did brought a twinge of guilt, but after days of turmoil, Tabby had come to accept that such feelings would be lingering there for some time.

Tabby hoped Joshua had found peace for his troubled soul. In her better moments, she even hoped he had found happiness, which made her feel better about finding her own. And she and Phillip would do so. They would rebuild and move on, and there was no escaping the fact that they were able to do so freely because Joshua was gone. A bittersweet blessing.

And there was the twinge again.

Opening her eyes, Tabby watched Phillip run circles around the garden. If only she could capture this moment and hold onto it forever, but Tabby knew their time at Rosewood Cottage was coming to an end. Without the fear that Joshua would assert his patriarchal rights, there was no need to hide in Farrow any longer. Tabby was free to find a position and home of their own.

Raising Phillip alone would not be easy, but it would be infinitely better than doing so while battling her husband. Another twinge struck her, but she batted it aside. There would be no more worries about moneylenders. No more fighting over his drinking and gambling. No more arguing. It would be difficult but more peaceful. She had never wished for Joshua's death, but there was no point in ignoring the fact that there were blessings to be found in it.

And then Tabby's thoughts strayed to the man who constantly lurked in the back of her mind.

Tabby stood and returned to the cottage, wishing to brush her memories aside as easily as she brushed the dirt from her skirt. But once again, Captain Ashbrook came to mind when she stepped through the kitchen door. It looked nothing like Gladwell House, yet just having the similar accoutrements strewn around her was enough to recall the memories of them baking together.

It was foolishness. A gentleman such as Captain Graham Ashbrook would not last long among the single ladies of Bristow. It had been nearly ten months since they had last met, and there was no possibility that he was unattached and free to pursue a further acquaintance.

Snatching the nearest rag, Tabby began scrubbing at the pristine table.

Heavens above, she didn't even know if he desired such a thing after everything that had happened. It was one thing for him to help Phillip in their time of need, but that was no indication that he wasn't infuriated at her deceit. He had a good heart, and anyone in his position would have fetched the physician. It meant nothing.

And yet...

Tabby froze, twisting the rag in her hands.

And yet, she had seen the look in his eyes at their final parting. She thought she understood it, but then again, Tabby was no longer confident in her ability to read men. Joshua had certainly taught her not to trust appearances.

"You should be out enjoying the fine weather, not sitting inside, fretting. Such lovely days are few and far between," said Mrs. Engle, bustling into the kitchen and pulling the rag from Tabby's fingers. "You are going to wear yourself out if you keep it up."

"I have a lot on my mind," said Tabby as she took a seat at the table.

"I'm certain you do," said Mrs. Engle, glancing at Tabby for a fraction of a second before turning her attention to the pantry. "You've had a lot of upheaval in your life, and I would be worried if you weren't at odds with yourself."

"At odds?" Tabby tried for nonchalance but failed miserably.

Mrs. Engle retrieved a tin and shut the pantry door. Popping open the lid, she offered a biscuit to Tabby. "It is no sin to be happy that your life has become less complicated."

Tabby shrugged and turned the biscuit in her hands. "Tell that to my heart."

Mrs. Engle sat opposite her, shifting in her seat and toying with the tin. "I know what it is like to be rid of a husband."

Stilling, Tabby stared at the woman who studiously avoided her gaze.

"It is not something I freely admit to most, but I was married before Mr. Engle."

The biscuit lay abandoned on the table, and Tabby waited for her to continue.

Mrs. Engle took a breath. "In truth, my story is not terribly different from your own, though I was never as posh as you, ma'am." At that, a shy smile stretched across Mrs. Engle's face. "But women of any class can be blinded by the men they love."

Leaning forward, Mrs. Engle took Tabby's hands in her own. "The truth is that I give thanks every day that my first husband is gone, and that I was able to find such a good man as Mr. Engle. At first, I felt wicked for being relieved that my burden was gone and I could start a new life without being dragged down by a selfish creature who cared only about himself.

"I allowed that guilt to keep me from moving on with my life," she said, her eyes shining. "I had men who wanted to court me, and I chased each one of them off. If Mr. Engle hadn't been so persistent, I would never have known what it was like to be cherished and loved the way a woman ought to be. And I have come to believe that he is my reward for making the best of a difficult situation."

"But I—"

Mrs. Engle raised a staying hand. "It has been nearly a fortnight since you arrived on our doorstep, and we have discussed much about your marriage. I know that you tried your best to make a go of it. There is only so much you can do about the actions of others, and you cannot allow yourself to get mired in guilt over being unable to love a man who treated his family so shabbily. In truth, I think you were far more patient with your husband than I ever was with mine."

"I appreciate the thought," said Tabby, picking up the biscuit and turning it in her hands. "But you did not meet your Mr. Engle until after you were free to feel such things."

Crossing her arms, Mrs. Engle gave Tabby a hard look. "So, I am right to believe that someone else holds your heart? Perhaps that Captain Ashbrook you've mentioned a few times?"

Tabby's shoulders slumped, and she abandoned the biscuit again. There was no hiding the truth anymore, so she laid out the entire tale to the sweet woman who sat so patiently throughout it. Though she asked a few clarifying questions, she simply listened as Tabby poured out all her troubles.

"And that's what you are tearing yourself up about?" asked Mrs. Engle. "I would have expected at least a little more impropriety."

"I fell in love with a man who is not my husband!" Saying the words aloud made Tabby press her hands to her mouth and blush until she was a deep scarlet.

"Oh, you silly goose," said Mrs. Engle. "It is true that in a perfect world your heart would have remained untouched, but then again, in a perfect world your husband would have lived up to the promises he made. Given the circumstances, I am quite impressed with your resolve. I don't know if I would have been able to do the same."

Tabby opened her mouth, but Mrs. Engle raised another staying hand.

"I know you are going to argue with me, but do not bother for you shan't convince me otherwise," said the woman. "Yes, you felt things that are reserved only for a husband. That happened, but we are not always in control of our hearts. What is important is that once you realized the situation you were in, you made plans to leave. There are not many people who would face such a temptation and remain true to their marriage vows even while their husband broke his. That is courageous, Tabby. Do not think otherwise."

With those simple, heartfelt words, Tabby felt her shame ease. She had carried it around with her since the moment she had discovered her feelings for Captain Ashbrook, a constant reminder that had become a bit of background noise in her life. Tabby had not even realized it was so entrenched in her heart until she felt it lighten. Only a touch, but it was a beginning.

"So, what are you sitting here for?" asked Mrs. Engle. "Go find your young man and tell him the truth."

And like that, Tabby's stomach clenched, her peace fleeing like a fox before the hunt. "I cannot possibly do that, Mrs. Engle."

"And why not?" she asked. "You are a respectable widow

now."

"Not so respectable," said Tabby, shaking her head. "Bristow was abuzz with scandal over our situation. Even if I could ignore that, to take up with anyone so soon after my husband passed would set the gossipmongers in a dither."

"Oh, for goodness' sake!" said Mrs. Engle with a huff. "To turn away such a gentleman simply because others wouldn't like it is ludicrous."

"I'm certain he has moved on, and I fear it is time that Phillip and I do the same," said Tabby, coming to the decision that she had been so hesitant to make. "We must leave Rosewood Cottage and make our own way."

"You cannot think—" she began, but Tabby stopped her.

"No, Mrs. Engle. It is the right thing to do," said Tabby, standing and heading to the door. "We cannot trespass on Mrs. Kingsley's generosity any further."

Mrs. Engle shook her head, crossing her arms with pursed lips. "Rubbish!"

···

Fingers tapping on his knee, Graham stared at the passing countryside, desperate for the carriage to move faster. Farrow came into view, and Graham did not know if his churning stomach was due to anticipation or agitation. He had certainly been in a constant state of both since the letter had arrived. Any semblance of peace he had found in his life had evaporated the moment he had read Mina's words.

Tabby was free.

But what if Mina were wrong? Or what if Tabby had no interest in renewing their acquaintance? Graham fell forward, his hands raking through his hair and scrubbing at his face. If he weren't sitting, he was certain his legs would give out from under him. Tabby was free. His heart thumped in his chest, pulsing through him as he fell back against the squab. He could not breathe.

And that was when the carriage pulled to a stop. Pinching the bridge of his nose, Graham took several steadying breaths. He had faced armed frigates and the threat of death countless times, yet none of it compared with the possibility of having Tabby taken from him again. Another breath and a few more on top of it, and Graham wrested his self-control into place. No matter how terrifying the prospect, driving away without speaking to her was not a possibility.

Popping open the carriage door, Graham looked at Rosewood Cottage. He could not remember the last time he had been there. They had visited various times when he was a child, but he had never felt a kinship for the place as Mina did. Now it was Graham's most favorite spot in the world, for it held his future.

Stepping onto the road, Graham made his way to the front door, listening for any sign of Phillip, but there was nothing. On such a sunny day, he would have expected the boy to be running about the fields of Farrow, but there was not a soul in sight. Graham rapped his knuckles against the front door.

No answer.

He knocked again and waited. Nothing.

His heart tapped a steady beat against his ribs as he tried again. Leaning over, he glanced through the front windows but was greeted by an empty room.

And then he heard a sound that was a blessing from heaven. Phillip whooped and laughed, drawing Graham around the side of the cottage into the garden. Sitting in the dirt, the lad marched his soldiers through the flowerbeds, waging war on the petunias.

As he was about to greet the boy, Graham caught sight of Tabby through the kitchen window, freezing him in place. She sat at a table, chatting with another woman. Neither noticed him, and he was free to enjoy the picture she presented. The turn of her lips, the way her eyes crinkled at the edges. The slope of her neck. Those slight dimples of hers. Graham knew them all so well, yet his memories had not lived up to her beauty.

Standing, she turned to leave the kitchen, but when she glanced over her shoulder, her warm eyes caught his, and it was as though an unknown weight lifted off his chest. For the first time in months, Graham was able to breathe again. Her eyes widened, and her hand inched upwards to cover her gaping mouth. It wasn't until he stepped forward that she moved to the kitchen door, stepping out into the garden.

His feet carried him forward without bidding, bringing him to stand toe-to-toe with her. For a silent moment, they stared at each other, Graham's mind unable to form thoughts. Tabby was before him, inches from his touch.

"Is it true? Are you free?" he whispered as he breathed in her scent, bringing with it a dozen memories of her.

Her chin quivered as tears gathered in her eyes. And then, she nodded.

His strength fled him, and Graham staggered, a bark of laughter bursting from him. Tabby spoke as she steadied him, but Graham's mind was unable to comprehend the words. She was free. That was the only clear thought in his mind. Another bout of laughter burst forth.

"I know I behaved abominably, but I can only hope that you can forgive me..." she said, gripping his forearm.

At that, Graham stilled and straightened, gazing into her eyes. "Why are you apologizing?"

Tears slipped from her eyes. "I never meant to mislead you. I had no idea that you believed me widowed, and I never thought I was risking your heart. If I had known what you felt for me I would have left long before—"

But she stopped when Graham took her hand. The feel of her skin on his set his heart racing, and he brushed his thumb across it. Slowly, he raised it to his lips, his gaze never wavering from her. A few more tears trickled down her cheeks, but Tabby's eyes glowed at the gentle kiss.

"You have nothing to apologize for," he said, stepping

closer to her, clasping her hand to his chest. With each movement, he watched, looking for any sign of trepidation or rejec-
tion, but he only found that glow of joy in her gaze.

"I have spent the last months fighting what I feel for you,"
he whispered, pausing to form the words he needed to say. "But
I couldn't. They are buried so deep in my heart that I could not
cut them out. And now that I am free to do so, I must tell you..."

Graham ducked his head, taking a deep breath at the wave
of gratitude that overwhelmed him. Clearing his throat, he met
her eyes again and said, "I love you."

The tears in Tabby's eyes brought a sparkle to them as her
gaze softened. She did not return the words, but Graham did
not need them. Given what she had suffered in her married life,
it was a miracle she was willing to open her heart again, and
Graham would not press her, but neither could he allow her to
doubt where his heart lay.

Leaning in, Graham watched her carefully as he pressed his
lips to hers. It was not the kiss he wanted to give her, but it was
the one he sensed she needed. It was filled with hopes and
promises for the future, and to Graham it was as much a vow as
one made before a vicar in a church. With that one chaste touch
of lips, Graham gave her a silent promise to honor and cherish
her for the rest of his life.

Stepping away, he gazed into her dazed expression and the
swell of color filling her cheeks. As her eyes focused on his, a
tremulous smile tickled her lips. The sight of it drew him in, but
Graham restrained himself, for Tabby needed time. At present,
it was enough to know that there were no more impediments to
their future together. The rest would be sorted out later.

Tucking her hand into his arm, Graham led her to the garden bench, her eyes never leaving his as they sat together. There
was so much more that he wished to do and say, but he knew it
was too soon. Phillip continued to run about the yard, chasing
butterflies and catching bugs, and Graham took Tabby's hand
in his.

Smiling at him, she squeezed it, the glow of utter contentment in her face.

Sitting there, there was no need for Graham to count his blessings. No need to remind himself to find the joys of his new life, for there was nothing better to be had than a lifetime of days filled with Tabby and Phillip. Even his happiest moments paled in comparison to the sublime pleasure he got from having this incredible lady at his side.

A French cannonball had stolen his naval career, but it had given him so much more in return.

Epilogue

Bristow, Essex
Ten Months Later

A pox on mourning rituals. A pox on wagging tongues. A pox on the Royal Naval Academy. And on all of Portsmouth. And if it were not for the fact that Tabby adored Graham's sense of honor and duty, she would curse that, too.

Tabby stared out at Avebury Park's burgeoning gardens, witnessing the clear sign of time marching onward. It was awful enough that she felt it in her heart with each long day stretching before her, but to see the budding trees and spring bulbs coming to life before her eyes was more than she could bear. How she missed Graham.

"He shall be free soon," said Mina from her place on the sofa.

Glancing over at her friend, Tabby gave a rueful smile. "I had not realized I was that transparent."

"You have been standing there sighing for the last ten minutes," said Mina, peeking up from her needlework. "As you do so regularly, it is not difficult to guess where your thoughts lay."

Coming over, Tabby sat on the couch with another sigh. "I

miss him terribly."

"I can imagine," said Mina, working her needle through the fabric. "In the years we have been married, I have only been apart from Simon for a sennight, and I cannot imagine being separated for longer than that."

"Even though you were glad to be rid of him at the time," said Tabby with a smile.

Mina shook her head, giving a mock scowl. "Of all the things I felt during that time, 'glad' was not one of them, and I should never have told you that story. I shan't tell you anything more if you insist on teasing me about it."

The sitting room door opened, and Jennings stepped inside to offer up a thick letter to Mina. Tabby leaned forward to glimpse at the handwriting, but she could not make out who it was from. A flutter of anticipation flitted through her, hitching her breath as Mina took it with a smile. Breaking open the seal, she pulled out a hidden secondary letter and handed it to Tabby.

"I suppose I should feel put out that yours is so much thicker than mine," said Mina. "But as Graham has written me more during the last ten months than in all his years in the navy, I will be satisfied with the shorter missive."

But Tabby did not respond. Hurrying towards the door, she rushed past a grinning Jennings and scurried to her room. Sitting on her bed, she pulled open her letter, savoring Graham's scent that lingered on the paper. Tabby absorbed each word, reveling in even the minor details he had to tell her. The exciting and mundane all held her in their grip as Tabby imagined all the goings on in his world.

She wished she were a part of it.

It had made sense ten months ago for them to undertake such a secretive courtship. Being newly widowed and far too fragile, Tabby had been in no position to contemplate anything more serious, but months of separation were becoming a torture. Perhaps it would be different if Graham were nearby, but his commitment to the Royal Naval Academy kept him in Portsmouth, which was too far a distance for regular visits. If it weren't for Mina conveying their letters hidden among her own, the courting couple would be denied even that little contact.

Tabby read the letter twice more before going to her dressing table to tuck it away with the others. Though not all of them contained anything romantic or sentimental, each was a precious piece of him, and Tabby would not part with a single one.

Two more weeks, and Graham would return. And yet there were several more before her mourning period was complete, freeing them to pursue a public courtship. Though it was no time compared to the previous months, it still felt too long.

Sitting at the table, Tabby stared at herself in the mirror and frowned at what she found there. Wrinkles that did not belong on so young a face, and a wariness in her eye that she did not like. Some of it could be blamed on her mourning clothes for the dark colors had quite a sickening effect on Tabby's complexion, but it was more than that. It was the physical manifestations of a life spent waiting.

Waiting for a child. Waiting for her husband to change. Waiting for the sadness to ebb. What was she waiting for now? Her heart had told her long ago where it lay, yet she had not moved forward in her life. Graham had made his intentions clear, yet they were waiting for something as inconsequential as a mourning period. They were waiting on the opinions of others.

Tabby glared at her mourning dress. Though she did not revel in Joshua's demise, she did not mourn it either. He was at peace, and she had come into her own; clinging to a tradition seemed a silly thing when she was ready to move forward with her life.

Stepping over to her wardrobe, she retrieved the first dress she found that did not require assistance and released herself from the dark, drab dress she had been wearing. Looking at herself once again, it was as though she were a new person. It was more than the light blue color that highlighted the rich brown hues in her eyes. It was a lightness in her soul, and a determination not to wait another day for her life to be all that she wished.

...

Eyes fixed on the passing scenery, Graham watched the landscape as it grew familiar. Knowing that Avebury Park was so close made the time pass even slower while he sat like an anxious child awaiting the arrival of a gift.

He was free.

Though the term would not be finished for another fortnight, Graham's commitment to the academy was fulfilled. It had taken precisely twenty-five minutes for him to pack after it was announced that his presence was no longer necessary. It had taken a further thirty before he had procured a carriage. Of course, all that hurrying had been for naught as it had taken two days to make the journey despite Graham's best efforts to get the coachman to drive through the night. And now that he was minutes from seeing her, it was impossible to sit still.

Graham imagined their reunion. Seeing Tabby and sweeping her into his arms and a passionate embrace. Of course, it was naught but a fancy for he would do no such thing. Reining in his wild imaginings, Graham reminded himself of the truth of his situation. Tabby needed time. They were free to properly court now and could fully explore their future together.

Grasping that thought, Graham reminded himself again that he needed to be careful. Cautious. Tabby had been through a terrible ordeal, and it would not do to run roughshod over her and hurry her to the altar. As much as he wished otherwise, he would give her all the time she needed.

But all other thoughts fled his mind as he saw Avebury Park drawing closer; he loved the place and was grateful for a happy harbor in which to plot out his future—with Tabby and Phillip. His face broke into a grin at that, but he steeled himself as the carriage rolled to a halt at the front door. He was liable to frighten poor Tabby if he was too forward. They had time, and Graham could be patient.

Stepping out of the carriage, he took the front steps two at a time and greeted Jennings, who had pulled the door open in anticipation. But as he was about to ask after his sister and her guests, Graham stopped at the sight of the breathtaking beauty standing at the top of the stairs.

He had hardly enough time to acknowledge her presence before she rushed down the stairs and threw herself into his arms. Graham stumbled back a step, but he kept them upright as she clutched him.

"You are home," she said with a contented sigh, and Graham caught the scent of lilacs in her hair.

"As you see," he whispered, his voice growing rough. "Am I..." Graham cleared his throat. "Shall I take this as a sign that I have been missed?"

"Terribly," she whispered.

Tabby leaned away to look him in the eyes, and Graham lost his voice at the sight of her. There was never a man more smitten with a woman than he, and he was eternally grateful to see the sentiment reflected in her gaze. Gone was the trepidation and worry. In her eyes, Graham saw the Tabby he had longed to see.

"Are you..." He faltered, clearing his throat. Graham cast a nervous glance around and found that the servants had abandoned their posts, leaving the pair without an audience. "Does this mean you have had enough time?"

A grin tugged at her lips, stretching into a full smile. "I am tired of waiting," she whispered. "Tired of holding onto the past. I love you, Graham Ashbrook, and I cannot stand the thought of waiting any longer to be your wife."

And that was all Graham needed to hear. Leaning forward, he pressed his lips to hers, feeling the weight of past worries and fears fall free from them. This was his love. His future wife. The woman he would spend his life with. The mother of his children. His heart and soul.

Tabby was making a spectacle of herself, but she could not find the will to care. Her path to this moment had been a rough and rocky one, but it was impossible to feel anything but gratitude at the pure felicity she felt in Graham's embrace. All the highs and lows of the past few years culminated in this moment, and Tabby poured every ounce of love and gratitude she had for this wonderful man into their kiss.

Yet no matter how much she wished to make him feel how profoundly humbled she was to claim him as her own, Tabby knew it to be impossible.

Here was everything of which her young heart had dreamt. A gentleman her father would have been proud to call his son-in-law. Her closest friend and confidant. The loving father her dear boy deserved. He was so much more than a mere partner in her life, and Tabby had no idea how she would ever convey how much he meant to her.

Luckily, she had the rest of her life to try.

Exclusive Offer

Join the M.A. Nichols VIP Reader Club at

www.ma-nichols.com

to receive up-to-date information about upcoming
books, freebies, and VIP content!

About the Author

Born and raised in Anchorage, M.A. Nichols is a lifelong Alaskan with a love of the outdoors. As a child she despised reading but through the love and persistence of her mother was taught the error of her ways and has had a deep, abiding relationship with it ever since.

She graduated with a bachelor's degree in landscape management from Brigham Young University and a master's in landscape architecture from Utah State University, neither of which has anything to do with why she became a writer, but is a fun little tidbit none-the-less. And no, she doesn't have any idea what type of plant you should put in that shady spot out by your deck. She's not that kind of landscape architect. Stop asking.

Website   Facebook   Instagram   BookBub

Printed in Great Britain
by Amazon

44999849R00179